The
Baron of Eastcastle

Quinn Hawk Series
Book 2

ISBN-13: 978-1492323921
ISBN-10: 1492323926

Cover art: Ken Corbett   www.kencorbettart.com
Digital photography: Kent Shelton   www.sheltonphoto.com

For all who dream,
and for all who make
the dreams of others possible

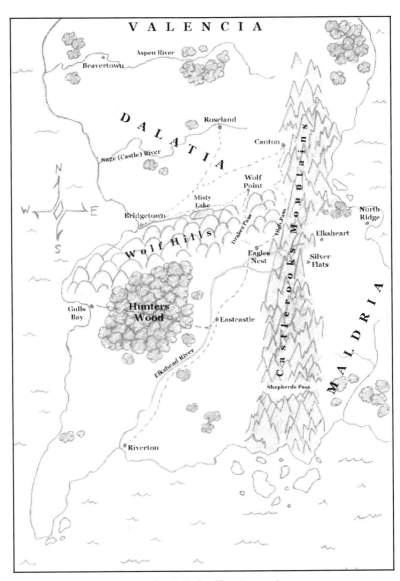

Map by Nicholle Pugmire

The bright moon had traversed across the sky and embedded itself in the cloud bank resting on the horizon. It was still early morning and the sun had not had a chance to purple the eastern sky. The fires had burned to embers and all but two pickets slept in their bedrolls.

Through the darkness, a shadow moved to the edge of the makeshift camp. Moving silently, he found where the young girl slept. Stealthily, a hand detached from the shadow and covered the girl's mouth. Her head jerked up, unseeing eyes wide. The shadow whispered in her ear.

"Rhiannon, I give you my word I will not hurt you. I need your help. Do you know who I am?"

Rhiannon nodded.

"If I take my hand from your mouth, will you promise me you will not make a sound?"

She nodded again.

The ranger slowly removed his hand, but Rhiannon made no sound.

"We need to move out of the field and into the woods without being seen. Leave your bedroll. It will be difficult enough without it."

Rhiannon carefully shed herself of the bedroll and silently followed Rowan into the darkness.

Chapter 1

The cries of the gulls woke Quinn in the morning. Sitting up, he was surprised to find Rhiannon was already gone. Perhaps she was using the privacy of the nearby trees. The men had rekindled the fire, but there was still no food to prepare a hot meal. Some of them had offered to go hunting, but the duke had vetoed the idea. He intended to leave as early as possible and did not want to be hampered by an involved meal.

As Quinn stood and stretched, he realized he was the last one to wake. In fact, his uncle's small tent was already down and stowed away. He gathered his bedroll and walked to where the horses were tethered. Finding his own, he strapped on his bedroll. At least he was not the last one since Rhiannon's still remained in the grass. He looked for Alexander, but he was nowhere to be seen. He had not been able to talk with him since the duke arrived and Quinn wondered how things had gone with his father. With nowhere else to go, he drifted over to the small fire.

"Good morning, Quinn," his uncle greeted him. "I trust you slept well."

"Yes, milord." Quinn noticed the duke had not been correcting him as of late. Either he was tired of doing so, or maybe Quinn had lost something in the relationship with his uncle.

"Grab a bite to eat, then. We will be leaving as soon as Bastian and his boy return. They are filling the water flasks for the ride back."

Quinn made one last scan of the field before asking, "Did Rhiannon go with them?"

"The kitchen girl? Not that I know of. In fact, no one has seen her since she went to sleep last night. She was gone before dawn. She may have decided not to return to Eastcastle. Maybe she thought leaving during the night was easier."

Quinn knitted his brows together. *Not want to return to Eastcastle? That didn't make sense.* "No, she was planning on going back. I talked with her last night and she thanked me for inviting her to live at the castle."

The duke shrugged, but not unkindly. "Well, then I am sure she will come back. If not today, well, she should know the way back to Eastcastle. And, of course, she will be welcomed when she does," he finished with a smile.

Still confused by Rhiannon's disappearance, Quinn walked back to her bedroll. It sat in a crumpled heap with no indication she had tried to fold it up for the trip back. Not knowing what else to do, Quinn rolled it up and took it back to the horses. While strapping it down, the approach of two other horses announced the return of Bastian and Alexander. No sooner had they entered the camp than Petric whistled his men to their horses and they prepared to leave. Quinn climbed upon his own mount and rode slowly around the field as the other men prepared for the ride back. There was no sign of Rhiannon anywhere.

"Hey bed-head! I see you finally decided to join the day!"

Quinn turned his horse to face Alexander as he rode up to him. As he waited, he tried to fix his hair, but gave it up as a lost cause.

"I should have woken you up so you could have enjoyed our little trip to the creek—along with the second half of father's lecture," he added quietly.

Quinn winced. "Sorry about that."

Alexander gave him a grin. "That's okay. I think you're probably still ahead of me in the 'undeserved lectures' category. Besides, ever since father heard you and Rhiannon actually found the jewelry box, he has been a little more forgiving."

"Speaking of Rhiannon, have you seen her?"

Alexander shook his head. "Not since before going to sleep last night. I'm pretty sure she was gone before I got up this morning."

"Gone where?"

"I don't know. I just noticed she wasn't in her bedroll."

The guardsmen and the duke mounted and guided their horses to the trail back to Eastcastle. Quinn watched for a moment before scanning the field again.

"My uncle isn't going to wait for her."

"Maybe she decided to leave now that you found the box. Or maybe she didn't like working in the kitchen. That would be too bad because I was kind of hoping she'd start sneaking us food."

Ignoring Alexander's last comment, Quinn said, "It doesn't make any sense. She told me last night she was happy at Eastcastle. She even thanked me for inviting her. Why would she do that if she was planning on leaving?"

"I don't know, but we better ride over and join them. I'm already on pretty thin ice with father. One more step out of line and he's likely to really blow his top."

They rode to where the last of the guardsmen were lining up.

"Who knows," Alexander continued, "Maybe last night she wasn't planning on leaving, but then she changed her mind this morning. It's no use trying to understand girls."

"I guess," Quinn murmured. "I hope she doesn't think we left her."

"Well, if she does, she should know it's her own fault. She could have told someone where she was going instead of just taking off."

Quinn realized Alexander was right. She could have at least told *someone* where she was going—except for the fact that Rhiannon always kept to herself and hardly talked to anyone. Still, it *was* her fault for taking off. And his uncle was right as well—she could find her way back to Eastcastle.

The trip back was a lot less pleasant than coming had been. The duke was anxious to get back to the castle after leaving so abruptly. Petric was his usual cheerless self, and the rest of the guardsmen were less than thrilled about spending two days in a row on horseback. Quinn gathered from their stares that most considered him the primary cause. During the morning ride, nobody talked, not even Alexander. Bastian was civil with Quinn, though not like he had been on their journey to the festival. Father and son rode along in near silence with the others.

As a consequence, Quinn spent the morning with only his thoughts for company. The excitement of finding the jewelry box faded as the day progressed. He was still anxious to find somewhere private to look at the letter, though his hope of actually reading it had disappeared with Rhiannon. The thought crossed his mind again that he should have shown his uncle the letter the night before. At least then he would have known what was written on it.

As the day progressed, Rhiannon's disappearance still bothered him more than anything else. He tried to sort through his memories of the night before to see if she had said anything that might have given a hint she was leaving. Had her kiss on his cheek been a kiss goodbye? He hadn't thought so. In fact, if anything, he thought she actually *liked* living at Eastcastle. Why would finding his mother's jewelry box cause her to leave without saying anything?

Quinn felt more and more deflated with each step of his horse. Now that they had solved the dead bishop's riddle, there was nothing to keep his uncle from sending him to Maldria. After yesterday's antics, the duke was probably more than happy to do so. The more he thought about it, the more he realized he could not think of a single excuse he could give his uncle for not going. By the time they reached Hunters Wood, Quinn accepted the fact he would be spending at least two years at some baron's estate.

By midday, despite the pleasantness of the summer afternoon, the whole party seemed as gloomy as Quinn felt. After traveling at a rigorous pace, the duke allowed them to stop at one of the many streams for a short rest and a bite to eat. Quinn separated himself from the group and sat on a log watching the water. After a few moments, his uncle joined him.

"Mind if I sit?"

Quinn shook his head. The duke sat on the fallen tree beside him and stared at the water. Finally, he looked toward Quinn with a small smile on his face.

"We are not a very cheery group are we?"

Not knowing how to respond, Quinn just shrugged. His uncle looked back toward the stream.

"I know you are probably a little upset we did not try and find your friend, so I thought you should know—according to Petric she left well before dawn. When you awoke, she had already been gone for quite some time. Much longer, I think, than she would have if she planned on coming back."

Quinn looked at his uncle, who was watching him carefully.

"Quinn, sometimes…well, sometimes people do things that do not seem to make any sense, except perhaps to them. Sometimes it is easier just to do things without explaining them to anyone else."

"Like running off to Gulls Bay looking for jewels?"

His uncle laughed. It was an honest, unforced laugh that brought a touch of mirth to an otherwise gloomy day.

"Yes, Quinn, exactly like that."

Silence broke out once again as both uncle and nephew watched the tiny sparkles of sunlight filter through the foliage onto the water. Finally, Renard spoke again.

"There is something else I need to talk to you about." He gave a short laugh. "And I am sure you can probably guess what it is. Quinn, I want you to seriously consider going to Maldria. I think it will be a good experience for you, and it will build more trust between our two countries. Now that you have found the jewelry box, I think you need to focus more on the future and start accepting the past for what it is. Going to Maldria might be a good place to do that."

Quinn did not answer, nor did his expression change. He almost told his uncle he had already resigned himself to the fact he was going to Maldria, but he just stared at the water instead.

The duke took a deep breath and let it out slowly. "Quinn, I know I have never really been a good replacement for your parents. In all honesty, I have not tried to be. A child should be raised by his own parents, but sometimes things happen that make it impossible."

Renard paused, as if trying to sort out his thoughts, and rubbed his bearded chin. "You have probably heard, or maybe even guessed, your father and I were not very close. We had little in common—unless you count our knack for arguing politics," he tacked on with a dry laugh. "I guess what I am trying to say is I know I am not your father.

Throughout your life I have tried not to dictate too much about what you should or should not do. In this case, however, I *do* think you should consider going. This is an unprecedented opportunity, one that could potentially impact Eastcastle for years to come. I know you probably do not see it that way, but I feel this will be a great thing for all of Dalatia…despite Petric's misgivings," he added as an aside.

Quinn blinked, surprised by his last comment. *Why would Petric have misgivings about his going?* Quinn would have expected the duke's bodyguard to be the first to agree to such a plan. In fact, he would not have been surprised if Petric volunteered to take him there just to make sure he actually went.

Renard took another deep breath and slapped his hands down on his thighs as if preparing to stand.

"Well, I will not force you to go. You know how I feel about it now, but it will be your choice whether to go or not. Unfortunately, I do need to know quickly. I am afraid our delay thus far may already be misinterpreted as something else. Think on it for the remainder of the ride and give me an answer when we reach the castle."

With that his uncle stood and signaled the guardsmen to mount up. Quinn stood also. Before he had a chance to talk himself out of it, he blurted out, "I'll go."

Renard turned back, his face softened by a small, tired smile. "No, Quinn, think about it for the rest of the day. We will talk again tonight."

Quinn shook his head and said more decidedly, "No. I'll go. I've already been thinking about it for the past couple of days and I've made my decision. I'll go."

The duke stared at him for a moment, and then broke into a wider smile. He put his hands on Quinn's shoulders and looked down into his face.

"You have never looked more like your father than you did just now. You looked and sounded just like him."

Quinn felt his heart quiver with emotion, but fought off any outward display.

Patting his shoulders, his uncle said, "Thank you, Quinn. You will do great things in Maldria. I know it."

The men mounted up and headed down the trail. Quinn followed, second thoughts screaming through his head. He felt as if his stomach was tied in knots. The momentary pride he had felt seconds before was completely swallowed by fear and depression. *What had he been thinking? What was he supposed to do in Maldria?*

Quinn's decision had a different effect on the duke. The second half of the day was more relaxed as the guardsmen picked up on Renard's newfound lightheartedness. They joked and ribbed with one another; except for Petric, who, if anything, grew more aloof. Although he rode near the duke, he would not have seemed less a part of the group than if he were twenty leagues away. In watching him, Quinn thought of his uncle's earlier comment and wondered why Petric was against the trip to Maldria. A voice behind him interrupted his thoughts.

"So, you must have promised the duke you would behave for years in order to cheer him up that much," Alexander said.

Quinn gave a dry laugh. "Sort of. I told him I'd go to Maldria."

Alexander blinked in surprise as he pulled his horse up next to Quinn's. "Oh," was all he said.

The two boys rode along in silence, listening to the chatter of the birds and the laughter of the men. Finally, Alexander asked, "How come?"

Quinn shrugged. "I don't know. I guess I kind of thought he was going to send me there anyway, so it didn't really matter."

"Did he say that?"

"No. Not with words, anyway. He said it was my choice, but sort of in a way that choosing to go was the only right answer."

Alexander leaned toward him and whispered, "I think adults like to do that. My father does it all the time. If you pick the other way, they just tell you it was the wrong choice and make you do it anyway."

They rode a bit further, before Alexander asked, "When do you leave?"

"I think as soon as possible. Probably tomorrow."

"*Tomorrow?* Why are you leaving so soon?"

"Somehow, Vareen messed up and the envoy came too early. He's been at the castle for almost a week already. He thought he was just coming to pick me up and return to Maldria. My uncle has been stalling him so far."

Alexander scowled. "Vareen is an idiot," he said under his breath.

"Besides, now that we found my mother's jewelry box, the duke wants me to start thinking of the future instead of the past. He thinks going to Maldria will help."

"So it really *did* belong to your mother? My father said he thought he'd heard that, but he was not sure."

"That's what everyone says."

"Do you think it means your parents really were…well…"

"Murdered? *I* think so. And so does Rhiannon."

"Rhiannon? How would she know?"

"She told me last night she was sure Marcus didn't steal the jewels. And if he didn't, then the only other explanation that makes sense is what he told the bishop. He somehow found them and decided to look into my parents' deaths."

Alexander was silent.

"What?" asked Quinn.

"Nothing."

"Yeah, right, nothing. I can see it written all over your face."

Alexander grinned. "It's just, how would Rhiannon know? She sure seems to have a lot to say about anything and everything."

"I don't know, but she was right about the church and the hiding place. In fact, nothing she's said has been wrong."

"Except you can't win a sword fight by just being stronger than the other guy," laughed Alexander.

"Well, yeah, there is that."

"So, where do you think she went? My father said Petric told the duke she was gone a long time before dawn."

Quinn shook his head. "I don't know. I talked with her last night right before we went to sleep and it sounded like she was coming back to Eastcastle with us. I don't know why she would change her mind."

"Maybe she remembered what a nice place Gulls Bay was and decided to stay."

Quinn gave Alexander a dirty look. "I don't think so."

"Well, she might have. She said she's lived on her own for a long time. Maybe she just decided she missed that kind of life. Maybe she didn't like working in the kitchen. Who knows, maybe she went with Rowan."

Quinn jerked as though someone had stuck a knife into his back. "What?"

Alexander looked over to his friend. "I'm only kidding."

Quinn thought back to the night in the church and tried to remember everything that had happened. Rhiannon had come up the stairs to let him know the duke had arrived. She had been surprised to find that Quinn was not alone and Rowan...*the ranger's face.*

Chills ran down Quinn's spine. Rowan's face flashed into his mind. It had changed when Rhiannon came out on the balcony. He had been intent on getting the parchment until Rhiannon arrived, but after that, he had given up. Quinn had thought it was because the duke and his men were entering the courtyard, but now he was not so sure. The ranger had changed his mind *after he saw Rhiannon.*

Quinn felt as if ice water were running through his veins. He thought he was going to throw up. Rowan had not given up on getting the parchment; he had simply taken a different approach!

"He took her!" Quinn gasped in horror.

"What?"

"Rowan. He came in the middle of the night and took Rhiannon." Quinn was shaking and sick with fear.

"What?" Alexander repeated. "Why would he?"

"Because he wants the parchment!" Quinn hissed.

Alexander looked at him with a confused expression. "Parchment? My father said you didn't find anything but the jewelry box."

Quinn was near tears. "I know, because Rowan made me promise not to tell anyone. I just thought...I don't know what I was thinking. I was just so scared, and he was leaving, so I just told him that I wouldn't. I didn't think he would do something like *this*."

Alexander looked over his shoulder to where his father rode with a couple of the guardsmen. No one was paying any attention to them. He rode as close to Quinn as he could.

"Look," he said quietly, "You don't know Rowan took her. You might just be jumping to conclusions. Maybe she really did just leave on her own."

Quinn shook his head, distraught. "No. She would have taken the bedroll. If she were leaving and not coming back, she would have taken it!"

"You don't know that. Besides, even if he took her, he's not going to hurt her. Rangers are obviously a weird set of ducks, but they aren't murderers. They live by a code of honor—at least among themselves. If he did take her and wants the parchment, then he'll come to Eastcastle to get it and he'll have to bring her. Just tell the duke and he can have his men watch for him."

"Tell him what? 'Uncle, I think Rowan took Rhiannon and won't give her back until I give him the parchment. You know, the parchment I told you I didn't find at the church.'"

Alexander winced. "Okay, yeah, that won't be pretty."

"How could I have been so stupid?!"

Alexander thought for a moment before asking, "What does it say anyway?"

Quinn looked at him incredulously. "*How should I know?* I can't read, remember! I was going to have Rhiannon read it, but obviously that didn't work out."

"What if we hide it somehow in the bottom of the jewelry box? Make it seem like you just didn't see it."

Quinn's face lit up for a moment, before realizing his uncle had taken the jewelry box. There was no way to get to it or to know if the duke had already searched it.

"I don't have it. The duke took it when we left the church last night. Besides, that doesn't help Rhiannon anyway."

"Well then, we'll just have to wait for Rowan to make a move. If he really did take Rhiannon to get the parchment, then he'll have to let you know somehow. Worst case, we can just trade it."

The idea seemed plausible until it dawned on Quinn he would not even *be* at Eastcastle. He fought to keep from falling into absolute hysteria.

"Alexander, I won't even be here! Even if Rowan comes to Eastcastle, I'll be in Maldria. I already told the duke I would go!"

Alexander scratched his head, before cracking a little smile. "I think we should go back to letting me get us into trouble. You're a little too good at it."

Quinn brought his hands up in balled fists and rubbed his forehead, letting his horse plod along after the others. He felt sick and could not stop shaking. Tears escaped from his eyes, but Alexander pretended not to see them.

"You'll have to go back," Quinn said finally. "Please, Alexander, you have to go back and see if you can find them. I'll give you the parchment and you can give it to Rowan. I know he took her. I know it! I keep seeing his face from last night and the way it changed when he saw Rhiannon. He took her to force me into giving him the parchment."

"Quinn, I can't. Father already wants to skin me alive for leaving yesterday. He'll absolutely kill me if I disappear again."

"Please, Alexander. It's the only thing I can think of."

Alexander swallowed. "I'm sorry, Quinn. I can't go back. It wouldn't make any difference anyway. You can't find a ranger who doesn't want to be found."

Quinn stared at the trail in front of him before conceding quietly, "I know. I know."

Alexander began to feel as miserable as Quinn. As they left the woods and approached the final stretch toward Eastcastle, his mind raced through all the alternatives. Quinn had given up all hope—his posture showed complete dejection. There had to be some way of getting the parchment to the ranger, though the likelihood of finding him still seemed small. Actually, Alexander was not even sure the ranger had taken Rhiannon at all.

It was not until they were crossing the bridge that Alexander finally started formulating a possible plan. The traveling party had spread out as they approached the environs of the castle, and the two boys crossed the bridge alone.

Thinking out loud, Alexander said, "So you're probably leaving tomorrow, right?"

"I don't know for sure, but probably."

"How are you going to go? Not over the Castlerooks, right?"

Quinn shook his head, "No. The baron sent a man and a chaise."

Alexander raised his eyebrows. "Oh, a *chaise*."

Quinn rolled his eyes.

Alexander smiled and continued, "Good. That means they'll have to take you through Shepherd's Pass."

"Why is that good?"

"Because it will take the better part of a day to get to the pass *riding in a chaise*," he ended in a mock pompous voice.

"So?" asked Quinn, ignoring his theatrics.

"I'm going to ask father if I can go with you, just as far as the border."

Quinn looked puzzled. "Go with me? What good will that do?"

"Well, if that's how you feel, I guess none," said Alexander with an exaggerated look of hurt on his face.

"Well, I mean…why would you want to?"

Alexander started laughing. "I don't. I said I was going to *ask* my father if I could go with you to the border, but that doesn't mean I'm actually *going*. But, if he thinks I am, then I have the better part of two days to try and find Rowan. Though, to tell you the truth, I could look an entire year and probably not find him."

"Maybe you won't have to. If he's really trying to get the parchment, he'll be following us. If you go back to Gulls Bay, you'll probably bump into him. Or at least he'll see you. Hopefully, he'll think it's strange to see you coming back and he'll stop you to ask why."

"Maybe."

The two boys reached the castle courtyard and slid down from their horses. Quinn's body cried out in pain, and the fear and depression only made it worse. They retrieved their gear from the horses before letting the stable hands take them.

As he carried his gear toward the barracks, Alexander called out, "See if you can stop by later tonight and we'll run it past father."

Quinn told him he would try and carried his packs to his room. His muscles were fatigued and he was mentally tired. He was no longer shaking, but only because his mind was in a fog. Dragging his gear the last few steps to his bedroom, he opened the door, piled it against the wall, and fell exhausted onto his pallet. Within moments he was asleep.

Chapter 2

It took a moment for the banging on the door to register. Sitting up groggily, Quinn tried to orient himself. The knocking continued.

"Quinn! Quinn! Are you in there?"

Quinn recognized his cousin's voice and called out, "You can come in. It's not locked."

The door opened slowly and Bertran sheepishly poked in his head. "Oh, sorry. Were you sleeping?"

"I guess so. How late is it?" he asked, rubbing his eyes.

"We've already had dinner and Father announced to everyone you are going to go live in Maldria."

"Oh." Quinn stared at the floor in front of him.

His cousin looked puzzled. "What's the matter?"

Quinn glanced up and tried to put a smile on his face, but his insides were in turmoil.

"Nothing. I was just wishing I hadn't missed dinner. I wonder if Melinda has anything left in the kitchen," he said as he stood.

Bertran accepted his explanation. "I don't know, but you'll have to wait. Father wants you to come to the library so they can get everything ready for tomorrow."

"Tomorrow?"

"For your trip to Maldria. You knew you were leaving tomorrow, right?"

"Uh, yeah," Quinn covered again. "I guess I thought you were talking about something else happening tomorrow," he ended lamely.

Bertran twisted up his nose. "Like what?"

"Nothing. Never mind, I guess I'm still not really awake."

"Well, try and wake up on the way to the library. Father wants you there right away."

The two boys hurried down the hallway toward the library. The butterflies in Quinn's stomach were out in full force. He was shaking as though he were bitterly cold, but the castle was still warm with the summer's heat. He had to consciously calm himself just to be able to walk. Luckily, Bertran never stopped talking the whole way. Quinn never had to say anything, only nod or shake his head at the appropriate times.

When they reached the library, the heavy door was open. Inside, sitting in his normal chair, was the duke. Petric stood behind him, while Vareen and a tall man stood to the side. Quinn guessed the tall man must be the Maldrian who had come to take him to the baron's home.

"Ah, here he is," said Renard standing, barely covering the relief in his face. "Quinn, come in and meet Tucker. He will be escorting you to Maldria tomorrow."

Quinn forced himself to walk into the room and was about to bow to the escort when Tucker shocked him with a low, formal bow of his own.

"Good evening, young master."

"Uh…good evening," Quinn replied, returning the bow, but looking sidelong at his uncle.

"Well, Tucker," said the duke, "As I was saying, Quinn has accepted the baron's offer, and I think he will be a great little ambassador for Eastcastle."

Other than a head nod to the duke, Tucker gave no reply. In fact, his face was completely unreadable. Quinn thought he might as well be looking at Petric.

Vareen, on the other hand, was overly animated. "Milord, now that it has been decided, I am sure Tucker will want to be on his way as quickly as possible." Shooting a thinly disguised sneer at Quinn, he added, "To delay him any longer would surely be nothing short of an insult to the baron."

Quinn swallowed and looked toward the tall Maldrian, expecting to see a similar glower. Instead, the envoy looked completely calm. If anything, he seemed a little bored. Quinn suspected Vareen's sense of urgency had less to do with Tucker's feelings and more to do with his own embarrassment.

"Vareen, I am sure Quinn will be ready to leave by tomorrow," said the duke, not trying very hard to conceal his annoyance. "Though, of course, *you* could leave tonight and let the baron know."

Vareen flashed his sour smile and with a forced laugh said, "No, I imagine tomorrow will be acceptable to the baron."

Tucker continued to look as interested as if they were discussing flower arrangements. In fact, the entire room went silent. No one seemed to have anything more to say. Personally, Quinn felt like screaming.

"Well then," the duke said returning to his chair, "I guess it is settled."

Looking at Quinn, he said, "I am sure you will want time to get your things ready and say a few goodbyes, so you may be excused— unless you have any questions."

"No, milord."

His uncle nodded. Tucker gave another deep bow, which Quinn again acknowledged with one of his own—though his was not nearly as formal. Quinn rose from his bow and slowly walked from the library. He hid his real desire, which was to flee the room in a panic.

When he reached the hallway, he expected to see Bertran snooping around, but his younger cousin was nowhere to be seen. *All the better*, thought Quinn, who no longer tried to hide his shaking. He walked a few paces to an adjoining hallway and stopped.

After several deep, calming breaths, he closed his eyes and leaned against the wall. He wondered what he was supposed to do to get ready for tomorrow. Everything he owned would easily fit inside one trunk, so packing was not going to be a problem. As he began to relax, he realized he was hungry. Pushing himself away from the wall, he made his way toward the kitchen, hoping something was left from dinner.

The kitchen girls were in the final stages of cleaning when Quinn poked his head through the door. Melinda was sitting on a high stool in the middle of the room, hair poking out from of her bonnet. She seemed satisfied with the performance of her staff and was content to watch as they finished. Quinn felt a lump come to his throat as he realized tomorrow would be the last day for several years he would be able to come talk with Melinda in the kitchen.

Catching the movement at the door, Melinda turned and saw him. She gave a smile touched with sadness and gestured him in.

"I was guessing you would come by sometime tonight, sleeping through dinner as you did. Come in and get some food. I had the girls save you a plate."

Quinn walked into the room. It was overly warm from the large ovens and the summer's heat. Seeing his face, Melinda stood up from her toadstool and enveloped him in a hug. Holding him, she said quietly in his ear, "So it's true. You *are* going to Maldria."

Quinn fought to hold back the tears, but gave up trying when she broke their hug and smiled down at him through her own. Giving him another hug, Melinda dismissed her staff for the night. Silently, they stood and cried together. Finally, she put her arm across his shoulders and walked him over to a plate of chicken and steamed vegetables.

"Well, all this blubbering won't do at all," she said with a sniffle. "Come eat your dinner and tell me what you've gone and got yourself into this time. I'm sorry it's not very warm anymore, but that's what happens when you skip dinner."

Melinda sat him down at one of the counters and wiped her eyes. "Well, go ahead. It's only going to get colder."

Between bites, Quinn related the little he knew about the Maldrian baron and the arrangement Vareen had orchestrated. Melinda was surprised he did not know more, especially when he could not even give her the baron's name. She tried to stay positive and even sounded a lot like his uncle when she talked about the good things that could come from it.

"So, when are you leaving?"

"Tomorrow," he said, relieved he said it without additional tears.

"*Tomorrow!* Why in creation are you leaving tomorrow?"

"Vareen feels if we wait any longer we might insult the baron."

"*Insult the baron*. Well, we will just see about that!" she said standing up from the stool.

"No," said Quinn quickly. He was afraid Melinda was going to leave right then and track down Vareen or the duke. "No, I already told them it was okay. There really isn't any reason to wait. Besides, I already delayed them by going to Gulls Bay."

Melinda sat back down, her face suddenly serious. "Yes, I heard about that. Quinn, where is Rhiannon? She did not come back to the kitchen today."

Quinn's throat constricted and he found it difficult to swallow. Luckily, Melinda had set out a mug of water and he quickly took a drink. He had forgotten about Rhiannon because he had been thinking so much about going to Maldria. He felt ashamed, and it must have shown on his face because concern flashed across Melinda's face.

"What is it? What has happened?"

"I don't know," Quinn started lamely. "I mean, not really. She just disappeared. When we got ready to leave this morning, she was gone. The duke didn't look for her or wait because Petric said she'd been gone for a long time—longer than she would have been if she were coming back."

Melinda stared into Quinn's eyes until he was forced to look down at his half eaten dinner.

"Quinn, I've known you since the day you were born. What aren't you telling me?"

His appetite gone, Quinn moved the vegetables around with his fork. "I think Rowan took her."

Melinda sat back confused. "Who's Rowan?"

"He's the ranger we met on the way to the Festival. He was at the church in Gulls Bay when we found my mother's jewelry box. I think he came in the middle of the night and took her."

"Why? I mean what makes you think he took her?"

Quinn continued to stare at his dinner.

"Quinn, what's the matter? What's going on?"

Finally, Quinn reached into his tunic and pulled the folded parchment from his inside pocket. "He wanted this."

Melinda carefully took the parchment and unfolded it. She quickly scanned it before reading it more slowly a second time.

"What is this?"

"It was with the jewelry box. The bishop said it was proof my parents were murdered."

She read it a third time, her face showing her confusion. "Where does it say that?"

"I don't know," mumbled Quinn quietly, tears forming again. "I can't read."

Melinda looked first at the parchment, then Quinn, and then back again. "Why do *you* have this and not the duke? Did he let you keep it?"

"He doesn't know about it," he whispered looking up at the kitchen master. Seeing her shocked look, he looked back at the plate. He planted his elbows on the counter and cradled his bowed head.

"How could he not know of it?"

Quinn told her the story of their trip to the church, finding the parchment and box, and the subsequent encounter with the ranger. He told her how Rowan had him promise to hide the parchment and how his face had changed when he had seen Rhiannon.

"Now I can't tell the duke because he'll wonder why I didn't tell him in the first place."

He risked a look back up at Melinda, but she was staring at the wall, her face paler than it had been.

"Mistress Melinda?"

She looked toward him, blinking, as if surprised to see him there. After a moment, she asked, "Quinn, do you think Rowan recognized her? You said his face changed when he saw her. Do you think he knew her?"

The question took him by surprise. He tried to remember back to the night before, tried to see the ranger's face again.

"I don't know. Maybe. Why would he?" Melinda did not answer. "Mistress Melinda, who *is* she?"

The kitchen master paused before turning to look at him again with a small smile.

"Quinn, we've been through this before. You introduced her to me, remember?"

"I know, but…it seems like you're not telling me everything. Like, why do you call her Ann to everyone else? And why do you worry about her all the time? *Who is she?*"

Instead of answering, she asked, "How many people know about this parchment?"

"Just me, Rhiannon, and Rowan. And Alexander," he added.

"But no one else? Not the duke or any of his men? Not even Alexander's father?"

Quinn shook his head in answer to each question. Melinda sighed and absently pushed the stray hairs under her bonnet.

"Why?"

"Quinn, this doesn't say anything about your parents. It's simply a vague reference of payment for services rendered. It doesn't even mention what was done or what the payment was. The only way this could be tied to those jewels was if it was found with them."

"But it was with them! I told you, I took it out of the box."

"But no one else knows that. Rowan may just have wanted to separate the two from each other. Now, even if you show it to the duke, everyone will still wonder why you didn't show it to him immediately. The only one who knows it was there is you."

"And Rowan and Rhiannon."

"Who have both disappeared."

"But *you* believe me, don't you?"

"Of course I believe you. First, you've always been an honest child—lacking in good judgment at times—but always fairly honest. Second, I know you can't read, let alone write. The only believable explanation is the one you have just given, but now it will always have doubts attached to it. And doubts are the enemies of action."

Quinn stood and reached for the parchment. "I'll go give it to the duke now. The longer I wait, the worse it'll get."

"If you give it to him now, will you get it back? What if you are right? What if Rowan *is* holding Rhiannon in exchange for it? The damage may already be done. It will not get any worse by waiting. What we need to do is find Rhiannon."

Quinn felt dread growing in his stomach. If Rowan had taken her, they would have better luck finding a certain pebble on a beach.

"I asked Alexander to go back and look for her. He's going to tell his father he's going as far as the border with me tomorrow, but he's really going back to Gulls Bay."

Melinda smiled. "I should have known the two of you would have something schemed up." Standing, she said, "We had better go see the weapons master."

Quinn looked panicked. "What for? You're not going to tell him, are you?"

"Come along, Quinn." She retrieved the parchment and headed out the door toward the gardens. Quinn's heart sank, but he followed her.

The evening air was still warm, though it felt cool after spending time in the kitchen. Melinda led them through the gardens and across the courtyard to the barracks. The off-duty soldiers were gaming and talking outside to escape the day's heat trapped within the stone walls. Some acknowledged them as they walked past, but most only glanced at them before going back to their entertainments.

The soldiers' barracks was a long building along the inner curve of the castle wall. It provided housing for the single soldiers. Those with families lived outside the castle on small plots of land, usually with a cabin and a small crop field. A hallway ran down the center of the barracks with doors on each side. Lining the hall were rooms containing three or four bunks, a few chairs, and sometimes a small table. Common rooms were at each end and served as gathering places for meetings or activities.

Bastian and Alexander shared a private room at the far end thanks to Bastian's position as weapons master. Melinda walked through the back door and led Quinn to the first door on the left. She knocked loudly.

They heard some shuffling before the door swung open and Alexander poked out his head. Seeing Melinda, his eyes went wide for a moment.

"Good evening, Alexander. Is your father in?"

"Um, yes, Mistress Melinda." Turning his head, he called to his father.

They heard the sound of a chair scooting along the wood floor and then Bastian appeared beside his son. Quinn bowed his head to hide a smile. Bastian's expression nearly matched his son's when he first recognized their visitor. Raking his fingers through his hair, he asked resignedly, "What has he done now?"

Melinda pushed herself through the door, pulling Quinn with her. Once inside she nodded to Alexander to shut the door.

"Not that my lack of knowledge absolves him in any way, but I am unaware of anything at the moment."

Bastian's face jumped rapidly through looks of concern, confusion, surprise, and finally stopped at relief.

"Oh. Oh, well, come have a seat at the table."

With just the two of them sharing the room, there was enough space for a small table with four chairs. A dresser and two pallets completed the sparse furnishings.

"Thank you," said Melinda and she took one of the chairs at the table. The others joined her, Bastian sitting directly opposite, the two boys facing each other along the sides. After they were seated, they each turned their attention to the kitchen master, not unlike a group of students facing their tutor.

"Has Alexander asked you yet? I mean, has he asked if he can accompany Quinn on the first part of his journey to Maldria?"

Bastian's face clouded, and he glanced over to look at his son. Alexander, on the other hand, was staring at Quinn.

"Yes," the weapons master said, slowly, "Why?"

Ignoring his question, Melinda asked, "And what did you tell him?"

"I told him I didn't think it was a good idea. I thought he could just say goodbye from here."

Melinda smiled. "I'm glad to see Alexander's notorious lack of good sense is not coming from his father. However, I have a new proposal for you."

She looked at Quinn briefly before turning back to Bastian. She pulled out the parchment he had found in Gulls Bay and held it across the table.

"Do you know what this is?"

Bastian looked down at the yellowed paper, but made no attempt to take it. "No."

Flapping it a little, Melinda said, "Well, take it and see what you think."

Still making no effort to take the parchment, Bastian said, "I, uh, can't read that."

Melinda sat with her arm out for a moment longer before she understood what he meant. She quickly brought back her arm. Setting the parchment on the table, she began to self-consciously smooth it out. Small spots of red showed up in her cheeks.

"Right. Anyway, this was found with the jewelry box at the church in Gulls Bay."

Bastian looked at her in confusion. "That's not possible. Nothing else was found except for the jewelry."

After a moment, he turned to look at Quinn, who suddenly found the wood floor very interesting. Luckily, Melinda related the full story of finding the parchment and meeting the ranger. She ended with the possible cause of Rhiannon's disappearance.

When she was done, Bastian asked, "What makes you think the ranger took her? What if she just decided to leave on her own?"

Melinda shook her head. "If she were planning on leaving, she would have told me."

The weapons master looked unconvinced. "Maybe she didn't want you to know."

"No," she said adamantly. "She would have said something."

Bastian let it go with a shrug. "So, what's your proposal?"

"Take this parchment back to Gulls Bay, find the ranger, and if need be, trade it for Rhiannon."

"If that was really found in Gulls Bay, then it needs to be given to the duke."

"I've read it. Nothing written on it is of any use to anyone, especially now that it has been separated from the jewelry box. It makes no reference to the jewelry or the box, nor does it mention a single name. It has no value. Certainly not when compared to the life of a young lady."

"What you are asking could easily be taken as treason. That parchment should have been given to the duke as soon as it was found."

Quinn kept his eyes averted, but he could feel the weapon master's eyes on him.

"Poppycock! There is nothing here that can be construed as treason. We are talking about ensuring the safe return of a young woman."

Bastian gave a wry laugh, "Be that as it may, it doesn't really matter. What you are asking is impossible. We cannot simply go to Gulls Bay and *find* the ranger. Nobody *finds* a ranger."

"No, but you *can* put yourself in a position to be found. You both know Rowan. He has met you and spent time with you. If he meets you on the way, chances are he will make contact with you."

Bastian took a deep breath and let it out slowly. After a long pause, the weapons master finally answered, "No."

"No?"

"No. I won't go."

"Bastian, we are talking about a girl's life…"

Bastian stood up abruptly. "No, we are talking about more than that! Do you know what that is?" he asked, pointing to the parchment. "That could very well be evidence of a murder—of several murders."

Melinda stayed seated and calmly said, "Bastian, you are overreacting."

Bringing his hands up and scrubbing his face, Bastian walked a few paces before turning back, noticeably calmer.

"You are asking me to give away possible proof Quinn's parents were murdered. That could sentence me to a life in the dungeon if the duke were to find out." After a pause, he added quietly, "We are talking about more than one girl's life. We are talking about *my* life, and possibly the life of my son."

The room sank into silence as Bastian held Melinda's eyes with his own. Alexander and Quinn felt as though they were eavesdropping on a conversation they were not supposed to hear. They both kept their eyes down, only glancing up at each other occasionally.

Finally, Melinda said, "I'm sorry, Bastian. You're right. We *are* talking about more than one life."

Bastian nodded, accepting her concession.

"However, it still needs to be done. I will make a copy of the parchment and give it to the duke after you leave, *and* after Quinn is in Maldria. I will not mention your name and will accept any blame the duke feels the need to dole out." She smiled as she added, "I suppose he owes me a few payback lectures for all the ones I gave him as a boy. But, regardless, we need to find Rhiannon."

Bastian just stared at her in unbelief. He had thought from her apology she had given up on her request.

"Melinda, this is insanity!" he finally exploded. "Besides the huge chance we are taking with the duke, there is another aspect you are not thinking about. What if Marcus *was* telling the truth? What if Quinn's parents really were murdered? That means the murderers are still out there, and we have no idea who they are! And what if *they* hear about this parchment? Creation, woman! They killed a duke! They won't think twice about killing anyone else."

He took a breath, expecting the kitchen master to retaliate; however, she only nodded. Her calmness only infuriated him more.

"Why does Rowan want the parchment? What's it to him? He claims to have known Rustan, but what do we really know about him? *Nothing!* For all we know, he could be working for those who killed them, trying to cover up tracks they thought were long since lost. Lord Rolands's ghost! He may even have done it!"

"Rhiannon is Marcus' daughter."

Melinda's quiet voice pierced through Bastian's rant, freezing him with his mouth agape. Quinn's head shot up, eyes directed at the kitchen master, but she was staring at Bastian. Slowly, Bastian stepped back to the table and sat down in his chair.

"Does *he* know that?"

Melinda shifted her eyes toward Quinn a second, before answering. "I honestly don't know. However, based upon what Quinn remembers, I would say it is certainly possible."

Quinn's own thoughts whirled like a spinning wheel. Inside he was hurt Melinda had not told him before; it would have explained a lot about the things Rhiannon always seemed to know. All this time, he thought she had been lying, that she was just making things up when it suited her. He had even made fun of her a couple of times. Why had she not told him? Then he would not have made such a twit of himself. His face started to redden as his temper rose, but he held his tongue. He was not the only one.

The room fell into silence. Each of them sorted through their own thoughts. The only sounds were the muffled laughter from the guardsmen outside.

Finally, Bastian said quietly, "We'll leave tomorrow. As soon as Quinn is on his way, Alexander and I will leave on a 'hunting trip'."

Melinda released her breath, the sound betraying the calm exterior she was portraying. With a nod, she stood, retrieved the parchment. "Thank you."

Bastian rose as well. "See that you get that copied tonight."

"Of course. Come, Quinn. We all have things to do before tomorrow."

Quinn stood without answering and followed Melinda to the door. Bastian beat her to it. Before opening it for her, he said, "May the Lord help us if this gets out."

Melinda nodded again and slipped through the door.

As they walked across the courtyard to the kitchen, Quinn's anger got the best of him. "Why didn't you tell me?"

Melinda did not stop or slow her pace. "Not here, Quinn. We'll talk in a moment."

For a brief second, Quinn felt like pushing the issue, but he swallowed his words. He followed Melinda through the gardens to the same door they had exited. The kitchen was still warm from the ovens and probably would be until the girls came back in the morning to prepare the next day's bread.

Melinda crossed the kitchen to the far doorway and glanced up and down the hallway. Satisfied that no one was nearby, she returned to Quinn. Taking him by the hands, she led him to a stool.

"Quinn, I'm sorry I didn't tell you. I thought I could keep her from…I don't know…from the gossip and the questions and everything else that would have happened had people known who she really was. I didn't think…"

Quinn's barely held anger escaped. "I told him who she was! I called her *by name* in front of him! Of course he's going to know her. He said he knew Marcus!"

Melinda shut her eyes and took a slow, deep breath. When she opened them again, they had watered. Her hands trembled slightly as she continued to hold on to Quinn's.

"I'm sorry, Quinn. I'm so sorry."

Looking at her haunted face, Quinn's anger faltered and tears began to wet his own cheeks. Torment racked his voice.

"It's my fault. I told him who she was. I was the one who took her there. We shouldn't have gone. We shouldn't even have been there."

Melinda pulled him tight against herself and stroked his hair. "It's not your fault, Quinn. It's not your fault. I should have told you."

Quinn broke down, the pent up heartache escaping through sobbing breaths. "Why didn't you tell me?" he whispered.

Melinda held him until his body stilled. Finally, she broke the embrace and looked down into his face, wiping away the tears. Through her own, she forced a smile,

"Quinn, it's going to be okay. Bastian will find her and she will be safe. I know it. Rangers are not murderers and from what you have told me of this Rowan, he doesn't sound like he will do her any harm. Bastian will give him the parchment and bring her safely back again."

Not knowing whether she was trying to convince him or herself, Quinn simply nodded.

"Now, we both have things to do this evening, so we need to straighten up and get to it. Okay?"

Quinn nodded again, though his heart was not in it. He was suddenly very tired, as though all his energy had flowed out in his tears. He was no longer angry; he simply felt empty. Everything was taking on a dreamlike quality—Rhiannon's disappearance, his trip to Maldria, even Bastian's acceptance of the nearly impossible quest of tracking down a ranger in the woods. Nothing seemed real. It was all just a long nightmare from which he needed to awake.

Emotionally spent, he allowed Melinda to lead him to the hallway and push him on his way. He walked back to his room in a near trance. When he finally arrived at his bedroom door, he could hardly remember walking there.

Pushing the door open, Quinn stepped into the middle of his room. A large wooden chest sat against the wall opposite from his pallet. The lid was open and several sets of leggings and tunics were neatly stacked inside. The castle servants had apparently provided additional clothing for his stay in Maldria. Nothing else seemed to be different, yet the room already felt deserted. His father's sword and bow still hung on the wall. He hoped they would stay until he returned—*if he returned.*

Hoping the servants had packed all the necessary items, Quinn sat down on his pallet. His travel bags and sword belt had been taken from the floor where he had left them and set on the end of his pallet. He pulled his sword from its sheath and held it out with the flat in front of him. Rotating his wrist back and forth, he was again amazed at its balance.

Carefully lowering the point to the floor, he let his mind wander aimlessly through thoughts of Maldria, Gulls Bay, Rhiannon, Rowan, Bastian, and Melinda. There was no real thread to his thinking, just one image after another, jumbled together like a mismatched tapestry. A thought of Rhiannon was swept away by the memory of the townspeople in Gulls Bay, which in turn gave way to the memory of Bastian's outbursts. He sat for a time before a knock at his door roused him from his stupor. He looked dumbly at the door. The knock was repeated.

Rising from his bed, Quinn felt the smallest glimmer of hope that perhaps it was Rhiannon. He crossed the room to the door, still holding his sword. A third knock came, loud and hard, just before he opened it.

The disappointment of not seeing Rhiannon was made worse when he found himself staring at Petric's stomach. Glancing up, he saw the bodyguard's face was devoid of expression as usual. Momentarily eyeing the sword in Quinn's right hand, he stepped into the room, forcing Quinn to step back. Once inside, Petric's eyes swept the room, taking in every detail. Satisfied they were alone, he turned back to Quinn.

"What do you want?" Quinn managed to ask.

"Shut the door."

More scared to disobey than he was to be shut in with his uncle's bodyguard, Quinn pushed it closed. Having done so, he looked back at Petric and waited.

The tall man squinted ever so slightly, the only change in the marble mask that served as his face. Suddenly, without warning, he drew his own sword from his scabbard and stepped to the door, forcing Quinn to retreat back toward his pallet in horror. Having secured the only source of escape, the bodyguard readied his sword and faced him.

Quinn's stomach lurched and adrenaline poured into his bloodstream. By simple reaction from his weeks of training with Alexander, he brought up his own sword, setting himself in a defensive stance. Coldly and methodically, Petric attacked.

Quinn's first thought was he must be dreaming; his second was he was about to die. His body automatically followed the forms Bastian had shown him, his mind screaming constantly that this was completely insane. He met each stroke as he had been taught, deflecting, blocking, always moving, concentrating on his defensive movements, ignoring any urge to strike offensively. He circled the room, avoiding corners and obstacles that would impede his ability to fall back. Petric, on the other hand, kept himself between Quinn and the door, never allowing Quinn the opportunity of making a mad dash toward escape.

As time passed, the fear and shock subsided and Quinn's pent up anger replaced them. The betrayal of being attacked in his own room by someone whose sole purpose was to protect his uncle from just such things blended with the hurt of being used by the ranger and kept in the dark by Melinda. A cool rage built inside him. It focused his thoughts and fueled his determination. If he was to die tonight, it would not be before he had used up everything he had in him. The anger offered an inner strength and an odd sense of calmness, which he funneled into his sword.

Using both hands, he wielded his sword with a swiftness that would have surprised him had he had time to think about it. He thwarted attack after attack, each time choosing the most efficient defense to save his energy. In his mind he could hear Bastian's voice. *Save your strength. Wait for his mistake. Never take a gamble. Watch for the openings. Always choose escape over chance. Never overextend. Never become unbalanced. Watch the eyes as well as the blade.*

Time wore on and Quinn felt his strength begin to ebb. He had hoped someone drawn by the distinctive ringing of weapons would come to his rescue. He did not expect to beat Petric; he was too good a swordsman. However, he had hoped to last long enough for someone to find them. That hope now waned like a candle burnt down to its nub. His vow to himself to use every bit of his strength was about to be made good. Just as he was about to give up, Petric stepped back and sheathed his weapon with a metallic *shunk*.

"Hold, young Hawk! Hold!" he said with both hands raised.

Quinn kept his sword up in both hands, wincing as his muscles drained the last of his energy reserves to keep the blade aloft.

"Your abilities are somewhat more than I was led to believe," the bodyguard said with a small smile that was more a sneer. "Perhaps you will survive after all." With a wave of his hand he added, "You may put away your sword. I give you my word that you have nothing to fear—*from me.*"

Quinn wanted to laugh. The man had just been trying to kill him. Unfortunately, he did not have the strength left to maintain his stance. With great effort, he lowered his sword to the ground, avoiding a complete collapse that might have damaged the point on the stone floor.

Petric's face changed back to his normal expressionless demeanor. "What do you know of Paddock?"

Quinn, who was still struggling to understand how a fight for his life had turned into a conversation, missed the question. "Of what?"

"Of the *Baron* Paddock. The man whose *hospitality* you will be enjoying for the next several years."

"Nothing," he managed to gasp between deep breaths.

His answer induced no change in the bodyguard's expression, as if he was not surprised. "Then I suggest you listen, if you care at all for your life."

Quinn's head was spinning worse now than it had been when he was locked in combat. Fighting had been rudimentary, simply using the forms he had been taught to block each attack. But now, his fatigue was taking its toll on his ability to understand what Petric was saying.

"Paddock is the most dangerous man you will ever have the displeasure of meeting."

"I don't believe you."

Petric gave a short, dry laugh. "A family trait. Regardless, it is the truth. Do not be fooled by his flowery words and appearances. He is ruthless and uncaring."

"The duke seems to think he will help extend the peace between our lands."

"The duke is a dreamer trapped under the memory of his dead brother."

The blunt, uncomplimentary description of his own employer shocked Quinn.

"He is the victim of carefully directed flattery and misguided hope. Do not think for a moment that Paddock cares a whit about peace. He cares only about power and will use anything or anyone to get it. To him, the world is nothing more than a game of Knights where people are simply pieces to be manipulated, captured, or sacrificed for his own purposes. Do not misjudge him. Fear him."

"Why should I believe you? How do you know so much about him when my uncle does not?"

Again he flashed the sneering smile. "Because Paddock and I have a lot in common."

With that, the tall man turned to the door and opened it. Before exiting, he looked back and said, "You have had your warning; do with it what you will," and then he was gone.

Quinn stared at the closed door. The sword fell from his right hand, clanging loudly on the stone floor. His body was shaking uncontrollably and he could barely stand. Staggering to his pallet, he fell across the matting and pulled the blankets around him. If the shaking had been caused by cold, the effort might have worked.

Quinn's rattled mind tried to sort through it all. Was Petric lying? He had to be. But why? And why had he attacked him? Would he have killed him? Why did he stop? Exhausted physically, mentally, and emotionally, Quinn collapsed into a troubled sleep.

Chapter 3

When the moon settled behind the bank of clouds just above the horizon, they had to travel by starlight. The ranger seemed to be unaffected and walked as though the noon day sun were shining. Rhiannon concentrated on distances and directions at first, intending to turn back if the need arose, but by the time the sun purpled the eastern horizon she abandoned the hope. Instead, she prayed she had made the correct decision.

They had circled the camp until they were beyond sight and sound before returning to the main trail. The ranger had led them into Hunters Wood, which now seemed more ominous than it had the previous afternoon. With virtually no light to see by, she had to trust in Rowan's ability to follow the trail. He slowed their pace only slightly, intent on getting as far from the Eastcastle camp as possible before sunrise.

As the sky lightened, Rhiannon still hoped they would be near the main trail when the others came by on horseback. If so, she would take whatever risk was needed to get back with them. Her hopes were dashed when the ranger turned left at one of the small offshoot trails that led higher into the Wolf Hills. After a few steps, he paused just long enough to partially snap a small branch of a fir tree, causing it to hang slightly. Satisfied, he once again started up the trail. Apparently comfortable with their distance from the main trail, he struck up a conversation.

"How are you doing? Are you cold?"

Rhiannon shook her head when he looked back at her. He nodded, his face set in an odd smile.

"Are you scared?"

The question surprised her. She thought about lying, but answered, "A little."

The ranger gave a short laugh. "Understandable. I suppose I would be as well, if I were in your shoes. However, I promise you have nothing to fear. Do you believe me?"

Rhiannon was not exactly sure, but she answered affirmatively anyway.

"Good. We are going to a place a little further up in the hills. Once we get there I will tell you how you can help me."

They came to a fork in the trail and he took the one to the left. After a few steps, he picked up three stones about the size Rhiannon used to skip into the ocean as a child. He lined the stones along the side of the trail and placed a stick next to them.

Looking up, he explained, "I am expecting a friend to follow and I want to make sure he does not get lost on the way." The casualness of his tone surprised her.

"The other ranger? The big man with the round face?"

Rowan quirked his eyebrow. "So, you have met Asher."

Rhiannon nodded. "Outside of Canton." Then, after a pause, she added, "He saved my life."

For a brief moment, his face softened. "Well then, perhaps you can thank him when he finds us."

The ranger led them higher into the hills, similarly marking each fork taken. Their conversation was light and meaningless, consisting mostly of questions of how she was doing and whether she needed a rest. Every once in a while, he would point out a deer or a fox before it was startled and bounded away.

It was nearing midday when Rhiannon first noticed the sinking feeling growing in her stomach. They had just crested a ridge of hills and were descending into a small valley dominated by a crystal blue lake. The sunlight sparkled on the surface making the lake appear as though it were full of diamonds. It would have been a beautiful vista if she had not seen it before.

As the ranger led the way down the switchbacks, Rhiannon dread grew. By the time they reached the edge of the lake, she was shaking. She could barely keep one foot in front of the other as she followed Rowan to a small, rustic cabin partially set within a natural cleft in the rocks. It was about a stone's throw from the edge of the lake, making it difficult to see unless you knew it was there. Upon reaching the door, Rowan turned back to Rhiannon.

"I am guessing from your face you have been here before."

Rhiannon said nothing and concentrated on hiding the terror she felt. Looking up, she steeled herself to meet his gaze. She was surprised at the seriousness of his expression.

"You know, you look just like your mother—though I can see Marcus in there too." When she did not answer, he continued. "I know both of them very well. I brought you here to prove that. How else would I know the location of your father's hunting cabin? It is actually their help that I need, particularly your father's."

Again, she said nothing, though she could no longer keep the shaking indiscernible. His face grew concerned. "Are you alright?"

Rhiannon did not risk an answer.

"Rhiannon, I promise you are in no danger from me, nor are your parents. I just need to talk with them, but I have not been able to find them. I need your help. I need you to tell me how I can find them."

"No," she choked out.

The ranger knelt down in front of her and took her hands, surprised at her distress. "Rhiannon, what is the matter?"

"My parents are dead," she said, barely above a whisper.

Rowan jerked back as though she had struck him. His face was an odd mixture of shock, sympathy, and anger.

"How? How did they die?"

"They were murdered!" She stared into his eyes, but he seemed to be somewhere else. "They were murdered by the man your friend killed—the one he saved me from in Canton. He was one of them."

The ranger's jaw clenched and his face grew hard, harder than any face she had ever seen. The rage was almost tangible, an unseen force trying to escape and threatening to destroy everything in its path. Rhiannon shrank back from him.

Catching the movement, Rowan blinked as if surprised to see her standing in front of him. Immediately, the anger disappeared from his face.

"I am sorry. If I had known…Rhiannon, I promise you, if I had known I would never have brought you here. I am sorry."

Turning his head from her, he stood and looked out over the lake. "I need to wait until Asher comes before I can leave here. If you will wait, I will take you back to Eastcastle myself." Looking down, he added, "If you would rather leave now, you may do so. I will give you directions back to the main trail if you need them."

Rhiannon stared at him, but did not say anything. When he realized she was not going to answer, he said, "I am going to go and find something to eat. If you are gone when I return, I will understand."

The ranger pulled the hood of his cloak over his head and melted into the surrounding woods.

Unsure if he had really left, Rhiannon watched the woods. Detecting no movement for some time, she turned to her father's cabin. If nothing else, the ranger's reaction to the news of her parents' deaths had stopped her from shaking. Whatever Rowan's relationship had been with her parents, she was sure the rage he had briefly shown was genuine.

Rhiannon walked to the door and pushed it open. Her father had never added a lock. He always felt if someone in need happened upon the structure, they were welcome to its protection. The inside of the cabin was covered with dust and cobwebs. It was a one room structure with a small stone fireplace built in the back wall. The furnishings consisted of a small table, a couple of chairs, a pallet, a chest, a half filled box of wood, and some small cupboards. Other than feeling smaller, the cabin looked exactly as it had the last time she had been here—shortly after her parents were killed.

As she walked in, the dust on the floor wafted up and was caught in the rays of light filtering through the gaps in the log walls. She glanced around the room in search of a broom, but found none.

She walked to the chest and lifted the lid. As expected, it was filled with folded blankets. Taking the top one, she swished it around the floor, but was only moderately successful at cleaning up the dust. Mostly, it just rose into the air and settled somewhere else. After several attempts, she gave up and sat on one of the chairs. Resting her arms and head on the table, she succumbed to the tears that came unbidden from the memories surrounding her.

∗   ∗   ∗

A noise at the door startled her. As she looked up, the backlit form of the ranger filled the doorway.

"So you decided to stay. You might be sorry once you try ranger cooking." The smirk was back on his face as he lowered his hood. "I am afraid all I could find were a couple of small rabbits and some berries."

Rubbing her arms to bring back some feeling, she asked, "Do you need any help?"

"Fixing dinner or finding something better?"

He gave a quick laugh and beckoned her outside. The rabbits were already skinned, cleaned, and hanging from a branch of a nearby tree.

"Too bad Asher is not here. His cooking is much better than mine."

Rhiannon searched the nearby area for wood while Rowan whittled two spits with his belt knife. When he was done, he collected the shavings and added them to the twigs and dead grass Rhiannon had placed in the fire ring. With the aid of a tinderbox, he lit a small fire. He gradually added larger pieces of wood until the flames rose several inches. With nothing left to do but wait for the coals, they both sat on the large rocks near the fire.

As they listened to the snapping of the burning wood, Rhiannon asked, "May I ask you a question?"

The ranger looked at her through the thin smoke. "I would wonder if you were actually Marcus' daughter if you did not."

"Why did you want the letter?"

The ranger looked into the flames and thought for a moment. "Probably the same reason Quinn was so adamant about keeping it. I guess we are both interested in finding out if it mentions who was behind what happened to his parents."

"Why do you want to know?" Rhiannon hoped she had not gone too far, but she needed to know something she could only find out by asking him directly.

The ranger laughed. "You are clearly Marcus' daughter."

His face grew serious as he stared once more at the crackling fire. Finally, he took a deep breath and answered vaguely, "It is important for me to know."

He threw a few more pieces of wood into the fire, more to clean up the area than to aid the progress of the coals. They were the unconscious actions of someone not completely comfortable.

To know what? she thought. *Who did it, or just whether the letter names the people involved?* Ignoring the possible consequences, she risked the question she needed answered.

"Did you do it?"

The ranger glanced up in surprise. "Is that what you think?"

She swallowed before shrugging.

He gave a small snort of laughter—a bitter one without humor. Shaking his head, he said, "You have your father's courage to go with your mother's looks."

Standing, he stirred the fire. Deeming it ready, he brought the two spitted rabbits over and laid them in two forked branches he had positioned earlier. Rhiannon watched him, her stomach tightening into knots. She thought she knew the answer, but she wanted to know for sure. Of course, now that the question was out, she wished she had not asked. The silence roared in her ears and she fought the urge to run.

As the tension became almost unbearable, he finally answered, his voice cold as death itself. "No. I give you my word, I did not do it."

His answer did not completely reassure her. She believed he was telling the truth, but her question had changed things. The warmth of the summer afternoon was now overshadowed by a dark heaviness.

Feeling the need to get away for a moment, Rhiannon said, "There is a small spring by that stand of trees. Do you want me to refill the water flask?"

Rowan's nod almost looked relieved. "Yes, please."

Rhiannon tried not to look too hurried as she retrieved the large flask from his gear and headed toward the stand of trees. The flask was still more than half full, but the heat of the day had made the water tepid. As she walked, she opened the stopper and spilled out the contents.

As she walked, the warmth of the sun helped calm Rhiannon's nerves. She had always loved this valley as a child, but after her parents' deaths the feeling of loss had been too strong to return again. The beauty of the lake and surrounding woods would always be tied to the memory of her father.

The flow of the spring was low at this time of the year. Rhiannon carefully lowered the flask under a small spout from the hillside, splashing water and freezing her hands. When it was full, she stood and drank, feeling the coolness run inside her. It tasted much better than the barreled water at the castle. After taking another swallow, she lowered the flask again to top it off. She then stood and replaced the cap.

When she returned to the cabin, the smell of cooking meat filled the air. Rowan was rotating the spits and whistling, though the tune choked off a bit when the smoke swirled toward him. She offered him the flask and he gratefully took a drink. When he handed it back, they were both relieved to find the earlier tension had dissipated.

"So, I have a question of my own."

Swallowing to wet her suddenly dry throat, she felt her stomach knot up again. Reading her reaction, he let out a mirthful laugh. "You may relax. I know you had no part in it either."

It took a moment for Rhiannon to understand what he had said, and she blushed when it finally registered. The ranger laughed harder.

"No, my question is simply whether you recognized the jewelry box?"

"Recognized it?" she asked confusedly. "It's supposed to have belonged to Quinn's mother."

The ranger nodded as he turned the spits. "And so it did. However, it was given to her as a gift."

"From my father?"

He smiled warmly, which was a nice change from his usual expression. "Yes. Your father carved it. He had a talent with all blades, carving and fighting. In fact, he was one of the best I have ever seen with a sword. I am very sorry to hear of his death."

Rhiannon stared at the coals of the dying fire and pulled her legs into her body. She tried to remember the box. With all that had happened that night, she had not really paid much attention to it. She remembered thinking it was beautifully carved, but now she wished she could look at it more carefully. Her father had loved to work with wood. He spent hours making furniture, bows, and even wooden toys, most of which were lost in the fire at the inn.

The ranger was content to leave her to her thoughts. He picked up his whistled tune again as he monitored the spits. Finally, he said, "There is not much to them, but they are done."

Taking the spits from the fire, he set the rabbits aside to cool. They brought out the two chairs from the cabin and set them in a grassy area near the lake. Rhiannon returned to search the cabinets and found two wooden cups, a small plate with curved sides like a bowl, and several small candles. One of the cups was split halfway down and the plate was discolored by some earlier meal. Realizing neither was of much use, she chose to leave everything in the cabin and went back out into the fading sunlight. With nothing to set the food on, they each took a spit and broke off pieces of meat as best as they could.

Rhiannon had not realized she was so hungry. The ranger had not used seasonings, but she found it did not matter. The long morning's hike and earlier tension had left her famished. The rabbit and berries disappeared all too soon, and she was left with only the spring water to finish sating her appetite. She drank several times from the flask, but ultimately was left wanting by its lack of substance.

By the time they finished, dusk had come and the air had grown considerably cooler. Intending to start another fire inside the cabin fireplace, Rowan had let the coals burn down after the rabbits were done. Rising to his feet, he gathered the two spits and the depleted water skin.

"I will take care of these, if you will light a few candles from the coals. We can use them to start another fire inside."

Rhiannon nodded and watched him walk toward the spring. She had grown more comfortable with the ranger since their earlier conversation. Although she knew he still had his secrets, she was also certain he intended her no harm. Picking up her chair, she carried it back to the cabin. With the loss of the sun, it was difficult to see inside. She waited a moment for her eyes to adjust before retrieving two candles from the cabinet.

As she stood in the cabin, she was suddenly overcome by a strong feeling of inner peace. The initial shock of being here had waned throughout the afternoon as she came to terms with the memories of her parents. Instead of the sharp, painful reminder of loss, the cabin now offered a warm, comfortable reassurance of their undying love for her. She felt as if they were present and wanted her to know they still cared for her and were watching over her. She stood still and let the peace wash through her, erasing her fears and pains.

"Are you okay?"

She turned and looked toward the ranger in the doorway. Wiping away tears she had not known she was shedding, she was relieved to find the feelings of love did not disappear entirely. They remained in place somewhere deep inside her where she could draw on them, if needed. The realization brought on a fresh set of tears, but she nodded to Rowan.

"Are you sure?"

She could hear the smirk in his voice, but she ignored it. The light of hope that had been kindled in Gulls Bay was burning brighter now, filling her with warmth, comfort, and love.

"I'm fine." Walking toward the doorway, she added, "Sorry, I didn't get the candles lit."

He took a step back, allowing her to exit. When she saw his face, she was surprised to see an odd mixture of sadness and sympathy.

"Whether Asher comes or not, we will leave for Eastcastle tomorrow."

"No. I mean…we don't have to…unless you want to…"

The ranger looked at her. Except for a slight tightening around his eyes, his face was once again unreadable. *So many masks*, thought Rhiannon. *Are any of them real? Or are they all real?*

Slowly, the odd smile crept back onto his face. "Well then, we will sleep on it and make the decision tomorrow."

While Rhiannon lit the small candles from the remaining coals, Rowan gathered more wood and filled the box next to the fireplace. Within moments, they had a warm fire burning beneath the carved wooden mantel. Rhiannon ran her hand along the front panel. It was wider than her hand and displayed birds resting or flying within a swirled design of leaves and flowers. She smiled as she remembered her father's care and precision in everything he did. The ranger's voice brought her back to the present.

"You may have the pallet. I will make do with a chair or the floor. Believe me; I have done with much worse."

She was about to say she had done the same, but gave only a simple, "Thank you."

With a nod, he went to his gear and began to rummage through his shoulder pack. Rhiannon grabbed a blanket from the box and spread it out across the small pallet, trying not to think of the numberless bugs that had likely made a home of it. Removing her boots, she lay down with her back to the wall and pulled the blanket over her. With the fire burning brightly, it was not especially cold in the cabin, but the blanket brought a sense of comfort.

The ranger finally found the object of his search and extracted a small wooden flute from his pack. Holding it up, he asked, "Do you mind if I play?"

Surprised he would even ask, Rhiannon shook her head in reply. Curling her legs in tight, she watched as he set a chair close to the fire and sat down. Putting the flute to his mouth, he played a few random notes before launching into a playful tune. When he looked over at her, he raised his eyebrows and she about laughed out loud. She tried to hide it by rubbing her face with her hand.

Rhiannon recognized a couple of the melodies the ranger played, but most were new. He transitioned smoothly from song to song so each one sounded more like a part of a whole work than an individual melody. The music brought a light feeling to the room and added to the warmth radiating from the fire. Rhiannon watched the dwindling dance of flames over the charred remains of wood. She remembered watching similar fires in this very hearth as her father carved, feeding the flames with his shavings.

As the coals began to break apart in occasional bursts of sparks, Rowan changed to a slow, melancholic tune. Almost instantly, the feeling in the cabin changed with it. The notes hung in the air and seemed to devour all thoughts of happiness, leaving an empty hopelessness in its place. The light of the fire darkened as if death itself had come to spirit it away.

Rhiannon's eyes watered and her soul ached with a deep sadness she had felt only a few times before. She glanced at the shadowed face of the ranger, which was oddly etched by the dying fire. He stared at the glowing coals while his fingers moved gracefully over the wooden instrument. He played as if in a trance, his mind and thoughts lost in the pool of sadness he was creating.

Tears rolled down Rhiannon's face as she watched him. Many times in her life, she had found herself immersed in self-pity, believing no one could possibly understand her depth of loss and sorrow. Yet as she listened, she knew whoever this man was, he did. The flute was no longer playing notes, but instead was weaving small threads of sorrow into a tapestry of terrible loss. No one could evoke such depths of sadness without having faced them personally.

Rhiannon stared at the ranger through blurry eyes and grieved for him and with him. Whatever mask he wore to hide himself, Rhiannon was sure of one thing—Rowan had experienced pain and sorrow in a way few had. She knew it because she saw herself in him.

Slowly, the tune faded. It was not as if he had stopped playing, only that the notes were no longer audible. He stared into the darkening coals, seemingly unaware the mouth piece had fallen from his lips. After a while, he turned to look at Rhiannon, his face all but invisible in the shadows.

"I am sorry," he said, his voice thick. "You have had a long day and I have kept you awake. Forgive me." He stood and made his way to the door.

Rhiannon meant to call to him and tell him she had not cared, but she could not find her voice. As the door shut behind him, she curled into a ball and wept.

Chapter 4

High, low, trill. High, low, trill. The bird call woke Rhiannon. She stayed under her blanket as her eyes swept the room, squinting in the half-light. High, low, trill, came the bird's call again. She wondered if it was welcoming the morning or mourning the arrival of another lonely day. Sitting up, she slipped on her boots and wrapped the blanket around her. The coolness of the morning surprised her.

Crossing the room, she pushed through the door and into the morning light. The bird called once more, but she was unable to locate it in the surrounding trees. She walked to the fire pit where Rowan had built a small fire and sat down on one of the rocks. The ranger was busy attaching some large roots on to new spits.

"Good morning," he said without looking up. "Did you sleep well?"

"Yes, sir. Thank you."

He glanced over to her with a small smile. "So formal?"

She looked down, slightly embarrassed. He gave a short laugh that was not unkind.

"Sorry. I am afraid I do not spend much time around people anymore. I hope you do not mind tubers."

"They're fine," she answered.

She watched as he slid two roots carefully onto the long sticks. He then placed the spits on the same Y-props he had used the night before. When he was finished, he sat back and stared down at the lake.

"I'm sorry," Rhiannon said quietly.

Startled, the ranger looked at her with a puzzled smile. "Sorry? For what?"

"For whatever causes you so much sorrow."

Rowan's eyes tightened slightly, but he held his smile. Glancing down, he breathed in through his nose. When he looked back up, there was a deep sadness in his eyes.

"Thank you," he said. It was stated sincerely, but it also carried a gentle caution he would not discuss it further. Instead he changed the subject. "There was a small group of deer across the lake earlier, but I am afraid I spooked them off while I was searching for these delights."

She smiled at his sarcasm.

"I could not justify killing one for just a single meal, as we will be starting for Eastcastle as soon as we have eaten."

"No. I mean, we can wait for your friend. Really."

"You do not want to go back?"

"No, I do. It's just, well, I mean we don't have to go right away." Quietly, she added, "No one will be missing me anyway. Except Mistress Melinda. And maybe Quinn."

The ranger looked at her, his face unreadable. "Melinda is still there, then." He gave another short laugh. "Is she still cooking?"

"Yes, sir. I have been working for her in the kitchen. She has never said so, but I think she knows who I am. I mean, I think she knows who my parents were."

Rowan's smile was back in full. "Oh, I believe you can count on that. Renard may think he runs the castle, but I am willing to bet it turns where Melinda steers it. Stay close to her. She is tougher than a tanned hide, but you will never find a truer friend."

"You know a lot about Eastcastle, then?"

"*Knew* is likely more correct. I have not been there for years and much has probably changed since then."

They talked of lighter things after that. They discussed the surrounding area, the wildlife, the weather, and even some happier memories of her parents and her father's sword tournaments. Through it all, the ranger showed no traces of the emotion from the night before.

Rhiannon listened intently to his stories, amazed he had known her parents so well—particularly her father. Some of the stories she had never heard, and the ones she had, were from her father's perspective. At times, he had her laughing so hard, she could hardly breathe. They talked through breakfast and before she knew it, the roots were gone.

Finally, Rowan stood and stretched. "Would you like to walk around the lake?"

"But your friend…if he comes, he might miss us."

Rowan gave a chuckle. "If Asher is within three leagues of us, he will not miss us. The man is part hound—at least the part that is not bear."

"May I put the blanket back first?"

"Of course. In fact, I think I will leave the bear a note, in case he arrives early."

They both walked back to the cabin. Rhiannon folded the blanket and replaced it in the large wooden box by the side of the bed. When she turned to leave, she noticed the ranger had spelled out "be back shortly" on the floor with twigs.

Standing to admire his work, he laid a hand on the carved wooden mantel. "What do you think?"

"Will he know it's you?"

"He will know," the ranger answered, slapping his hand on the mantel with a dull, hollow thud. Surprised by the sound, Rowan turned to look at the carved mantel.

"These are not just birds, they are *hawks*."

Stepping closer, Rhiannon saw he was right. She was alarmed when the ranger pulled out his belt knife, but watched curiously as he carefully slipped the thin blade between the top shelf and the front panel. Slowly, he pried up one end of the shelf, slipping a candle stub underneath to hold it open. Working from the other side, he managed to free the shelf completely and propped it against the wall. Reaching in, he pulled out a long bundle wrapped in oiled leather. He laid it carefully on the floor and slowly unrolled it. When he was finished, a sword glinted in the sunlight shining through the open door.

Rowan rocked back to a squat, his hand rubbing his bearded chin.

"Is it my father's?"

Seemingly startled, the ranger glanced up at her and shook his head.

"But you recognize it. Whose is it?"

"That is the wrong question," he said quietly. "The real question is: what is it doing here instead of lying on the bottom of the ocean?"

Rhiannon look at him, puzzled. The ranger's face was hard again and the same veiled anger she had seen the day before flashed in his eyes.

"This is the Flame of Eastcastle. It was last seen with Rustan Hawk."

"But, that means…"

"Someone took it off the boat before it sunk."

Rhiannon sat down on the small pallet. "Then the bishop was right," she said almost to herself. "Quinn's parents were murdered. How else could the sword have been taken?"

The ranger stared at the girl. Suddenly, Rhiannon realized what she had said. "What do you know of what the bishop said to Quinn?"

"Not very much. Just that he said his parents had been murdered and my father had provided him with proof."

"The jewelry box and the letter."

Rhiannon nodded.

"Did he say anything else?"

"I don't remember anything else. Just about the box and that it was hidden in the church. He tried to tell him exactly where, but he was too hurt to talk. Quinn didn't say anything else that I can remember."

The ranger rubbed his face and stared down at the sword. The hilt was inlaid with gems and covered in gold leaf. It may not have been practical for fighting, but it was impressive to look at. After a while, he carefully rewrapped the sword and set it in the mantel box.

Forcing a smile, he said, "Still care to walk around the lake?"

She gave a quick nod and stood. Walking toward the door, she tried to figure out what the presence of the sword meant. She was fairly certain her father was the one who had hidden it. No one else would have known of the mantel box, and the carvings on the front were clearly his. But how did he get the sword in the first place? The thought popped into her head that perhaps he had stolen it, but she quickly discarded it. She had heard her father talk many times of Rustan Hawk and it had always been with admiration. He could not have had any part in the plot that took his life. So, if he had not taken it himself, then he must have found the person who had. That was the only thing that made sense. Finding the sword would have tipped him off that something more than a storm had killed the duke and his wife. Rhiannon realized she was standing outside the cabin completely lost in her thoughts. Rowan was watching her, but said nothing.

"Sorry. I was just thinking."

"As far as I am aware, that is not a crime." The smirk was back, the anger dispelled again.

"If my father had the sword, why didn't he tell anyone? Why did he run away instead?"

The ranger smiled. "How like your parents you are, young Rhiannon." He paused for a moment before answering. "I honestly do not know. Perhaps he feared people would think he had done it."

"He didn't."

Rowan gave her a sad smile. "I know."

Rhiannon looked down, suddenly embarrassed.

"Perhaps he did not know who he *could* tell. Without knowing who had done it, how could he be sure he was not telling the murderer? He would have needed to be very careful." The ranger looked out at the sunlight reflecting off the surface of the lake. "Perhaps he simply ran out of time."

"Why didn't he just tell the duke? I mean, the new one, Renard."

Rhiannon noticed Rowan had put on his ranger cloak. He looked at her from underneath his hood. "As I said, he would have had to be very careful."

Rhiannon looked at him, shocked at what he had just implied. "But he's his brother!"

"Yes," Rowan said quietly and walked toward the lake.

Rhiannon tried to make sense of everything, but it was impossible. No wonder her father had fled from the castle. Possession of the Flame of Eastcastle would have cast him as a murderer in everyone's eyes except those who had actually done it. And to them, he would have been a threat. Without knowing whom to trust, he had been forced to trust no one—except the priest of a small church in Gulls Bay. Sadly, it would later cost the bishop his life.

The girl followed the ranger as he led them along the small, overgrown trail around the lake. They headed in the opposite direction of the spring, passing the trail back to Eastcastle. They walked in silence, both lost in their own thoughts.

Looking out at the lake, Rhiannon was surprised at how much smaller it looked. Her father had taken her on this trail the last time they were here together; however, he had carried her on his back for the better part of it. The peacefulness of the place was the same. The area seemed untouched by the hate and madness she had witnessed over the past few years. It was as if the Creator made such places in the tops of the mountains for people to escape from the world and become renewed.

They had just rounded the bend to a point where they could look back at their camp when Rowan stuck out his arm. Startled, Rhiannon caught her breath. She looked at the ranger, who had his finger up to his mouth and then pointed ahead.

At first, Rhiannon did not see anything except the narrow trail that wove through the long grass. Then a movement caught her eye and a large, antlered buck moved cautiously toward the lake edge. He was a massive creature and moved with elegance and nobleness. For a moment, she wondered if the ranger intended to slay it, but he made no effort to string his bow. The buck lowered his head to the water and drank.

"He's beautiful," Rhiannon whispered. It turned out to be a mistake. The deer's head snapped up, eyeing the surrounding area. Both girl and ranger stood absolutely still, but after a brief moment the buck bolted into the trees.

"Sorry," Rhiannon said.

"Do not be. I am certain the outcome was inevitable. It was simply a matter of time."

"Well, I'm sorry I made it come sooner than later."

The ranger started walking again. The appearance of the stag had interrupted their previous silence and they began to talk. They both laughed when Rowan, distracted by a swarm of gnats, walked straight into a marsh and sunk almost to the top of his boots. Stepping clear with a loud *shwup*, he tried to wipe them off as best as he could in the tall grass. Rhiannon laughed even harder when he stumbled and almost fell after stepping in some rodent's hole during the process.

"You know, it is not polite to laugh at the trials of others," he said with mock sternness.

"I know, I'm sorry," Rhiannon said, between laughs. "Really, I am."

"Yes, your sincerity is overwhelming. Come on, then."

They walked around the remainder of the lake without further incident. Rowan pointed out various plants, birds, and other creatures as they walked, always testing her before giving their names. She knew only a handful of the plants, but almost all of the wildlife that they saw or heard. Concentrating on the scenery around them, she was surprised how quickly they arrived at the springs. The walk with her father had seemed to take almost the whole day.

Stopping at the springs, Rowan pulled the water skin from under his cloak and refilled it. Rhiannon took the opportunity to rest on one of the large rocks and look out over the lake. It really was a tranquil place. No wonder her father had loved spending time here. Closing her eyes, she listened to the gurgling of the springs, letting the light breeze blow through her hair.

The past several weeks were a wonder to her. It had been a long time since she had felt such peace. She let the feelings wash through her, healing areas within herself she had not even realized were suffering. It was good to finally let the pain, the fear, and the anger go, each conquered by the quiet force of peace inside her. She was so caught up in the warmth she did not hear the distant baying of hound dogs.

"Rhiannon. *Rhiannon*." The urgency in his voice surprised her. "We have to get back to the cabin. Now."

They hurried back to their camp, the barking of the dogs coming closer as they jogged. Rhiannon was relieved to find a small spark of the peace she had been feeling had not left her. Whatever the future held, she now felt a calmness that would carry her through it.

"Go inside and stay," Rowan said when they reached the cabin. "Do not come out until I call you."

She obeyed without argument, shutting the door behind her. Pulling a chair to the wall, she sat where she could see out one of the many small gaps in the wall. Her heart raced faster as the baying of the dogs grew louder.

Within moments, two hound dogs appeared at the head of the trail they had used yesterday. Alternating between smelling the ground and playfully bouncing along, they paused for a moment at the trail around the lake. The darker of the two turned along the path away from the cabin, while the other began to bark and come closer.

Rhiannon held her breath, hoping the lighter dog would follow the other's lead. Unfortunately, while they circled the area, each trying to convince the other, a third dog bounded out of the woods, followed by two men leading horses. One of them whistled to the dogs while scanning the area around the lake. It was not long before he led his horse directly toward the cabin.

Rhiannon tried to calm herself as she watched them approach. With the recently used fire pit and matted ground, she knew it would be impossible for them not to find the cabin. She was about to hide under the pallet when she got a good look at the approaching men. Her fears instantly dissipated as she recognized Alexander and his father.

With a small laugh of relief, she jumped to the door, opened it, and stood on the threshold. Rowan stood several paces ahead, his back to her. She noticed his bow was strung and he was wearing his arrow sack. She was about to say something when he spoke.

"So you found me after all?" he called out.

The weapons master and his son paused momentarily, surprised at his greeting. The dogs looked briefly at the ranger before passing him and coming forward to where Rhiannon was standing. Bastian looked as if he were about to answer when a voice spoke from behind them.

"Well, it's not as if your markers were all that subtle. Though, I must admit, the going became a bit easier once I decided these chaps and I were headed to the same destination."

Father and son turned quickly, right hands unconsciously moving to sword hilts. Almost casually, the large ranger they had met outside of Canton melted out of the woods. He carried a strung bow, his hooded cloak pulled back to show his boyish, round face and curly locks.

"Well met, Rowan."

"And to you, Asher."

Gesturing with his arm, Asher said, "Please don't let me interrupt. It appears you have other business. I shall wait over here and rest a bit."

Finding a large rock outcropping, he heaved himself up and sat. The bow rested easily in his lap.

Finally acknowledging Bastian, Rowan asked, "So, good weapons master, what brings you into the hills?"

Slightly shaken by Asher's unexpected appearance, Bastian turned back to Rowan and said, "We have come to take Rhiannon back to Eastcastle." His hand remained on his sword hilt.

Eyeing his sword with a smirk, the ranger asked, "And if she does not wish to return?"

Bastian shrugged. "I suppose that's her choice; if it's truly *her* choice."

"Well then, I suppose we should ask her." Turning halfway towards her, but keeping Bastian and his son in sight, the ranger said, "Are you ready to return to Eastcastle?"

Rhiannon was squatting down in an attempt to get one of the hounds to come to her. Still smiling with relief, she nodded and said, "Yes, sir."

Turning back to the weapons master, Rowan said, "Then it is decided." After a pause he added, "I suppose I should thank you for saving me the trip. We were planning on heading there ourselves as soon as Asher arrived."

Bastian's face did not change, but doubt was written all over Alexander's face.

Rowan gave a laugh and said, "Alexander, your candor is refreshing!" Unstringing his bow in one quick motion, Rowan added, "Come, rest for a bit. I would offer you something to eat if I could, but I am afraid the best I can do is point you to a fresh spring."

Still wary of the other ranger's presence, Bastian reluctantly took his hand from the pommel of his sword. Tying off his horse to a nearby tree, he tucked a piece of material into one of the saddlebags.

Watching them, Rowan said, "Of course, Rhiannon's abandoned bedroll. Still, these must be pretty extraordinary hounds."

"Some of the best I've ever worked with," answered Bastian, whistling them over. "They make a good team. What one misses, the other two tend to find." He scratched each one on the head and patted them.

The ranger's face softened a little watching them, but just for a moment. His mocking expression returned quickly.

"You are welcome to stay the night. Asher and I will be leaving shortly, so there will be plenty of room inside. Provided of course, you do not mind sleeping on the floor. However, as I said before, there really is no food."

"We brought enough along with us, though I don't expect to stay much longer than you. As soon as the horses are rested and watered, I imagine we will be off. Will that be a problem?" he asked Rhiannon.

"No, whenever you want to leave is fine. I don't have anything to get together."

"Well then, I will leave you to see to your horses," said Rowan. "If you will pardon me, I unfortunately am *not* without some required preparations."

With a quick nod, he left them, beckoning to Asher. In a smooth motion, Asher hopped off the rock and entered the cabin with Rowan.

When they disappeared inside, Bastian quietly asked Rhiannon, "Are you okay?"

"Yes."

"Does he know you are Marcus' daughter?"

Wrinkling her brow in surprise, she answered, "Yes, but it's okay. He says he was a friend of my father's and based upon the things he knows I think he probably was."

Bastian gave a deep sigh. "Good. I'm glad you're safe."

Taking a few water skins, he excused himself, and headed toward the spring Rowan had pointed out.

"How long have you known who my father was?" Rhiannon asked Alexander.

"Only since last night, when Melinda told us."

"Melinda?"

"She said she knew from the first day you started working in the kitchen."

Rhiannon did not answer.

"By the way, Quinn left this morning for Maldria. He said to say goodbye if we found you."

"So he went, then?"

Alexander nodded. "He wanted to wait for us to come back, but he was afraid to wait any longer after our stunt to Gulls Bay. Besides, that twit Vareen keeps telling the duke the baron will be offended if Quinn doesn't get there as soon as possible."

"How long will he be gone?"

Shrugging, Alexander said, "I don't know. No one has really said. I don't think anyone really knows."

Rhiannon felt disappointed. "I'm sorry I didn't get to tell him goodbye in person. I hope he'll be safe."

"He will be. The duke sent an escort of a dozen men to see him to Shepherds' Pass. From there, he's supposed to get an even larger escort of Maldrian soldiers—according to Vareen, anyway."

The two youth sat down on the stones around the fire pit and watched Bastian make his way towards the spring. Alexander kicked up some small stones with his heel and chucked them into the lake.

"How did you end up with Rowan anyway?" he asked after a while.

"He came and asked me to go with him in the middle of the night."

"And you *went?*"

Rhiannon shrugged and made a face. "I was so scared; I didn't know what else to do."

Alexander shook his head and threw another stone into the lake. "You have guts."

"Thanks," she said smiling.

"Maybe not brains, but certainly guts." He ignored the dirty look she gave him. "What did he want, anyway?"

Rhiannon's face grew serious again. "He wanted me to take him to my parents," she said quietly.

"Oh. He didn't know that they were…"

She shook her head.

Throwing another stone, Alexander gave a short laugh. "We thought he'd taken you to make Quinn give him the letter he found. Melinda guessed Rowan recognized you when Quinn used your name at the church. She thought you might be in danger, so she convinced my father to bring the letter and try and trade it for you."

"He has the letter with him?"

"He has a copy of it. Or, at least there's another copy back at the castle. I think my father has the original."

"Will he let Rowan have it?"

"Are you crazy? You don't seem like you're in danger, so why would he? Giving the letter away could be taken as treason. At least, that's what my father thinks."

"Maybe he could just let him read it?"

"I don't think so. I probably shouldn't even have mentioned it. My father will skin me alive if he ends up losing it."

Rhiannon sat quietly for a moment. "I don't think Rowan would keep it. I think he's trying to figure out what happened to Quinn's parents and just wanted to read it."

"Well, that's not the impression Quinn got at the church."

"He's not like that. Really." Suddenly, Rhiannon sat forward. "Oh! I almost forgot! Guess what Rowan found in the cabin?"

Alexander scrunched up his face, "I don't know. A dead bear?"

"No! He found the Flame of Eastcastle! It was in the fireplace mantel."

"The Flame of Eastcastle! The duke's sword? What in the world is it doing here?"

"Instead of lying on the bottom of the ocean? Exactly!"

Alexander looked at her, his mind whirling.

"Somebody got off that ship," Rhiannon said.

"Or Quinn's parents never got on it. Or at least the sword didn't."

Rhiannon's face clouded. "I hadn't thought of that. Maybe you're right. Maybe the sword was taken from the duke *before* he got on the boat. Then they still might have died in a storm and the whole thing really was an accident."

"Rustan would have never left or lost his sword."

Rowan's voice caused them both to jump. The two rangers stood behind them cloaked and shouldering their supply bags.

"Its presence can only mean one thing: the priest and your father were telling the truth."

Alexander stood, resisting the urge to move his hand to his sword. Neither ranger had made a threatening move, but he felt uneasy around them. Although he had spent time with Rowan before the Spring Festival, the warnings Quinn had given him this morning were fresher in his mind. Whatever had happened in the choir section of the church had changed Quinn's feelings about the ranger. Now, with Rowan standing in front of him, Alexander's nerves were on edge.

"You're leaving then." Alexander tried to hide the relief his father's voice brought. Bastian approached with a full water skin slung on each shoulder.

Rowan glanced at him, his customary smirk etched on his face. "The camp is yours, weapons master. Good travel to you."

"And to you."

"Give my best to Quinn. I am sorry to see he did not accompany you."

At the same time Bastian said, "I will," Rhiannon blurted out, "Quinn is in Maldria."

The ranger's face froze making his smile even more odd than normal. "What?"

Bastian shot Rhiannon a look, eyes on fire, before turning the same look on his son. Alexander began to study the ground.

"Quinn's gone to Maldria. He left this morning."

Looking at Bastian, Rowan asked, "Is this true?"

Bastian nodded, trying to maintain his temper.

"Why is he going to Maldria?"

The weapons master weighed his options and decided nothing was to be gained by lying. "He's gone to live with a baron there in hopes of improving relations between our two countries."

Rowan glanced over at Asher, before asking, "*Which* baron?"

"I believe he said his name was Baron Paddock."

"The *fool!*" Rowan exclaimed.

The verbal explosion caused Bastian to take a step back. "The boy is trying to build upon the peace his father put in place!"

Rowan looked at him as if he had just grown another head. With quiet rage he said, "I was not referring to the boy, but to his so called uncle, the duke!"

Both Bastian and Alexander were shocked at the sudden fury in the ranger's eyes. Rhiannon was uncomfortable, having already seen the fiery anger of the ranger. Only Asher seemed completely unfazed.

Leaning forward, he said quietly, "It appears time has become a precious commodity."

Turning to look at him, Rowan gave a quick nod. His teeth clenched tightly together, causing a muscle to twitch in his cheek. The two rangers turned to leave. After only a few steps, however, Rowan paused and returned to stand before Bastian. His eyes and face were still as hard as flint.

"I am presuming you know who Rhiannon's father was."

"Yes," the weapons master answered.

"Then I am leaving her in your charge. If *anything* should happen to her, you will answer to me. Do not trust all is well inside the walls of Eastcastle, not even at its highest levels. The duke is either a snake or a fool. Either one makes him deadly."

"We will keep her safe."

The ranger's face showed no sign of being set at ease. Quirking an eyebrow, he said, "See that you do."

He turned to look at Rhiannon. "Be careful," he said. Then, with just a hint of a fierce smile, he added, "Probably unnecessary words for the daughter of a king's champion."

"I'll be fine. Just by being here, Bastian has shown his courage. They thought you had taken me as ransom for the letter. They came risking both harm and treason."

Rowan's eyes narrowed slightly. "Then you have brought the letter with you?" he asked Bastian.

Bastian stared at the ranger, his face revealing nothing. Alexander glared at Rhiannon trying to burn holes into her with his eyes. After a moment, Bastian nodded.

"May I read it? I give you my word, I will return it."

Again Bastian held the ranger's eyes; eyes that were still tinged with fury, but which also reflected a quiet dignity and a lack of deceit.

"Zander, get the letter from the pack."

"But father…"

"Zander."

Alexander walked slowly to the horses, blasting one last look at Rhiannon. She casually looked away as though she had not noticed. Upon Alexander's return, he gave the letter to his father, who in turn offered it to Rowan.

The ranger accepted it with a nod and carefully opened the fold. Asher walked to where he could see over his shoulder. After a few moments, Rowan glanced up at the other ranger, indicating nothing with his blank expression. Asher gave a nod and Rowan returned the letter to Bastian.

"I thank you for your trust. Did Quinn honor his promise? Is the duke unaware of its existence?"

"Yes, he honored it."

Bastian did not feel the need to tell him of the other copy or what Melinda intended to do with it.

The ranger gave a tight smile, eyes softening. "Then I apologize to both you and your son and whoever else *is* aware of it. My actions that night have put you all at risk, for there is now no easy way to inform the duke of its existence. I promise, that was not my intention. In fact, quite to the contrary, my only hope was to keep Quinn from potential harm. I have obviously failed miserably in both respects. My recommendation is you keep that letter hidden, at least for a time. I am sure I do not need to impress upon you the fact that lives have already been lost because of it."

Bastian handed the letter back to his son, but said nothing, his face as blank as a stone wall.

"Well, then," Rowan said, "May the Creator keep you each safe on your journeys. Farewell."

With that, both rangers pulled their hoods over their heads and walked toward the trail back to Hunters Wood.

Bastian paused only a moment before saying, "Rhiannon, gather your things together. We will leave as soon as you're ready. I wish to be back to the castle before dusk if possible."

Bastian looked to where Rhiannon was standing, but she had not moved. Instead, she watched as the two rangers disappeared into the surrounding foliage. They both wore similar cloaks, though Rowan's smaller size made him easily distinguishable from Asher. As did the long, narrow bundle wrapped in oiled leather strapped to his back.

Chapter 5

Quinn awoke with a start when the chaise drew to a stop. He groggily wiped the dust from his face as he looked out the window and tried to determine where they were. He was surprised to see several soldiers, which meant they were already at Shepherds Pass. Stretching as best as he could, Quinn realized he must have been asleep for hours. His mouth was dry and felt like it was lined with dust. Thankfully, Melinda had included a water skin with the food she had packed.

Taking a long drink of tepid water, Quinn thought back on his morning. Even now, several hours later, it did not feel real. He had not slept well the night before, which caused him to wander about in a daze. Melinda had made him a special breakfast of sausage, eggs, and hashed potatoes, but his stomach had not allowed him to do it justice. Melinda seemed to understand and did not push him to finish as she normally would have. In fact, she seemed to be barely containing tears the whole morning.

After breakfast, he had met one last time with the duke in the library. Petric was there, of course; though nothing in his demeanor revealed he had just tried to kill Quinn the night before. Unfortunately, he had been too scared to say anything about it to his uncle while the bodyguard was standing next to him. Then again, it may not have made any difference as Renard had been all smiles and compliments. He had spent the morning reciting trite advice regarding manners, obedience, and good impressions. When he had finally finished talking, he personally led the party out to the courtyard where the stable hands had prepared the Maldrian's chaise. Quinn figured the duke was not going to take any chance of something going awry.

Within moments, the courtyard had flooded with various well-wishers. Quinn's aunt had come with both Bertran and Jens. Melinda had brought several wrapped treats and a water skin, which she gave to him with several hugs. She had struggled to keep her emotions in check, which only made it harder for Quinn to do the same.

Alexander and Bastian were already in the courtyard with a pack of hounds, presumably preparing for a hunting trip. Alexander had needled his father about letting him ride in the chaise for a while, but Bastian was adamant that it was not a possibility. Their "hunt" would take them in the opposite direction almost immediately upon leaving the gates of the castle.

Throughout the ruckus, Tucker had leaned against the chaise, appearing neither anxious nor hurried. His face gave nothing away, though his eyebrows dipped a little when the servants brought out Quinn's trunk. After loading it, he finally asked with a puzzled look if more was coming. After being informed to the contrary, he had shrugged and leaned back against the chaise again.

The pit in Quinn's stomach had grown worse as the morning wore on. One part of him wanted to get in the chaise and be done with it, while the other wanted to go screaming back to his room and stay in bed forever. Finally, the duke had hinted it was time to go. One last round of hugs, handshakes, and goodbyes was had before Tucker held the door open for Quinn to climb into the chaise. Within moments, the tall envoy was aboard and the chaise started toward the gates of the castle.

Quinn leaned out the window for one last wave. A small part of him hoped the duke would change his mind and call him back. Alexander had wanted to ride out with them, but the farewells had delayed Bastian's final preparations. He had waved wildly, but was forced to stay within the castle gates.

As they traveled, the butterflies in Quinn's stomach settled. The anxiety he felt earlier seemed to have been tied more to anticipation of leaving than the actual event. The view from the window had alternated between small homesteads with their summer crops and shadowy patches of wooded areas. Occasionally, they had met travelers headed in the opposite direction, and Tucker would slow to let them pass.

After a while, Quinn had grown accustomed to the bounce and sway of the chaise and closed his eyes to rest them. He had doubted he could fall asleep, but within moments his head began to nod. The rest of the trip had been spent in a half-sleep.

It was early in the evening when they reached the barracks on the Eastcastle side of Shepherds Pass. They would spend the night here and leave early the next morning for Maldria. Stopping the chaise, Tucker hopped off the bench and opened the door for Quinn. A grizzled old man with a large moustache greeted him.

"Well met, Quinn Hawk. My name is Saladar. I am the commander here." Quinn braced himself for what he knew was coming. "I knew your father. He was a great man and a true friend to Eastcastle. Welcome to Shepherds Pass."

"Thank you, sir."

"We have some food ready for you and your driver. Please follow me."

Saladar led them into the barracks, which were even more rudimentary than those at the castle. Soldiers milled about, many stopping to look at Quinn as he followed the commander. They were led to a small room with a table and chairs and two pallets. Two bowls of stew had been set out with a small plate of hard rolls.

"Please eat. If you want more, just let one of the men know. I am guessing you are tired from your day of traveling, so I will take my leave. When you are finished, simply set the bowls and plate outside the door and they will be attended to. It is an honor to house the son of Rustan Hawk, if only for a night."

Quinn thanked him again and Saladar gave him a small bow before disappearing through the door.

After he was gone, Tucker said, "Sir, by your leave, I will look after the horses and find some suitable lodgings for the night." He formally bowed and turned to the door.

"Wait," Quinn called to him. "There is stew here. Why not eat first? Besides, I'm sure the guardsmen have already seen to the horses."

The tall man looked at Quinn, his face somewhat puzzled. Returning to the table, he picked up one of the bowls and took a roll.

"Thank you, sir," he said bowing again.

He then walked to the door and left. Quinn stared at the shut door for several moments after Tucker had disappeared. He hoped all Maldrians were not so odd.

Quinn ate quickly, enjoying the warm food after a day filled with only the small snacks Melinda had packed. When he was done, he set the bowl and plate outside the door as he had been instructed. He thought briefly about exploring the barracks, but decided against it. Instead, he selected one of the pallets and sprawled out on it. It felt good to stretch out without the constant swaying motion of the chaise. He doubted he could sleep, having dozed for most of the afternoon, but when he closed his eyes, he found he was mistaken. With the warm stew in his stomach and the comfortable pallet beneath him, he drifted off to sleep.

*   *   *

Quinn never got his chance to explore the barracks. Before he awoke, Tucker had already prepared the chaise for another day's travel. They had a brief breakfast and some small talk with Saladar, but it was not long before Quinn found himself sitting in the chaise again. He took a drink of the refreshing water from his recently refilled water flask hoping to settle his nerves.

As it worked its way down, Quinn stuck his head out the window. A soldier standing at the front of the chaise was talking with Tucker. By the wide grin on his face, Quinn guessed there were no unforeseen problems. After waving to Tucker, the soldier walked back to where Quinn was sitting.

"Good morning, young Hawk. Everythin' all right?"

"Yes, sir."

The middle-aged man stepped close. Speaking softer, he said, "It's a great thing you're doin'. Somethin' your father'd be proud of, that's fer sure." He paused a moment before adding with a warm smile, "You're startin' ta look like 'im, ya know. After all the years, we 'aven't forgot 'im. Well then, take care an' good luck."

The soldier stepped back and whistled a signal ahead. As the chaise pulled forward, he gave Quinn a wave. Quinn returned the wave and sat back against the wall. He thought about what the man had said. The words were actually not much different than those his uncle had been reciting the past several days, but they meant more coming from this grizzled soldier—a man who had probably fought alongside his father. A cry from outside interrupted his thoughts.

"FOR EASTCASTLE! FOR HONOR!!"

Lurching forward again, he looked out the window. A large group of soldiers was standing in formation with their drawn swords held over their hearts in salute. Acknowledging their salute with a wave, Quinn whispered back in a choked voice, "For Eastcastle, for honor."

As he passed, the men raised their swords and cheered. "HURRAH! HURRAH, FOR THE HAWK! HURRAH!"

Quinn waved to them as long as he comfortably could without leaning too far out the window. Finally, he returned to his seat, eyes brimming with tears. They had cheered for him as they had for his father. For the first time in his life, Quinn really felt like he was his father's son—the son of a duke. He always feared his parents would have been disappointed in his life, given his failures in schooling, weapons training, and everything else he tried. He thought back to the soldier's words and smiled. Maybe his father would have finally been proud of him.

Shepherds Pass was the only natural break through the Castlerooks. It was longer than Drake's Pass, but at a much lower altitude. In years gone by, men had herded their flocks from one side to the other, giving the pass its name. Currently, it represented the biggest risk of attack other than by sea. As such, garrisons of soldiers were posted both in Dalatia and Maldria. The pass was long, but fairly wide as it meandered through the high, rocky cliffs on either side. Even at The Narrows, forty men could comfortably walk side by side.

From above, the pass looked roughly like a goblet turned on its side. The Dalatian side opened quickly from the juncture of The Narrows into a roughly round, bowl shape. The wide, semicircular field sloped down gradually to the river valley. The barracks were built against the northern edge of the bowl along the lower edge of the Castlerooks. Additional lookout camps existed throughout the cliffs on both sides.

From The Narrows to Maldria, the pass was not as wide and opened much more gradually. As the chaise started through the high cliffs, the butterflies returned to Quinn's stomach. The high cliffs blocked most of his view, and he had an eerie sense of being eaten by the mountains. He knew when the cliffs were no longer visible, he would be in Maldria.

He took another drink from the skin, closed his eyes, and tried to calm his body. Once he almost called out and told Tucker to turn around—a task that would have been tricky over the shattered rock on the floor of the pass. Breathing deeply, he fought back the fears until he reached a tenuous stability.

After a while, the chaise began to descend into Maldria. Looking out the window at the land before him, Quinn was struck with the thought that it looked a lot like Eastcastle. For some reason, he had thought there would be a noticeable difference, as if he would know he was in Maldria simply from the land itself. He chided himself. *Did you expect the trees to be purple and the grass to be red?*

As they approached the Maldrian garrison, they were stopped by soldiers dressed in green and gold. Glancing discreetly out the window, Quinn could see three men talking with Tucker. Their expressionless faces were in stark contrast to the soldiers on the other side of the pass. After a few words, the men returned to their posts and the chaise lurched forward again. Quinn watched the three soldiers as they passed; however, none of them looked in his direction. In fact, none of the soldiers milling around the area paid him any attention. Each seemed content to go on about his business.

Tucker drove the chaise slowly through the garrison before turning left onto a road following the edge of the mountains. Quinn was surprised that none of the guardsmen joined behind them. Apparently the chaise would be unaccompanied from this point on. He tried to reassure himself that he was not in any danger. Logically, it would not make sense to bring him to Maldria and cause him harm; at least he hoped that was true.

Quinn sat back in his seat, but continued to look out the right window at the land of Maldria. As time progressed, he reassessed his first impression—the land *was* different from Eastcastle. Much of it was barren and rocky with little vegetation. Occasionally, where a stream ran out of the mountains, small thickets of trees grew in green ribbons across the land. Usually at these places, large fields had been cleared on each side of the band of trees. The offending rocks had been piled into low fences, which crisscrossed the land. People of all ages were working the fields, their drab colored clothing standing out against the earthy greens and yellows. At first, Quinn thought a party of neighbors had gathered to help a friend in need, but each successive field was the same. Scores of people worked in each, and they were clearly more than just one family.

As they traveled, Quinn also noticed each farm area contained a large manor house, which could be seen from a great distance. They were each unique in design, but all were magnificent. Even from afar, the timber and rock work were impressive. Most had tall columns and arches, numerous windows, and were surrounded by beautiful gardens, which contrasted sharply with the land around them. Based upon the number of people in the fields, Quinn figured the manors must be the home of multiple families who had banded together to farm the land.

They continued on the road throughout the afternoon. Each time they approached one of the turnoffs to a manor, Quinn's stomach clenched, but Tucker invariably continued on. Quinn realized he had no idea of how far they were going. He had assumed they would be there shortly after exiting the pass. Now that the shadows of the Castlerooks were creeping across the fields, Quinn wondered whether they would be spending the night somewhere again before continuing on the next day. He was not very good at directions, but he guessed they had come at least as far north as Eastcastle was on the other side of the mountains.

As he watched the darkness grow, his stomach growled. Unfortunately, Quinn had eaten everything Melinda had packed for his trip. Even the water skin was empty. Closing his eyes, he tried to rest again, but was too uncomfortable from sitting all day. He finally gave up when he realized he could not keep his eyes shut for very long before watching for more lights.

Finally, when Quinn could barely see because of the darkness, Tucker turned off the road toward some lights burning in the distance. Quinn was so relieved by the thought of finally getting out of the chaise that he no longer worried about meeting the Baron Paddock. As they continued on, the lights separated into scores of lanterns and torches that lit up the front of a large manor house. The front of the building was all stone and was dominated by a huge columned porch, which sheltered a massive arched doorway. Two ornately carved doors of dark wood stood open and a tall, broad-shouldered man stood between them, backlit from the light inside.

Tucker brought the chaise to a stop directly in front of the giant man standing on the porch. Immediately, two footmen rushed to the door of the chaise and opened it. With trepidation, Quinn slowly climbed out, stretching his legs and back as he stood straight for the first time in hours.

"Good evening, Quinn Hawk," a deep voice resonated into the night. "Welcome to Elksheart."

The man stepped out of the doorway and crossed the porch. The light from the hanging wrought iron lanterns splashed across his face. He was a bear of a man, nearly twice as tall as Quinn and easily three or four times his girth. However, from his stance and movements Quinn could see he was mostly muscle. He wore a black, fur-lined robe, which came all the way down to his black velvet evening slippers. His tunic and pants were also black, though they sparkled with silver embroidery. On his left hip, he wore a decorative scabbard that was discordant with the rest of his outfit.

"Thank you…mi…um…sir," Quinn stammered, unsure of the proper address. He wished he had listened more carefully to Vareen's long-winded lectures on Maldrian culture.

The large man laughed a deep, full guffaw, which sounded more like an animal's roar. "'Sir' will do just fine, or if you prefer, milord, lord, baron, Baron Paddock, My Lord Baron Paddock, or just Paddock. I have been called each at one time or another by friend and foe alike— though the latter generally prefer not to use titles."

Unsure of how to answer, Quinn nodded and averted his eyes to the ground in front of him.

The baron looked over his head to the two men standing at the chaise. "Buck, Sanders, help Tucker with the boy's things. He will be in the Green Room."

Turning back to Quinn he said, "Well, where are my manners? Come inside and get something to eat. I am sure you are probably hungry after your day's journey. The men will take care of your horse and baggage."

Quinn looked up at the baron. "My horse? I...I didn't bring a horse. I'm sorry, I didn't know I was supposed to."

Paddock looked at Quinn in apparent disbelief. "No horse? They sent you here without a horse?"

"No, sir. I mean, yes sir, they didn't send a horse." Quinn's heart began to beat rapidly until he realized the baron was trying to contain a laugh. Finally losing the battle, a deep rumble escaped.

"No matter, young Quinn. We will go to the stables tomorrow and you can pick out any that you fancy—except mine, of course."

Surprised, Quinn managed a feeble, "Thank you, Baron Paddock."

The large man laughed again, but stopped when he glanced over Quinn's head. His face grew hard in a flash.

"Sanders, you are to be getting the boy's things," he said in a quiet voice as hard as flint.

The man bowed quickly and said, "Forgive me, my lord baron, but the boy has brought only one trunk, which Tucker and Buck have managed."

The baron stared at the man for a moment longer, before glancing back down at Quinn. "Is this true?"

"Yes, sir."

Paddock screwed up his face and said, "Well, that will not do." Shaking his head, he added, "What has become of Eastcastle since her revolt? Do even the nobles live as paupers in the 'new society?'"

Again, Quinn had no answer, so he looked away instead.

"Well, no matter. We shall remedy that tomorrow as well. Sanders, please inform Abigail we shall need her skills tomorrow."

The man bowed again and walked away briskly, apparently relieved to be dismissed.

"Here I have kept you outside even longer. My apologies again, Quinn. Come inside and let us see if we cannot find you something to eat."

Quinn followed the baron through the large doors into the anteroom. As impressive as the outside of the manor had been, Quinn was unprepared for the interior. Paintings, tapestries, rugs, vases, and statues were visible everywhere he looked. The walls and furniture were covered with ornate woodwork. Silver and gold glinted in the light cast by scores of candles in expensive candelabras and chandeliers. A large staircase went up both sides of the entryway and met in the middle.

"Are you hungry?" the baron asked.

Startled, Quinn realized he had been gawking. "What?"

The baron laughed and asked again, "I asked if you were hungry."

"Oh, uh, yes sir."

"Excellent, because I am afraid the kitchen staff has gone all out. The dining room is through here."

The baron led him down a long hallway beneath the staircases. The walls were lined with paintings. Beautiful landscapes were combined together with detailed hunting and battle scenes, as well as an occasional portrait. Each one looked like a masterpiece to Quinn.

The hallway ended in a huge room with a large fireplace at the far end. Though there was currently no fire due to the summer's heat, Quinn guessed a small tree could be burned in it during the winter.

Turning to his left, the baron took them to an adjoining room where a long table was laden with all sorts of food. Quinn's stomach growled loudly, much to his embarrassment. The baron only laughed his deep throated chortle again before clapping his hands together. Immediately, a small woman stepped through a doorway at the other end of the room and gave a low curtsy.

"Please inform the Lady Carmen and Alysse our guest has arrived and is ready for dinner."

"Of course, my lord," she said, bowing out of the room.

Quinn looked up and down the table in amazement. It looked like a holiday feast. Pheasant, ham, and a beef roast were displayed with vegetables, candied fruit, and several kinds of bread with an almost artistic touch. Quinn was not sure whether they were supposed to eat the feast or just admire it. Of course, the aroma made him hope fervently it was the former. There were easily a dozen chairs around the table, but there were only four settings—two at the far ends and two in the middle. The plates, goblets, and silver were of the finest quality and added to the splendor of the table.

As Quinn was taking it all in, a woman and a girl came in through the doorway the servant woman had just exited. Both wore satin gowns, the lady in black with silver highlights that complemented the baron's garb, and the girl in dark green. Both were beautiful and Quinn felt his face grow warm just looking at them. The woman was slender and her dark black hair was caught up in a net sparkling with diamonds. The girl looked to be a couple years older than Quinn with copper hair, which was set off by her dark green dress. She had a sprinkling of freckles across her nose and an air of gloominess.

The baron walked over to greet them. "Ah, Carmen, may I introduce Quinn Hawk. Quinn, my wife, the Lady Carmen."

Quinn bowed awkwardly, and in doing so, realized he was considerably underdressed in the current company. He felt his face grow even redder.

"Hello, Quinn," she said in a musical voice. "Welcome to Elksheart. We are so pleased you could come."

"Thank you, my lady," Quinn managed to get out.

"And this is our daughter, Alysse," Paddock said, standing behind her with both hands resting lightly on her shoulders.

Quinn bowed again, only slightly better than his first attempt. The girl gave a small, forced smile in acknowledgment before looking away. Quinn looked up at the baron, whose eyes tightened ever so slightly before saying, "Well, I believe it is time to eat. Quinn, you may sit here," he added, pointing to one of the middle chairs.

As he sat, Quinn looked up and down the table, unsure of where to even start. "Are the others eating later?" he asked.

The baron stopped in the process of sitting in his chair and looked at Quinn. After a moment he looked down the table to where his wife had sat. She gave a small shrug of her shoulders and the baron looked back to Quinn.

"The others?" he asked.

Quinn swallowed and then cleared his throat. "I mean…well, I just thought that with all this food there were others who will be eating."

The baron stared at him for a bit before a smile broke out across his face. As he sat, the smile soon gave way to laughter.

"No, Quinn, no. This is all for you. You see, we did not have any way of knowing what sort of food you preferred, so we simply had the cooks make, well, everything." He chuckled again. "Go ahead and eat whatever you want and as much as you want. You will find life in Maldria is probably a bit different than what you are used to in Eastcastle. But, I think you will like the differences."

Quinn nodded and looked down at the food, hoping he looked as if he were deciding what to have first rather than hiding his embarrassment. He was about to reach for some glazed ham when the baron rang a small bell set near him on the table. Instantly, several men and women appeared at the far door. They were there so quickly, Quinn realized they must have been waiting right outside.

Their clothes were immaculate, though not as showy as those worn by the baron's family. Instead they were made from a sturdy black or gray cloth with no finery. As Quinn watched, the baron, his wife, and his daughter began to point at the various entrees. The men and women would then add a serving of each entrée selected to their plates. Quinn looked to each side of his chair and saw servants waiting. Timidly, he pointed at the glazed ham. Immediately, the man to his right stepped forward, retrieved a slice, and placed it on the plate in front of him.

"Thank you," Quinn said.

The man gave a small nod and backed away to his previous spot. Looking up, Quinn caught the baron's eye. He was watching him with a broad smile on his face. Quinn returned the smile and pointed at a dish of garlic potatoes and some sliced cheese. Again, the servants on both sides promptly added helpings of each to his plate. Quinn thanked each of them.

After several more selections, his plate was full. Glancing across the table, he felt embarrassed when he noticed Alysse's plate was only half-filled. With her head resting on the palm of one hand, Alysse was looking down at her plate and picking through the food with her fork.

"Alysse, manners," her mother reprimanded in her musical voice.

The girl quickly sat up, pulling her elbow from the table. "Sorry, mother," she said quietly.

She glanced in Quinn's direction and caught him staring at her. He gave her a sheepish grin, but she had looked back down. Feeling his face grow red again, Quinn concentrated on keeping his eyes on his plate.

"So Quinn, what do you know of Maldria?" the baron asked.

Quinn hurriedly chewed and swallowed the large piece of ham he had just put into his mouth. "Not very much, sir."

"Really," Paddock responded with a surprised look on his face. "They did not teach you about our country?"

Trying to avoid the subject of his aborted schooling, Quinn simply shook his head and filled his mouth with a bite of fish.

The baron scrunched his face, his eyebrows lowering. "Nothing about Maldria? The land? The people? Our history? Nothing?"

Quinn shook his head once to every question.

"Nobody has told you about anything, not even about me?"

The night before flashed through his mind, but he was not about to bring that up.

"Not even Petric?"

The last question froze Quinn's hand on the way to his mouth. For a brief moment, he feared the baron could read minds. Realizing a second too late he was holding a fully loaded fork in the space between his mouth and the plate, he slowly lowered the utensil hoping the baron had not been watching him. Clandestinely, he raised his eyes only to find the baron staring at him. His stomach flopped and he suddenly felt sick.

Watching Quinn carefully, a small, thin smile slid across the baron's face.

"It is all right, Quinn. Your uncle's bodyguard and I share a common past. I can only imagine what he would have to say."

The smile left Paddock's face in the blink of an eye, but he continued on in an almost casual tone. "However, we do need to have an understanding, you and I. First, I must tell you I know more about you than you may think. I am aware of the disappointments you have had in your schooling and training. I am guessing you probably feel as though you have been written off and given up on. In fact, that is primarily the reason you are here."

As he listened to the baron, Quinn successfully fought off the shame he felt, funneling his emotions instead to anger. It was easier to control the outside appearance of anger than the dread and hurt he felt buried deep inside him. He concentrated on trying to bore a hole through the plate with his eyes. He ignored the impulse to look at the man sitting at the head of the table until he called his name.

"Quinn."

His voice was not angry, but carried a strong compulsion in its quietness. Quinn raised his eyes straight ahead. Alysse was watching him, her face devoid of expression. He wondered what she was thinking, but she gave nothing away. Turning his head to the baron, he tried to match her expression. The baron's face was contemplative, his chin resting lightly on top of his folded fingers.

When their eyes met, he continued, "You should also know I do not believe most of what I have heard."

Quinn, unsure of what to say, said nothing.

"You see, I knew your father and I have a hard time believing his son would be so different from him—the apple not falling far from the tree, so to speak. This was the primary reason I asked if you might come and stay here at Elksheart."

Quinn was still not certain how to respond, but thought he should at least thank the baron.

"Thank you, milord."

"Think nothing of it. After all, it is the least I could do for your father." After taking a bite of fish, he added, "Starting tomorrow, we will begin your training." Dread washed over Quinn, but he successfully maintained his blank expression. "Alysse will help you with your letters and numbers, and I will personally see to the rest."

Concentrating on holding in his emotions, Quinn almost missed what he said. When it finally registered, he looked back at the copper-haired girl in front of him. She was still watching him with a blank expression, though he wondered if the small tightening around her eyes meant her feelings regarding his training were the same as his. After a moment she looked back to her food, swirling the vegetable soup with her spoon.

Feeling the baron's eyes still on him, Quinn realized he was probably waiting for him to respond. Belatedly, he said, "Thank you, sir."

Paddock nodded and summoned a servant for additional wine. Quinn tried to return to eating, but his appetite had fled. Despite the high quality of the food, he found he could no longer enjoy it. He was worried about facing failure all over again, only this time among strangers. He knew in the pit of his stomach he would ultimately fail the baron's unrealistic expectations. He wished he had never agreed to come.

The rest of the meal consisted of meaningless small talk. The conversation was dominated by the baron and his wife, while the two children mainly just answered questions. In fact, Quinn thought he could probably count the number of times Alysse spoke on one hand. Even when asked a direct question, she responded nonverbally if she could.

After what seemed like an eternity, the baron excused them from the table. Calling a maid, he asked her to lead Quinn to his room so he could unpack and get situated. The effects of the day's journey, the food's richness, and tomorrow's worries had left Quinn exhausted. Standing, he bowed to the baron and his wife and again thanked them for their hospitality. He would have said goodnight to Alysse as well, but she had disappeared immediately upon being excused.

Following the maid through the ornate hallways, Quinn was led to a large room where everything was highlighted in dark green. A large bed with four hand-carved, wooden posts sat against the far wall, its overstuffed bedding clearly expensive. A small couch and two chairs were on one side of the room, while the other was dominated by a large set of oaken drawers. Quinn's chest sat dwarfed in front of it. Next to the dresser sat a smaller set of drawers topped with an ornate mirror. A small padded bench faced it. The green walls of the room were set off by intricate woodworking, and large paintings of forests and animals hung everywhere. Quinn stopped at the doorway and took it all in. The maid, seeing his reaction, covered a small smile.

The room actually looked even bigger once he entered it due to the large, mirrored armoire sitting against the wall shared with the hallway. Quinn wandered the room gazing at the different paintings, amazed at how real they appeared. Halfway through the circuit, he realized the maid had not left. He turned back to face her and asked, "Is this really my room?"

"Yes, my lord. This is your room," she said with a curtsy. "I was wondering if you needed assistance to change into your bedclothes."

Quinn felt his face begin to grow red again. "No! I mean no, thank you."

The maid gave another quick curtsy and backed out of the room, pulling the door closed behind her. Still feeling like he was daydreaming, Quinn walked to the bed. The covers had been pulled back, exposing a large, overstuffed down pillow and satiny white sheets. He sat on the edge of the bed and removed his boots. Kicking his legs up, he sprawled out on the mattress. It was the most comfortable thing he had ever laid on. Drawing the covers around him, he decided to enjoy at least this night. As soon as the baron realized he really *was* incapable of learning, he was sure he would be on his way back to Eastcastle.

Quinn closed his eyes and tried not to think about it. After several months of finally coming to a shaky acceptance of himself, he was about to revisit it all again. Hoping and praying this time would be different, he drifted off to sleep.

Chapter 6

Quinn woke to a blast of sunlight when the maid opened the heavy curtains. Shielding his eyes, he was struck by two thoughts. First, he thought he had just barely closed his eyes moments before; and second, despite the first, he was surprised how completely rested he felt.

"Good morning, young master," the maid said with a curtsy. "I am sorry to bother you, but the Baron Paddock has requested your presence in the receiving room as soon as you are available."

Quinn's spirits immediately sank. For a moment, in the brightness of the morning, he had forgotten his worries of the new day. Climbing from the covers, he saw he was still wearing his traveling clothes from the day before. The maid looked at him with disapproval, but said nothing. Instead she laid out several tunics and leggings, each colored in the scarlet and gold of Eastcastle.

"We were unsure of your exact size, so we made several different ones. Come here and I will help you find the one that fits best."

Somewhat embarrassed, Quinn walked over in his stocking feet to where she had laid out the clothes on the small divan. The maid looked him up and down, her arms akimbo. After a few moments, she selected a tunic and held it up to him.

"Stand up straight, please." She leaned back as far as her arm's reach would allow her, squinting and wrinkling her nose. "Maybe a size smaller," she said and swiftly changed to another tunic. After another brief appraisal, she nodded with satisfaction. After repeating the process with the leggings, she asked, "Will you need assistance in dressing?"

"No ma'am."

"Like the bedclothes, then?"

Feeling his face turn red, Quinn mumbled an apology.

"Well, be quick about it, anyway. The baron does not like to be kept waiting. I will be outside the door when you are finished."

As soon as the door closed, Quinn hastily changed into the new clothes. The material had a soft, silky feel to it, unlike the heavy, coarse cloth of his normal clothes. The maid proved to have a good eye as both the tunic and the leggings were a near perfect fit. Scrambling quickly back to the bed, he stuffed his feet into his boots and practically ran to the door. Pulling it open, he stepped into the hallway.

The maid had been standing with her back to his door when he opened it. Turning, she took one look at him and asked, "Is there a problem?"

Baffled by her question, Quinn answered a simple, "No."

"Then what are you doing?"

"I...I thought you said...well, I thought you said the baron was waiting for me."

The maid looked at him as though he were mad, before bursting out into laughter. "Oh no, I don't think so. Not on my shift. March right back in there this instance."

Spinning him around, the maid pushed Quinn back into the room.

"First of all, take off those hideous boots. You are going to meet with nobles, not clean out the stables. There are house slippers over there," she said, pointing toward the side of the divan. "Then, sit yourself down in front of the mirror."

Quinn did as he was told. It took a couple of tries to find the right size slippers as the first ones fell off his feet when he tried to walk to the mirror. He found a good fit on the third try, and then hurried over to where the maid was waiting.

"Have a seat, young master."

Sitting down on the padded bench, Quinn looked at himself in the mirror. His hair was standing straight up in every direction, stiffened by the dust of yesterday's journey. Shrinking down slightly, he glanced at the maid in the mirror. Armed with a comb and a jar of water, she looked like a king's champion set to do battle.

"Honestly, do they teach you any manners at all in Eastcastle?" Quinn winced, as much from the jibe as from the first few strokes through his dirty hair. "If you ask me, what you need is a good dunking first, but we haven't the time for it. Sit up straight, young master."

"My name is Quinn," he managed to get out between flinches.

"I am fully aware of your name, milord."

"What I mean is, you can call me Quinn."

"I am sure I could, but I am just as sure I won't, milord. Lord Baron Paddock's order—you are to be addressed as nobility."

"Oh."

"Now do try and hold still. You are worse than one of the master's hounds."

After a few painful minutes, the maid finally sighed and said, "Well, I suppose that's the best we can hope for in the time that we have. Here," she said, dipping a cloth into the jar of water, "Best wash up your face a bit too."

When he was done, they left the bedroom together. Quinn tried desperately to match her step without running. She led them toward the dining area, but opened two double doors before reaching it. Quinn was disappointed. He had been hoping to grab something to eat before seeing the baron. Looking at the maid, he realized she was not going in. Instead, as she held the door she jerked her head toward the room and mouthed, "Go in!"

The double doors led to a raised platform on one end of a large room. The remainder was filled with wooden benches, much like a small cathedral. About half of them were filled with people dressed in drab brown and gray outfits. They sat talking quietly amongst themselves. Several cushioned chairs had been set on the dais against the front wall. Paddock and another man were sitting in the center two behind a large, sturdy table of dark wood.

"Ah, here he is," said Paddock rising. "Quinn, come take this seat next to me. This is Baron Trimble from the Silver Flats Barony to the south."

Trimble gave him a token nod and smile, which quickly evaporated back to the scowl he had been wearing when Quinn came in.

He looked very uncomfortable in his chair, though Quinn wondered if he would be comfortable in *any* chair. The man was easily wider than Quinn was tall; in fact, he might have been wider than he himself was tall. Quinn gave a quick bow toward both men and sat in the proffered chair. He became very uncomfortable when he realized most of the people in the room were now looking at him.

"I believe we can start now," said Paddock, still standing. "Daniel, please come forward."

A tall, young man with broad shoulders and the largest arms Quinn had ever seen stood and walked toward them. He stopped in front of the small railing, which divided the dais from the rows of benches. He was dressed in clean, sturdy clothes, which were drab brown in color. The straw hat in his hands looked as if it were about to be reduced to horse feed from his constant wringing.

"My Lord Paddock, Lord Trimble…and Master Quinn," he added with a slight bow of the head. "Begging your time and pardon, I have come to ask permission to marry Caroline, the seamstress from Silver Flats. I have discussed it with both her and her mother, her father being deceased, and they are both agreeable to the proposal. I have come this morning to formally submit my proposition to you."

Quinn guessed Caroline and her mother were the two women clasping hands and staring intently at the young man before them. No other emotion showed on their faces except for a hint of anticipation.

"Thank you, Daniel. The proposition of Daniel the smith from Elksheart marrying Caroline from Silver Flats is now before us. What say you, Quinn Hawk of Eastcastle?"

The question took Quinn completely by surprise. Suddenly, every eye in the audience was back on him. He wished he could melt into the chair. He looked at Paddock, but found no help there. The man looked as if he had just asked Quinn to pass him some butter. He glanced back to the audience again and caught the eye of Caroline, who now wore a small, pleading smile.

"Um…I…um…I guess, yes. Sure, if they both want to, I mean…then I guess they can get married."

Inside Quinn felt lost and stupid. What was the baron asking *him* for? In fact, why were they asking *anybody*? He felt even worse when

Trimble coughed loudly and said under his breath, "Paddock, what games are you up to?"

Paddock turned to the round man next to him.

"No games, neighbor. I am interested in the boy's opinion. I would request your silence while he has the floor, please."

The last word came automatically, but without feeling, much like the back of a knife follows the blade. It was clear to Quinn there was obviously no love lost between these two men.

Turning back to Quinn, Paddock asked, "Do you know the profession of the man before you?"

"I believe you said he was a smith."

"Correct, and quite a good one. In fact, one of the best we have at Elksheart. And the woman he wishes to marry?"

"She's a weaver."

"Very good; *however*, she is a Silver Flats' weaver."

"One with years of training, mind you," Trimble added.

Paddock visibly fought off the urge to respond to the man behind him, but continued. "You see, the dilemma before us is I do not wish to lose a fine smith, nor does the Baron Trimble wish to lose a weaver—as he has been quite clear about." The barb cut off an interjection from the rotund man. Instead, he harrumphed. "But they wish to marry. So what do you propose we should do?"

Quinn shifted in his chair. Briefly eyeing Daniel and his sweetheart, he saw they were obviously not going to say anything more. Both of them watched him quietly, though the straw hat was still getting a terrible wringing. Quinn's mind raced as he tried to put together some kind of intelligent answer before opening his mouth.

Clearly, from Trimble's reaction, his first response was lacking. He shut his eyes as much to think of a solution as to ignore the fact everyone was looking at him. For a while, nothing came to him. His mind simply whirled around in a building panic. *What am I doing here? I am not my father.* But then a thought came to his mind—a thought in Melinda's voice.

"When two parties have different ideas and neither one is really wrong, there has to be a compromise. And that was what your father was best at; he knew how to work a compromise."

"A compromise," Quinn almost whispered and then added a little louder, "There has to be a compromise." Opening his eyes, he looked at Paddock. The Baron of Elksheart leaned back into his chair and played his fingers on the table.

"Excellent. So, what is the compromise?"

Quinn looked down at the table, his eyes following the grain back and forth. He fought down his fears again and tried to think it through.

Two people, who want to be together, but have to be apart. Why do they have to be apart? Because they have to work. But that's insane; they should be able to go wherever they want. I don't understand this place at all. Why is he asking me? Two people, two years of work...What if they traded? A year for a year? Or even half a year?

"Maybe they can trade work."

"Trade work? What do you mean?" Paddock asked, but a smile grew on his face.

Bolstered by the baron's reaction, Quinn slowly talked it through. "Maybe they can be married, but share time at each place. Half of the time at Elksheart and half of the time at...the other place. Sorry, I don't remember what it's called."

"It is Silver Flats. So you propose they trade a week? A month? A year? And for how long? Forever?"

"Not every week, that would be too short. Even a month would be hard. I would say maybe every six months? And maybe for several years? Probably until they have a family and it's too hard to move back and forth."

Paddock rubbed his chin, his eyes twinkling. "Each half year they will switch from one place to the other for, say, five years?" Quinn nodded. "Now, where do they start?"

Quinn stopped and thought again. *Did it matter? A weaver and a smith. The smiths in Eastcastle like to work in the colder months when the forges' heat was a blessing. A weaver needs to work when the sheep are sheared. The smith in the winter, the weaver in the summer.*

Continuing out loud, Quinn said, "Spend time at Elksheart in the winter months because the sheep will need their wool and the forges can run hot. In the spring, they can move to Silver Flats. That way, both places will share half of each trade."

Throughout Quinn's explanation, Paddock's smile grew. "And after five years, where do they end up?"

"Can they choose?"

Paddock gave a small shrug. He then gave him a wink, before turning to Trimble. "Neighbor, what say you to young Master Hawk's proposal?"

"It is very much the same as every…"

"What say you?" Paddock asked again, cutting him off, in a slightly raised voice.

Trimble rose slightly in his chair, but flung out a hand when he saw Paddock's face. "Of course, I accept the proposal."

Paddock thumped the table once with his closed fist and said, "The proposition of Daniel the smith marrying Caroline the weaver is accepted. It may transpire at a time and place of their choosing. Following their union, they will follow the compromise as outlined by Master Hawk. Next item."

Caroline gave her mother a hug before standing. She then gave one to Daniel after he made his way back. The couple nodded to the two barons. Caroline caught Quinn's eyes and gave him a quick smile embracing her future husband again. The three of them walked out the door at the rear of the room.

The rest of the morning was spent listening to various requests, complaints, and suggestions. Paddock never again addressed Quinn as he had during the first. Most often he would listen to the presenter and make a decision, some in favor, others not. However, regardless of the ruling, there was never an emotional outburst, just acceptance. In some cases that involved both baronies, Paddock and Trimble discussed the matter until they agreed upon a solution. Occasionally, they asked questions of the presenters, but most of the time they simply took what was stated at face value and made the ruling.

When it became apparent he was not going to be actively involved in all of the discussions, Quinn's nerves began to settle. At first, he listened carefully, in case Paddock asked questions as before, but after several cases Quinn's mind began to wander. Many of the items seemed trivial, such as requests over dead chickens, garden space, or the need for household items. Their seeming insignificance was surprising at first, but as the morning dragged on, they started to sound redundant. Quinn's stomach growled several times, but if Paddock heard it, he chose to ignore it. By the time the last presenters stood, Quinn's bottom was sore as well. He hoped this last one was decided quickly.

The only people left in the room were four men, all dressed in the now familiar drab brown and gray clothing. One of them spoke and explained how a family of beavers had dammed the river and caused it to flood across their allotted farmland. Many of their crops had been ruined, and the land was still partially under water. Quinn listened half-heartedly to the complaint, thinking mostly of lunch.

When the man was done, the two barons began to discuss it among themselves. Apparently, the river served as the boundary between the baronies, and the discussion centered on who was responsible for the clean up. Quinn sat holding his head in his hands, his elbows resting on the top of his knees, barely listening to either one. It turned out to be a mistake.

After a while, the discussion became heated. Paddock's obvious disdain for his counterpart finally got the better of him. The four men standing before them grew uncomfortable, as if fearing the sudden explosion of anger would be turned on them. Quinn tried his best to be invisible.

Suddenly, without warning, Paddock turned to Quinn, his face hard. "Perhaps we should get an unbiased opinion."

"*Unbiased!*" scoffed Trimble, his large round face beet red. "The boy lives and breathes on your whim. He is…"

"Silence, you fool," Paddock hissed, whirling on the rotund man. "Do not try my patience further."

Returning his gaze to Quinn, he asked, "Now, my young friend, what are your thoughts on this matter?"

Bile dumped directly into his empty stomach. A hundred thoughts instantly spun out of control in his mind, not one of which was useful. He struggled to remember what they had even been discussing. *Something about the river flooding.*

"Um…I guess the dam will need to be removed."

"Yes, of course," Paddock said dismissively, with a slight cock of his head. "But by whom? The cleanup and reparations, who is responsible?"

Quinn was not even sure what "reparations" meant. He wished he had been paying better attention to what Paddock had been saying. For Quinn, the "right" answer was probably the one that matched closest to what his host was thinking.

Unfortunately, Quinn could not remember any of the discussion. While his mind fought to replay the last few moments in his head, he blurted out the first answer that came to his head.

"The beavers?"

Paddock stared at him. Quinn tried to sink into his chair. After what seemed like an eternity, a smile crept across Paddock's face. He turned his head down and to the side to look at Trimble askew.

"Of course, Trimble. Your complaint is with the beavers. I suggest you take it up with them." Paddock slapped his open hands down on the table and raised himself up. "You are welcome to use this room for any further discussions with Lord Trimble on how to proceed with the beavers. However, as has been announced several times by Young Master Hawk's emphatic stomach, I believe it is time for lunch."

Motioning for Quinn to follow him, Paddock walked to the side door.

"We are not done here, Paddock!" Trimble growled from behind them. "Paddock!"

The tall baron simply held his left hand up in a dismissive wave without turning around.

"*Paddo…!*"

The door slammed shut with a resounding crash. The baron led them down the hall toward the dining room. As they grew closer, Quinn's stomach reacted to the smell of spices and his appetite began to return.

"Well done today," Paddock said, and then, shaking his head he added with a chuckle, "The beavers."

Quinn chose to hold his tongue, not wanting to risk the chance of the baron figuring out he had not really been listening.

When they entered the room with the large table, Carmen and Alysse were already there, standing against the wall. The baron nodded to them on the way to the head of the table and then gestured for them to sit. Quinn sat where he had the night before, facing Alysse. There was not nearly the quantity of food from the previous evening; however, the large pheasant in spiced berry sauce was still more than enough for a party two or three times larger.

The meal progressed as it had the night before. Each member of the family pointed to an item and it was quickly added to their plate by one of the servants. The servants were never addressed by name or even thanked by the baron, his wife, or his daughter. After a while, even Quinn stopped thanking them, based upon looks he received both from Alysse as well as the servants themselves. Neither the baron nor his wife seemed to care one way or the other.

"So Quinn, how was your first morning?" asked Carmen.

"Um, fine, thank you."

Paddock chuckled and related the story of the beaver dam. "The look on Trimble's face was almost worth the drudgery of enduring his presence."

"You ought not to provoke the man."

"Trimble is a pompous parasite…" Paddock looked as if he were going to add more, but decided against it.

Changing the subject, he said, "Quinn, I have asked Alysse to start your lessons immediately following the lunch meal. She will take you to the library."

Quinn nodded and hoped his forced smile covered the sudden sickening he felt. Glancing at Alysse, he saw she was staring at him with an odd expression on her face. It was the same look the two Maldrian ladies had at the dinner in Eastcastle weeks before. At that moment, deep inside, something changed. A determination grew. Whatever they thought about him no longer mattered—he would prove them all wrong. Bastian had taught him how to fight and he had learned. He would learn to read as well.

"After your lessons, I will take you on a ride through the barony. I think it will help you understand life in Maldria a little better."

"Thank you, sir. I look forward to it."

Actually, Quinn was not really sure he did. He was still unsure of his host. Obviously, he was a powerful man by the way people acted around him. But was he more than that? Not just powerful, but dangerous as well. Somewhere in the back of his head, Petric's words kept fighting to be heard, but he ignored them.

The remainder of the meal was much like the night before. The baron and his wife bantered back and forth while their daughter answered questions in as few words as possible. Given the lack of conversation, Quinn ate more than he should have and his stomach felt overfull.

When Paddock appeared to be done, he effectively ended lunch by standing. The servants immediately began to clear the meal. Quinn stood up as well when he saw Carmen and Alysse rise to avoid being the only one still sitting at the table. Obviously, things started and ended with Paddock and everyone else was better off to follow—and do so quickly.

"Until this evening then, Quinn," Paddock said. "Alysse will take you to the library. Feel free to read any of the books you find of interest." With a head nod, he exited toward the receiving room.

Alysse on the other hand simply walked out the other door without a word. Quinn gathered he was not getting a formal invitation to follow and hurried around the table. He worried he would lose her in the maze of halls. The Lady Carmen wished him luck in her sing-song voice before following her husband.

Walking quickly, he was able to catch up with Alysse. Quinn tried to commit to memory the various furnishings around him so he would be able to find his way again if the need arose. At the same time, he racked his brain trying to think of something to say to Alysse to break the silence. Unfortunately, nothing came to mind. The girl continued on as though she were the only one in the hallway. Quinn wondered if he would have been less uncomfortable if she were not so pretty.

After what seemed like an impossibly long walk through the manor, Alysse finally opened a large door and stood to one side. She had stopped so abruptly that Quinn barely managed to avoid running into her.

"Sorry," he mumbled embarrassedly.

Quinn entered the library first, but only went in a couple of steps before stopping. The library was one of the most beautiful places he had ever seen. All of the walls were done in polished, light-colored wood, which reflected the sunlight from the large leaded glass window panes in the ceiling. The windows were peaked in an inverted "V" down the length of the room and flooded it with natural light.

Instead of having bookshelves along the walls, the room was filled with small free-standing bookcases arranged in precisely spaced rows. Each had two finely carved front panels and held books or rolled parchments in between. Some of the panels were filled with delicate patterns while others seemed to depict a scene of a story. Any one of them would have been a masterpiece, but the whole collection together was astounding. Quinn's eyes wandered from one to the next, discovering each was unique. He figured he could spend the entire day just going from one to the next.

Atop each of the shelves were smaller pieces of art: sculptures in marble, wood, or metal, as well as other pottery and glasswork. Paintings and exquisite tapestries adorned the walls, each more impressive than the next. He wished he could take the time to look closely at each of them.

At the center of the room, several couches and chairs were arranged around a large, circular table. Even the furniture appeared to be works of art. Smaller tables were mixed with the chairs, presumably to be used as reading desks.

"It's impressive, isn't it?" Alysse said.

Quinn turned to face her. She had a small smile on her face—the first Quinn remembered seeing.

"Yes," Quinn exclaimed, "I've never seen anything like it. I mean, we have a library in Eastcastle, but it's *nothing* like this."

Alysse gave a small, musical laugh. "No, I imagine not," she said scanning the room. "You are not how I pictured you, I mean, from the way you were described."

Not knowing what to say, Quinn simply said, "Oh." He was suddenly very uncomfortable and averted his eyes to the art around him.

"You are...I don't know...smarter I guess. The baron told everyone you would be, but still..." Quinn felt his face begin to grow red. "At least you don't drool as much as they said...oh, I'm sorry," she said abruptly, seeing his reddened face and taking it for anger. "That wasn't very polite at all."

"Don't worry about it. It's fine," Quinn answered tersely.

"Well," she said, changing the subject, "What do you want to do first? The baron asked me to help you with reading, numbers, history..." With another short laugh, she finished, "Pretty much everything."

Quinn shrugged his shoulders in response. None of the above sounded very appealing.

She smiled again and said, "Okay, well, why don't you just pick out a book. We'll work on both reading and whatever subject is covered by the book you choose."

Nodding, Quinn went to the first bookshelf and looked through the leather bound tomes. Each sat flat on the slightly sloped shelf with the front side showing the title of the work. Unfortunately, not a single one made any sense to him. Selecting a large one that seemed thinner than the rest, he brought it carefully back to the round table in the center of the room. Climbing into an empty chair, he placed the large leather book in front of her.

"Um, these are maps," she said after looking at his selection.

Growing red again, Quinn tried to cover. "I know. Is that okay?"

Looking at him, she asked, "You really can't read, can you?"

Playing with the corner of the leather cover, Quinn quietly said, "No."

"Did they just not teach you, or can you really not...um...?"

Quinn dug his fingers into the palm of his other hand, fighting down the tears that usually came during these times. He was not going to cry in front of Alysse.

"No, they did. I…I just couldn't figure out all the different rules. There were just too many to keep straight, and they seemed like they changed all the time. I decided I was never going to learn how, so I stopped trying."

"Oh. Well, do you want to try again? It's not hard, really. I mean, once you get the hang of it."

Taking Quinn's silence as a yes, Alysse said, "Here, let me pick one out."

She walked to a different shelf and returned a short time later with a small packet of papers held together between light-colored leather panels. The front one was decorated with an etching of a flower.

"These are some observations a man made about different plants and flowers." She smiled and gave her little laugh, "Not really very interesting, but it's easy to read."

Quinn stared at her. He had known she was beautiful the first time he met her, but with a full smile, her face was angelic. She was more striking than anyone he had ever met. Slowly her smile faded like the sun falling below the horizon into darkness. The cool somberness returned.

Forcing his eyes to the parchments Alysse had spread in front of him, he tried to concentrate on the manuscripts. The letters were written in a curvy script, but they meant no more to him now than they had with Rhiannon at the river.

Rhiannon! He had completely forgotten about her. He hoped she was all right. He knew Bastian would keep looking until he found her because that was the way he was when he committed to something. He hoped his perseverance did not lead him and Alexander to harm. A little voice in his head kept telling him Rowan would not hurt her, but he wondered if it was just his guilty conscience.

"Are you okay?"

"What?"

Alysse's face was touched with concern. "I asked if you were okay. You looked…I don't know, worried about something."

Quinn forced a reassuring smile to his face. "No, I'm fine."

Unconvinced, Alysse let it go. "Okay, well let's start here."

They worked together through the afternoon. At first, Quinn was disheartened and worried more about looking foolish than learning. As the day wore on though, he started to make progress. He began to align the letters with their different sounds and even recognized some of the words. When a servant came and called them to dinner, he told Alysse he could hardly believe the whole afternoon had already passed.

She laughed. "You know, if not for your honest face, I would swear you faked your inability to read all along. You learn very quickly." Then, as before, her face saddened and she said, "We had better head to dinner. He does not like to be kept waiting."

She led them down the same hallways and Quinn realized the manor really was as big as it appeared to be. Quinn had to nearly run to keep up with the longer-legged girl.

"I don't think I'll be able to find the library again."

"Don't worry about it. I will come and find you before each lesson. It takes a while to learn your way around. I remember when…" She cut off unexpectedly with a small, embarrassed smile. "We really need to hurry."

After a couple more turns, they entered the dining area. The baron and his wife were already standing at their respective ends of the table. The baron's face was unreadable, though his eyes were as hard as flint.

"I am sorry, father," Alysse said with a small curtsy. "Quinn was doing so well with his reading we did not realize how late it had grown."

Paddock stared at his daughter for an exaggerated moment before the corners of his mouth twitched slightly. "I am glad to hear you are making such good progress."

He then sat in his chair with the aid of a servant behind him. The others followed suit. The silence of the first half of the meal was only disturbed by the sound of silver on porcelain. Quinn's stomach felt tight despite the wondrous smells around him. It was easier to cut the meat than the tension in the room.

After a while, Paddock questioned Quinn about what he had read and learned. The oppressive feeling in the room lifted, and both the baron and his wife chuckled frequently. Alysse, however, still only spoke when addressed. The radiant smile was missing from her angelic face, as it had been at the other meals. Even though Quinn could not help glancing at her throughout the meal, they seldom made eye contact as she was almost always looking down.

Quinn actually felt a sense of relief when the baron finally stood and invited him to the stables. He noticed Paddock acknowledged his wife as they left, but ignored his daughter. They walked together to the front door and then around to the side of the manor. The building looked even larger than Quinn remembered, but then he had never seen it in the daylight. Workers around the grounds stopped and bowed as they walked past.

"So you are learning quickly, then?"

"Um, I guess…I don't really know."

Paddock gave a short laugh. "Yes, perhaps that was an unfair question. Well, keep at it—hard work and patience are the two keys to accomplish anything worthwhile."

"Yes, sir."

When they arrived at the stables, two horses were already saddled and waiting out front. The giant black stallion covered in silver regalia clearly belonged to the baron. It was the largest warhorse Quinn had ever seen, and a warhorse it clearly was. Its eyes gleamed with fierceness reminiscent of its owner. The other horse, a smaller roan, struck Quinn as being a bit dull compared to its magnificent companion.

As the stable hands helped him mount, Quinn noticed Paddock carried his large sword as usual. Three other mounted men joined them, each armed similarly with a sword. Crossbows hung on the side of their saddles. Quinn tried to match the baron's obvious indifference to them, though he was not nearly as successful.

"I will take you around the barony, and please, if you have any questions, just ask. This is as much to help you learn about our ways as it is to show you your way around."

With that said, Paddock kicked the flanks of his horse and it bolted forward with unmistakable power. Quinn and the men followed, the latter taking care to hover just beyond the range of casual conversation, but near enough to be at hand should they be needed.

"We will go to the village first so you may see how the people live."

They took a small dirt road, which led away from the manor. As they rode, various maids and servants stepped aside, each bowing or curtsying as they passed.

"The servants do not live in the manor?" Quinn asked.

The baron smiled. "No. Each of them lives in the village and returns at their assigned work hour."

"Why don't they just stay in the manor? There must be enough room."

"Certainly there is enough room; however, there is not enough room for *all* of the people. You see, Maldria is very different from *your* Eastcastle. Here, none is treated any different from the rest. Each person is given the same home, the same provisions. Everything is equal to their needs." After a pause, he added, "Go ahead and ask the question."

Quinn looked at the baron in surprise. "What question?"

"The obvious question that would follow my explanation."

Quinn replayed in his head what Paddock had said. "Everyone is equal, except for you."

"Ah, touché, Quinn. Touché! Yes, all are equal, except for the nobility. And why is that, do you think?"

"Um," Quinn started. He was not completely sure how much liberty he had.

As if reading his thoughts, the baron said, "You may say whatever you think around me, Quinn. Do not worry about causing offense. After all, you are in the process of learning, and when learning, no question should ever be taken as an offense."

"Well then, because you are in charge?"

"Well, yes, partly because we are in charge. But, in charge of what?"

"Of everything, I guess."

"Exactly. I am responsible for everything that happens in Elksheart. *Everything*. For example, three years ago, a very late freeze destroyed much of the early crops. Our overall harvest was half of normal." Quinn remembered the year. It had impacted Eastcastle as well. "Do you know what happened as a result?"

Quinn shook his head.

"Effectively, nothing. No one went without food. In fact, no one even missed a meal because I have stores in reserve. How long do you think those stores will last if I need to use them?"

"Six months?"

"Longer."

"A year?"

The baron shook his head. "*Five* years. At Elksheart, we could easily go five years on our reserves with careful planning and execution. So, you see, I am in charge of everything—even the weather!

"I am responsible for making sure every need is met. In order to do that, I must make the best use of every part of Elksheart: the land, the resources, even the people. If everyone farmed, then how are we to be protected? Or if all were soldiers, where would we live? What would we wear? And what would we fight with—our hands?

"You see, I must make sure we have not only farmers, but soldiers, smiths, weavers, craftsmen, cooks—everything needed to make a barony run. And for that, I live in the manor." After a pause, he asked, "What did you think of the library?"

"It was very nice."

"Just nice?"

"Well, no, I mean it is a very beautiful place."

"Everything in that library was made here by our own people. We may have traded for some of the materials, but the craftsmanship is all here. So, you may look at the library and think it is extravagant, a waste of wealth built for my whims, but you would be wrong. In reality, the library is a perfect example of how Maldria works. I supply men and women the opportunity to perform labors to learn their trades. I do not spend money merely to surround myself with trappings, but to make the barony successful. In so doing, the people live well when others find it hard to do so. Now, here is the peoples' village."

The village consisted of rows and rows of houses, each one identical. Made of wood, they were clean and in excellent repair. Small children played in front of many of them, laughing and running. Their clothing was made from the same drab, sturdy cloth Quinn had seen everywhere. The mothers of the children were watching, consoling, or playing along with them. When they saw the baron, they stopped what they were doing and curtsied. Many of the children did as well, though they were less polished. The baron stopped when they were about halfway through the village.

"So, Quinn, tell me what you see."

The question immediately triggered Quinn's memory back to the Cathedral when Elias had asked the same thing. What had he said? *When you are looking for something, what you don't see may be more important than what you do.*

"A man once told me what I see is not always as important as what I don't see."

The baron's smile lost a fraction of its fullness and his eyes tightened slightly. "A wise man."

"Well, what I mean is, well, everything is clean. No one looks...poor, I guess. It's not dirty and I don't see a single house that needs to be repaired or that looks like it might fall over if the wind blows too hard." Quinn paused before adding, "I once went to a place back home near the ocean. The people were very poor. It felt horrible there."

"And here? What do you think of our people?"

Quinn shrugged. "They look happy. And healthy, the people all look healthy. I don't feel sorry for them like I did in Gulls Bay."

Paddock nodded and flashed him a smile, which showed his teeth. Nudging the flanks of his warhorse, he started forward again. Quinn and the others followed. After leaving the village, Paddock led them down the road along the edge of the fields.

"How much do you know of the history of your land? For example, did you know that it was once part of Maldria?"

Quinn had heard of the disputes between the countries on both sides of the Castlerooks, but he did not know much of the specifics. He was surprised by the baron's comment, but figured he was simply referring to the land disputes.

"No, but I really don't know very much."

"Really?" Paddock looked surprised. "I would think the son of a duke, the *heir*, would have been taught more about the land he will someday rule."

Quinn looked away from the baron. "I don't think that will ever happen. At least, I hope it won't."

"Why not?"

Uncomfortable, Quinn gazed out at the fields. He could see countless workers attending to the crops under the hot sun. Finally, when he realized Paddock was still waiting for an answer, he said, "Because I don't think I could do it."

The baron rubbed his bearded chin with his gloved hand. "I see. Well, do not sell yourself short. You realize, of course, no one is expecting you to rule right now. What you think you lack will likely be discovered over the next several years—with the proper training and experience. Based upon your first day with Alysse, it is obvious you possess a quick mind. Perhaps after your stay here, your feelings will change."

Quinn nodded, but did not reply.

"Let me share a little of our history—and yours. If you want to read about it further, I will have Alysse show you where the books are located in the library. Of course, if you do, you should know there are very few references to *East*castle." The added emphasis struck Quinn as odd. "You see, Eastcastle is not really very old."

Confused, Quinn said, "But the castle has been around for hundreds of years."

"I did not say the castle was new, just the name. If you go through the history books, you will see your home referred to as *West*castle."

"*Westcastle?*"

"Yes, Westcastle. You see, years ago, before you were born—well before any of us were born—the castle was built by Maldrians. The duchy of Eastcastle, as you know it, was really two baronies: Westcastle and Riverton."

Quinn was not sure he believed what he was hearing. It sounded ridiculous.

"About forty years ago, the two barons decided to break from the others and form their own country. The lands on the west side of the mountains are full of wood, ore, and fertile land, and they decided they could survive on their own.

"Have you never wondered why your land is called Eastcastle? I mean, what exactly is it *east* of? You see, Vespian Hawk, the *Baron* of Westcastle...yes, your grandfather...renamed it Eastcastle in order to emphasize the break in everyone's mind. He wanted to make sure everyone understood it was no longer part of Maldria."

"But my grandfather was not a baron."

Paddock laughed, but there was no warmth to it. "Actually, he was, before he became the King of Eastcastle."

"*King!*"

"Quinn, you really should study your land's history," the baron said, but not unkindly. "Yes, Vespian was the first and only King of Eastcastle. Of course, the other barons were not happy with his defection. Many of their lands were dependent upon the raw materials from the west, and trading with another kingdom is more complicated than with an equal barony.

"Within months of the declaration, the other barons mustered their armies together and sought to force the return of the two wayward baronies to Maldria. Of course, this would have required replacing the rogue barons as well. Unfortunately, or fortunately depending upon which side you are referring to, Vespian knew an attack was imminent and prepared his people to stand against it."

"At Shephards Pass."

"Precisely. Without a way to flank Vespian's army, the Maldrians were forced to fight in the close quarters of the pass where they were decimated by the longbows of Eastcastle. The battle was over virtually before it began and the barons retreated.

"What followed were years of infighting among the barons as each blamed the other for the failure. Many of the northern barons had not been committed to the campaign from the beginning, as they were fairly self-sufficient. However, those in the southern parts lacked good land and resources. Before long, the barons formed alliances among and against themselves, effectively destroying the strength of Maldria.

"Of course, over the years, other campaigns were launched, but each one ended in failure. An attempt at a sea attack around the tip of Cape Hook was aborted when an unexpected storm smashed half of the fleet against the rocks. Other attempts through the pass were also repelled. Each demoralizing failure was devastating to the poorer baronies, and after a time, the campaigns were abandoned altogether. Vespian had successfully created a kingdom for himself."

Quinn tried to absorb everything. It was like hearing one of the fairy tales his nurse had told him when he was young, only Paddock did not appear to be telling children stories.

"But Eastcastle is not a kingdom. It's a duchy."

Paddock's smile only touched his mouth. "Correct. There is obviously more to the story, but first there is something I want to show you. We will have to walk from here as it will be too dangerous for the horses."

Quinn lowered himself from his horse and followed the baron. They climbed a large rock formation, which stood in the middle of the fields like a joke played by the Creator. There was no real path, and Quinn often had to use his hands to climb from one ledge to the next. When they reached the top, Quinn experienced a wave of vertigo. He had not realized how high they had climbed.

"Are you okay?"

"Yes…yes, sir. I was surprised at the height, is all."

The baron nodded, before looking out at the scene in front of them. "From here, you can see all of Elksheart. It stretches all along the Castlerooks over here to the sea over there."

Quinn looked to where he was pointing and could see a thin wavering line along the eastern horizon. It looked to be half a day's ride away. Behind him, he saw the patchwork fields surrounding the village. Further in the distance, he could just make out the manor house, though it was hard to pick it out of the encroaching shadows.

"Along the edge of the sea is another village for those who work the docks and the fisheries. In truth, it was once its own barony called Northridge. The baron and his wife were tragically killed when their manor caught fire in the middle of a winter's night. The streams and springs were frozen over and no water could be found. The manor was completely destroyed. Rather than build again, Northridge was absorbed into Elksheart, which doubled my responsibilities.

"The land to the south belongs mostly to Silver Flats, under the Baron Trimble whom you met this morning, though you can see some of Salmon Run and Deerfield as well."

After giving Quinn the chance to take it all in, he said, "We had better start back or we will be riding in the dark."

Descending took longer than climbing. Knowing how high they were, Quinn's legs grew shaky. He felt a wash of relief when he was finally on his horse again. As soon as they started riding, Paddock picked up his narrative again.

"When Vespian created his new kingdom, he also changed the traditional Maldrian way of life. Instead of providing trades, protection, and provisions, he decided to model his kingdom after his Dalatian neighbors to the north. He gave his people their *freedom*." The scorn in the last word was obvious. "He no longer concerned himself with their day-to-day trials. Instead, he forced his people to fend for themselves.

"After only a few years, large differences in wealth emerged among his people. While some grew rich through their enterprises, others found themselves struggling just to survive. Towns such as the one you described were little more than overgrown poorhouses. Hunger and poverty existed everywhere, and crime spread throughout the kingdom. The only *freedom* Vespian created was his own—freedom from the responsibilities that should have been his."

Quinn had never known his grandfather, though he had seen his portrait in the library back home. He thought he had been well respected by his people. *Could it be true? Was Eastcastle really created from two baronies of Maldria?*

"So was Eastcastle taken over by Dalatia?"

"Taken over? No, not taken," Paddock said with contempt. "It was given…by your father," he ended quietly.

Quinn's stomach began to churn. *None of this can be true, or at least not entirely. Why would my father have given over his kingdom?*

"After many years of separation, a baron named Philip decided it was time to reclaim the lost lands for Maldria. He was a strong man with much influence and managed to unite the barons once again. He studied the past failures and was determined not to make the same mistakes. Unfortunately, the planning took too long. Before he was fully prepared, someone close to him betrayed him and warned the Hawks.

"At the time of the warning, Vespian was sick and rarely left what would become his death bed. He left the kingdom in the hands of his two sons, Rustan and Renard—your father and his brother. Renard argued for gathering the troops again and stationing them at the opening of Shephards Pass, the only real option for a land invasion. Rustan however, thought differently. He proposed to make Eastcastle a duchy under the rule of Dalatia.

"At first, the people of Eastcastle were appalled and cries of treason rang throughout the halls of the castle. However, your father was a powerful orator and no one could stand against his logic. By becoming part of Dalatia, the united baronies would no longer merely be invading the wayward lands of their past, they would be declaring war on Dalatia. The bulk of Philip's plan was built around the creation of a fleet, which would provide two fronts for the invasion. Unfortunately, he only possessed half as many ships as Dalatia. Within days, a formal proposal was drawn up and messengers were dispatched to Roseland.

"Sadly, the decision was not without a cost. Renard was in violent disagreement with your father. When Rustan's plan was selected, Renard stormed from the castle, seemingly never to return. With him went the informant who had thwarted Philip's surprise invasion. He would later become his bodyguard."

"Petric," Quinn whispered.

"Yes, Petric, the Betrayer of Maldria." The baron's hate-filled eyes glinted in the early dusk. "But Rustan's plan worked. The invasion was aborted and Philip was disgraced. He never again commanded the same power. In fact, he died in relative obscurity.

"Rustan became Eastcastle's first duke under the rule of Dalatia, Vespian having died before the agreements were fully established. The people of Eastcastle became subjected to Dalatia instead of choosing to embrace their past. Anthony gave the duchies some autonomy, but required their allegiance and monies. Rather than giving his people a chance at stability and equality, your father subjected them to a country which sees them as little more than a land of traitors."

Keeping his eyes forward, Quinn tried to sort through what he was hearing. Why had he not heard it before? He did not want to believe what he was hearing, but he certainly had no way to refute it. He knew very little about his father and mother, just bits and pieces really. He had been told Rustan Hawk was a great leader and had done great things for Eastcastle, but never anything specific. What if Paddock was telling the truth?

"I take it from your silence you were taught none of this?"

Quinn shook his head. "No," he said quietly.

"Well, I will not apologize for being the one to tell you. I think it is vital for you to understand how things were if you are to lead someday. No, do not protest. I am an excellent judge of a person's worth and character. You sell yourself too short, Quinn Hawk."

The light faded completely when they rode into the stable yards. After the customary bowing, the stable hands took their horses. Paddock walked Quinn back to the manor.

"I know that was much to hear in one sitting, but as I said, it is extremely important for you to learn it. Take some time and think about what I have said. We will get together later and I will answer any questions you may have."

"Thank you, sir."

"For now, I think you have had a full day. Dalia will show you back to your room. Good night, young Master Hawk."

"Good night, sir."

Chapter 7

The next several days passed quickly. At first, Quinn was homesick for Eastcastle, but it faded as the days went on. He still missed Alexander and the others, and he hoped Rhiannon was safe, but his mind was now preoccupied with other things.

His lessons with Alysse continued and what he had feared would be a trial soon became the best part of the day. After only three days, he was able to sound out most words and recognize over a hundred by sight. He enjoyed the lessons mostly because it was the only time Alysse broke out of her somber shell. Everywhere else she wore the same solemn face he had seen when they first met.

Horseback rides in the evening were Alysse's reward for progress. At first, she presented it as a motivation to help Quinn accomplish more each day. However, when it became apparent Quinn did not need additional prompting, they used it more as free time. As the late summer days shortened, fewer daylight hours were available, but Quinn cherished them. Soon, the shadows cast by the monumental Castlerooks would probably end their rides until next spring.

In addition to his reading, Alysse also helped him learn his numbers, the geography of the surrounding countries, and more of the history of their two lands. Quinn noticed none of the written material he stumbled through contradicted what Paddock had said. The more he read, the more Quinn wondered about his father's actions. The more he wondered the more disloyal and guilty he felt.

Paddock had not yet talked to him about it again. In fact, except at mealtimes, Quinn rarely saw the baron. Often, Paddock entertained men from other baronies. Quinn guessed they were probably other barons, but he did not feel comfortable asking. If Trimble had been one of them, he would have known the answer, but the heavy baron from Silver Flats was never present.

In addition to spending time with Alysse, Quinn also enjoyed getting to know the different servants around the manor. Apparently they were not accustomed to being addressed or acknowledged. He began to use their names and the effect was amazing to him. They brightened and wished him a good day with a bow or curtsy. The stable hands were particularly helpful by having the horses ready for their evening rides so Quinn and Alysse had as much daylight as possible. The only time they were non-responsive was when the baron was present, which was usually limited to mealtimes. At those times, Quinn followed Paddock's lead, keeping the focus off him and the servants.

After two weeks at Elksheart, Quinn had learned his way around the manor. The turns and hallways to the library had taken the longest to memorize, but the servants helped him when Alysse was not present. He was allowed to go wherever he wanted, except when Paddock held one of his conferences. Quinn had been told rather sternly to avoid interrupting them. Usually, he was in the library or out riding anyway, so it had not been a problem. Quinn had met the group only twice in a hallway, and Quinn might as well have been one of the servants for all the acknowledgment Paddock had given him. Apparently, the baron was not interested in conducting introductions, which was just fine with Quinn.

It was after the first two weeks that his schedule changed. Instead of spending most of the day in the library as he had been doing, he was now to start weapons training in the morning. He was informed of this over breakfast, which of course ruined his appetite.

After Quinn had forced food into his knotted stomach, Paddock took him to the weapons yard and turned him over to a stocky man named Dominic. The weapons trainer was a full head shorter than the baron with sparse black hair sprouting from his balding pate. His surly face belied a surprisingly pleasant demeanor.

"So, have you trained before, young Master Hawk?"

"Uh, a little," Quinn stammered, hoping he would not realize just *how* little.

"Excellent. What would you like to start with? The sword? Crossbow? Perhaps, the staff?"

Quinn chose the only weapon he thought he could handle without completely embarrassing himself. "I think I would like to start with the bow."

"Of course, the weapon of Eastcastle. And the favorite of your father, I understand."

"Yes, sir."

"Well, to the archery range then. There are several longbows to choose from."

"Um, actually, may I use a short bow?"

The weapons trainer eyed him carefully, one eyebrow quirked up. A small smile slowly crept across his face. With a nod, he said, "The short bow it is, then."

The two walked to the range together. Dominic whistled a light tune causing Quinn to wonder if whistling was the habit of every weapons master. The thought of Bastian brought a smile to Quinn's face. He decided he was going to like Dominic, if for no other reason than he reminded him of Alexander's father.

Dominic brought Quinn to a little outbuilding and led him inside. The walls were lined with shelves of finely carved bow sticks and well-crafted crossbows, all in immaculate condition. The weapons master let him choose one of the smaller sticks as well as a sack of arrows, while he retrieved a bow string from an oiled bag. Dominic handed the string to Quinn, who quickly strung the bow. A curious expression crossed the older man's face.

"You are pretty familiar with bows, then?"

"Uh, yes, sir. Well, a little bit. I shot in the tournament at the Spring Festival in Bridgetown." Seeing the confusion on Dominic's face, he added, "Oh, that's the big tournament in Dalatia every year."

"I see," said Dominic.

"I didn't do very well, though."

"Well, let's see if we cannot help you do better the next time."

The bulk of the morning passed with Quinn firing arrows at targets until his arms were sore. It reminded him of the first time he practiced with Alexander on the way to Bridgetown. Quinn was surprised to find that between the trip to Gulls Bay and the two weeks here his arms had lost some of their conditioning.

Quinn was generally able to hit the targets, sometimes in their centers. Dominic offered pointers here and there, but mostly he just complimented Quinn on his form and style. Quinn's first assessment had been correct—the weapons trainer of Elksheart was very similar to Bastian.

Quinn shot arrows until he felt he could no longer draw back the cord. Finally, Dominic had him unstring the bow, and they returned the equipment to the outbuilding. Quinn hoped it was time for lunch. He looked to see if anyone had been sent for him. Unfortunately, Dominic had other plans. He led him to another part of the training grounds.

"I think we will end this morning with some sword work. Bows and arrows are a great choice at a distance, but they do not work well when the snake comes at you from behind. Many fine archers have found their deaths on the end of a sword."

Quinn reluctantly followed the stocky man to another outbuilding, this one nearly three times the size of the one at the archery range. Inside were hand weapons of all sorts: swords, daggers, pikes, maces, and quarter staffs. Again, the room was neatly organized. All of the metal blades were smooth and oiled without a trace of rust anywhere. Quinn found himself wishing he could show the room to Bastian, who would have appreciated the obvious care that had been taken.

"The armor is actually kept in the next building; however, we will not use armor today. In fact, select one of the wooden swords from the far table. We will just go through some forms today. Fair enough?"

Quinn nodded and walked to a table stacked with carved wooden swords. Each had been hardened, but most bore small dents from previous use. Quinn felt Dominic watching him as he selected a smaller sword about the size of the one Bastian had given him. He waved it slightly to judge its balance. He found it suitable, though somewhat lighter than the one he had in his room.

"Will that one work?"

"Yes, sir."

"Excellent. Give me a moment to grab one as well and then we can go out to the yard."

Dominic selected one of the longer wooden swords, testing it with a few measured strokes. He flashed Quinn a closed-mouth smile and nodded him out the door. Leading him to an open area of the dirt yard, Dominic showed Quinn several stances and forms. Many of them were identical to the ones Bastian had taught, and Quinn followed them easily. After a while, Dominic stood straight, resting lightly on his sword like a cane.

"You have done this before." A statement, not a question.

"Yes, sir."

The weapons master looked at him for a moment with a puzzled look on his face. Then he shrugged and said, "How about we spar for a while? Nothing fierce, mind you, just an easy, good-natured fight."

"Okay," Quinn said hesitantly.

After the first few parries, Quinn could tell Dominic was exaggerating each move for his benefit. He found he could easily block each advance by instinct. The first time Quinn lightly struck the stocky man, Dominic was surprised, but shrugged it off to luck. The second time, he realized Quinn was not the novice he had taken him to be.

Slowly, the weapons master adjusted his style, smoothing out his movements, speeding up his strokes and advances. Any thoughts Quinn had that the man before him was not a master quickly fled. However, Quinn's instincts did not abandon him.

The training with Alexander came back as if he had just fought him yesterday, and though his arms and lungs burned with exertion, he managed to fend off each attack. He relied heavily on the techniques Bastian had taught him, covering and withdrawing from the reach of the longer sword. He tried to minimize his movements, conserving as much strength as he could, but always looking for a mistake or an opening. Unfortunately, Dominic offered neither.

Finally, after several attacks and repels, the weapons master withdrew and lowered his sword. Quinn lowered his slightly as well, but only as far as he thought he could without losing the ability to defend against a surprise attack. Dominic noted his stance and laughed.

"Good boy, but I give you my word we are done. Well fought, young Master Hawk. You are full of surprises."

"Yes indeed," the baron's voice said from behind him. Quinn flinched, but lowered his sword the rest of the way in an attempt to hide it. He had not heard Paddock approach.

"Hand your practice sword to Dominic and follow me. Lunch has been prepared."

Quinn loosened his grip on his wooden sword, just now realizing how tight his hold had been. Spinning the sword around, he handed the hilt to the weapons master, who accepted it with a bow.

"Until tomorrow then, Young Master Hawk."

"Thank you, sir," Quinn said. Turning, he joined the baron and they walked toward the manor house.

"You have a unique fighting style. It seems especially well-suited for you."

"Yes, sir."

"Who has been training you?"

"Bastian, our weapons master at Eastcastle."

The baron nodded. "I have not heard of him before. Perhaps someday we can meet. At least it is good to know your training has not been completely neglected."

Paddock led them through a side door and down the hallway to the dining area. Quinn was disappointed to find only two plates were set and loaded with food. Apparently, they were eating the midday meal alone.

"Carmen and Alysse will not be joining us today, so I thought we could take this opportunity to talk more. Do you have any questions about what we talked about before?"

"Um…no, not really."

"Well, then I have one for you. Do you know why I invited you here?"

Quinn thought about it for a moment as he sat in his chair. The baron was at his customary spot, but Quinn's plate had been moved closer to it.

"To help build better relations between our countries?"

Paddock smiled and crooked his head. "In part, I suppose, but not entirely."

Quinn waited for him to take his first bite so he could begin his lunch. He particularly needed a drink from the large goblet of water in front of him. Finally, after Paddock lifted his fork, Quinn reached for the metal cup. He took several short sips, hoping the baron was not waiting for another guess from him. He breathed a small sigh of relief when Paddock started talking again.

"My personal belief is that some decisions need to be made in the next few months, which will impact Eastcastle for years to come. And, as the future heir of Eastcastle, I think it is imperative you participate in those decisions. In order to do so, you will need to be taught *all* the history and heritage of your land—something I feel is being severely neglected, unknowingly or otherwise." His tone made it perfectly clear which he thought. "So, I think you should…well, actually, before that, I have another question. Why do you think your uncle agreed to allow you to come here?"

The first answer that popped into Quinn's head was the same one he had given before. Racking his brain, he tried to think of something else, but finally had to repeat himself. "He said he thought I could help build a better relationship between our two countries."

The baron smiled, but it was the smile of a tiger spotting helpless prey. "And he was correct. But *why*? Why build better relations with a country that has stood at odds with yours for so many years?"

Quinn looked down to his plate, absently moving food around with his fork. He never thought there needed to be a reason, other than just to get along better. *Wasn't that good enough?*

"I don't know," he shrugged. "Maybe he's hoping there won't be any more wars."

"Perhaps," Paddock said with the customary crook of his head. "Or perhaps he wants to be king."

The statement caught Quinn completely by surprise. Jerking his head back up, he said, "But that would be treason."

Paddock's cold smile did not fade. "Again, perhaps *or* perhaps not. I do not think he wishes to be King of Dalatia, but I think he does wish for a return of the Kingdom of Eastcastle. Is it really treason to take back something freely given?"

"But you said my father became subject to Anthony in return for his protection. So it wasn't really free."

"Point taken. However, protection against what?"

"Against Maldria," Quinn exclaimed, momentarily forgetting to whom he was speaking. Embarrassed, he looked down and said quietly, "I mean protection against the possibility of another attack."

"It is quite alright, Quinn. Never feel embarrassed for stating a truth, for you are always right regardless of whether or not you are popular. And in this case, you are correct. The deal was made to save Eastcastle from falling into the hands of Philip. He would have most certainly executed the ruling family—*your* family. So, I ask you again, why would Renard suddenly be so interested in developing better relations with Maldria?"

Quinn thought it through. Was his uncle really trying to reestablish Vespian's kingdom? Could it even be done? Surely, King Anthony would not simply let them split off again, not after saving them from Philip so many years before.

"You see," continued the baron, "There are two ways to neutralize an enemy. Either you amass a larger army through strategy and alliances, or you turn the enemy into a friend."

"But it won't work. King Anthony will not just let Eastcastle become a kingdom again, will he? I mean, my father offered his allegiance in return for protection. My uncle can't just end his allegiance because he no longer needs protection, can he?"

Paddock templed his fingers together and rested his chin on them. He looked at Quinn, his eyes hard. "Precisely," he said in a cold, quiet voice. "Which is why you must find a better solution."

"*Me?*"

"Yes, you. You are the rightful heir through your father's line. Whether you are to be the heir to a duchy, a kingdom, or a barony must be your decision. I fear your uncle's ambitions will ultimately turn Eastcastle into a wasteland. It will become a buffer between two great armies, each doing what they feel is right: Anthony, because of your father's treaties, and the Maldrians, because of your uncle's schemes. In the best case, Eastcastle will be thrashed and trampled by war; in the worst, it will simply cease to exist. Unless, of course, you stop it."

Quinn had stopped enjoying his food, which seemed to be happening a lot these days. "How can *I* stop it? I can't do anything."

The baron's face softened. "Forgive me. I can see perhaps I have gone too far with my grim predictions. There is certainly still time for you to learn more and make decisions later, but I feel it is important you understand what you are facing. Perhaps for no other reason than to help motivate you in your studies.

"As for what you can do or should do, I will help you anyway I can. I will give you everything you need to make the best choice, the most informed choice, but I will not make it for you." With a broad smile, he added, "Obviously, *I* would like to see you become the new Baron of Eastcastle, but again, only you can make that decision."

Quinn went back to picking at his food, the meal ruined. At first, the history lesson had been interesting and he had wanted to know everything he could about his grandfather and the Kingdom of Eastcastle. Now, he wished he had never heard of it.

He tried to convince himself it was possible that none of what Paddock had said was true. After all, he had never been taught any of it before. Maybe the baron had made it all up or at least twisted it in some way. He hoped it was so, but something in the back of his mind hinted at its truth. Memories of the festival at Bridgetown kept replaying in his mind. His uncle at the sword tournament with the king, the man at the archery shoot, the constables at the bazaar–each one's actions fit well with what the baron had said. And if it were true, what did it mean? Was the baron right? Would Eastcastle once again go to war? What did the baron want him to do about it?

"What can I do?" he asked quietly without looking up.

"For now, nothing. As I said, there is time yet. Your uncle will not move without being convinced he has the support of the Maldrian barons—support he will not get until *I* give it. Never, if need be. You see, I have some influence with the nobles of my country. I will see to it they waffle and delay any serious commitments to your uncle for as long as necessary. At least long enough for you to prepare and decide your own course of actions. And, as I said before, I will help you anyway I can by answering questions, providing information, or even raising an army if you choose. But it will be *your* choice. Agreed?"

Quinn looked at the large man sitting at the head of the table. His face for once did not have the hardness that usually frequented his eyes.

Quinn nodded. "Agreed."

The baron set down his fork. "Well, enough of this. For now, I will show you where you can find the information you need in the library. I have informed Alysse you will not be having your normal lessons today, so you are free to peruse it. I understand you have made great advances during your reading lessons."

Quinn nodded, but did not say anything. In actuality, he was disappointed to hear he would not be meeting with Alysse. He looked forward to their time together. The baron must have seen his disappointment.

"Do not worry. You will still be able to go riding together this evening."

Quinn felt his face redden, but managed to say, "Thank you, sir."

The baron smiled and chuckled. "Quinn, the sun will come up tomorrow and things will be much the same as they have been. Life does not move so quickly that choices must be made in a heartbeat—at least, not yet."

Standing, he said, "Come with me. I will walk with you to the library."

Quinn followed him out of the dining room. He had little hope of actually being able to read the material Paddock was going to show him. They walked through the halls, servants bowing at their approach and averting their eyes. It was very different walking through the manor with the baron. Quinn decided he liked walking alone better.

When they reached the library, Paddock took him to the far corner where several documents and parchments had been gathered together on top of the furthest bookshelf.

"I have gathered together many of the pertinent documents and have instructed they not be moved. Feel free to read through them. Simply return them here when you are finished. Alysse will allow you time each day to study. Will that be acceptable?"

"Yes, sir. It's just...well, lots to think about, I guess."

"Of course. Well, take your time and do not worry too much about what we have talked about. We still have time."

"Thank you, sir."

"I will let the stables know to expect you. After you have had time to read we will talk more." With a nod, the baron excused himself.

The library was lonelier without Alysse. He had only known her for two weeks, but it felt longer. He wished Paddock had let her come today. He wished there was someone he could talk to about everything the baron had said. He missed Alexander and Bastian, and even found himself wishing Rhiannon was here. For the first time since coming, he wished he was back at Eastcastle, and that he could forget everything he had learned in the last two weeks. Of course, he knew that would never be the case. Even if the baron let him go back, he knew his life would never be the same now.

Thumbing through the parchments, Quinn tried to make sense out of the various titles. Most of them contained long words he could not sound out. He used all the sounds Alysse had taught him, but they just did not seem to form any words he knew. After a while, he became frustrated and stopped trying. Even as far as he had come, he realized he was still dependent upon Alysse to be able to really read.

With nothing else to do, he dug through the parchments and pulled out several of the maps Paddock had included. After taking a moment to orient them correctly, Quinn began to study them. The maps were mostly of Maldria, though one or two included parts of Dalatia and the surrounding oceans. After a quick look at each, Quinn decided he needed more room. He carefully carried them to the center table and spread them out side by side.

Although the maps generally showed the same thing, it was apparent the map makers had different ideas regarding the size and shape of the lands. As Paddock had mentioned, most of them referred to Quinn's home as Westcastle rather than Eastcastle. The other baronies of Maldria were also identified. Quinn counted sixteen of them, including Westcastle and Riverton. On the far coast, he found the outline of the Northridge barony, which had been absorbed by Elksheart. For the most part, the baronies were equal in size, though Elksheart had become much larger after annexing its neighbor.

The borders of Westcastle changed from map to map. In fact, on one or two of the newer ones, the name was even shown as the Kingdom of Eastcastle. Quinn was about to return them when something caught his eye on one of the older maps. The baronies of Westcastle and Riverton were much smaller than his uncle's current duchy. Small dots representing Eagles Nest and Gulls Bay were actually *outside* their borders. Quinn had assumed the Westcastle Barony would have gone all the way to the Wolf Hills.

After a final look, Quinn carefully gathered the maps together and returned them to the bookshelf. He tried reading some of the shorter documents one more time without success. He could make out many of the smaller words, but without knowing the bigger ones scattered among them, it was difficult to understand. Going back to the table, he sat back down and looked around.

He had examined all the different carvings over the past couple of weeks, and though they were still remarkable, he did not feel like wandering through them again. Actually, with lunch and his weapons training catching up, what he really wanted to do was take a nap. He moved to one of the small couches, kicked off his shoes, and nestled into the cushions. Before long, he was asleep.

*   *   *

"Quinn. Quinn, wake up."

Quinn jumped awake and his body immediately complained. His muscles had stiffened from the workout with Dominic. Through sleep-filled eyes, he could see Alysse looking down at him.

"How long have you been sleeping?" she whispered.

"I don't know. How late is it?"

"It's time for dinner. In fact, we need to hurry and get there before the baron." When he sat up, Alysse rubbed the side of his face. "You have sleep marks! Did you do any reading at all?"

Quinn was groggy and his muscles hurt. He slowly stretched and yawned. "A little bit, but I couldn't read a lot of the words. I looked at some of the maps though."

"Come on. The baron is going to ask you what you learned, so you'd better think of something. And try and get those marks off your face."

Alysse's frantic manner surprised Quinn. He hurried after her until they reached the doorway to the dining room. She stopped before entering and gave him one more cursory look.

"There's no help for it. He's going to know you fell asleep," she whispered. "Have you thought of anything you can talk about?"

"Um…just about the maps and stuff."

Alysse gave him one last desperate look. "Come on, then."

They slipped in and Alysse was relieved to find they were the only two in the room. Quinn went around the table and was about to pull out his chair when Alysse hissed at him. Motioning with her hand, she beckoned him back to the wall on her side. Quinn turned red and scurried back over.

"Sorry, I forgot!" he whispered.

"You *can't* forget. Okay? You can never forget."

Carmen arrived moments later and stood next to her daughter. As they waited for the baron to arrive, Carmen asked Quinn about his day and his training.

"It was okay," was his only answer.

Alysse kept glancing at his face, and Quinn realized she was still worried about his sleep marks. She seemed to grow calmer as they waited for Paddock. In fact, when the baron finally did walk in, Alysse seemed her normal, if morose, self.

The baron sat and began to select his food without acknowledging he had kept them waiting.

"Quinn, how was your afternoon? Do you have any questions regarding the material?"

The first thought that popped into Quinn's head was "No," but he briefly caught Alysse's eye and changed his mind.

"I thought Eastcastle—well, Westcastle—always went all the way to the Wolf Hills, but the barony maps show it as being much smaller."

Paddock looked at Quinn for a moment, his eyes tightening as they often did.

"No," he said shaking his head and stabbing a piece of ham with his fork. "No, Westcastle was considerably smaller than what is now called the Duchy of Eastcastle. Long ago, many Dalatians came over the mountains and down the coast and formed small settlements. I am sure you are familiar with Eagles Nest. It was founded by Dalatians who found the mountains a nice barrier between themselves and the edicts of the king. Of course, they still considered themselves Dalatians, but if every coin of tax money did not make it to Roseland…," he left off with a shrug.

"But Eagles Nest is now part of Eastcastle."

"Yes. It and the other outward settlements were dropped into your father's lap when he gave his allegiance to Anthony. They had been a constant thorn in Anthony's side anyway, so why not kill two birds with one stone, so to speak. Anthony was tired of their constant calls for help, especially when he was getting little else from them to begin with. They were a 'lose-lose' situation for him. Your father's new duchy provided the perfect solution. Besides, I think he was also hoping his new duke would clean up the social cesspools most of the settlements had become.

"Unfortunately, the people had experienced too much *freedom* for Rustan's policies to have much effect. After all, they had crossed the mountains to escape the full reach of Roseland in the first place. The last thing they wanted was someone telling them how to act again. The fact that the settlements regarded the Hawks as leaders of a foreign country only made it worse. It was quite a shock to suddenly be expected to show fealty to them. And then, when your father introduced his trade regulations…," the baron left off with a meaningful silence.

"Do you think the smugglers killed my father?"

The baron's fork stopped halfway to his mouth. He set it back down still fully loaded. "What do you mean?" he asked.

"The smugglers, the ones in Eagles Nest who were upset about the new trade laws; do you think they killed my father?"

After taking his previously aborted bite, the baron said, "First, you should be careful about your word choices. If a person sees an advantage or a chance to turn a profit, should he not be free to pursue it? After all, the popular…explanation…for the rebellion of Eastcastle was freedom. So, is it really fair to label these men as 'smugglers' when they are really nothing more than traders—albeit, outside the mainstream?

"Second, it is my understanding your father died at sea, the result of his ship being lost in a storm. I am curious why you would think differently?"

Quinn looked up to see the baron staring at him. His face was more puzzled than hard, but Quinn berated himself for having asked the question. A part of his brain blamed Alysse for egging him into this, but he knew deep inside his current awkward position was his own fault. He took a drink from his goblet in a stalling tactic as he thought about how much he wanted to say.

"I met a man who said he thought my parents had been murdered."

"Really? And did he say who he thought was responsible?"

Quinn shook his head. "No. In fact, he said he didn't know."

The baron looked at him for a moment longer before giving him a sad smile and looking back to his own food. "Do you know what the word 'conspiracy' means?"

"I think so."

Paddock looked back at Quinn. "Rumors of conspiracies are an unfortunate byproduct of almost all tragedies. No one wants to believe that fate, bad luck, or whatever you want to call it, is responsible for terrible things like unexpected deaths. So people begin to see things in other people's faces or read between the lines of correspondences. Almost anything can be turned into fuel for the flames of suspicion. However, in almost every case, there really is no fire at the heart of it, only smoke."

"So, you don't think my parents were murdered?"

The baron shook his head. "No, I am afraid I do not."

The silence that followed provided Quinn the opportunity to once again fill his mouth to avoid saying more. The roasted duck was superb anyway, so it was easy to keep his mouth full. In his mind, he thought through the events of the past summer. The bishop had been sincere, even at death's door, and the letter had been where he had promised. He decided he was not as sure as his host seemed to be about the cause of his parents' deaths. He wondered if the baron would change his mind if he knew all that had happened since the Festival, but decided not to find out.

Quinn reached for his goblet and caught Paddock staring at him, his face expressionless. Embarrassed, Quinn tried to give him a smile as he drank his grape juice.

"You made good progress today, Quinn—good questions. Hopefully, in the future you will be able to read more than just the maps. You will find written material does not always need to put you to sleep."

Quinn quickly averted his eyes, willing his face not to redden. From the top of his vision, he saw Alysse flinch slightly as well.

"You two should hurry if you want to get in your nightly ride. The days are growing shorter with the approach of the Harvest. Colder, too."

"Yes, sir. Thank you, sir."

Paddock stood and with a head nod to his wife, left the room. Quinn quickly finished the rest of what was on his plate, noticing Alysse was already done. As she waited, her left leg bounced slightly, but her face was stoic. When his plate was empty, Quinn stood and gave a small bow to Lady Carmen, before turning to Alysse.

"I'm going to get my cloak from my room. Do you want to just meet at the stables?"

"That's fine," she said and excused herself from the table.

Now that he knew his way around the manor, it did not take long for Quinn to retrieve his cloak from his room and head back to the stables. In fact, he was there well before Alysse arrived.

As usual, their horses were already saddled. Quinn climbed on his and walked it slowly in a circle. It felt good to be on horseback. The change from the hot summer days to the cooler evenings of autumn was refreshing. High in the mountains, the first signs of fall colored the slopes with red, orange, and yellow. Quinn smiled as he looked at the mountains already shadowed from the descending sun. The best part of his day was always the evening ride.

Alysse came out as he was staring at the fall colors. She carried her cloak instead of wearing it. She wasted no time mounting her horse, and with a devious smile, rapped her boots against her horse's flanks. Quinn laughed and spurred his own horse after her. Behind them, the usual three guardsmen followed, each bearing a sword and a crossbow.

Alysse steered her galloping horse into the field of wild grass between the manor and the foothills of the Castlerooks. After a while, she slowed her pace and allowed Quinn to catch up. Riding alongside, he said sarcastically, "Thanks for waiting."

She made a face and stuck her tongue out at him.

"Oh, that's nice."

Alysse laughed and looked at the mountains. When she looked back at him, her face had grown serious.

"You still believe your parents were murdered." It was a statement of fact, not a question.

Quinn was so surprised by the abruptness of the question he did not know how to respond.

"So? Is he going to tell me what I can think?"

The girl looked behind her discreetly, judging the distance between the guardsmen and themselves. Seeing that they were beyond hearing range, she noticeably relaxed.

"Don't say things like that, not even in jest."

Taken aback at her seriousness, Quinn apologized. Hoping to clear the air, he asked, "Do you think it's a problem? I mean, if your father knows that?"

Alysse shrugged. "I don't know. I really don't know much about what he thinks or does. I only know he likes to be listened to and he is not very tolerant of opinions contrary to his."

"Hopefully, we won't have to talk about it again."

"Maybe."

"Well, *I* won't bring it up, anyway."

Alysse gave him a small smile, but it looked patronizing. Quinn decided to change the subject.

"So, what did you do today?"

Alysse described her day of meeting with her tutor and being fitted for her new winter wardrobe. "I'm sure you'll be next, seeing as you didn't bring enough clothes with you."

"It would have been enough in Eastcastle."

"Well, you're…"

Alysse did not finish her sentence. She was staring at the two cloaked figures who had risen up from nowhere. The larger one whispered quietly to the horses, stilling them both as he took hold of their bridle straps. Another similarly dressed, but smaller figure spoke in a hushed voice.

"Do not react or signal your guards. You have my word we mean you no harm."

Both men stayed low, keeping the horses between them and the guards. Looking up, the smaller man pulled back his hood to reveal a bearded face with a buckled scar on the side.

"Hello, Quinn."

Chapter 8

Alysse's eyes were wide as she turned to look at Quinn. "Do you know them?" she hissed. But Quinn was not looking at her.

"Where's Rhiannon?" Quinn asked with an angry voice, surprising Alysse.

The smaller man smirked and said, "I have many talents, Quinn, but I am afraid seeing through mountains is not one of them." Looking up at the fading sunlight, he added, "Though I would guess she is probably helping Melinda and the others clean up from the evening meal."

"Quinn, who are they?" Alysse whispered.

Quinn ignored her. "Why should I believe you?"

The man's smile grew. "Because *I* have never lied to you." Quinn flinched at the barb, but did not respond. "And I imagine that is where Bastian and your friend Alexander would have taken her."

Turning to Alysse, the man said, "In answer to your question, young lady, my name is Rowan, and this is Asher. We met Quinn earlier this summer. In fact, at different times, we have each saved his life."

Alysse turned to Quinn, uneasiness still evident in her voice. "Is that true? Are they friends of yours?"

Still smarting from Rowan's jibe, Quinn answered, "I wouldn't say they are my *friends*." He turned back to Rowan. "Why are you here? What do you want?"

"Actually, right now I would be much obliged if you would point to the mountains and act as if you are showing your friend something on the hillside. It seems your escorts are becoming a bit curious as to what you find so interesting on the ground in front of you."

"Not until you tell me what you are doing here. Why did you take Rhiannon?"

Rowan's face grew hard. "Please point to the mountains."

"No."

"*Quinn!*" the ranger hissed, "Your life is in danger here. Now look away and point to the mountains before they come closer!"

Quinn looked down, his eyes as hard as the ones he stared into. He made no movement. Behind them, the three guardsmen began to wander closer. It was their habit to stay about a stone's throw behind, but their unanticipated stop had raised their interest.

"*Quinn Hawk! Do it now!*"

The riders grew closer, forcing the two rangers to sink lower behind the horses. Behind him, Quinn could hear the clinking of their gear, but he remained motionless. His eyes bored into those of the smaller ranger. The smirk was gone and in its place was a visage of barely controlled anger.

Suddenly, Alysse casually raised her arm and pointed toward the hillside. She turned to Quinn as if pointing out a bird or wild animal, but she addressed her question to the rangers.

"What do you want?"

Behind them, the guardsmen slowed and stopped. The hum of their conversation and laughter was just audible over the beginning song of the crickets. Rowan looked toward the larger ranger, whose head bobbed slightly, assuring him they had stopped. His face softened a little.

"We have come to once again save this young man's life. Tomorrow, you will bring as many traveling supplies as you can successfully hide. We will meet you at the foothills and help you escape."

"No."

Rowan snorted through his nose. "You have absolutely no idea the magnitude of danger you are in, do you?" Softening his expression, he added, "Quinn, you must trust me on this. I would not lie to you. You *must* come with us tomorrow."

"I don't believe you."

Alysse began to look like a weather vane, her arm swinging from point to point on the mountain.

"Is it true, Quinn? Did these men really save your life once?"

Her voice was oddly agitated, causing Quinn to look at her. Slowly, as if not wanting to acknowledge the truth, he nodded; though, a scowl remained on his face.

Alysse swallowed and risked a look down at the rangers. "Take me with you," she whispered.

Rowan almost hid his surprise. "I think not, young lady. I imagine the baron will be sufficiently angered by Quinn's sudden disappearance. I will not do more to raise his ire even more."

"Please. We must go *now*. He will find out. Please. *Please!*" Alysse's voice took on an air of hysteria that shocked Quinn. He stared at the girl as if he had never seen her before.

"No. Conditions are precarious enough. I will not sway them unnecessarily on the whim of a daughter who does not see eye to eye with her father. It seems to be a universal problem."

"Please!" she whispered again, on the verge of a complete breakdown. Fighting back sobs she said, "We have to go now. Paddock will never permit us to go riding alone again. He will know. He always knows…" Her small frame began to be wracked with sobs.

Rowan stared up at the girl, his face blank. Quinn wondered what he was thinking.

"Asher, she may be right. We will leave now, though we will need the girl's horse," he said quietly.

"No!" she shrieked, head jerking up. "Take me with you!" She yanked on the reins in an effort to pull the horse from the large man's grasp.

"Your father will…" Rowan began.

"*He's not my father!*" Her shrill voice pierced the evening sky. Stunned by the revelation, they all stared at Alysse. A flood of questions filled Quinn's mind, but he could not voice a single one. Instead, the larger ranger broke the silence.

"I am afraid our time is up, my friend." The dull thuds of horse hooves confirmed the guardsmen's approach.

"Asher, climb behind the girl. We will have to try for the hills."

"No, I'm…," Quinn started, but never finished his objection.

The two rangers leaped fluidly behind the two children and spurred the horses forward. The unexpected appearance of the two cloaked figures brought a cry of alarm from the guardsmen. One of the three peeled off to return to the manor, while the other two galloped toward them, reaching for their swords. The sound of a battle horn rang out across the valley.

Quinn leaned forward and tried to hold on as best as he could. A quick look behind confirmed Alysse was doing the same. They rode faster than was safe for the uneven grasslands, but the two armed men behind provided great motivation. As they neared the Castlerooks, the evening shadows deepened and made the ride even more treacherous. The only consolation was conditions were just as bad for their pursuers.

Rowan led them straight toward the hills. At the last moment, he veered to the right between several large rock formations. Small trees and brush hampered their way, but the ranger weaved through them like a shuttle on a loom. Their surprise start had granted them a small lead; however, the weight of extra riders was beginning to take its toll. They were not going to be able to outrun their pursuers, especially in the foothills.

As Rowan led them past a standing rock three times their height, Asher wheeled his horse around. With his right arm, he picked up Alysse as though she were a rag doll and lowered her to the ground. Screaming, she clawed at his arm.

"Stay here little bird, until I return."

Realizing she was not being left, she collapsed to her knees. Lowering her face into her hands, she began to sob.

Sitting upright, Asher pulled the large bow stick from under his cloak and headed back around the rock. He met the two surprised guardsmen on the other side. The first went down quickly with a blow to his head. His horse rolled to one side and left him in a crumpled heap before running off. The other man drew his horse up short, causing it to rear. Unable to reach him with the bow stick, Asher rode by. After several strides, he turned back sharply, sending rocks flying.

Spurring his horse, he rode directly toward the remaining guardsman, who had also turned. Coming up on his left side, Asher's only option with the bow stick would be a backhanded swipe, which would leave him open to a well-placed sword stroke. Instead, the large ranger rode by again, grabbing the man's cape at the last moment with his left hand and twisting it around his forearm. The man was yanked backwards, somersaulting off the end of his horse and landing flat on his stomach. His sword clattered across the rocks.

Asher turned his horse again and rode straight at the man as he struggled to get to his feet. The guard was forced to roll to one side to avoid being trampled. The first guardsman moaned on the ground as Asher rounded one last time. Taking the reins of the horse he had just unmanned, he headed back into the gap between the mountainside and the rock formation.

Once on the other side, Asher drew up short where Alysse now stood composed. The splotchy colors of her face showed the remnants of her breakdown, but her demeanor was that of a statue.

"Climb up," Asher said, pulling the spare horse toward her.

"Did you kill them?" she asked.

"No, milady, though the one will likely see double for a while."

Alysse mounted the horse, her back straight, and her face emotionless. "Then you have done them no favors."

Asher glanced toward her, but she was not looking at him. Instead, she clipped the flanks of her horse with her heels and rode after Rowan and Quinn. Asher let out a low whistle, and with a shake of his head, followed after her.

They rode along the base of the foothills, avoiding the areas of loose rocks. As they approached a particularly treacherous area, a bird trilled from above. Alysse was oblivious to the call, but Asher replied with a similar whistle. A cloaked shape detached itself from the shadows in the rocks and became Rowan, his longbow held loosely in his left hand.

"We have gained a little time and another horse," Asher said.

"Good. We will make use of each. Quinn, bring your horse to me and ride with the girl."

Quinn led his horse out from a nook in the rocks. His face was still masked with anger, but he held his tongue. They quickly mounted and worked their way further north. Every so often they would hear the sounds of horns behind them, but none were very close. The shadows deepened into darkness, which slowed their progress even more.

"Are you okay?" Quinn whispered to Alysse, who sat in front of him. She nodded, but said nothing. Quinn sat silently for a few more paces before asking, "If you're not the baron's daughter, then who are you?"

Alysse did not answer, and Quinn began to think she was not going to. Finally, she said, "My father was the Baron of Northridge."

"The one who died in the fire? I'm sorry."

"Yes, the one who died in the fire—just like your parents *died* when they were lost at sea. I was given to Paddock, along with my father's lands, ships, and people."

"But you…he calls you his daughter."

"I was officially *adopted* when the two baronies merged under Paddock."

The two rode in silence, trying to keep sight of Rowan in front of them. They could hear the sound of the hooves of Asher's horse clicking on the rocks behind.

"You don't think your parents died in an accident then," Quinn whispered after a while.

"Did yours?"

The sound of water ahead of them ended the conversation as much as Alysse's cool response. Within moments, they heard splashing from Rowan's horse. Alysse guided their horse into the small stream, which ran from the foothills. In the middle of the stream, Rowan materialized from the darkness.

"Dismount here," he said, just loud enough to be heard over the gurgling of the water.

"In the middle of the stream?" asked Quinn.

"Yes. In fact, see that you stay in the water."

Since neither of them had the will to argue, they climbed down from the horse. Quinn alighted first and then held the reins for Alysse. The frigid water penetrated their riding boots immediately. Icy water encompassed their feet and calves with instant shots of pain.

"Your legs will numb soon and it will be tolerable," Rowan said, hearing them both inhale sharply. "We will stay in the water only as long as necessary."

As Quinn and Alysse jostled from foot to foot in an effort to fight the cold, Asher joined them.

"We will part here, my friend," said Rowan. "You must get to Anthony as quickly as you can. Everything will depend upon your speed. Ride as far north as you are able before you set the horses free. It is a shame you cannot take them all the way, but they will never make it up the trails to the High Pass."

"Will he believe me?"

"He must or everything will be lost. If you cannot make him believe you, Eastcastle will become a wasteland." Rowan turned to Quinn. "I need your father's ring."

Instinctively, Quinn reached for the ring hanging around his neck. "No," he said through teeth clenched more from cold than defiance.

"I would not ask if it were not of the utmost importance. Eastcastle is on the verge of war. Only a thin thread of hope stands between it and ruin, and our little escapade tonight will push it even closer to the latter. Your ring may be the key to saving it from destruction. I promise, Asher will return it when he is able."

Quinn wanted to ask how his father's ring was important, but the talk of war reminded him of what Paddock had said.

"Because my uncle wants to be the King of Eastcastle?" he asked.

The darkness was too great for Quinn to see Rowan's face, but after a pregnant pause, he snorted.

"Only if he were a fool. No, your uncle may be prone to bouts of unrealistic optimism, but not even he would be that reckless. He would know such an insane move would put Eastcastle between the hammer and the anvil. Better to be joined with one or the other than to occupy the space between."

"Quinn, please just give him what he wants. I can't feel my feet anymore."

Looking at the near featureless shadow he knew to be Alysse, Quinn grudgingly lifted the necklace over his head and held it out to the ranger.

"Thank you," said Rowan. He handed it up to Asher. "Let us hope it is enough. Quinn, hand Asher the reins of your horse. Take anything you can carry that will be of use—cloaks, gear, food if you have it—and then follow me."

Quinn did as he was asked and then followed the smaller ranger upstream. Alysse trudged through the shallow water at his side. Behind them, the horse hooves splashed momentarily before going silent and all they could hear was the gurgling of the stream.

The numbness of their feet made it hard to walk. The streambed was lined with slick rocks, and it was not long before Quinn was thoroughly soaked from several falls. He also felt several bruises forming on his shins from bashing into the large boulders hidden in the dark water. From the amount of splashing to his left, he gathered Alysse was in no better shape.

Every so often, Rowan stopped and made sure they were still with him. He warned them of dangers as he found them, but even his heightened senses were not foolproof. More than once, they had to scale small falls found only after nearly running face first into a cascading sheet of ice cold water. After what seemed like an eternity, Rowan finally led them from the stream and into a thicket of trees.

"I am sorry for the walk in the stream," Rowan said, "But it will make it more difficult for Paddock's hounds to track us. With any luck they will follow Asher all the way to the High Pass, though they will likely lose his trail before then. I will build a small fire as soon as we are deeper within the trees. The darkness should hide the smoke."

"Where are you taking us?" Quinn asked, his teeth chattering.

"Back to Eastcastle."

"*Eastcastle?* But that's a two day ride, and you've given away our horses."

"We would never have been able to ride them out of Maldria. I am sure couriers have already been sent to the ports and Shepherd's Pass."

"Then how…"

"We will go over the mountains."

Quinn stopped and stared into the darkness in front of him. Alysse bumped into him from behind, not realizing he was no longer moving.

"We have to go back," Quinn said. "You have to take us back. It will take days to cross the mountains, maybe even weeks and we don't have food or blankets or anything."

The dark shadow in front of them stopped and turned back. "I am afraid that will not be possible. These mountains are full of food if you know where to look, so we will be fine. Now, try and get out of anything that is wet and wrap yourselves in your cloaks. The night will only get colder and your wet clothing will make it worse. I will build a small fire to dry them as much as possible."

Alysse and Quinn wrapped themselves in their cloaks before slipping off their riding boots and outer clothing. It felt good to get the wet leggings off, but their underclothes were also uncomfortably damp. They could hear Rowan snapping off the dead undergrowth from the pine trees around them.

"How do you know Rowan?" Alysse whispered as she huddled near him.

"We met him on the way to the Spring Festival. I…uh…ran into some wolves and he rescued me."

"Can we trust him?"

"I don't know. I thought so once, but that was before he kidnapped a friend of mine."

"The girl you mentioned."

Quinn nodded, but then realized she probably couldn't see him very well. "Yes. We found something he wanted, but we didn't give it to him. I thought he took her to get it from us. It's kind of a long story."

"Do you believe him? That he let her go?"

"I don't know. My friends were supposed to take the parchment, the thing he wanted, and try and get her back. He said they came and got her, so maybe they did. I don't know."

They sat quietly together trying to warm up under their cloaks. Quinn's was wet from his numerous stumbles in the creek, but it was better than the open autumn air. Every so often they heard noises in the darkness as the ranger continued to collect wood for the fire.

"Quinn," Alysse whispered after a while. "He's right about not being able to go back. He's also right about Paddock being dangerous. I don't know why he brought you here, but it wasn't to help you. Paddock doesn't help anyone unless he gets something else in return. He's not really like what you've seen. He can be terrible."

"So why *did* he bring me?"

A soft clatter of dropped sticks behind them caused them both to jump. "My guess is he plans to take control of Eastcastle," answered Rowan.

Recovering from the ranger's sudden appearance, Quinn asked, "How would my living at Elksheart help him do that?"

"Because you have a claim to the duchy; a claim Paddock can exploit to his favor."

"But I don't want to be the duke."

The ranger paused in the shadows. "Perfect, because Paddock does not want you to be duke either."

"But..."

"I said he needs your *claim*, not you. Here, huddle around me and block the breeze."

The ranger worked his tinderbox until a spark caught. He carefully nursed it into a small flame. After transferring the flame to a pile of twigs, he slowly added some small sticks. Within moments, the fire began to consume the larger branches Rowan had gathered. As the flames grew, the light spread and illuminated the surrounding trees.

"Quinn, gather some larger branches to hang the wet clothes on. Hopefully they will dry out. They will also help block some of the light. Do not go too far though. Keep the fire within sight."

Quinn pulled his cloak tighter and replaced his wet boots. Though the fire was small, it generated enough heat to provide some warmth. He felt the chill seeping back as he moved away. The light from the fire cast eerie shadows in the tall trees around them. Quinn tried not to think about what might be hiding just beyond the reach of the glow. Using both hands, he broke off several large boughs and dragged them back to the fire.

"Good," Rowan said, pulling out his belt knife. With a few sure strokes, he fashioned a point on each. He then pushed them into the ground, forming pickets around the fire. Quinn gathered their wet clothes and hung them on the branches. Alysse watched quietly as she sat huddled under her cloak. When they were done, the draped clothes formed a semicircle around the flames.

"With any luck, they will be fairly dry by morning," Rowan said. "Now we need to see about finding something to eat. Stay by the fire. I will be back momentarily."

Quinn watched as the ranger disappeared into the surrounding darkness. When he could no longer see him, he returned to where Alysse was staring into the fire.

"Are you okay?" he asked.

Alysse gave him a little smile. "You asked me that already."

"Oh, sorry."

"It's okay," she said with a little laugh. "I'm just scared."

"Scared? Of Rowan? I don't think…"

"Not of Rowan, of Paddock." Her voice dropped quieter, and she said, "If he catches us, he will kill us."

Quinn's stomach lurched at her seriousness. "He won't *kill* us. We didn't do anything. We'll just tell him they took us."

"The guards will tell him we didn't fight and we were talking with them. They will say we went willingly, if for no other reason than to try and save their own lives. But I doubt it will," she added after a pause.

"You're serious. But that doesn't make any sense. I'm sure he'll be mad, but he won't…"

Alysse turned on him. "You don't know him, Quinn. You don't know anything about him. Everything you've seen and heard is a lie. Well, not a lie, but an act. He is using you just like he uses everyone. He says things and does things, just to get what he wants. Rowan is right about him. You were only safe because he needed you for something."

Quinn sat quietly looking into the flames and remembered the experience with Petric the night before he left. He had all but forgotten it during his time at Elksheart, but hearing Alysse echo the same sentiments brought it back to his mind. Had he been blind? Was he really in that much danger? The night suddenly felt cooler and he pulled his cloak tighter. He felt small and lost like his early years at Eastcastle.

The two sat quietly until Rowan returned. He found a few edible plants, but nothing more.

"I am afraid the animals see better than I do in the darkness."

"That's okay," Quinn said, "We've already eaten dinner."

"I hope it lasts," Rowan answered. "Because breakfast will likely be more of the same."

They sat around the fire for a while, but no one seemed very interested in talking. Besides the crackling of the flames and an occasional noise from the woods, the evening wore on in silence. Had circumstances been different, it might have been a peaceful night.

Finally, Rowan stood.

"You should probably try and get some sleep. The next few days will be long and the more rest you can get, the better off you will be. I will keep watch, so do not worry about Paddock's men." The last was directed at Alysse, and Quinn was surprised at the concern shown on the ranger's face. "I will wake you if there is a need."

With no better options, Alysse and Quinn laid down near the fire, drawing their cloaks around them. Dangerous or not, Quinn found himself missing the bed back at Elksheart. The ground was uncomfortable and it took several turns to find the spot with the fewest lumps. The cloak was more troublesome than warm and made a poor blanket. At least some of the heat of the fire still reached him. Quinn stared into the flames and replayed the events that had brought him to his current predicament. He hoped he had not made a mistake.

"Quinn, are you asleep?" Alysse whispered.

"No."

"Thanks."

Confused, Quinn asked, "For not being asleep?"

"For being my friend."

"Oh. You're welcome," he said awkwardly.

It made him think of the last time he had seen Rhiannon and he once again hoped she was truly safe. He rolled, trying to move off the rock digging into his side. It was going to be a long night.

Chapter 9

Quinn awoke several times during the night, and each time, he was disoriented. He alternated between thinking he was in his bed at Elksheart or on his pallet in Eastcastle. He was almost relieved when Rowan gently shook him awake in the gray half-light of morning.

"It is time to go. Get dressed as quickly as you can."

Quinn sat up and stretched. He felt bruised and tired from sleeping on the hard ground. Looking over, he saw Alysse was already dressed and lacing up her riding boots. "Are they dry?"

Alysse shrugged. "Almost. Did you get any sleep?"

"It doesn't feel like it."

Rowan kicked out the remaining embers of the fire and then pulled a fallen tree over it.

"It will not fool a tracker, but it might escape the eye of the casual looker. Are you ready?"

Alysse nodded, but Quinn was still scrambling into his outer clothing while trying to stay under his cloak. His clothes and boots felt damp and cold. When he was dressed, he stood and tried to stretch out some of the kinks from the night before.

Glancing around, he was surprised by how different everything looked from the night before. Rowan had set up camp within a stand of trees, but he could see a meadow of tall grasses just beyond them. A small creek, presumably the one they had walked through the night before, ran through it. Behind him, the trees extended nearly twice as far before ending at a steep slope of rock. Quinn marveled at the ranger's ability to choose such a secure location in the dark.

The ranger led them out toward the field. As they walked, Quinn's clothes warmed and became more tolerable. They walked along the creek rather than in it, which was a welcomed improvement over the previous night. If there was a trail, only the ranger could see it.

Quinn wondered at the different plants and trees that grew in abundance along the creek bed. Birds and squirrels came out with the sun along with scores of flies and other bugs, which kept them swatting constantly.

Quinn had always thought of the Castlerooks as two dimensional—they simply marked the east side of his country. He was surprised to find they were actually a series of peaks and valleys linked together. They climbed several steep slopes, finding meadows at the top, many of which were interlaced with pools formed by industrious beavers. He never saw one of the nocturnal creatures, but they had clearly been left to themselves for quite sometime.

By late morning, they had climbed high enough to see much of Maldria below them. The coast was a thin, wavering line at the horizon. Quinn tried to pick out Elksheart and its village, but Alysse never looked back. The heat of the day made their cloaks unnecessary, so Quinn and Alysse bundled theirs under their arms. Rowan shared his edible plant stash from the night before, which was a far cry from the meals at the manor.

"We will stop and rest here for a while," Rowan said, noticing that both Quinn and Alysse were lagging behind.

Quinn sat down heavily on a rock near the creek. Using a cupped hand, he took several drinks of the ice-cold water. The last handful he dumped over his head. He arched his back as the cold water dripped down his neck.

"Do we have to go so fast?" he asked. "I don't think Paddock could find us even if we spent a week right here."

"Unfortunately, I doubt Paddock is even looking for us."

"Why would that be unfortunate?"

Rowan stared down at Quinn for a moment. "There are several things you should know." He came and sat in the grass. "Paddock and the other barons have formed a large army, one bigger than necessary to merely defend the borders of Maldria. It is divided among all the baronies, but it is clearly an invasion force."

"An invasion force? To invade Eastcastle?"

"Yes, that is my belief. As Maldria is surrounded by the sea on the east and south, there really is no other possibility. In addition, they have also rebuilt his father's fleet. Within a few days, Paddock could easily overwhelm all of Eastcastle's defenses—even if they were prepared. Their only warning will come from us, which means they will have only the time we give them."

"Paddock's father had a fleet? Like Philip's?"

A look of surprise flashed across the ranger's face. "Philip *was* Paddock's father," he said quietly.

"Oh," said Quinn. He felt his face start to redden. "He never told me that."

The smirk returned to Rowan's face. "Not surprising. He likely sees his father as a failure, and Paddock has very little tolerance for such things. Come, we need to keep moving."

Rowan led them through a ravine with high peaks on either side, which gave Quinn the same claustrophobic feeling he'd had in Shepherds Pass. He knew the Castlerooks were tall, but seeing them from within made them immense. The higher peaks were snow-capped throughout the year, but according to the ranger, they would not have to cross any snow fields. The air was colder and thinner now, and Quinn found he was breathing harder. Although the sun was out, the shadows were cool enough that he thought about putting on his cloak. The creek ran through the ravine, which at times became so narrow that Quinn thought they were going to have to walk through it again. Luckily, Rowan found paths along the rocks and ledges, allowing them to keep their boots dry.

When they reached the top of the ravine, Rowan once again allowed them to rest. A large lake sat nestled between the ridge they had just climbed and the one behind it. The lake was fed by a large glacier on the peaks to the north, and drained to the east creating the creek they had been following. It was a deep blue and smooth as glass. Quinn tested the water with his hand and immediately pulled it out. It felt as though it were liquid ice.

The ranger laughed. "I suggest not bathing here."

Quinn smiled back. "Good idea."

"It is called Ice Lake, which seems appropriate as it is covered with ice almost as often as not. I have never felt it be anything but frigid. Rest here while I fill up the water skins. We will not have a water source for a while on the other side."

The ranger walked back down the ravine to where the creek moved swiftly. Leaning out on a rock, he lowed the skins one at a time into the flow.

"I'm exhausted," Quinn whispered to Alysse as he straightened out his legs to stretch them. "I feel like I could sleep for a week."

Alysse gave a small laugh of agreement, but did not say anything. She had grown more morose throughout the day.

"What are you thinking about?"

She shrugged. "I don't know. Nothing. Everything. I have never been outside of Northridge and Elksheart."

"Well, it will be better when we get to Eastcastle, though it isn't as nice as Elksheart," he added somewhat embarrassed.

Alysse stiffened a little. "I don't care. I'll never go back there."

"When we get to Eastcastle, I'll introduce you to Rhiannon—that is, if Rowan was telling the truth. You remind me of her."

"The kitchen girl?"

"Uh, yeah. But she is…well, I mean her father was once the weapons master for Eastcastle," Quinn finished lamely.

Alysse gave him a reassuring smile. "I'd like to meet her."

When Rowan came back, they started around the lake. The sun dipped behind the western ridge and the temperature dropped. Both Alysse and Quinn stopped to put their cloaks on again. Rowan had worn his the entire day.

The bowl that formed the lake was covered with sparse trees and scraggly bushes. The ground was covered in cracked rock from years of freezes and thaws. They made it to the other side of the lake just as the light began to fade. Rowan wanted to set up camp over the next ridge where there were better areas for sleeping.

"We will need to climb out of the valley here," Rowan said in the half light. "The loose rocks make it dangerous to climb behind one another, so spread out to each side and try to stay with me. If you need to stop or you feel like you are falling behind, let me know. Are you ready?"

The two nodded, and they began to climb. The broken rock was unstable and shifted constantly as they ascended. After only a few steps, they were using their hands in addition to their feet. Rowan warned them to be wary of smashed fingers. Occasionally, they started small rock slides, and sometimes they could hear the rocks splash into the lake below them.

Quinn's lungs began to burn, but he decided he would not be the first to ask Rowan to stop. If Alysse could do it without resting, he could as well. Little did he know, Alysse was having a similar argument with herself. Thankfully, about three-fourths of the way up, the ranger turned and carefully sat on a large rock. They quickly followed suit.

"I hope you do not mind if I rest a moment here before continuing," Rowan said wryly. Quinn shook his head, breathing hard. Alysse was stooped forward, her head down between her knees. "Do either of you need a drink?"

Quinn shook his head again and closed his eyes, trying to will his heart to slow down. He was not thirsty as much as he was hungry. The sporadic snacks Rowan had foraged along the way were nowhere near what he had become used to over the last couple of weeks. Of course, the extra expenditure of energy was not helping either. He felt famished and his muscles twitched painfully. When the ranger announced it was time to continue, Quinn reluctantly stood and followed.

As they neared the crest, there were fewer rocks to deal with and the climbing was easier. Rowan stopped at the top and allowed them to look back the way they had come. The lake was just visible in the shadows as the first stars dotted the sky.

"We will have to be even more careful going down the other side. The terrain is about the same, but the light is now worse. Stay side by side again in case we dislodge a slide. When we reach the tree line, we will go in a little further and set up camp. I have saved some jerked meat that we can eat."

The prospect of real food motivated them to make the descent quickly. In reality, it became little more than riding a controlled slide of loose rocks down the hill. Quinn's cloak was constantly in the way, but the extra padding was a blessing each time he landed on his rear end.

They reached the tree line in half the time it took them to climb out of the lake bowl. Rowan led them to the right, away from the rock slide, and into the darkness of the trees. He did not go very far before he stopped. A large rock jutted out from the mountainside and formed a natural shelter. Rowan dumped the wood he had gathered along the way near its base. Alysse and Quinn dropped unceremoniously onto the ground while Rowan retrieved his small tinderbox. Before long, he had a small fire burning.

Once the fire was going well, Rowan rummaged through his packs and pulled out a small, cloth sack. Opening the drawstring, he took out several pieces of jerked meat and gave them each two. The meat was tough and salty, but tasted much better than the plants and berries they had been eating. Quinn's first piece was gone before he realized it. He concentrated on rationing the second.

"Is Paddock attacking Eastcastle because of what happened to his father?" Quinn asked, as he nibbled the end of his second piece.

"Maybe partly," answered Rowan, "But mostly Paddock is his father's son. He was not an innocent bystander when his father decided to invade. In fact, he was in full support of the decision. If anything, he is even more power-hungry than his father."

"But if he's Philip's son, how could he assemble an army? I thought the other barons were against him."

The ranger glanced at Alysse. "Paddock can be very persuasive," he said quietly. "My guess is he has them convinced you are trying to reclaim the rule of Eastcastle, and that in return for his help, you will come back to Maldria."

"But that's not true!"

Rowan gave a snort. "With Paddock, what is true is not nearly as important as what people *perceive* to be true. He tells people what they want to hear so he can use them for his own purposes."

"Like a game of Knights," Quinn said quietly, watching the flames.

Rowan looked over to him with a raised eyebrow. "Yes, exactly like a game of Knights."

"Petric told me that. He's my uncle's bodyguard." The ranger nodded, but said nothing. Watching his face, Quinn asked, "Do you know him?"

Rowan was quiet for a moment. He placed more wood on the fire before answering.

"Yes, I know him," he said finally.

"Why did he betray Philip?"

The question caught the ranger off guard, and his face briefly flashed his surprise. Both youths looked at him, waiting for an answer. "I suppose because Paddock pushed him too far."

"How?"

The ranger smiled more fully, still throwing bits and pieces of wood into the flames. "That is not my story to tell," was all that he said.

"But Petric won't tell me. He hates me."

Rowan glanced at Quinn, his face suddenly unreadable. "Really? What makes you say that?"

"He just does."

"Did he talk your uncle into sending you to Maldria?"

The question surprised Quinn, and he answered without thinking. "No. In fact, as far as I could tell, he was trying to talk the duke *out* of sending me. He came to my room the night before I left and…well…he said he was warning me—about Paddock."

The ranger looked at him for a moment, but said nothing. Instead, he turned to where Alysse was sitting and asked, "Are you thirsty, Alysse?"

Having finished her portions of jerked meat, Alysse had been content to just watch the fire and listen. She was surprised to hear her name.

"Yes, thank you," she said.

Rowan stood and retrieved one of the two water skins from the pile of gear and held it out to her. Opening the top, she took a long drink before handing it back with another, "Thank you."

"Quinn?" Rowan asked, holding the skin to him.

Quinn likewise took a drink. The cold water was refreshing after the salty meat he had just finished. After a quick breath, he took another drink and handed it back to the ranger. Rowan returned it to the pile of gear.

"We have another long day tomorrow. You should try to sleep while you can."

Quinn stood, only to have his body and legs complain bitterly. He had not realized how much he had stiffened in the cool evening air. Gathering his cloak around him, he looked for a spot to lie down. The ground was somewhat flat in front of the outcropping rock, but did not look very soft.

Alysse stretched out on the ground almost immediately after the ranger's suggestion, her face away from the fire. Quinn wondered if she was alright, but did not want to ask her again. She was different than she had been at Elksheart. She had always been quiet, but she was more withdrawn now than when he had first met her.

Following her example, Quinn was relieved to find the ground more comfortable than he thought it would be. Years of fallen needles had formed a cushiony layer, which was almost tolerable. Not long after he settled in, the day's long journey caught up with him. His eyes grew heavy, and he began to drift off to sleep.

During the small gap between sleep and consciousness, he thought he heard the sound of a wooden flute. The tune was familiar, but his mind was too weary to remember exactly what it was or where he had heard it. Within moments, the airy notes melted into the developing dreamscape, and Quinn fell into a deep sleep.

As with the night before, Quinn was more than happy to get up when Rowan woke him. The temperature had dropped during the night and his cloak had not been enough to keep him warm. The ground had grown harder as each hour passed. When Quinn sat up, the smell of sizzling meat was a welcomed surprise. Alysse was already awake, huddled in her cloak near the fire. Pulling his own tighter, he joined her. They watched as Rowan tended to the small ground squirrels he had caught sometime earlier.

"Good morning," the ranger said. "Did you sleep well?"

"Not really," Quinn mumbled.

Rowan chuckled. "Well, I guess that makes it unanimous. Breakfast will be ready in a minute."

Quinn watched the meat drip and sizzle on the spits and his stomach growled loudly. Embarrassed, he tried to cover it up by asking, "Do you play the flute?"

The ranger looked over the fire at him, his eyes unblinking.

"Not really," he said. "Sorry, did I keep you up last night?"

Quinn shook his head. "No. It's just I thought I recognized what you were playing, but I was too tired to wake up and ask you what it was."

"You play very well," Alysse said, surprising them both. She had not said more than a couple of words since the first night they had fled from Elksheart.

Rowan gave her a mock bow. "Thank you, milady, but in reality I am afraid I only tinker where others excel."

Standing up straight, he lifted the spits from the fire. "These will take a while to cool. While we are waiting, if you would both be kind enough to follow, I have something to show you."

They stood and followed the ranger as he led them back the way they had come the night before. As soon as they broke out of the trees, he led them higher onto the shattered rocks.

"Now," he said stopping, "Look behind you."

Quinn and Alysse turned and stared at the vista before them. It was the most majestic panorama Quinn had ever seen. The slope dropped off into a deep wooded valley that was bordered on every side by mountains. The various peaks were interlaced like fingers down the length of the valley as far as the eye could see. Autumn had painted bright reds, oranges, and yellows across the canvas of green. A single large eagle glided in great circles across the sky.

"It's called The Creator's Garden," said the ranger from behind.

"It's beautiful," said Alysse in a voice just above a whisper.

Quinn simply nodded, absorbed in the view.

"Go ahead and have a seat. I will fetch breakfast, and we can eat here."

Quinn and Alysse sat carefully on the loose rocks while Rowan walked noiselessly back to their campfire.

"Do you believe in Him?" Alysse asked quietly.

"In Rowan?"

Alysse gave a quick laugh that reminded Quinn of the days back at Elksheart. "No, I meant the Creator. Do you believe in the Creator?"

"Oh. Uh, yeah, I guess. Don't you?"

She shrugged. "I don't know. They don't really talk about Him in Maldria."

"We don't really talk about Him in Eastcastle either; though, I did go to the big cathedral in Canton this year. It was incredible."

Alysse nodded, but she didn't seem to be listening. "Sometimes," she said in a whisper, "when I see things that are beautiful, I forget about the ugly, hateful things in the world. And then I can almost believe He exists."

Quinn didn't know how to respond. He had heard a little about the Creator and His care for the world and its people. It was something he never really thought about *not* believing. The memory of his trip to the Cathedral brought back the feelings he had felt there. He was about to tell Alysse about them, but Rowan returned with the cooked squirrels.

They each took turns tearing off pieces of meat. The squirrels were small, and the edible portions were quickly consumed. The flavor was gamey, but the meal was warm and substantial compared to what they had been eating.

"Do you see the break in the mountains over there," asked Rowan pointing nearly straight across the valley. "That is Smugglers Gap. On the other side are the headwaters of the Elkshead River and the trail down to Eastcastle."

Quinn tried to orient what the ranger was saying with his memory of the Castlerooks from the other side. "If that's where the Elkshead runs, then Eagles Nest must be just beyond the gap. We could spend the night at the Golden Boot. The keeper is a good friend of Bastian's, and I know he would let us stay."

"No," Rowan answered tersely, before adding in a softer voice, "We will not need to stop in Eagles Nest."

"But…" Quinn started. His memories of the pallets at the inn were much more favorable than those of the past two nights.

"No."

There was an unmistakable air of finality in the ranger's voice. Standing, he said, "It is time to move on. We should be able to make it to the Gap by this evening."

The three travelers went back to their camp. Rowan stamped out the remains of the fire and buried it with dirt and rocks. He collected his various satchels and the water skins, and put his bow stick on his back.

"Ready?" he asked.

Quinn nodded and they started down the hill between the trees.

The second day of walking was easier than the first as most of it was downhill or flat. Unfortunately, the downward slopes used different muscles than those Quinn had used for climbing, so by the end of the day everything hurt.

Luckily, the scenery was beautiful enough to keep his mind off the fatigue building in his limbs. The woods were full of birds, squirrels, and deer. A moose wandered by when they stopped for a lunch of edible plants and overripe berries. As they walked, Rowan whistled or talked loudly to lessen the likelihood of surprising one of the many black bears that roamed the mountains. His conversation was mostly about the various plants or wildlife rather than the circumstances that had led to their journey. It reminded Quinn of the first time he had met Rowan on the way to the Festival. Alysse was generally quiet, though she talked more than she had the day before.

Several times during the day, the ranger allowed them to rest in an open glen or near one of the many small lakes and ponds. While Rowan dug out several cattail roots with his belt knife, Quinn and Alysse rested in the tall grass. It felt good to lie down, though the insects ruined any chance of a peaceful nap. The small, cool brooks provided fresh water for drinking and cooling their faces.

The canopy of trees made it difficult for Quinn to discern any direction as his view of the mountains was blocked. Each time they broke into a meadow, Quinn worried they were walking in circles. More than once, he had almost asked Rowan if he knew where they were going, but decided against it. He had led them this far. There was no use doubting him at this point.

By the time they started climbing the other side of the valley, the sun had disappeared behind the imposing peaks in front of them. The temperature fell with the setting sun, and Rowan decided to make camp at the base of Smugglers Gap. Quinn slumped down immediately after the ranger stopped. His entire body hurt and his stomach grumbled for something besides the bitter plants they were subsisting on.

While Rowan built a fire to cook the starchy roots he had been collecting, Quinn waffled between waiting for him to finish and simply falling asleep. He decided if he did not sit up, the choice would be made for him.

Forcing himself up with his feet stretched out before him, he watched as the ranger skillfully transformed a spark into a small fire. Once the fire was burning on its own, Rowan stripped some small branches for cooking. Quinn watched the flames in front of him, mesmerized by their hypnotic dance. Before long, he was once again lying down and losing the battle of keeping his eyes open. Not even the drop in temperature could keep him awake. He was softly snoring before Rowan even had the roots prepared for cooking.

Chapter 10

"Quinn. Quinn."

At first the call was part of his dream as he walked across a large mountain meadow. His feet felt as though they were made of lead. It was an effort just to drag them through the long grass.

"Quinn, wake up," Rowan said, gently shaking him.

Quinn opened his eyes, but could not see anything through his rapidly blinking eyes. The world was enveloped in darkness, except for the soft light that came from the remains of the fire. The ranger was a dark shadow outlined by the glow behind him.

"We need to leave now. We need to get out of the mountains."

The urgency in Rowan's voice was unusual for the ranger. Quinn tried to focus on Rowan's face, but after failing to see anything, it finally registered that he had his hood up.

"Are you awake?"

Quinn nodded and sat up, his body protesting. His legs hurt and he felt as though he had not rested at all. The vestiges of sleep were still pulling at him as he rolled to his feet. Rowan moved over to a small mound to his right. Quinn's guess was confirmed when the dark mass became Alysse.

As Quinn stretched, his mind finally registered what his ears had been telling him since he awoke. Wind. The trees were alive with it, and its rush through the branches was a constant hiss. Looking up, Quinn could make out one or two stars through the thrashing canopy above.

"Are you ready?" came the ranger's voice. Quinn could see his form as he stamped out the remainder of the fire. "It will be dark for several hours yet, so you need to stay close to me. If you fall behind or get lost, I may not be able to find you. Do you understand?"

Quinn was again surprised at the seriousness of the ranger's voice. "What's wrong?" he asked, swallowing hard.

"There is a storm coming that we are completely unprepared for if it catches us in the mountains. We need to find the Elkshead. It will lead us out."

"I can't see you," said Alysse in a small voice.

The ranger stopped. "Follow my voice. Walk slowly so you do not trip on anything. Hold on to the back of my cloak and Quinn will hold onto yours. We will walk slowly, but do not let go of the cloaks. It will be better once we get into the gap and out of the trees."

They walked forward carefully with Rowan in the lead. As they moved, he relayed back the presence of potential hazards. After a while, Quinn's eyes adjusted to the remote bits of light, which filtered down from the stars above. He still could not see far into the distance, but he could make out Alysse in front of him and the obstacles as they were pointed out by the ranger. Their travel was tediously slow.

Finally, they broke out from the cover of the trees and onto a rocky slope. The starlight was eerily bright compared to the relative darkness they had been traveling in. It suddenly seemed silly to hold onto the cloaks and both Quinn and Alysse released their grasps. Quinn rubbed his hand with the other, not realizing how tight his grip had been.

"This is the base of the Gap. We need to climb for a bit, but it will not be as high as before. It will be several hours until we are through the mountains. Do not fall behind."

It did not take long for the howling wind to chap their faces as they began to climb. Unlike the days before, the air was not simply crisp, it was chilly. Quinn kept his head down and his hood in place. He held his cloak tightly together with his hands, but the air was growing painfully cold. He hoped Rowan had overestimated the time it would take to get out of the mountains.

The trail, if there was one, was not straight, but meandered with the stream that trickled down from the slopes. Often, they had to climb over large boulders, which had fallen from the cliff face and had become wedged into the cleft they were following. The rocks felt oddly warmer than the frigid wind now rushing down the gap. Before scaling the larger ones, Quinn would rest near the base out of the biting air. Each time, Rowan would prod him on, moving them as quickly as the conditions allowed. The weak light from the stars above dimmed as the sides of the gap grew higher.

Finally, thought Quinn as the gap leveled out. The small stream they had been following ended at the base of a waterfall on their left. The wind carried the spray from the crashing water and it felt like shards of ice pelting their faces. Rowan quickly led them past.

Within moments, the wind died down and the air felt warmer again. Quinn's relief turned to disappointment when he realized why the wind had stopped.

"We need to climb here," Rowan said, standing in front of a vertical wall. The gap had led to a dead end. "It is not terribly high, but enough to be dangerous. Quinn, you will go first and then Alysse. I will bring up the rear. Do not try to go too fast, but remember, time is against us."

Quinn made his way over to the wall and found there were many nooks, cracks, and knobs for hands and feet. It was not as hard as he thought it would be. Additionally, between the poor light and having two people behind him, it was hard to tell just how high he actually was.

The climb did not take very long. He knew he had reached the top when a blast of frigid air caught him full in the face. The temperature was so cold now that he had to catch his breath before pulling himself up to lie on his belly on the ground. Within moments, Alysse and the ranger were also atop the cliff wall.

Taking advantage of the small rest Rowan allowed them, Quinn sat on a nearby rock and tried to stretch his tired body. The lack of sleep and food was catching up to him, and he felt more tired than he could ever remember. As he sat and slowed his breathing, he realized why the ranger was so anxious. The sky to the west was completely dark. One by one, the small specks of starlight were being obliterated as the darkness swallowed them up. It would not be long before the clouds reached them.

"Come, we must keep moving," Rowan said.

Quinn and Alysse stood and followed as the ranger led them through the jumble of rocks, brush, and trees. They had not gone far before the first drops of rain fell from the ever-darkening sky.

The ranger stopped and turned to them. "Cover up as much as you possibly can. Try to keep your hands and face dry. We need to make it to the Elkshead before we lose all of the starlight. Stay close." With that, he turned and once again led them into the blackness.

The longer the night wore on, the more difficult Quinn found it to put one foot in front of the other. The sprinkling raindrops changed into a torrent. The wind did not subside, but drove the droplets into their faces, stinging them with its icy force. Before long, Quinn felt as though he had just climbed out of the river. Finally, just as he was despairing that they were lost, he heard the churning of the river over the rushing of the wind.

Rowan brought them to the river's edge. They huddled under a stand of pine trees, which offered partial protection against the storm's fury. The rushing water of the Elkshead was all but invisible in the darkness.

"We cannot stop here for long. The temperature will continue to drop, and as it does, it will become more dangerous. Our only chance is to keep going and get out of the mountains."

"Are we going to die?"

Quinn was shocked by Alysse's question, and grew more worried when the ranger paused before answering. "Not if we keep moving. We will have to hold onto cloaks again as there is no light to see by. Are you ready?"

He did not wait for an answer before moving back out into the night. Alysse held the ranger's cloak and Quinn held hers. The wind lessened some as they left the shelter of the trees, but the rain changed to hail. Quinn kept his head down to protect his face from the stinging pellets.

Rowan followed the edge of the river as best as he could, occasionally stopping and retreating slightly when he stumbled into mud or water. The darkness was now complete as the storm clouds blocked all the light from the stars above. Quinn's hands began to go numb as the cold penetrated deep into his bones. His body shook and he wondered whether Alysse had been right—maybe they were going to die up here. He stumbled along as if in a trance, his mind cloudy from lack of sleep. Alysse's voice brought him back to awareness.

"It's snowing."

Looking out from under his hood, he was surprised to find she was right. The wind had subsided, and huge flakes landed on his upturned face. He wished it were light enough to see. He had always enjoyed watching snow fall. Of course, watching from a castle wall was much different than wandering through the mountains.

"Can we rest?" asked Alysse. "I'm so tired."

Rowan's answer was quick and direct. "No. We must keep moving."

"I don't think I can. I'm too tired."

Quinn said, "I am too. Can't we just stop for a minute?"

"No. Not yet."

"Please, can we just rest," Alysse pled again.

The ranger ignored her and kept moving along the side of the river, carefully placing his steps.

"I don't think I can hold on to your cloak anymore, father. I'm too tired. It's so cold." Alysse's voice was soft and her words were starting to sound slurred. "Please, father."

"Father?" Quinn asked. "Alysse, what are you talking about? Rowan, I think we need to stop. Something's wrong with Alysse."

As the girl continued to ramble, the ranger pushed on into the night. "We have to keep moving."

"Please...please..." Alysse murmured.

"Rowan, please, can't we stop?" Quinn asked.

The ranger sighed and said, "Only for a moment, but do not sit down."

Quinn wrapped his arms around himself, pulling his cloak tight. The snow continued to fall, but it was hard to see in the darkness. Quinn jumped when a voice whispered in his ear.

"Have you heard of snow fever?" the ranger asked.

"No."

"When a person gets too cold, their mind starts to fail them. They cannot think clearly. They say things that do not make sense. When their mind fails them completely, they die."

"Is that what Alysse has? Is that what's happening?"

"I do not know for sure, but that is my guess. If she is allowed to fall asleep, she may never wake up. You must keep her awake, keep her talking and moving. If you do not…" he left off.

"But, I don't…"

"Quinn, her only chance of survival is getting her off this mountain. You must help me keep her moving. Besides, there are more lives at stake than just ours. If Eastcastle is not warned of the danger it faces, many more lives will be lost." Louder he said, "We must keep moving."

Alysse protested, but moved forward. Her words were becoming more slurred and she seemed to babble more than talk.

Quinn thought through what the ranger had told him. He was supposed to keep her talking, but she was already doing that on her own. His stomach hurt and he was suddenly terrified that she was going to die.

"Uh, Alysse, do you, um…" He realized he probably sounded worse than she did, but he could not think of anything to say to her. Finally, he asked, "Do you remember the carvings in the library? You know Paddock's library? Which one…" He never finished his question.

"NO!?" Alysse screamed. In fact, she went completely berserk. "I won't go back! I won't!! NO! NO!!"

Completely surprised by the sudden outburst, Quinn was at a loss as to what he should say. "I…you don't have to…I mean…'

"Good, Quinn, good," Rowan said over her wailing, "Make her angry. She will not remember any of this, so do not be concerned about making her upset. It may be the only thing that saves her life."

They continued on, the ranger leading, Alysse railing against her past, and Quinn trying to convince himself that none of it was real. The snow was sticking now, and Quinn could feel his feet sliding on the accumulated flakes. He wondered if he would ever feel warm again.

Every so often, he asked Alysse about Elksheart or Paddock and tried to draw out her rage. Each time, it felt more surreal and he began to think he was catching the snow fever too. Unfortunately, Alysse was becoming less and less responsive. The last time, she simply whimpered under her breath.

Quinn was wondering what he should do when Alysse suddenly fell in front of him. Before he could let go of her cloak, he was pulled down on top of her in the snow. She did not move. Rowan turned immediately and helped him to his feet, brushing the snow off as best as he could.

"Get it off of your face and then put your hands back under your cloak. We need to keep going."

"What about Alysse?"

There was a long pause.

"We can't leave her," Quinn said incredulously.

"Quinn, we have to make it to Eastcastle or many people will die. Sometimes…sometimes doing the right thing, the best thing, is the hardest choice you'll ever make."

"No! I won't leave her here."

"Quinn, I did not ask her to come…"

"*No!*" Quinn repeated.

The ranger's temper began to slip. "Look, we may *all* die up here and if that happens, Eastcastle will fall. *I will not let that happen.* Do you understand? You are the son of a duke—*now act like one!*"

"Fine, then go. Maybe *you* can live knowing you let her die, but I can't. I *won't.*"

The ranger recoiled as if Quinn had shoved him. For a few moments, Quinn thought Rowan truly had left them. Tears of anger and fear welled up in his eyes, bringing heat to his frozen face.

"Hold these," Rowan said suddenly from the darkness.

Quinn reached out and felt the ranger place his bow stick and a small satchel in his nearly numb hands. "Try to keep them dry."

Quinn tucked them under his cloak, but the bow stick was too long. He hoped the ranger did not notice. Quinn heard the sound of ripping cloth in front of him and then the ranger said, "Hold this as well. When I tell you I am ready, put it over both of us."

"I will have to set these down first."

"Fine. Just do not lose them."

The ranger lifted Alysse on to his back, pulling her arms around his neck. He lowered himself down onto his knees so the girl was leaning against him. Taking a bow string, he looped it around them both and tied it in front of his chest.

"Now, put the cloak over us."

As Quinn draped the ranger's cloak over them, he realized what the ripping cloth had been. The ranger had removed the hood and widened the hole of his cloak so that it now fit over both their heads. Alysse still wore her own cloak and hood.

"Gather the bow and the satchel. If we are to save her, we must be quick. Hopefully, my body heat will be enough until we reach Eastcastle."

"How far is Eagles Nest? We can stop at the Golden Boot, just to get warm I mean."

"No. Eagles Nest is too dangerous. We cannot go there. We will find somewhere else along the way."

Quinn wanted to protest, but the ranger set a faster pace than before, and Quinn had to concentrate to keep up. The snow made the uneven ground slick and treacherous. As they walked, Quinn's eyes played tricks on him, and he thought he could see flashes of light. He feared it was the beginning of the snow fever. It was quite a bit later before Quinn realized that small gaps were appearing in the clouds above, allowing pin pricks of starlight to shine through. These bits of light were reflecting off the snow, which covered everything except the river.

Rowan plodded on, rarely speaking. Quinn knew he was angry, but he also knew he could not change that. He had been serious about staying with Alysse, which scared him more now than it had at the time. What if Rowan had left them? He decided not to think about it.

As time passed, Quinn found it harder and harder to stay awake. Moving his feet was a chore and without Rowan talking, his mind was becoming as numb as his body. In the back of his head, something tried to warn him, but he could not think straight. He could not remember where they were going or why. He just knew he was tired and he wanted to sleep. He did not even feel cold anymore, just exhausted.

At the edge of the hillside, Rowan paused. Small glimmers of firelight burned down in the valley.

"Look, Quinn," he said, laboring for breath, "Eagles Nest. We made it."

Silence answered him.

"Quinn?" he called turning. "*Quinn?!*"

His stomach tightened. When had he lost him? He staggered back through the snow, calling the boy's name.

He had only gone a short distance when he saw the small mound lying directly in the path of his footsteps. Fear gripped him as he ran forward, Alysse's weight seeming to increase with each step.

"Quinn! *Quinn!!*"

He knelt in the snow, still impeded by the young girl on his back. Feeling the boy's face, Rowan was relieved to feel small puffs of breath, but his skin felt ice cold.

"Wake up, Quinn. Wake up." He shook him gently, which brought a small moan, but nothing more. "Come on, son. Get up. I cannot carry you both. Wake up."

When Quinn still did not move, the ranger looked to the heavens and roared, "*Will you take them all?*"

*   *   *

The ocean waves crashed against the sides of the ship tossing it first one way and then the other. Lightening flashed outside the small, leaded windows in the back of the stern cabin. The storm was not fierce, but it had enough wind to make the evening meal interesting. It had already produced more than one chuckle as the dinner party found their food moving on its own across the table. Luckily, at least the table and benches were pegged to the floor.

Rustan and Catherine Hawk sat on opposites sides of each other while the ranger Landon, Rustan's friend and bodyguard, sat at the head. The dried fruit, sharp cheese, and jerked meat made an unappetizing meal, which was fitting as their appetites had long since been carried away on the waves. They picked at the tray of food as they talked.

"I do not think I can take many more of these cursed waves," Rustan said with a laugh as he peered at the slice of jerked meat in his fingers. "We *will* be taking the pass on the way home."

"You are more than welcome to ride for three days, my love; however, I will be sailing back. Given the choice, I much prefer several hours of stomach abuse than several days of bruising my backside."

Rustan laughed. "You just have not built up the necessary calluses."

"You know," said Landon through templed fingers, "We could walk back. The scenery alone would make the journey worthwhile."

Catherine wrinkled her nose as she was wont to do. "I think not."

Rustan leaned forward across the table, pointing at his wife with the piece of jerked meat. "There, you see Cat? Trust a ranger to come up with something worse than the two choices being considered. Though, if I had my hunting bow, I might just opt for it. This stuff is terrible," he said flinging the meat onto the table. "I might as well be eating my boot."

"Bow or no bow, I am not considering anything," Catherine said. "I will be sailing back."

A knock on the door interrupted their discussion. Landon rose from his bench to stand facing the door. Rustan called out, "Come!" The next few moments became forever etched into Rustan's mind.

The door was thrown open and three men barreled into the room, loaded crossbows held at the ready. There were no words of warning, no demands, no explanations. Each man simply turned and released his bolt. Catherine fell dead immediately, the shot true to her heart, her head slumping onto the table. Landon instinctively threw himself in front of the duke, bending him over backwards. The bolt meant for Rustan buried deep into the ranger's lower back. The third bolt thumped harmlessly into the wood below the windows.

With lightening reflexes, the ranger rolled over Rustan and onto his feet. No sooner had he landed than his right arm flicked out, his belt knife on its way into the neck of the first attacker. Stumbling backward, the man fell into the other two, allowing Rustan time to roll off the bench onto the floor.

Landon flung himself at the nearest of the two remaining men, but found his strength failing. The man pulled a dagger, and both men struggled over it. Four hands wrapped around the small blade.

"Cat! *Cat!*" Rustan called to his wife from his crouch at the head of the table, but there was no response.

The final attacker jumped onto the table and used his momentum to kick the duke under his chin. Rustan stumbled back against the windows, catching himself on the leaded panes.

The man came at him with a short sword, pressing his advantage. The cramped quarters of the cabin made it difficult for Rustan to dodge his thrusts, and the second one caught him on the chin, slicing up to his ear. Realizing if he stayed put it would only be a matter of time before the man killed him, Rustan waited for the next thrust before pushing off the wall straight toward him. The two men stumbled backward until they ran into the table. The attacker folded backward, his eyes wide with surprise.

Landon's stamina was quickly failing. He knew his wound was fatal; however, while he was still breathing his obligation was to the duke. Without warning, the ranger buckled his knees and rolled backward, pulling his attacker to the side of him. Instantly, pain lanced through his body as the bolt was driven deeper into his back. Only years of strenuous training kept him from blacking out altogether.

Rolling to his side, he threw his body across the man as the unknown attacker tried to climb back to his feet. Using his dead weight to his advantage, Landon lay heavily on the man. He pulled the man's right arm back awkwardly over his head and pried the dagger loose. Within moments, the fight was over and the man lay dead beneath him.

The duke was struggling with the final attacker near the windows, but Landon crossed to the door instead. Shutting it, the ranger dropped the latch and jammed a discarded crossbow underneath. Judging from the blood running down Rustan's face, neither of them was in the position to face more opponents.

Dropping to the floor, Landon pulled himself to the first dead man and retrieved his belt knife. Turning to the back of the boat, he let the knife fly just as Rustan shoved his attacker against the table. The blade buried into his back between his shoulders. The short sword dropped from his fingers.

Throwing the man away from the table, the duke went to his wife's side. Cradling her lifeless body in his arms, he carefully brushed her hair back from her face. Tears mingled with his blood and dropped onto her dress.

"Milord," Landon rasped, pulling himself to the bench opposite the duke and his dead wife. "We are still in danger."

At the same moment, as if in response to the ranger's words, the door was tried from the outside. Pounding and cursing followed. Rustan glanced up at the ranger and Landon was shocked at the transformation. His face was contorted with rage and hate, made all the worse by the ugly gash along the side of his face. His eyes burned with a dark flame that would devour the world if only it could escape.

"We will kill them all," the duke said in a voice cold as death.

"Not today, milord. We cannot win."

Rustan looked at his bodyguard, angered by his contradiction. Seeing his state for the first time, the duke's demeanor softened slightly. "How bad is it?"

"It is mortal, my friend. I am sorry."

Rustan accepted the confession with a blink, but said nothing.

"Your only chance is to break out the windows. There is no weakness in living to fight another day."

Outside the door a man called to them. "A pity I cannot see you die, Hawk, but no matter. Death *will* come. Enjoy the last moments of your life!" Then to someone else outside the door, the man said, "Light the oil. Burn everything. Farewell Hawk!"

Rustan laid his wife's body down gently, and walked purposefully toward the door.

"Rustan, do not open that door," Landon said quietly, pulling himself once again to his feet, wincing with the effort.

The duke seemed to ignore him and reached for the latch, resting his hand upon it. Staring at the door, head lowered, Rustan stopped.

"Only death waits outside that door."

"I will have my vengeance."

"Then live to have it."

Rustan turned to the ranger, his face a mask of death. "*I will have my vengeance!*"

Retrieving the short sword from the floor, Rustan used it to hack the bench at the head of the table. After several blows, it came loose. Tossing the blade as if it were a thing of evil, Rustan picked up the bench and hurled it into the lead framed windows in the back. The panel of windows cracked and splintered, but stayed intact. It took another blow before a break opened.

The ranger seated himself across from Catherine's body. He called to Rustan.

"Here, take this," he said, handing him a small, metal square. Both sides were embossed with the same symbol, an arrow with branches of leaves instead of feathers. It was small enough to sit easily in his palm. "Show this to any ranger and you will be treated as a brother."

"I have no claim to this."

"You have claim to it because I have given it to you. You are more ranger than you know. A man you can trust implicitly is sometimes worth more than an army."

The duke nodded, and looked toward his dead wife.

"I will stay with her," Landon said, following his eyes.

"Thank you," Rustan said quietly.

The ship had grown quiet as smoke seeped under the door. It would not be long before the flames completely consumed the dry, wooden innards of the vessel.

"Take the bench with you. We are far from any shores. Farewell, my friend."

Rustan looked back at the ranger, his eyes welling with tears that refused to fall.

"Farewell, my brother."

He circled the table and raised his wife's head to his. With eyes closed, he kissed the top of her head.

"Forgive me," he whispered. "Farewell, my love and my life."

The duke walked quickly toward the back of the ship and retrieved the bench. After smashing the opening wider, he threw the bench into the rain and darkness beyond. Glancing back for one last look, he etched the image into his mind. It would keep him alive through the devastating trials he faced in the following years. He would have his revenge. Hunger, thirst, fever, confinement, and slavery would not take it away.

Turning, he dove through the hole and into the chilly waters. The salt water caused his face to burn with pain. Locating the bench, he threw an arm over it and watched as the flames consumed his ship. Behind it, a smaller unrecognizable vessel disappeared into the night. He forced himself to watch until the flames were no longer visible. The coldness of the water penetrated deep inside him until his very soul was deprived of warmth.

I will have my vengeance.

*   *   *

The pounding on the door was incessant. Grobeck finally could ignore it no longer and walked from his bedroom. Stopping only a moment to grab the large cudgel he kept behind the counter, he went to the front door. As he walked, he yelled, "We're closed. You are either too late or too early, but we're closed."

The knocking came again. With a sigh, he asked, "What do you want?"

When no one answered, he fingered the cudgel and opened the door a crack. A man stood in the darkness, long hair dripping with water, his bearded face marred by a long scar from his chin to his ear. He looked a wreck, his body stooped with fatigue.

"Move on, sir. I'm afraid we have no room tonight," Grobeck said, keeping the cudgel from sight.

The man looked up, his head partially bowed. "Please…save the children."

"What?" Grobeck asked, but the man had already turned to walk unevenly down the boardwalk.

Grobeck watched him go, fully expecting him to fall into the drifted snow. He shook his head and started to shut the door. At the last moment, something caught his eye. A pile of cloaks sat on a makeshift sled of evergreen bows, wet with melted snow. Grobeck opened the door wider and his blood turned cold. A small booted foot hung off the side of the sled.

"Gwendolyn! *Gwendolyn!!*"

Chapter 11

Quinn opened his eyes and blinked several times. When they finally came into focus, he found himself staring at the white plaster ceiling above him.

"It's about time you woke up."

Quinn turned his head toward the voice. "Alexander?"

"Well, I'm certainly not the good looking girl next door."

"Huh? Oh, Alysse." Quinn sat up, his body protesting the sudden movement. His head felt swimmy. "Is she okay?"

Alexander stood up from the chair he was sitting in and crossed the room. "How should I know?" he said with a shrug. "Gwendolyn won't let anyone near her."

Quinn lowered himself back down onto the small pallet and rubbed his face. "Is Rowan here?"

"Then it *was* Rowan. My father thought so from Grobeck's description, but no, he's not here. He dropped you off and left."

Quinn stared back up at the ceiling. "He saved our lives."

"If you ask me, he darn near cost you your lives," Bastian said coming in through the open door. "Hello, Quinn. How are you feeling?"

Sitting back up more slowly this time, Quinn turned so his back rested against the wall. "Okay, I guess, just tired."

Alexander laughed. "Tired? You've been sleeping for over two days!"

"Two days?"

Bastian explained how Grobeck had sent Tomkin to Eastcastle with instructions to find him. The roads had been a muddy mess from the falling rain and snow. Tomkin had found Bastian in the barracks and they met with the duke immediately afterward. Early the next morning, Bastian, Tomkin, and Alexander set out in the drizzle for Eagles Nest. The temperature had warmed enough to turn the snow back into rain, but the conditions were still miserable. Alexander had spent all evening in front of the big hearth trying to feel warm again.

"So my uncle knows I'm here?"

"Yes, of course," said Bastian.

"Is he angry?"

It was Bastian's turn to shrug. "He wasn't exactly happy about it."

Quinn sighed and his stomach growled. He suddenly realized he was starving. "Is there anything to eat?"

"You mean, besides the broth you've been drinking?" Alexander laughed. "Gwendolyn's had to force you awake to drink it."

"Really? I don't remember."

"I'll see if I can find you something," Bastian said. "It's good to see you awake, Quinn. You had us worried."

"Thanks. And thanks for coming. I'm sorry for causing you trouble."

"Don't worry about it. Just get better."

Bastian left the room and Alexander pulled his chair over to the bed. "So, what *are* you doing here? Why were you with Rowan? And who's the girl next door?"

Quinn did his best to answer his friend's questions as briefly as he could, but each one seemed to lead to more questions. It was hard to explain everything without telling him everything about Paddock, Elksheart, and Maldria. Quinn was relieved when Bastian returned with Grobeck, who was holding a large plate filled with food. The smells wafting across the room made Quinn's mouth water.

"Hello, Malthus," the large man said with a wink and a grin. "I'm glad to see you're awake. In fact, after that first morning, I am glad to see you're alive. You are both very lucky."

"Hi, Grobeck. Thank you for helping us."

"I have to tell you, you had us pretty scared."

"Have you seen Rowan since he brought us here?"

"Rowan's the man who brought you here?" Grobeck shook his head. "No, I'm afraid not."

He set the plate down in front of him, and Quinn felt like eating everything at once. "Eat slowly. You haven't eaten for several days, and your body may need to get used to it again."

Quinn started slow, but soon was eating as fast as he could. Apparently, his body was a quick learner.

"How soon do you think he will be well enough to travel," Bastian asked Grobeck.

Grobeck shrugged. "I would think soon, as long as you keep him warm. I guess it really depends on Gwendolyn."

"What depends on me?" Gwendolyn asked coming into the room. She spied the half eaten plate and bustled over. "What do you think you are doing? You're going to kill the boy just when I finally have him back in the world of the living."

Quinn stuffed in several more bites before she snatched the plate away.

"In fact, you all need to let him rest. Out, out," she said herding them with her arms. Alexander rolled his eyes before giving a quick wave and darting out the door ahead of Gwendolyn's raised foot.

After she had ushered them all to the door, Gwendolyn turned back. "You still need more rest, young man. Marching you across the mountains in the middle of a winter storm…honestly, what was the man thinking? And without winter clothes!" She shut the door with a harrumph.

His stomach satisfied, Quinn promptly followed Gwendolyn's order for more rest.

Quinn awoke several times, but it must have been night because the room was dark. Finally, on the fifth time, he heard movement below him, and he figured it must be the early morning. Swinging his legs out of the bed, he yawned and stretched before standing up. The floor felt cool, and he realized that his legs were bare. He was wearing an oversized tunic that came down to his knees.

Probably Tomkin's, he thought.

He wondered if his own clothes were somewhere in the room, but he had no way of finding them in the darkness. Instead, he started across the room, his arms out in front of him. It took some feeling along the wall, but he finally found the door.

Sticking his head out, he saw he was in one of the upstairs rooms near the staircase. The hallway was dark, but a small, thin light emanated from downstairs. Slipping quietly out the door, Quinn made his way down the stairs.

The light was spilling out from under the door behind the counter. He walked to the door and poked his head in. Grobeck was kneeling down placing wood inside the stone oven.

"Good morning," Quinn said.

Grobeck jumped and scattered kindling across the floor.

"Sorry."

Grobeck laughed and pulled himself up. "Quite all right, quite all right. Just goes to show how much of my heightened senses I have lost over the years," he chuckled. "How are you feeling?"

"Better. Just hungry, really."

"Well, let's see what we can scratch up. If you'll prepare the wood for me, I'd be much obliged. I'm afraid these old joints just aren't what they used to be."

Quinn walked over to the oven where Grobeck had been working. As he knelt down, Grobeck said, "Actually, you had better go back up and get dressed. Gwen will have my head if she sees you down here like this, though I don't expect to see her soon. She's been up late with the young lady who came with you."

"Is she okay? I mean, is she going to…?" Quinn left off without finishing.

Grobeck glanced at Quinn and saw the anxiety on his face. "To die?" He smiled and shook his head. "No, not with Gwennie pulling for her. She just needs a little more time, but she'll perk up. Don't you worry about it."

Just then, the back door opened and Tomkin came in with a pile of split wood. "Sorry for the delay, sir, but the top layers are fairly well soaked. I had to dig down some."

"Quite alright," Grobeck said. "I've been shooting the breeze with young Malthus here, anyway. Just set them in the box on top of the others. Hopefully our guests won't be too ornery this morning," he said, winking at Quinn. "By the way, Tomkin, I'm probably going to need your help again in the kitchen. Gwen had another late night."

"Yes, sir. Just let me wash up."

"Here's a candle, Quinn. Your clothes should be on one of the chairs in your room. Hurry back and perhaps the three of us will be able to pull together a breakfast worth selling."

When Quinn returned, Grobeck had fires burning in both the oven and the stove. He assigned Tomkin the breakfast hash and Quinn the sweet rolls. Tomkin was a quiet, efficient worker and accomplished everything he was asked to do quickly. Quinn just struggled to keep up. Grobeck assured him that Tomkin was more familiar with what it takes to keep an inn running, but Quinn felt embarrassed anyway. He wished he had paid more attention to what Melinda did all those times he had visited her in the kitchen. While Tomkin minced the potatoes for the hash and Grobeck sliced off slabs of bacon, Quinn rolled out the sweet rolls.

"The man who brought you here, the ranger?" Grobeck asked while they worked.

Quinn concentrated on the rolls in front of him. "Yes?"

"What do you know of him?"

"Not much really." Quinn wondered how much he should tell him. Bastian seemed to trust the large man, but Quinn was hesitant to talk too much about Rowan. "He has helped me once or twice in the past. We met him last spring on the way to the festival."

Grobeck nodded. "That's probably thin enough. Use that towel to grab the butter pan from the stove and spread it lightly on the dough."

After Quinn started spooning on the butter, Grobeck continued. "You probably know this already, but innkeepers, well, we hear a lot of things—it seems people always like to talk with bar keepers," he said with a chuckle. "Anyway, I'm not sure why your ranger friend felt the need to take you out of Maldria, but do not judge him too harshly for it. He could not have known about that early winter storm, and I'm afraid there's a bigger storm brewing in the east."

"What do you mean?" asked Quinn, trying hard to pay attention to what he was doing with the butter rather than looking at Grobeck.

"There's been a lot of talk about…well, about armies and plans and schemes. Nothing definite, just rumors really. But, for now, it's probably better to be on this side of the mountains."

Quinn nodded, but decided not to share what Rowan had told him in the mountains.

"I guess what I am trying to say is, no matter what happens back at Eastcastle or with your young lady friend, do not judge the ranger too harshly." He gave Quinn a tight smile and a nod, which Quinn returned. "I think we're ready for the ground sugar."

Quinn worked with Grobeck and Tomkin until the light crept through the window at the rear of the kitchen. Soon afterward, Bastian knocked on the door and stuck his head in.

"There's a small group out here wondering if you're making breakfast or just eating it." Spotting Quinn, he said, "Good morning. How are you feeling?"

"Better."

"Good. We'd better plan on leaving soon after breakfast—unless, of course, that's not happening until after noon."

Grobeck tossed the towel he was using toward Bastian's head, but missed. "I don't see you stepping in to help."

Bastian suddenly jumped through the door as though kicked. Gwendolyn followed on his heels.

"Honestly, Grobeck," she said shaking her head, "Heaven help you if I ever die. Tomkin, please go out and see what the masses will be wanting this morning."

"Yes, ma'am," he said with a head bob and darted out the door.

Spying Quinn on a stool, Gwendolyn furrowed her brows. "And what exactly are you doing down here, young man? Grobeck, we are supposed to be taking care of our guests, not working them into an early grave. Scoot, scoot," she said, gently pushing him from the stool.

"I'm feeling better now, ma'am."

"Oh you are, are you?"

"Gwendolyn, he's been with me all morning. I think he's fine," Grobeck put in.

"Yes, and we all know how good *your* judgment is, don't we."

"Now, come on Gwen."

"Actually," Bastian said, "We really do need to return to Eastcastle as soon as possible." Gwendolyn turned and glowered at him, causing him to add, "It's a beautiful morning out there."

Gwendolyn looked as if she were going to argue the point, but at last conceded. "Fine, but the girl stays here. Beautiful morning or not, she's not leaving."

Grobeck caught Bastian's eye from behind his sister's back and tried to will him into conceding with his facial expression. Bastian took the hint, much to the innkeeper's relief.

"Fair enough. I don't have an obligation to bring her back with me, only Quinn."

This statement made everyone feel better, except Quinn, who was not looking forward to meeting with the duke. They all looked at one another until Tomkin came back. Sensing the tension, he delivered the orders and disappeared again as quickly as he could. Quinn and Bastian took the opportunity to slip out after him, leaving Grobeck to deal with his sister. The large innkeeper mouthed "Yikes!" before smiling.

Out in the main room, Bastian and Quinn found Alexander sitting by himself at one of the tables. Bastian excused himself to make sure the horses would be ready to leave right after breakfast. Quinn sat down across the table from his friend.

"Where have you been?" Alexander asked.

"I was helping Grobeck get the food ready for breakfast."

"Serious? Bogs! I *was* looking forward to eating it."

Quinn screwed up his face and said, "Very funny." Taking a deep breath, Quinn asked the question he had been dreading ever since waking up at the Golden Boot. "Did you find Rhiannon?"

"Rhiannon? Oh, you mean after you left. Yeah, we found her up in the Wolf Hills at some cabin."

"So she's safe?"

"As safe as she can be in Melinda's kitchen."

Quinn laughed, more out of relief than anything else. He had been afraid the answer was going to be different.

"So, who *is* the girl upstairs, anyway?" Alexander asked, sitting forward.

"She's the baron's daughter—well, step-daughter, I guess."

Alexander whistled. "No wonder the duke was furious."

"He's really angry then?" Quinn's heart sank.

"Oh, uh, yeah, sorry," Alexander said.

"Great," Quinn sighed.

"Alexander." Bastian's voice was low, but pointed. "I told you, this is not the place."

"Sorry, father," the older boy said, looking down at the table. Bastian sat down between them and asked quietly, "Quinn, are you really up to traveling today? If not, we can probably wait a bit longer."

"No, I mean, yes. I'm fine."

The three of them sat with their thoughts until Gwendolyn came out loaded with plates. She circled through the tables, spending just long enough with each customer to pacify any upset feelings. Within moments, the spirits of everyone in the room lifted, and the inn was filled with chatter and laughter. When Gwendolyn finished with the others, she brought three plates to Bastian, Alexander, and Quinn.

"Still planning on leaving after breakfast, then?" she asked.

"Yes," answered Bastian.

"And you're okay with that, Malthus? If not, just tell me, and I will make sure you don't leave until you're ready."

"No, ma'am. Really, I feel fine."

"Okay, then. Eat up. You might as well have something substantial in your stomach before you're on the road relying on whatever it is Bastian has prepared."

She turned and went back to the kitchen while the three of them dug into the hash and sweet rolls. The rolls were warm and the icing had melted into a sugary pool at the base. The hash was heavily spiced and contained bits of crumbled bacon. Everything tasted wonderful. It was not long before they were scraping the last remnants from their plates, and Bastian stood.

"The sooner we're on our way, the sooner we'll be home."

"I'm not so sure Quinn sees that as a good thing," Alexander said with a laugh.

Bastian flashed his son a stern look. "Zander, why don't you go up and get all of your stuff ready. It looks as if a bear slept in our room."

"Yes, father," he said scooting out his chair.

"Quinn, Grobeck said you didn't have any travel packs with you the night you arrived."

Quinn shook his head.

"Okay, well, just wait down here until we're ready. Don't go outside, okay?"

"Yes, sir."

The weapons master walked to the staircase and followed his son up the steps. Apparently, he did not trust Alexander to ready his packs in a timely manner. Quinn decided to go back to the kitchen rather than wait at the table. He was not sure whether it was simply a result of Bastian's paranoia or whether the customers really were watching him, but he decided he would rather wait with Grobeck.

Knocking on the door, he stuck his head into the back room. Grobeck and his sister were quietly talking near the oven, but waved him in.

"So you're done, then? How was it?" the large woman asked.

"It was wonderful."

Grobeck gently nudged his sister. "See, we men are not completely incapable."

"Let's not even go there, brother," Gwendolyn said on her way to meet Quinn. When she reached him, she put her hands on his shoulders. "Now that it's just us, are you *sure* you're okay? I will not have it on my conscience if something happens to you on the way to Eastcastle."

"Yes ma'am, really, I feel fine."

Gwendolyn gave him a quick smile and patted his right shoulder, before giving it a gentle squeeze. "Good."

"Gwendolyn, may I say goodbye to Alysse?"

She looked down at him, her eyes tightening slightly. After a drawn out moment, she gave him another smile and patted his shoulders once more.

"Of course. Come with me." Turning to her brother, she added, "Grobeck, try and keep things under control until I return. You may need to walk past the counter and actually mingle with the customers. If young Malthus here is done, there are probably others as well."

As they walked across the room, Gwendolyn stopped at various tables and chatted briefly. She deferred a couple of questions to her brother, who she assured them would be out shortly. As if prearranged, the innkeeper came through the door. Seeing her brother, Gwendolyn and Quinn went to the stairs. When they reached the top, she ushered him into the room where Quinn had been staying. Shutting the door behind them, she turned back to look at Quinn.

"I need to ask you a couple of questions, if that's okay?"

Quinn nodded and swallowed. He hoped she had not noticed the latter.

"Who is Alysse?"

"She's Baron Paddock's step-daughter."

Gwendolyn flinched in surprise. She filled her cheeks with air and blew it out slowly. Raising her hands to her face, she rubbed her eyes and cheeks with her palms. "Did the ranger—Rowan? Did he kidnap her?"

Quinn shook his head, "No. In fact, he didn't even want her to come. He said it would make the baron even angrier."

"Well, he's probably got that right. So, why is she here?"

"She made him take her along. We weren't supposed to leave the night we did. Rowan wanted me to prepare better and then leave the next night, but Alysse made it so we had to leave right then. She said we would never have been allowed to go riding again, so she alerted the guards and we had to run."

"Why would she do that?"

Quinn thought for a moment, wondering how Alysse would feel about him telling everything. Finally, he said, "She thinks the baron killed her parents. They ruled another barony, and she thinks he killed them so he could add it to his."

Gwendolyn nodded and looked away, her lips pursed. After a moment, she looked back at him with a small smile. "Before we go in, you need to know she is a very sick little girl, okay? She'll probably look different than you remember, even though it has only been a couple of days."

"Is she going to die?"

"I don't know, Quinn," she said surprising him by using his real name. "If it were just the effects of the storm, I would say no. But she is fighting other demons, and I don't know how to help her with those. We just need to keep hoping and praying, I guess." She took a deep breath and said, "Well, come on then. We probably need to hurry before Bastian…"

She was interrupted by a knock on the door, followed by the weapons master's head. "You'll have to wait a little longer, Bastian," Gwendolyn said. "Quinn wants to say goodbye to the girl."

Bastian looked from one to the other, before nodding. "We'll be waiting downstairs."

They followed him out the door, but turned the opposite way. Gwendolyn led Quinn to another room and gently opened the door. The room was lit only by a two candles, and the window shade was drawn tight. As his eyes adjusted, Quinn could see Alysse sleeping on a small pallet covered with quilts. He walked over to the pallet.

Quinn told himself the paleness of her face was due to the poor light, but he knew it was not the truth. Her face was drawn and sunken, her copper hair matted. The fingers of one of her hands were wrapped in linen. Quinn suddenly felt lightheaded and began to waiver. Gwendolyn's hand on his back steadied him. Leaning down, she rubbed Alysse's cheek with the back of her hand.

"Alysse? Alysse?" she called quietly.

Quinn let out the breath he had not realized he was holding when she stirred awake. Her eyes blinked as they tried to focus in the poor light. Gwendolyn nudged Quinn in the back with her other hand.

"Hi Alysse. It's me, Quinn. How are you feeling?"

The fragile-looking girl found his face with her eyes. She smiled very weakly. "Hi Quinn," she said in a hoarse whisper.

"How are you?"

"I'm thirsty."

Gwendolyn moved quickly to a small end table where a glass and pitcher sat. She poured the glass about half full and brought it back to the girl. Seeing she would not be able to sit up by herself, the innkeeper handed the glass to Quinn and helped her up. She then took the glass and held it to her mouth.

"Not too fast," she said, as Alysse tried to raise it up quickly.

"Thank you," she whispered. "Where are we?"

"We're in Eagles Nest. We made it. You're safe now."

Alysse's face slackened and she lay back on the pallet. "Am I?" she said in a humorless tone.

"Yes. Alysse, this is Gwendolyn. She's been taking care of you— she and her brother, Grobeck. They won't let anything happen to you."

She turned and looked at them both. "I wish that were true. Quinn, you don't know him. No one ever is safe from him. He'll find me."

"When you're better, you can come and live at Eastcastle and it won't matter if he knows. My uncle will keep you safe. But you need to try and get better."

"I wish I could just die."

Quinn stepped back shocked.

"No child," Gwendolyn said firmly, turning her face toward her. "No. You are a beautiful girl with too much to live for. The world is not as ugly a place as you may think, but you will never know if you give up now. Do you understand me? If you want to see it, you must fight for it. No one but friends knows you're here. We will keep you safe from Paddock, but I cannot protect you from yourself."

Quinn was surprised at Gwendolyn's tone. She sounded almost angry, as if upset by the girl's lack of will to live. He was worried Alysse would grow worse because of it, but she looked into the older lady's face and found something there to hold onto. Her face softened from its hardened sheen and she began to cry. Tears rolled down her cheeks as her small body was increasingly racked with sobs. Gwendolyn sat on the edge of the pallet and pulled the girl to her, kissing the top of her head.

"That's right child, let it out. Let the bad out and give the good room to get in." She rocked her back and forth slowly.

Quinn decided it was time to go and walked silently toward the door. Before leaving, he turned toward Gwendolyn and mouthed, "Tell her I said goodbye." Gwendolyn nodded, still stroking Alysse's hair and kissing the top of her head. Quinn slipped out, stopping in his room one last time to grab his cloak.

Downstairs, Alexander and Bastian were waiting by the door with Grobeck. As Quinn joined them, Grobeck opened the door letting in the cool air.

"Well, young Malthus, good luck to you. I'm afraid there are probably more storms on the horizon. Stay close to your friends."

He held out his hand. Instead, Quinn wrapped his arms around the wide man's stomach.

"Thank you, Grobeck, for everything." The large man laughed and patted Quinn's back.

"You are very welcome. Safe travels to you."

They walked out onto the boardwalk and Quinn, Alexander, and Bastian mounted the waiting horses. Grobeck stood in the doorway and waved as they rode up the street. Quinn turned one last time and waved at the large man. Despite the fact he knew his uncle would be waiting at the castle, when he turned back he was smiling. He was going home.

The ride back to Eastcastle was muddy. The snow and rain from the storm had left standing water all along the road. Quinn was glad Bastian had not brought the cart with him or it would have been even worse. They met very few travelers along the way, though the farms were dotted with workers hoping to save as much as they could. Quinn thought back to their trip to the Festival and was surprised how quickly summer had passed. The fields had just been plowed then, but now many were full of crops. He hoped they would dry out enough to be useful to the farmers.

While in the proximity of Eagles Nest, Bastian limited their talk. He was not interested in having anyone stop them to ask questions. Quinn did not think it was likely, but rode along in silence anyway. When they reached the foothills, Bastian finally asked Quinn how he had ended up in Eagles Nest.

The weapons master listened as Quinn told them first about the fateful night Rowan and Asher had come. He later added everything he could remember about Paddock and Elksheart. Alexander asked questions throughout. He found Quinn's description of the manor and its wealth unbelievable, but his father was more reserved. As Quinn told him what he could remember, his face grew tight with concern, but he did not say very much.

The morning developed into a beautiful, autumn day. The sun warmed them as they rode, but the air had a crisp, refreshing feel to it. Other than a short break to eat a small snack of fruit and cheese, they rode without stopping. As the day progressed, the road began to dry out and they were able to travel faster. By mid-afternoon, Quinn could see Eastcastle's towers growing on the horizon. His stomach began to flip-flop. He was excited to be home, but dreaded the inevitable meeting with his uncle.

Suddenly, Alexander looked at Quinn. Flashing his toothy grin, he spurred his horse forward. Quinn followed suit, trying in vain to catch his friend. Quinn continued to race his horse, even when it was clear Alexander was going to get there first. By the time Quinn reached the turn toward the castle, Alexander was already well on his way to the front gate. When Quinn entered the courtyard, Alexander still sat astride his horse.

"I guess they don't ride very fast in Maldria," he laughed.

"Or maybe you just took the faster horse," Quinn countered. Alexander's grin made his protests less believable.

The two boys dismounted and walked their horses to the stable. Bastian, who had chosen a more sensible speed, was just now turning off the main road. The stable hands met them halfway, and they waited while Alexander retrieved his gear. Quinn waited too, as he had none of his own. He offered to help carry something and was given a small pack and his friend's sword.

"I had to leave mine at Elksheart," Quinn said, turning the sword back and forth in his right hand. "Do you think your father will be upset?"

Alexander heaved two large packs onto his shoulder and walked toward the barracks. "I don't think so. It wasn't like you had any choice."

"Do you think he will get me another one?"

Alexander laughed. "Now *that's* a different question. Your fault or not, Father doesn't like to lose equipment." Quinn's face fell and Alexander laughed again. "I'm just kidding. I'm sure he will…someday."

Quinn swung the small pack at his friend, who dodged it.

They were halfway between the stables and the barracks when Melinda found them.

"I see I was correct," she said with a forced sternness, which threatened to break into a smile. "Only Alexander would ride in with such reckless abandon."

Giving up the fight, she smiled broadly and opened her arms wide. "Welcome home, Quinn."

Quinn gave her a loose, awkward hug, impeded by the sword and the pack he held. Melinda broke the hug and held him at arms length, using one hand to brush his hair off his forehead.

"We've been so worried. How are you?"

"I'm fine."

"And the girl who was with you?"

Quinn's smile quivered a little as he remembered his last visit with Alysse. "She's still sick, but she…um…I think she'll get better. She just needs more time."

The kitchen master read the worry in Quinn's eyes and pulled him close again. "I'm sure she will," she whispered. As she pulled back the second time Quinn saw someone else had come with her.

"Hi, Quinn. I'm glad you're safe."

"Hi, Rhiannon. Thanks."

Quinn stood stupidly. Hugging Melinda was one thing, but he was not going to hug Rhiannon, even though he was glad to see her. Her hair had grown even longer and was now braided the way the kitchen girls wore theirs. She looked happier and healthier than he remembered.

"I'm glad you're safe too," he added.

Rhiannon laughed at him, before rushing forward and giving him a hug. Quinn self-consciously looked over at Alexander, who was making the most of it by pursing his lips together and kissing the air. Quinn felt his neck and face flush.

"Well, I had better help Alexander get his stuff put away," he muttered awkwardly.

"Of course," she said, still smiling. "Come and see me later, though. I have some things to tell you."

"That's okay, Quinn," his friend said, dropping his packs to the ground. He gave Quinn an innocent smile. "There's no reason to hurry."

Quinn turned even redder. He was almost relieved when he heard his uncle's voice behind him. "So, you are back, then."

Quinn whirled around as Rhiannon took a step backwards. Melinda took the young girl by the shoulders and said, "We'll talk with you later, Quinn. We have things to attend in the kitchen, but welcome home."

Quinn acknowledged them with a nod, before turning to face his uncle.

"Good afternoon, milord," he said with a bow.

Renard's face was unreadable as he looked down at him. "I am glad to see you are well."

"Yes, sir."

"Well, get cleaned up. It is almost time for the evening meal. We will talk later."

"Yes, milord," Quinn said.

Alexander had retrieved his gear and high-tailed it away as soon as he had seen the duke. Quinn hurried to catch up. When Alexander heard Quinn approaching he turned and said, "Too bad the duke showed up. You might have gotten a kiss out of it."

"Yeah, you're hilarious," Quinn responded, sarcastically.

Alexander mocked surprise. "What?"

"Twit."

They arrived at the entrance to the barracks, and Quinn handed the sword and small pack back to Alexander. "I guess I should go get ready for dinner."

"Yeah, sort of like your last meal."

Quinn grimaced.

"Come see us after. I want to know what he says."

"You should already know what he's going to say. You've been through it several times before."

Alexander gave a short laugh. "Yes, but *I've* never ticked off a baron—or kidnapped his daughter."

Quinn sighed. "Don't remind me." His stomach hurt. Lately, it always seemed to hurt.

"If I don't see you again, it was nice knowing you."

Quinn could not find it in him to laugh. A part of him actually believed that was possible. "See you later," was all he could say, hoping it was true.

He walked to the side entrance of the castle and made his way to his room. He hoped it was still empty and not filled with somebody else's things. As he walked, the people he met either gave him a sad smile or ignored him altogether. When he finally made it to his room, he was relieved to find his pallet was still there. In fact, the room was exactly as it had been, minus his wooden chest of course.

He sat down heavily on the pallet and stared at the fireplace. Part of him was glad to be sitting in his own room—the part that ignored his upcoming meeting with his uncle. Quinn wondered what he would say. He had not shown it during their brief meeting in the courtyard, but according to Alexander, he was furious. Quinn sighed again.

Standing, he draped his travel cloak over the bedpost. It was the only stitch of clothing in the room besides what he was wearing. He realized he would have to be measured by the castle weavers for a new wardrobe. *One more thing to look forward to.*

He was glad his father's bow stick and sword still hung crossed above his bed. They identified the room as his. It was surprising to think he had only been gone for a month. It seemed much longer.

With no clean clothes available to change into, Quinn decided to wander down to the dining hall. He hoped by going early, he could find a place to sit out of the direct line of his uncle's sight. Quinn tried to stay as inconspicuous as he could as he walked, but unfortunately, he met Vareen at the entrance to the dining hall.

"You little fool," he hissed, before making his way into the large room.

Quinn dropped his eyes and headed to the opposite side of the room. Luckily, there were still some unoccupied tables. He chose one and sat down with his back up against the wall. As the various castle dwellers entered, a few acknowledged him, but most were either ignorant of his presence or consciously avoiding him. It seemed odd to have so many people at dinner after his time at Elksheart.

The duke and his family arrived next and sat at the head table. Bertran waved, Jens pointed, his aunt smiled, and Petric glanced at him briefly with no expression. *Great*, thought Quinn and began fiddling with his fork.

The room continued to fill with people. Quinn tried to keep his own eyes down, but he could feel many others on him. He was beginning to wish he had just taken his meal in the kitchen. Finally, the food arrived and everyone's attention turned to the roasted chicken and seasoned potatoes. Quinn ate as quickly as he could, trying to ignore the fact that no one had chosen to sit anywhere near him. Returning home was not turning out to be all that wonderful.

The meal progressed as countless ones before. The hall was filled with chatter and laughter mixed with the clanking of glasses and forks. Quinn tried to concentrate on enjoying Melinda's cooking rather than thinking about his meeting with the duke. He finished the last of his chicken when a disturbance arose at the door.

Several of the castle guards entered, dressed in armor and carrying swords. They were arrayed around a man wearing a hooded ranger cloak. *Rowan*, thought Quinn. The room grew quiet as the newcomers walked up the center aisle to where the duke sat with his family. Quinn saw Petric stand and move toward his liege.

"What is the meaning of this?" Renard asked, also rising from his chair. The ranger did not answer, but continued to walk deliberately toward the duke. "Guards, if this be treason, then at least be men enough to state it!"

"There may indeed be treason, but it is not among the men before you," the ranger answered.

He stopped when he reached the duke's table. With a sudden, fluid movement, the ranger pulled a sword from beneath his cloak. Screams shattered the silence, and benches and chairs scraped against the floor as the people scattered. Petric smoothly vaulted the table, his sword drawn. The ranger deftly slapped down the bodyguard's sword, but instead of pressing the advantage, the ranger retreated.

"Hold, Petric. I am no threat."

The ranger then turned back to the duke and tossed his sword on the table between them. A metallic ring echoed through the hall as it came to rest with its point toward Renard.

"Do you recognize the blade?" the ranger asked.

Renard looked down warily, periodically glancing back at the hooded figure before him. After a moment, his eyes grew wide.

"It is not possible," he said barely above a whisper. His head jerked back to the man in front of him.

"I am afraid this is going to be a day full of impossibilities," the ranger answered, pulling back his hood. His hair was cut short now, and his face was clean shaven, but the hideous scar still buckled his cheek from chin to ear.

"Well met, brother."

Chapter 12

Renard stared, seemingly frozen in time. Finally, he sat slowly back into his chair.

"*Rustan.*"

With one word, the duke unleashed a flurry of activity. The hall exploded into a din of noise with the words "dead", "ghost", and "returned" prominent throughout. Quinn stood, thinking he had misheard. He stared at the man who had just claimed to be his father.

"How?" the duke asked quietly.

"That tale will have to wait for another day, for we have little time to accomplish what we must. The forces of Maldria will soon stand at your gates if we fail."

Regaining some of his composure, the duke sat forward. "Rustan, I will not pretend to understand where you have been or why you have chosen now to return, but I assure you times are not as they once were. We are in the midst of building a peace between our countries."

"You are building a tower of lies that will crumble just as surely as the sun will rise tomorrow. You are either deceived, or you are a traitor to your land and your people. Which is it?"

The duke tried a small laugh, but it did not ease the tension. "Rustan, times have changed…"

"*Which is it?*" his brother lashed out, coldly.

"I…I do not know what you mean. Your own son has just returned from Maldria." The duke paused for a moment. "He was brought back by a ranger," he said to himself as the realization set in.

"The errand of a fool. You *know* Paddock. You knew his father."

"Again, Rustan, times are different…"

"They are *not* different, Renard! Only your inexplicable blindness is new! Paddock and his minions have assembled an army and navy twice the size of his father's. At this moment, it stands ready to wash over Eastcastle like the wave of the ocean. Surely, you know this. Surely your spies have told you?"

"We have no need of *spies*. We deal diplomatically with each other."

"Then where are your *diplomats*," Rustan replied in a voice as cold as death.

Renard stared at his brother, eyes locked in a battle of wills. "This is not the place for this discussion. Perhaps we should retire to the library."

Rustan gave him a mock bow, gesturing to his brother to lead the way. The duke motioned to Petric and scanned the hall for Vareen as he walked around the table. Failing to find his counselor, the duke turned to one of the guards who had entered with Rustan.

"If you still find you owe any allegiance to Eastcastle," the duke said caustically, "Then find Vareen and tell him to meet us in the library."

The guard bowed and left, ignoring the barb.

As the ensemble left the room, Quinn stared at them in shock. The whole episode was over so quickly that he was still trying to come to grips with it. Luckily, no one seemed to be aware of him as they were all talking intently among themselves. Well, almost no one.

"Quinn," Rhiannon said, suddenly appearing beside him.

He turned to look at her as if in a trance. She held a serving tray piled with empty dishes and utensils. Her eyes were bright with excitement.

"Is he really your father?"

Quinn let the question hang as he thought about it. He finally realized he had no idea.

"The duke seemed to think so."

Rhiannon was positively beaming. "That's great, isn't it? Quinn, Rowan's your *father!*"

Quinn did not know what to say. He just stared at her dumbly.

"Quinn, are you okay?" she asked, concern growing on her face.

He did not answer, but instead asked, "Why didn't he tell me?"

Rhiannon took his hand and led him from the hall, bypassing people who recognized his relationship to the recently returned duke. A couple of them called out to him, but Rhiannon bullied her way through to the door.

"Come on," she said. "Let's talk with Melinda. She'll know what to do."

Quinn followed, his mind too completely fogged to do anything else.

*   *   *

Renard, Petric, Rustan, and several guardsmen gathered in the library. Vareen had not been found. As soon as the door closed, Renard asked his brother, "Where have you been?"

"Everywhere, nowhere. It does not matter."

Renard laughed without humor. "Rustan, you have been gone for years and it does not *matter?* We thought you had perished in a storm. Is Catherine alive as well?"

The hardened look that flashed across Rustan's face was answer enough.

"I am truly sorry, brother."

"It has been a long time coming, but the hour of vengeance is here."

"Vengeance? For what? It was a storm—a terribly unfortunate storm."

Rustan whirled on his brother. "*A storm? You know nothing!* We were betrayed and boarded. Catherine was murdered in front of my eyes!"

The duke shrank back from his brother. In his mind, he began to question whether Rustan was even sane.

"I am sorry, brother. We did not know. If we had, we would have done something, but…"

"Marcus knew."

"Marcus? The man was obsessed with conspiracies. It was all talk—no evidence, no proof."

"*He knew!*"

Renard swallowed. He raised his arms palms up and dropped them to his side.

"There was no proof of anything, Rustan."

The ranger stared at his brother for a moment, composing himself. Finally, he said quietly, "It does not matter. We cannot change the past, but we must look to the future. Paddock will attack as soon as he is able. Pray the storms have set him back as well."

Renard rubbed his chin, relieved his brother's temper had cooled.

"Why would he?"

Rustan looked at his brother and then to Petric, who stood at his side. "Because that is what drives him. To succeed where his father failed."

"But why now? You have been gone for *years*, Rustan. Why when you return are we suddenly facing war? Perhaps you have misread the situation."

For a moment, Renard feared he had once again set off his brother's anger, but the ranger only clenched his teeth, cheek muscles flexing.

Rustan gave a humorless snort. "I do not know why now. Perhaps fate still plays with my life. But do not fool yourself into thinking there is no threat. I have been to Maldria, Renard. The armies are real. The ships are real. They are gathered for only one purpose."

"We can talk through this diplomatically. Confound it, where is Vareen?" the duke asked the room in general.

"You have been duped, brother. It has all been a sham, a game of Knights. Paddock has hidden his offense under a pretext of peace."

"I cannot believe it," Renard said with a sigh, sitting in one of the chairs. "I *will* not believe it. It makes no sense. What is to be gained? Why set up negotiations and goodwill only to dash it to pieces with war? For heaven's sake, he even housed Quinn, until you took it upon yourself to remove him—with the baron's daughter no less."

Renard paused and looked at his brother. "Does he even know? I mean, before tonight, did he even know who you were? Lord Roland's ghost, Rustan, *he's your own son!*"

Rustan waved it off. "I did it to keep him safe. Knowledge is a dangerous thing, especially when you do not know who your friends are," he said, staring at Renard.

"Me? You think *I* am behind any of this." The duke shook his head in disbelief. "Have you gone completely mad?"

"Have *you*? You sent a boy, your own nephew, into the hole of a snake. What am I supposed to think?"

"I have told you already, things are not how they once were. Times have changed."

"And I have told you that they have not. You may call a snake a flower if you choose, but it will still bite you in the end. Paddock will move as soon as he is able. Heaven help us if he successfully crosses the mountains before the snow sets in."

The duke sighed. "What would you have me do?"

"Take your armies to the south. Meet Anthony in Riverton and stop the Maldrians from over-running Eastcastle."

"Anthony?"

"I have sent a friend requesting he honor our agreement."

It was Renard's turn to grow red with anger. "You had no right!"

"*I have every right!* I will do whatever it takes to keep Eastcastle free."

The duke set his teeth and looked away. When he was composed again, he asked, "What makes you think he will come? We have not integrated as well as you might have imagined."

"Because I sent my ring and my word."

Renard smiled incredulously, shaking his head. "Of course, Quinn's ring—how convenient."

"And because I told him Eastcastle may be revolting."

The duke's head shot up, his face distorted in anger. "*What?!* You truly *have* gone insane!"

The ranger bore his full smirk. Raising an eyebrow, he said, "Anthony will come quickly. In fact, he may already be on his way. I suggest you meet him in Riverton and convince him otherwise."

"This is madness!"

Renard and his brother stared at each other, neither willing to back down. Finally, the duke turned to one of the guards.

"Tell the men to prepare for war. We will leave tomorrow, as soon as we are ready."

The guard suddenly looked as if he wished he were somewhere else.

"What is it?" the duke asked.

The man swallowed and said, "The men are already mobilizing, milord."

The duke gave a snort and shook his head. "Of course. Why should I think anything would be different? The great Rustan has returned."

Standing, he walked slowly to the door, Petric following. "If you will excuse me, I need to try to explain to my wife why we suddenly find ourselves facing the horrors of war despite all of our efforts to the contrary."

The two men left the room, the door closing with an ominous thud.

Rustan watched them go, his face expressionless. He sat down on a nearby chair and leaned forward, holding his head in his hands.

"Milord?" one of the guardsmen asked.

Without moving, he said quietly through his hands, "Your lord has just left. I believe you have your orders."

The guardsmen bowed and exited the room. Again the door closed with a thud.

Rustan sat alone, head resting on his palms. Despite their differences, Rustan believed his brother was telling the truth. He had not wanted to believe Renard could have been behind something so heinous, but he had needed to be sure. Renard had been sincere, unless he had developed the ability to cover a lie in the years he had been gone. No, all things now pointed to Paddock and a game of Knights masterfully played.

His eyes moved slowly around the room before stopping on a painting on the wall. He remembered when his wife had sat for the portrait in her red dress. The artist had been a master, capturing her playful smile and the wit in her eyes. He looked until he no longer could, and shut his eyes against the memories.

He was tired. The trek across the mountains was just the latest ordeal in years of hardships, pain, and despair. Through it all, he had kept his anger and his desire for vengeance burning. It was what kept him alive when food was scarce or when a lash struck his back. He had latched on to it and nurtured it. When he felt like giving up, it returned to carry him through. So many years, so much pain. The anger was always there, even when the hope withered.

It will end now, he thought. *It will end.*

*   *   *

Quinn and Rhiannon hustled toward the kitchen. Melinda met them coming the other way.

"Is it true?" she asked Quinn. "Has your father returned?"

"I think so," he answered.

"Quinn doesn't remember him," Rhiannon added.

"No, I guess he wouldn't. Is he still in the dining hall?"

"No," Rhiannon answered before Quinn could speak. "They went somewhere else to talk."

"Who?"

"His father, Duke Renard, and some of the guardsmen."

Melinda looked from Rhiannon to Quinn and back. "Well, that's probably best for now. Come with me back to the kitchen."

When they entered, the serving girls were talking excitedly among themselves, but doing very little work.

"Excuse me, girls," Melinda said in a loud voice. "I believe there is still work to be done." They immediately scattered to various cleaning jobs around the room. Turning to Rhiannon she said, "That goes for you also, young lady."

"Yes, Mistress." She curtsied and hurried toward the scrubbing buckets.

"Now, Quinn, come over here." She sat him down on a stool, like she had so many months before. Pushing her wayward gray hair back under her bonnet, she squatted down. "From your uncle's reaction, I can only assume that he is, in fact, your father. So how are you doing with all of this?"

"I don't know. I guess I should be happy."

Melinda gave him a small smile, "But you are not."

Quinn looked at her. "I don't know. I just...I don't understand why he didn't tell me who he was. Why didn't he tell me last summer when he saved me from the wolves?"

"Quinn, I knew...know...your father very well. He has one of the best minds of all the people I have ever met. I do not know why he chose to hide his identity, but I do know he has a sound reason for doing so. You will have to trust him on that, okay?"

"I guess so."

Melinda patted his knee. "Good. Now listen. Your father and uncle will likely talk late into the night. I know you probably have questions—we all do—but for tonight, I think it would be best to try and get some sleep. I am sure he will talk with you tomorrow. Besides, you must be tired from your ride here today, right?"

"A little."

She smiled and stood. "Would you like an extra dessert? It seems dinner was interrupted and we have some left over."

"No, thank you." He stood and walked toward the door.

"Okay. Let's talk again tomorrow. Oh, and Quinn?"

"Yes?"

"Welcome back. It's good to have you home." He came back and gave her hug.

"Good night."

"Good night, Quinn."

"Quinn!" Rhiannon called. She came back over from cleaning dishes. Melinda looked as though she was going to say something, but changed her mind. With a smile and a nod, she went back to overseeing the after-meal activities.

"Quinn, I…well, I just wanted to say I'm sorry for disappearing like that after Gulls Bay. Melinda said you were worried."

Quinn felt his face start to redden.

"That's all right," he said with a shrug, trying his best not to look embarrassed. It must not have worked, because Rhiannon's face broke out in a funny smile.

"Anyway," she continued, "We found something. Rowan, well, *your father* and I, found something at my father's hunting cabin. I guess it doesn't really matter anymore, with everything that has happened, but my father had hidden your father's sword in the fireplace mantel. He had carved the whole thing with hawks, and your father found it inside!"

Quinn stared at her dumbly while his mind tried to decipher what she had said. No wonder his uncle was so shocked when his father dropped the sword on the table. It was supposed to be on the bottom of the ocean. Someone must have taken it off the ship; maybe his father had. But then how did Marcus end up with it?

"I guess I should get back to cleaning," Rhiannon said. "I'm glad you're back."

"Me too. I mean, I'm glad you're back too."

Rhiannon's smile widened and she returned to the cleaning buckets. Quinn's stomach lurched as a jumble of emotions hit him—happiness, confusion, embarrassment, and excitement. He wanted to scream, laugh, and disappear all at the same time. Discounting the first two, he opted for the last and headed for his bedroom.

*　　*　　*

It was in the early morning hours when Rustan finally left the library. A messenger from his brother had stopped in and informed him that room arrangements had been made, but he declined them. He had spent few nights sleeping in a bed over the last several years. One more was not likely to make a difference.

He was standing just outside a small wooden door holding a candle lantern. He'd had to ask where the room was, but it was easy to find. Pushing on the door, he was relieved to find it unlocked. The candlelight filtered into the small room, illuminating a fireplace, a small pallet, and not much else. Metal glinted on the wall above the pallet. A small form lay underneath the blankets, rising and lowering in a steady rhythm.

Rustan rubbed his face, feeling the small scabs from shaving after so many years. He had hoped to tell Quinn earlier, but it had not worked out. The storm had changed everything. He knew when he dropped him off at the Golden Boot that he had lost the opportunity to tell him who he really was, but it could not be helped. Quinn's safety was more important. Besides, had he been recognized and killed, what good would it have done for the boy to lose his father twice?

As his eyes adjusted, he recognized his sword and bow stick crossed on the wall. He allowed himself a small smile. For a split second, he thought about taking them, but left them where they were. They belonged to Quinn now, memories more than weapons. He could have used the bow stick though, having lost his own in the Castlerooks. The armory would have many to choose from, of course, but none would surpass the bow hanging on the wall in front of him. Marcus had crafted it for him, and he had never pulled its equal.

Quinn stirred momentarily on the pallet before settling back down into sleep. Rustan shielded the lantern and stepped back into the hallway. "Good night, son," he said quietly before pulling the door shut.

Chapter 13

The sun crept over the mountains and commenced a beautiful fall day. Seemingly overnight, the trees had begun to change color. The sky was blue with sporadic white clouds, and the air had a crisp, fresh feel to it. Summer had been replaced by autumn, but this day was going to be glorious.

Outside the castle, men and horses gathered in groups that continued to grow as the morning progressed. Couriers had been sent throughout the dukedom calling all to stand and protect their homes from invasion. Most had come out of curiosity rather than the belief of a real threat.

Inside the courtyard, the standing army was a blur of activity. Soldiers gathered their weapons and armor. Pikes, lances, maces, and swords were dispensed. Some transferred whatever was left in the armory into multiple carts, while others saddled the horses or harnessed them to wagons.

Quinn sat on a bench near one of the carts. He had helped Bastian, Alexander, and others fill it with bow sticks, arrows, and cords. Now he watched as Alexander and his father tied down the oiled tarp. Despite the clearness of the day, Bastian never took chances with the fletchers' wares.

Quinn had looked for his father hoping to find him alone, but no one had seen him or the duke. Presumably, they had gone somewhere together to hammer out how things should proceed. Rumors were flying around the castle that Rustan had taken back the dukedom and sent Renard packing. Quinn chose to ignore them.

He had sat by himself again at breakfast, but quickly tired of the guarded looks and whispered comments around him. After wolfing down the pancakes, he decided to see if he could find Alexander amongst the chaos growing in the courtyard. Unfortunately, he found him just in time for Bastian to put them both to work loading the wagons.

"What's wrong? Missing your previous life of luxury already?" Alexander asked when he saw him resting on the bench.

"No," Quinn answered simply, when he couldn't think of a snappy comeback. He actually was not in the mood for Alexander's humor. He had come outside because he thought he would be ignored in all the commotion. Except for Alexander, he had been correct.

"Zander, you've let the line go too slack. Pull it again and hold it this time."

"Sorry, father," the boy sighed.

Quinn stuck his tongue out at him. It was petty, but surprisingly it made him feel a little better. Alexander, of course, responded with his usual hurt look.

"You know, now that you're back, it's only a matter of time before we start sparring again."

"Whatever," Quinn replied.

Alexander laughed.

As he sat forward with his head resting in his hands, Quinn continued to sort through his memories. The ranger who had saved him from the wolves, shown him how to shoot a bow, and entered him in the tournament was his father. He was the same man who had surprised them in the balcony of the old church and taken Rhiannon. All that time, Quinn had thought he was just a stranger, a traveler who happened to be at the right place at the right time. And what about the dead bishop—*had* his father been involved? Had he been trying to get information from him? But no, he already would have known. In fact, he *was* the secret, kind of. Quinn's head began to pound.

"What's with the scowl? You're not really mad are you?" asked Alexander.

Quinn looked up and sighed. "No, I'm not mad. It's just…"

"Your father?"

Quinn nodded.

"Have you talked with him? I mean, since you found out who he was?"

Putting his head back down into his hands, Quinn stared down at his feet, scraping them in the dirt.

"No, not yet."

"Well, maybe you can talk with him now. He just came out with the duke. Or is *he* the duke again?"

Quinn stood and looked over at the commotion near the front gate. The duke and his father sat upon horses. His father was still wearing the garb of a ranger, while Renard looked every bit the duke.

"I guess not."

The two youth joined the gathering crowd of soldiers and tried in vain to push their way to the front. Bastian followed more slowly, wiping the oil from his hands on a piece of cloth. As Quinn got closer, he suddenly felt a pang of jealousy. Bertran sat on a horse behind the duke.

Word of Rustan's appearance spread to the men gathered outside the castle walls. They began to throng to the gates, each trying to catch sight of him. Efforts to hold them back and create order were failing until Rustan pushed his horse through the masses as though he were fording a river. When he reached the stairs on the inside wall, he left his horse and climbed them. No sooner did his head appear above the wall than cheers of "Hawk!" and "Eastcastle!" rang across the valley. Holding out his arms, Rustan tried without success to quiet them.

"Men of Eastcastle! Men of Eastcastle!" he yelled above the cheers. Finally, the chants and cries dwindled. "Men of Eastcastle, it is good to be with you again."

A fresh cheer sounded and Rustan again raised his arms. When they again quieted, he added, "Though I fear you will not cheer me once you know the tidings I bring.

"Years ago, my father offered you your freedom—a chance to choose your own life. But such freedom is not free, and today it hangs in the balance. The barons of Maldria and their armies would take it from you. *Will you let them?!*"

The shouts of "NO!" reverberated across the land.

"Friends of Eastcastle, will you stand with me?"

"YES!"

"FOR FREEDOM! FOR EASTCASTLE!"

Quinn watched in awe as his father descended from the castle wall. With just a few words, he had energized them all. Renard circled his horse and shouted commands to the various captains, organizing them into groups and preparing them to march. The men listened for a moment before bowing to the duke and calling their groups together.

"LONGBOWS! LONGBOWS TO ME!"

"PIKEMEN TO THE ARMORY!"

"CAVALRY TO YOUR MOUNTS! WE RIDE FOR SHEPHERDS PASS!"

The chaotic throng of men organized both inside and outside the gate. At the bottom of the steps, Rustan looked for his horse. Quinn pushed his way toward him. His insides were roiling. Ever since the night before, he had tried not to think about this moment, but felt compelled to face it all the same. By the time he reached his father, he was about to mount his horse again.

"Father?" The word sounded odd coming from his mouth.

Rustan turned toward the voice, his foot already in a stirrup. Recognizing his son, he lowered his foot to the ground again.

"Hello, Quinn. How are you feeling?"

"Fine. I…" His mind went blank. He had rehearsed several things he wanted to say to his father, but he could not remember a single one. Instead, he just stared dumbly at the man he had thought dead for most of his life.

The moment was just as awkward for Rustan, who immediately flashed his customary smirk.

"Good."

Not knowing what else to do, Quinn rushed forward and hugged his father around the waist. After a brief pause, Rustan gave him a tentative hug back. He then pushed Quinn out to arms length and rested his hands on his shoulders.

"I am sorry I did not tell you earlier, but given the circumstances, I felt it best not to do so. When I return, we will talk more. I promise."

"When you return? But I'm going with you."

Rustan clenched his jaw, before relaxing.

"No, Quinn. War is no place for a boy." Then, half to himself, he added, "War is no place for anyone."

Quinn began to protest, but his father cut him off with a wave of his hand. "Quinn, do not press me on this. I will not change my mind."

"But I have been training…"

The arrival of Renard, Petric, and Bertran offered Rustan the opportunity to turn away. Quinn eyed his cousin and felt the sting of jealousy. He turned and disappeared into the throng of men. Rustan saw the movement through the corner of his eye and looked back, his cheek muscles flexing as he once again clenched his teeth together. Closing his eyes for a moment, he regained his composure before looking again at his brother.

"Shall we wait for him?" the duke asked.

Rustan shook his head. "No, he will be staying. I will not take him into war."

Mounting his horse, he turned the stallion toward the front gates, effectively ending the conversation.

Renard watched his brother as he steered his horse through the soldiers. Many stopped to shake his hand or wave a greeting. Turning back, he called to Bertran.

"Son, take your horse back to the stables. It will be needed."

"No, father, I'm going."

"Bertran, I will not discuss this. Take your horse back to the stables, now!"

The duke stared at his son. He was angry with himself for not having crossed this bridge in private. Unfortunately, the time for a quiet discussion with his son was no longer available. *At least his mother will be relieved.*

Bertran glared back at his father, his mouth opened in shock. Clamping it shut, he looked to Petric for support. The tall man looked straight ahead, his stone face completely unreadable. Finding no help from the bodyguard, Bertran tried his father one more time.

"Father, please…"

"No. Return the horse to the stables."

The duke's voice was quiet and cold, and his face reddened. Bertran knew instantly he had gone too far. He immediately turned his horse and spurred him forward. Soldiers scattered, shouting oaths as the boy rode through them.

"The boy…"

"Petric," said Renard, cutting off his bodyguard, "I respect your opinions; however, I have no interest in hearing them right now."

The expressionless man took the rebuke with a nod. Sudden cheers from without the gates let them know Rustan had left the courtyard.

"May the heavens smile upon us," the duke said quietly, nudging his mount forward. Petric followed him silently toward the gate.

Bastian and Alexander sat together on the seat of one of the archers' wagons. The tarp had been securely tied down, and they now waited for the area to clear enough to gain access to the front gates. They watched as first Quinn and then Bertran returned to the castle. Alexander found it hard to suppress a grin as the latter rode off in a huff. His father watched quietly as the duke and his bodyguard left through the front gate of the castle.

"Zander?"

"Yes, father?"

The weapons master turned to look at his son, his face conflicted. Alexander knew the look. It meant his father was going to tell him something he knew would make Alexander mad, but felt he needed to say anyway. Bastian always struggled to find the right words, as if it would make a difference. Without Bastian saying a word, Alexander knew where this conversation was headed.

Bastian took a breath and let it out slowly. "One of the most important things I have tried to teach you is to be loyal to your liege—to stand by him and to protect him. All of the weapons training I have given you was to make you more capable of doing that."

"Yes, father," Alexander said guardedly.

The weapons master swallowed. "The time has come for you to demonstrate that loyalty to your liege."

"And we will, as soon as the way is clear."

Bastian looked down and shook his head. "No, son…"

"Father, my *liege* has just left. Granted, I don't know which one he is exactly, but it doesn't really matter since they're both together."

The weapons master's face grew solemn. "No, Zander, *your* liege is still here," he said quietly.

Alexander glared at his father. In his heart, he had already known what his father was going to ask, though he had not expected this tack.

"Quinn. You're saying my liege is Quinn."

"Yes."

"You are asking me not to go to Shepherds Pass, not to fight for Eastcastle, not to use all of the training *you* have given me, but to stay here and baby-sit instead." Alexander's voice grew harder with each word.

Bastian sighed and nodded once. "Yes, Zander. I'm sorry, but yes, I *am* asking you to stay with Quinn. Things are moving quickly, too quickly, and I'm not sure things have been thought through. Rustan is rushing the army down to fight the very people Renard just sent Quinn to live with. I'm a simple man, Zander, but something doesn't sit well with me about any of this."

Alexander looked away. If he was honest with himself, he knew a small part of him was relieved, but it was vastly overwhelmed by the disappointment of being left behind. He had been trained in every weapon imaginable, and now was the time to put his training to the test. Not in a tournament, but for real, for something that mattered. For Eastcastle. For honor.

Bastian put his hand on his son's shoulder, but Alexander shrugged it off. Using the same motion, he leapt off the high wagon bench and landed softly on the courtyard dirt. Without turning around or acknowledging his father's farewell, he walked back toward the barracks.

The courtyard cleared with military efficiency. Within moments, Bastian was able to pull forward with the other carts and wagons. Giving one last glance toward the barracks where his son had disappeared, he said quietly, "Fare well, son."

With a slap of the reins, the sturdy pack horses lurched forward. Bastian stared ahead, his face somber. He could not find it in him to whistle as was his habit when traveling. Instead, he concentrated on forgetting the look of betrayal on Alexander's face when he had told him to stay behind. Try as he might, he failed. Inwardly, he hoped he had done the right thing. In fact, he hoped they were all doing the right thing.

∗   ∗   ∗

Quinn was angry. He was also hurt and embarrassed, but mostly he was just angry. The hot tears that ran down his face only made things worse as glances were thrown his way. People were everywhere, each on an errand that obviously needed to be done as quickly as possible given the way they hurried through the hallways. At least none of them was stopping and asking him what was wrong. Finally reaching his room, he slammed the wooden door behind him, only to belatedly realize that he had plunged the room into nearly complete blackness.

Growling, he re-opened the door to let in the light from the hallway lanterns. As the room lit, he was reminded that everything he owned was leagues away in Maldria. *Unless, of course, Paddock burned it all.*

Feeling his fury begin to grow again, Quinn went to the small pallet and tossed himself onto it. The stiff, uneven padding was just one more reminder of being dragged away from Elksheart by his father. Quinn lay on his back and pounded his fists backwards into the padding, uttering a yell of frustration. *A boy?* He was *older* than Bertran!

Finding no solace in beating his pallet, Quinn kicked his legs off and sat on the edge. His room was one of the last in the hallway that led to a castle tower. At least he was unlikely to be bothered by anyone. He laughed bitterly to himself. Everyone in the entire castle was on their way south. His father, his uncle, Bertran, Bastian, Alexander.

Quinn froze. *Bastian.* Why had he not thought of it before? He could ride in the wagon with Bastian and Alexander until they got to Shepherds Pass. Once they got there, his father would have to let him stay.

Quinn's mind raced. He would have to think of a way to convince Bastian to let him go with them. He stood and began to pace the room, knowing he would have to hurry to catch Bastian before he left. Maybe he could just tell him there were no more horses left—in fact, that was probably true. But why would his father not have taken him? One would think the brother of the duke could get a horse for his son, especially when many still considered him to *be* the duke.

Quinn brought his hands to his mouth and tapped his fingers together under his nose. He racked his brain, trying to think of a good excuse. His eyes came to rest on his father's bow stick. A small smile crept across his face. *Of course, his father would want his bow!*

Jumping onto the pallet, Quinn removed the bow stick from the wall. For a moment, he debated bringing the sword as well, but he was afraid he would not be able to carry it. It would only highlight Quinn's diminutive size if he dragged his father's sword behind him.

Stepping off the pallet, he examined the bow stick in the light from the doorway. It was intricately carved and looked more like a piece of art than a weapon. It was missing a cord, but Bastian would have ample to choose from in the cart. Quinn's only worry was that the stick had stiffened and lost its flexibility hanging on the wall for so many years. If the bow were no longer usable, Bastian would notice and doubt that Rustan had requested it.

Standing beside it, Quinn was surprised to see the bow was taller than he was. After all the years of looking at it on the wall, he had not really thought about its length. Setting one point on the inside of his foot, he tried to pull the other down as if stringing it. Quinn's heart sank. The bow stick did not even bend.

Knowing he was running out of time, Quinn argued with himself. Maybe the bow was fine, and he was simply not strong enough to pull it. He could never string the bows Malcolm had given him, why would he think he could draw his father's? If he brought the bow to Bastian, *he* would know without pulling it whether it was still usable. Quinn ran his hands along the smooth, light wood, wishing he could do the same. Of course, if he waited much longer, it would not matter one way or the other. Then again, maybe the bow's condition did not really matter anyway. His father had not seen it. He could just tell Bastian he had offered to retrieve it for him.

Quinn was about to run and find Bastian when he had another thought. Climbing onto his pallet again, he brought the bow stick close until it was standing vertically on the floor in front of him. Putting both hands on the top of the bow, just under the notched end, he jumped into the air and tried to balance all of his weight on the stick. Quinn smiled as he felt the bow flex under his weight. Suddenly, a loud *crack* echoed through the room, and Quinn fell hard, hitting his back on the side of the pallet. The next thing he knew, he was lying on his stomach on the floor.

Tears began to fill his eyes, partly from the pain in his back where he had hit the pallet and partly from the realization his plans were now ruined. Sitting on the ground, he berated himself for his stupidity. Any hope of convincing Bastian now lay shattered at his feet.

"No. No. *NO!*" Quinn screamed.

He picked up the nearest piece of the bow and was about to throw it across the room when something caught his eye. He held the end up to the light from the doorway. The break had occurred near the top flex point.

What caught Quinn's attention, however, was not so much *where* it had broken, but *why* it had broken. A small section of the stick had been hollowed out, leaving a gap in the wood. The thin remaining sides had snapped when he had applied pressure to it. Confusion overtook the anger as he looked closer at the bow through tear-blurred eyes. He had played with his father's bow many times. It had never had a gap in it before. He was sure of it.

Searching the floor where he sat, Quinn found a small wooden plug, shaped and smoothed on one side, not much bigger than his little finger. He compared the plug to the rounded part of the break and found it was a perfect match. Someone had hollowed out the bow stick and covered it with a wooden plug to make it look sound.

Quinn's first thought was that someone had done it to put his father at risk, hoping his bow would break when he needed it. The more he thought about it though, the less sense it made. The bow would have broken as soon as his father tried to string it. No, it was more likely someone had tampered with his father's bow *after* he and his mother had disappeared.

Wincing, he stood and rubbed his back. From the stinging sensation, he guessed the pallet had scraped off layers of skin. Dropping what remained of the top of the bow stick, he gingerly walked over to the other piece. He bent down and picked it up, wincing as his back stretched in the effort. Carrying it back to the light of the doorway, his breath caught. A small rolled parchment stuck out of the hollow in the stick, its top slightly crumpled.

Quinn carefully extracted the parchment and unrolled it. The script was small, but finely printed. Quinn wished he remembered more of Alysse's reading lessons as his eyes skimmed over the words. He recognized some of the smaller ones, but realized he would not be able to read all of it, at least not quickly. Ignoring the pain in his back, Quinn held the top and bottom down firmly to keep it from rolling back up.

When he found the top of the note, the hairs on the back of his neck stood up.

Quinn.

The note was addressed to him. Instead of trying to read through the text, his eyes dropped immediately to the end of the writing. He felt his heart begin to beat harder as he sounded out the name just above his fingers: *Marcus.*

Quinn let go of the parchment and sat back on the floor. He stared at the rolled note as it rocked back and forth on the ground. *Of course*, he thought to himself. Bishop Jerome had mentioned Marcus had left other evidences of his parents' murder in case he was killed. Who better to tell than their own son?

Quinn knew Marcus was a master woodworker in addition to being a weapons master. It would have been easy for him to hide the parchment in the bow. He must have counted on Quinn trying to string his father's bow someday. All these years, it had waited in plain site for the day when he was old enough and strong enough to try.

Leaning forward, he stretched out the parchment again. He tried to read the words, but it was painfully slow. *Quinn, If you are reading this, then I am sorry for I have failed you as I did your parents.*

Frustrated, Quinn rolled up the parchment and stood. It would take him forever to read all of the text, or at least longer than he had to catch Bastian. His heart sank with the thought. Without the bow, his plan to convince Bastian was worthless. Unless, of course, he wanted to show his father what was *in* the bow.

His face brightened and he slapped the rolled parchment in the palm of his other hand. Bastian would have to take him to his father. He would want to know what Marcus had written. He stuffed the parchment into his pocket and grabbed the smaller piece of the ruined bow stick. Hurrying out the door, he pulled it close with a thud. He took two steps before freezing.

Vareen and two men he did not recognize had just come around the corner at the end of the long hallway. A sneering smile slowly crept across his old tutor's face as he recognized Quinn. He said something to the guards that Quinn could not hear, but the message was clear enough from their actions. Both stepped forward, drawing the swords from their scabbards.

Quinn did not wait to find out what they wanted. Turning, he ran the opposite way to the end of the hall, still carrying the piece of his father's bow stick. He panicked when he realized there were no other exits in this direction. The hallway turned to the right and ended in a small anteroom before the stairwell to one of the castle's many towers. Quinn had climbed to the top enough times to know the round room at the top offered neither escape routes nor places to hide.

Skidding to a stop in front of the first stair, Quinn quickly scanned the small foyer. Two unlit lanterns and an old tapestry hung on the wall of the otherwise empty room. The tapestry was of a harvest scene and hung over the first of many archer slots. Behind it was a small alcove built to give an archer greater range.

Quinn slipped behind the heavy material as carefully as he could and hoped the darkness of the room would hide any lingering movement of the fabric. Years earlier, Quinn and Alexander had hidden here when one of Alexander's escapades had gone poorly. Alexander had used his knife to cut a small opening so they could see out. At the time, Quinn had been sure his uncle would find out about the damage and punish them both. Now he found himself silently thanking his mischievous friend.

Within moments, the two guardsmen rounded the corner, trained eyes taking in the small room and the doorway to the tower. Vareen joined them almost immediately.

"What are you waiting for?" he hissed in his whiny voice. "Go up and bring the brat down. Do whatever it takes short of killing him."

The men darted up the stairs toward the tower room. Quinn watched in dismay as Vareen began to pace in the small entry room instead of following them. Quinn's whole body was shaking and his heart was pounding so hard he was sure the small man would hear it. He knew it was only a matter of time before the guards returned empty-handed from the room above. After that, it would not take long for them to find him. He wondered if he could sneak around Vareen without getting caught, but decided against it. The man would have to be blind to miss him.

Quinn's eyes began to water, both from the strain of looking through the small hole as well as from the dust he had stirred up. The musty smell made it hard to breathe, and Quinn felt his nose begin to tickle. Dread filled him as he futilely tried to ward off the oncoming sneeze. Fighting the urge as long as he could, he pinched his nose, covered his mouth, and closed his eyes, trying to stifle as much sound as possible. Blinking, he peered through the slit. His stomach clenched. Vareen was coming straight toward him.

Chapter 14

The trek south was going as well as could be expected, but it was still too slow for Rustan. He pushed as hard as he could to get the column of men moving in a timely manner, but the condition of the road was working against them. Boughs had been cut and thrown down in the worst of the muddy areas to lend traction to the cart wheels, but even so the heavier ones bogged down. Men and beasts worked together to free them, but precious time was lost.

Renard rode between his brother and his bodyguard. Rustan's hood was pulled up, hiding his face in its depths—a sign of the coolness that remained between them. Renard had finally conceded to marshal the armies, but his lack of belief in the necessity was obvious. In fact, his only real motivation was to try and deflect as much of Anthony's wrath as possible, should the king actually answer the paranoid call of his recently-returned sibling. The risk was too great that Rustan had indeed notified the king of his insane conspiracy theories and Anthony would actually show up. At least with his army in tow, Renard could safely claim to have been duped by the same madness.

He had hoped to send word to Paddock explaining the embarrassing circumstances surrounding Quinn's disappearance and his daughter's kidnapping, but Vareen could not be found. The blasted man had simply disappeared. The thought crossed his mind that perhaps he was somehow involved in all of this, but he quickly discarded it. Vareen had been with him for years, even before he had become duke. Grimacing, he tried to shake himself free of the same paranoia that obviously consumed Rustan.

He glanced over at his hooded brother before looking back ahead with a scowl. *Rustan and his ridiculous ranger fascination. He's worse than Petric—at least I can see where he is looking, if not what he is thinking.*

Renard scanned their line and was amazed it was still moving well. If nothing else came of this little trek, at least he was reassured the army could respond quickly. Sighing, he tried to erase all the expression from his face. *How did Petric do it?*

They had only traveled a little further when Petric broke the silence.

"A rider, milord."

Renard looked past the front guards and saw his bodyguard was right. A single rider sped toward them at a reckless pace. Petric quietly slid his sword from its sheath, resting it lightly on the front of his saddle. Before long, the rider closed the gap between them.

He talked quickly with the lead men and then continued on toward them. He was middle-aged with thick brown hair, which was currently a windswept mess. He had clearly been riding hard for some time. He wore the uniform of the Eastcastle border guards.

"Milord, thank the heavens," he cried with a small head bow. His breath came in quick gasps and his voice was raspy. "I have been riding since the gray light of morning. I bring dire news, though from the looks of this, you already know it. The Maldrians are in the Pass."

Renard refused to look at his brother. "Perhaps they intend to talk or negotiate trade?"

The man shook his head, swallowing hard to wet his throat. "No, milord. They are armed and pressing forward. Several of our distant outposts were overrun before we even had warning. I am afraid their intentions are hostile."

"Have you seen any ships?"

The startled guardsman glanced at the hooded ranger. "Pardon?"

Rustan brought his horse closer and pulled down his hood. "Have your outposts relayed any messages regarding Maldrian ships?"

To the man's credit, his eyes stayed in his head when he recognized the man before him. "No…no, milord."

Renard grimaced again. He wondered if he was angrier about his brother's dramatics or the fact he had been right. Recognizing the pettiness of either answer only made him more upset.

"How many men are in the pass?" he asked curtly.

The man looked back to Renard, but his eyes darted to Rustan occasionally as he answered. "The reports said several hundred, milord. Well above what the treaty allows."

Renard felt his brother's eyes on him. Turning, he steeled himself for the worst. He was relieved to only find a determined look on Rustan's face.

"We thank you for your warning," he said to the border guard. "You are free to return to the castle for rest and nourishment."

"With all due respect, milord, I wish to return to the Pass and relay the news of your approach. It will bolster the men to hold, provided it is not already too late."

The duke nodded. *And to bring word of The Hawk's miraculous return, no doubt.*

"Of course. Exchange your horse and Godspeed."

The man bowed again before pulling his horse to the right and riding off. Renard looked back to his brother. "So, it has begun," he said with a sigh.

Rustan gave a short nod and they continued on.

*　　*　　*

Quinn watched in dread as Vareen stopped on the other side of the tapestry.

"Come out, boy. You're not fooling anyone."

Quinn pushed the tapestry up with his left arm, holding the broken bow stick behind his body in his right hand. A sneer widened across the small man's face.

"That's right, brat, come out. You're my guarantee out of this ignorant land. Get out here!"

Quinn edged out sideways, hiding the stick.

"What have you got…"

Vareen never finished. As soon as Quinn was clear of the tapestry, he swung the bow stick with both hands, smashing it down on the counselor's head. The small man stumbled backwards, and Quinn took the opportunity to run past him. Behind him, he heard Vareen's cry.

"Aaghh! You fools! He's down here!"

The tromping of the guards' booted feet faded as Quinn passed his bedroom. His mind whirled as he tried to think of a safe place to run. He reached the stairs at the end of the hallway and started down, taking the last four in a jump. Turning left, he hurried toward the main entry of the castle keep. He hoped he could find help in the courtyard.

He rounded the last corner and skidded to a stop on the stone slabs. Two guardsmen dressed in the same uniform as those with Vareen stood on each side of the double doors. Beyond them, the courtyard was almost empty. The two men looked at him, though neither made a move in his direction.

Quinn stood still, breathing hard from fear and exertion. He knew he would not make it past them if they chose to stop him. Even if he did, there appeared to be no one to help him outside, anyway. When one of the guards called out and took a step toward him, he decided the risk was too great. Besides, Vareen would likely come here first. Turning, he fled back into the heart of the keep.

He slowed his pace when he reached the inner hallways and staircases of the castle. From his countless adventures with Alexander, he knew there were several ways to any one place. It was a fact that had saved them from punishments numerous times. Now that he had gotten away from Vareen and his two henchmen, it was entirely possible to run into them solely by accident. He stopped briefly at every intersection and doorway and listened before continuing on. He feared he would see Vareen whenever he rounded a corner.

His first thought was to hide. He knew of many places, some where he could probably stay for a week, but what good would it do? The only ones looking for him would be the counselor and his two guardsmen. His father had most likely left with the bulk of the army, as well as his uncle, Bertran, Bastian, and Alexander. There was no one left in the castle he really knew, other than his aunt and Melinda. As he had never felt overly close to his aunt, he headed for the kitchen.

As normal, the kitchen was a flurry of activity. In fact, it was even more hectic than normal. The entire staff was busy piling breads, meats, cheeses, fruits, and vegetables into crates. In the middle of the room, Melinda called out directions and admonishments. Within moments, she caught sight of him.

"I'm sorry, Quinn, this is not a good time. We have several carts left to load—Amelia, be careful with those apples! You'll bruise some and ruin the whole barrel. Jillian, those rolls are done!"

Quinn leaned against the inside wall of the kitchen and closed his eyes. His heart was still beating rapidly, and he could feel the panic starting to creep over him again. Where else could he go? He thought about heading back to the duke's chambers and finding his aunt, but he worried he would run into Vareen. For all he knew, they were already on their way to the kitchen. An involuntary yelp escaped his lips when someone laid their hand on his shoulder.

"Quinn, what's the matter?" Melinda asked quietly.

She was squatting down so her face was near his. Fighting back the fear that threatened to overtake him, Quinn told her everything that had happened. Melinda's face hardened as she listened. When he finished, she stood and huffed.

"Well, we will get to the bottom of this!"

Taking him by the hand, she stepped out into the hallway. Quinn was about to follow, when she quickly pushed him back.

"They're coming this way," she hissed. Taking his father's broken bow stick from him, she quickly scanned the kitchen. "Quickly, climb into the last oven."

Quinn looked at her in shock. Looking down, she wrinkled her face and gave a short laugh.

"It's not in use. Your uncle has never fixed it. Quickly, now," she said pushing him toward the back oven. "Stay there until I find out what is going on."

Quinn hurried to the stone oven and climbed inside. The space was barely larger than he was, and he quickly became uncomfortable. Worst of all, he could not turn all the way around. He would not be able to see what was going on in the kitchen. In fact, he could barely hear. If Vareen found him here, he had no chance of escaping again. Beads of sweat started to form on his forehead, either from fear or the heat of the adjoining oven—likely both.

Melinda bustled back to the center of the kitchen gesturing frantically to the kitchen girls to ignore the fact Quinn had just climbed into an oven. The scowl on her face caused even the most insolent to look away and return to their tasks. She had just finished hiding the broken bow stick in a pile of firewood when the counselor and two large men entered with a loud, "Ahem."

Melinda twirled with what she hoped was a passable look of surprise. "Ah, counselor, forgive me. Things are in a bit of a tizzy right now, as you might expect."

The small man smiled his pained smile. "Of course," he said with an arrogant head nod. "I was wondering if perhaps you might have seen young Quinn Hawk around."

Melinda prayed the girls swarming the kitchen would not react. "No. Though, if I do, I will put him to work. Heaven knows we can use the help. My guess is he probably left with his father."

Vareen forced a bigger smile, which made his face look as though it would crack. "Of course," he said again.

His eyes scanned the kitchen meticulously. Melinda breathed shallowly. Many of the kitchen girls successfully ignored the visitors, but most were clearly agitated. Their guarded glances displayed more anxiety than they should have. The longer Vareen watched them, the more suspicious he became.

"Perhaps, I may offer the assistance of my two guardsmen. After all, it is the least we can do to help support the efforts."

Melinda tried not to sound desperate. "No, of course not. They clearly have better things to do than spending time bundling food." Hoping to gloss over the refusal, she asked, "Vareen, what have you done to your head?"

The counselor reached up and gingerly touched the large, purpling bruise on the side of his forehead. Wincing slightly, he laughed humorlessly, "Just being careless." Taking a step forward, he said, "However, I think we *will* stay and offer a hand."

Melinda walked quickly to him. "No, really. Do not concern yourselves. We will manage. Besides, I would not want to keep you from finding Quinn."

Vareen's eyes tightened slightly. "I thought you said he was with his father?"

"Well, I…I am sure he is. I…"

The counselor sprung forward and grabbed the kitchen master's arms. "Where is he, you old hag?" he hissed in a voice as cold as ice. The kitchen became as quiet as a mountain lake.

Melinda tried to push him back. "Take your hands off of me! I already told you, he is not here!"

"Search the kitchen," Vareen spat out, still not releasing the kitchen master.

"No! I said he is not here, now leave! We have work to do."

The small man flashed his teeth. "You will forgive me if I do not believe you. Search the kitchen!"

The two guardsmen started forward, one down each side of the large kitchen. All the kitchen girls but one backed away, many heading toward the door to the garden.

"Let her go," Rhiannon said quietly, her face set in stone. She held a knife loosely in her right hand.

The counselor's eyes narrowed. A hideous smile crept across his face. "Or what, little girl?"

"I said, let her go."

The guardsmen continued to look around the kitchen, ignoring the scene developing in the middle of the room.

"Let me give you some advice, girl. Stay out of things that do not concern you. You will have a much better chance of living a long life." Then he snorted, "For whatever your pathetic life is worth."

Rhiannon's arm moved in a blur. The motion was so quick and so smooth that Vareen had little chance to respond. With his hands still grasping Melinda's arms, he was unable to move quickly. The knife embedded into his thigh.

"Aaghhh!" he screamed and threw Melinda across the floor. The old woman slid several feet on the stone floor before crashing into some stools. She lay without moving.

Vareen's face took on a feral look as he glared at Rhiannon. "Kill them! Kill them all!"

The metallic sounds of swords leaving their sheaths mixed with the screams of the kitchen girls. Most of them ran wildly toward the garden door, while others stood frozen with shock. Rhiannon quickly gathered up all the knives she could and worked her way to the back wall.

From within his stone hiding place, Quinn tried vainly to back out of the oven. His yells reverberated off the oven walls.

"No! *NO!!*"

Chapter 15

Alexander was furious. He stalked through the courtyard bumping into anyone who did not move out of the way fast enough. Luckily, no one responded with more than just an angry word or glance because Alexander was looking for a fight. Had someone challenged him, he would have been more than happy to give them a piece of his mind as well as his sword.

By the time he reached his room, he had worked himself into a full blown rage. A small part of him knew his father had been telling the truth when he cited his concerns for Quinn, but the rest of him saw it as nothing more than an excuse to leave him behind. Slamming the door, he picked up a chair and threw against the stone wall, an action he immediately regretted when he heard the wood splinter. With a roar, he flung himself onto his pallet. Had he known Quinn was on his own pallet in nearly the same disposition, he might have found it funny. Instead, he stared at the ceiling, feeling his heart pump hot blood through his veins.

Closing his eyes, he tried to slow his breathing, much as he would at a sparring contest. In his mind's eye, he pictured his father seated on the cart bench, reins in hand. He wondered what his face would show if he could see it. Relief? Sorrow? Probably neither. His father's face would likely show nothing. He was the duke's man through and through. His personal thoughts and feelings would not change that.

When Alexander had calmed his rage, he left his pallet and went to look at the chair he had thrown. When he lifted the back it broke off completely.

Alexander grimaced and said out loud to no one, "Great."

Putting the back of the chair under his arm, he reached down and righted the seat and legs. Testing it lightly with his foot, he was relieved to find it was still sound. At least he would not have to repair that part. Not that it mattered. By the time his father returned, he could probably make several chairs from start to finish. Feeling his anger blossoming again, he tossed the remains of the chair's backing onto the table and sat on another.

Resting his elbows on the table, Alexander propped his head on his hands and stared at the wall. His leg bounced as he scanned the room. He thought about disobeying his father, but deep inside he knew would not. As furious as he was, he knew he could not cross his father on this, not when he had couched it in *duty*. His father's weapon training was always laced with the importance of a soldier's duty and his loyalty. He could challenge his father's patience with greased pigs and practical jokes, but he knew his father would never accept shirking one's duty.

Alexander's foot bounced quicker as he felt the room become more and more confining. He knew eventually he would have to go and find Quinn, but he would wait until the courtyard cleared. By living in the barracks, Alexander was friends with most of the soldiers stationed there, and the last thing he wanted was harassment or pity.

As he waited, he thought about how he was going to pass the time stuck at the castle. The realization that the entire place was likely to be nearly deserted brought him a small smile. There would certainly be a number of things Quinn and he could get into with such a lack of supervision.

Finally, he decided the courtyard was probably clear enough. Even if it was not, he no longer felt like staring at the walls of the small room he shared with his father. Besides, his eyes kept tracking over to the broken chair. If nothing else, he could borrow some tools from the woodworking shop. Standing, he was about to unbuckle his sword belt before he changed his mind. He wanted to foster the perception he was still getting ready to follow the army later if there were still soldiers around.

Alexander left his room and was relieved to see he had been correct. Only a few soldiers remained in the courtyard, mostly those left tending to the supply carts. Putting on his best look of nonchalance, he walked toward the castle's main entrance. He decided to ask Quinn if he was interested in helping repair the chair. If not, they could find something else to do. His father had only said to stay with him, not to keep him out of trouble.

The guards at the main entrance let him through without a smirk or comment. In fact, he might have been an ant crossing the floor for all the attention they gave him. Once inside, he took a moment to let his eyes adjust to the lantern lights before walking to Quinn's room.

The entire castle was unusually quiet and he met no one along the way. Apparently, those who had not gone to war had decided to spend their time in solitude. Even the guards at the door had talked in low whispers. It was as though a blanket of gloom had fallen over Eastcastle.

The door to Quinn's bedroom was shut. Knocking on the door, Alexander called out, "Quinn? Quinn, are you in there?"

He waited a moment and when no one answered, he tried the door. It opened easily. Poking his head inside, he called Quinn's name again. The room was dark with only the thin shaft of light from the doorway slicing across the room like a sword. Wondering if perhaps Quinn were sleeping, Alexander pushed the door open wider so the flickering lantern lights from the hallway illuminated the small pallet. It took moment for Alexander to determine the bump he saw was not his friend, but only messed up blankets. Stepping back, he was pulling the door closed when something caught his eye. A piece of wood lay on Quinn's pallet.

Checking again to see if anyone was in the hallway, Alexander slipped into his friend's room. Alexander had been around enough weapons to recognize the broken end of a bow, but it took him a little longer to realize *which* bow had been broken.

Letting out a low whistle, he smiled to himself. Whatever his chance was of actually fixing the broken chair, it was infinitely greater than Quinn's was of replacing his father's bow. He had seen bows shatter before and when they did, they were pretty much only good for firewood afterwards. Picking up the smooth piece of wood, he scanned the room for the other half. Unable to find it, he took a closer look at the end of the bow in his hand.

It did not take long for Alexander to realize someone had tampered with the stick at the break point. Instead of the expected jagged end, much of the break was smooth, as though the bow had been hollowed out. Wrinkling his brow, Alexander dropped the ruined weapon back onto the pallet and walked toward the door. He would have to ask Quinn about it when he found him.

Pulling the door closed, Alexander decided to try the dining hall and the kitchen. Even if Quinn were not at either place, he at least should be able to scrounge up something to eat. In the morning's excitement, he had neglected to have breakfast. As long as he was being forced to stay in the castle, he might as well make the most of it.

He walked through the halls of the castle toward the kitchen, and he was again surprised at how empty they seemed. Nobody was out. He occasionally heard soft, indistinct sounds proving the castle was not completely devoid of life, but it sure seemed to be. In fact, he was probably free to get into any mischief he wanted. Unfortunately, one had to be in the right mood for such things, and Alexander was not.

He reached the dining hall and poked his head inside the archway. The large room was empty except for some maids wiping down the long tables and Bertran. The duke's son sat on a bench, tossing his sword from hand to hand. His face was red and splotchy. The tears were gone, but his black mood was still readily apparent.

"Hey pouty boy, where's Quinn?"

Bertran turned and glared at Alexander, firing daggers with his eyes. "Why should I care?"

"Because I care, you little twit."

Bertran stood abruptly, swinging his sword loosely in his hand. He shrank back only slightly when Alexander stepped fully into the room, his own sword belt clearly visible. The two boys stood silently staring each other down, neither making a more menacing move. They might have stood there for some time if the screaming had not started down the hall. With one last snort, Alexander turned quickly and ran toward the screaming. It sounded as if it were coming from the kitchen area. Behind him, he heard the soft thuds of Bertran's boots.

They reached the wide doorway of the kitchen in seconds, both boys sliding to a halt. Neither was prepared for the scene in front of them.

Two guardsmen stood with their swords drawn as maids ran screaming in utter terror toward the garden area. In the middle of the room, Vareen was hunched over, grabbing his leg and bellowing, "Kill them! Kill them all!" From somewhere else in the room, a muffled voice that sounded like Quinn's was yelling, "No!" It wasn't until Alexander spotted the crumpled form of Melinda that he was able to move. Fighting the gorge that rose, he unsheathed his sword with a metallic *shing* and bellowed, "FOR EASTCASTLE! FOR HONOR!!"

Surprised by the battle call, Vareen whipped around. His face was contorted with rage and pain.

"You fools," he laughed. "Die with the rest of them."

The two guardsmen turned just as quickly, relief showing briefly on their faces. The thoughts of killing kitchen maids had clearly not been palatable. Alexander and Bertran may have been boys, but at least they were armed.

Alexander took a defensive stance, his peripheral vision telling him Bertran had done the same at his side. He only had time for one momentary thought of the insanity of it all before metal rang on metal.

Alexander faced the larger of the two guardsmen and realized almost instantly that it was going to be nothing like sparring in a tournament. The man was taller and had a longer reach than anyone Alexander had fought before. The man was also well trained. Alexander concentrated on simply deflecting each of the guardsman's attacks. There was little else he *could* do.

He carefully navigated the kitchen, avoiding the corners and walls that would impede his ability to move his sword fully. Unfortunately, he was forced to consistently give up ground. He was not able to attack in any way; the man was too quick and too strong. A completely foreign feeling crept up inside of him. It took a moment to realize it for what it is was—mortal fear. He could feel it growing, attempting to consume him. *I'm going to die. I'm going to die.* The thought echoed through his head in time with the clash of metal before him.

The other guardsman was smaller, but also well-trained. Fortunately for Betran, the man was also overconfident. Unimpressed by the boy's small stature, the soldier paced forward as though he were about to kill a downed animal. Had he recognized the composure on his smaller opponent's face, he might have been more cautious.

For Betran, it was nothing more than one of the countless drills he had done with Petric. Standing with perfect balance, resting lightly on the balls of his feet, sword held firmly with both hands, Bertran simply waited for the man to close the gap. As soon as he goaded him with a "Come on then, boy," Bertran attacked.

As Bertran flowed from form to form, the man realized his mistake. This was not an untrained boy pretending to be a soldier. Caught completely off-guard, the man stumbled backward, clumsily blocking each stroke as Bertran performed a graceful dance of flashing metal. His only advantage was his larger step and reach, which helped only slightly in his hasty retreat. Each time he moved back to recoup, Bertran smoothly closed again. It was only a matter of time before Bertran expertly knocked the man's blade aside and buried his own in the guardsman's stomach.

The man's face flashed shock and pain, his eyes and mouth going wide before he collapsed to his knees. Instinctively reaching toward the wound, his own weapon clattered loudly on the floor. The man fell to his side. As he slid off Bertran's sword, he left a swath of red on the exposed blade.

Only then did Bertran's composure fail him. He abruptly dropped his own sword, recoiling from it as though it were a deadly copperhead. Stumbling back, his back hit the wall of the kitchen and he slowly slid down, eyes locked on the weapon he had dropped.

Vareen had slunk back toward the door when the fighting started. His eyes darted from one pair to the next while he clutched his leg wound. When he saw Quinn emerge from the oven, he started forward, only to be cut off by one of Alexander's retreats. Snarling, he debated about clipping him from behind, but the opportunity was lost in a flurry of swords. With one last glare toward where Quinn now stood with Rhiannon, he hobbled out the kitchen door and was gone.

Through the ringing of metal, Quinn asked Rhiannon, "What happened?"

Rhiannon pulled him around the corner of the island in the middle of the kitchen. "Vareen has gone crazy. He was threatening Melinda, so I threw a knife at him."

"*What?!*"

"I threw a knife at him! Come on! Melinda's hurt." She pulled him over to the far wall where several stools stood in disarray. Quinn's stomach lurched when he recognized the small form in light blue.

Rhiannon ran the last few steps and knelt, pulling the old woman's head into her lap.

"I'm sorry, I'm sorry. Oh please, please. I'm sorry…" She brushed back the kitchen master's hair which was matted in blood from a gash on her forehead.

Quinn began to feel dizzy and had to look away. The clang of metal on stone drew his attention to the other side of the kitchen. One of the guardsmen was down and Bertran was slumped against the opposite wall, tears running freely down his face.

"No…," he murmured. *This is madness!* He felt like closing his eyes and screaming, hoping it would all go away, but all he could do was stand and stare dumbly at his cousin. "No," he repeated stupidly to no one in particular.

To his right, Alexander continued to trade blows with the larger of the two guardsmen. Quinn's attention was involuntarily drawn to the sound of their struggle. Somewhere in the fog of his mind, he realized his friend was outmatched. Alexander was losing and was about to suffer the same fate as Melinda and Bertran. The man had backed him into a corner and Alexander's defenses were clearly lagging. His movements were impeded by the walls around him. The man had him beat and he knew it.

With a roar, Quinn grabbed one of the stools and flew across the room toward his friend. Using all his strength, he swung the stool by its legs into the back of the man's knees. Caught completely by surprise, the guardsman crumpled. With impressive strength and skill, he kept his sword arm up to block any thrust by Alexander.

Unfortunately, Alexander's strength was gone, and he was unable to mount any kind of attack. Instead, he held his sword with both hands in front of him, arms quivering. Luckily, Alexander's threat was enough of a diversion and allowed Quinn to swing the stool again, crashing it down on the man's neck and shoulders. The large man fell forward and lay still.

For a time, the only noise was Rhiannon's soft sobbing. The two friends stared at each other until a small, reserved grin broke across Alexander's face.

"Thanks."

Stepping over the fallen guardsman, Alexander mopped the sweat from his face. He walked slowly toward where Melinda lay in Rhiannon's lap.

"Is she…"

Rhiannon looked up and shook her head. Tears were streaming down her face. "No," she whispered hoarsely.

Suddenly, the old woman's eyes fluttered open. "Alexander? Alexander?" she called quietly.

Surprised, Alexander knelt down so she could see him. After a moment, her eyes focused on his face and she gave him a small smile. "Alexander. You must keep them safe. Quinn and Rhiannon. You must keep them safe…" Her voice gave out. She swallowed with difficulty.

"Yes, Mistress Melinda," the young man said respectfully.

The old woman raised her hand to his cheek. Tapping it softly, she whispered, "You are a good boy, Alexander. A good boy." She smiled again and then said, "Hurry, you must go now."

"No!" Rhiannon cried. "You need help. We need to find you some help."

"No, child. I will be all right. Go with Alexander. Hurry."

With tremendous effort, the kitchen master raised herself from off the girl's lap into a sitting position. "Hurry," she repeated.

Standing, Alexander looked to Quinn, his eyes moist, but he held in the tears. "Where's Bertran?"

Quinn's stomach clutched, and his heart hurt as he turned to look at his cousin slumped against the wall.

"Bertran," Alexander called. "Bertran!"

Relief flooded through Quinn as the younger boy raised his head, his eyes red and puffy.

"Are you hurt?"

Bertran shook his head before looking back down. Alexander saw his bloodied sword and guessed the rest. Glancing back to Quinn and Rhiannon, he said, "Come on, we have to go."

"No!" Rhiannon said again, holding Melinda's hand. The kitchen master had closed her eyes again, but her breathing was steady.

Alexander looked at the girl, but said nothing. Instead, he turned to Quinn.

"We can't stay here. Vareen may come back and who knows how many goons he has working for him." While he talked, he walked over and picked up Bertran's sword. After wiping it on the back of the fallen man, he held it out Bertran.

"Here, Bertran. Take your sword."

The young boy looked at Alexander and then at the sword held out in front of him. Slowly, he shook his head.

"You did well, Bertran," Alexander said quietly. "Take your sword."

Hesitantly, Bertran reached out and retrieved his sword. Tears rolled down his cheeks again. Alexander gave him a pat and repeated, "You did well."

The sounds of boots pounding in the hallway caused them all to jump.

"Quinn, Rhiannon, it's time to go!" Rhiannon began to protest once again, but Alexander cut her off. "Bertran, you take the lead. We are going out the garden door."

The younger boy stood, wiping the tears onto his sleeve and nodded. The sound of the running boots grew louder.

"NOW!" Alexander yelled.

The three of them followed Bertran, who made a beeline for the outside door. Alexander pushed Quinn and Rhiannon ahead of him and out the door. Stopping at the threshold, he turned to look back to where

Melinda sat with her back against the wall. Her eyes were closed. Clenching his jaw, Alexander sprinted through the doorway.

They ran quickly through the garden that lined the wall of the kitchen. Many of the herbs and vegetables Melinda used were grown here. It was not a large garden compared to the vast farms surrounding the castle, but it kept the kitchen staff busy when they were not cooking.

Once outside the small enclosure that surrounded the garden, they heard the shouting of men behind them. A small knot of soldiers ran toward them from the direction of the barracks, apparently alerted by the kitchen girls.

Alexander led the others toward a side gate in the castle wall. It was primarily used for deliveries to the kitchen. The two doors, one on the inside of the wall and one on the outside, were almost always left open. Alexander prayed the threat of war had not changed that.

They ran on, ignoring the shouts and calls behind them.

"Where are we going?" Quinn asked in gasping breaths.

"Out of the castle. Out to the woods."

"But…"

"Just keep running!"

They made their way around a corner and Alexander breathed a heavy sigh of relief when he caught a glimpse of the open doorway. Three guardsmen stood at the gate, wondering about the disturbance they could hear. As they drew closer, one of them laughed and said to the others, "Bastian's son! I should have guessed."

Under his breath, Alexander said as quietly as he could, "Just keep running through the gate. Do not stop. Run to the woods. Even if I don't make it, keep running to the woods."

Alexander used his longer legs to run ahead of the others, his sword still held in his right hand. Putting distance between them, he ran as though he were going to run past the gate.

"Hey, Alexander! What d'you do this time? You might as well stop now and take your dues. It will only be worse when your…*Hey*!"

At the last moment, Alexander turned and charged directly at the two men standing closest together. Keeping his sword down and away, he lowered his left shoulder into the stomach of the first man and sent him sprawling into the second. Both went down in a heap. Luckily, Alexander was able to stay on his feet after a few wild steps.

The third guard pushed away from the wall and lurched toward Alexander. Bertran, Quinn, and Rhiannon had caught up by then and ran directly at him. Bertran's sword was still out, and he waved it dangerously as he ran. The guardsman withdrew his own a few inches before realizing the boy with the sword was the duke's son. Wondering what he should do, he finally opted to simply step out of the way. All four of the youth ran through the gateway and out into the fields. Some cursing followed, but they ignored it and ran on.

The gate led to the fields that surrounded the castle and the large expanse of woods behind them. They were not as vast as Hunters Wood, but offered enough trees and brush to hide in—at least until someone brought dogs or a tracker.

Alexander tried not to think that far ahead, and urged them onward. His lungs were burning, both from the run as well as the fighting in the kitchen, but he forced himself to continue. Their only hope was to make it to the woods before anyone followed. Once inside, they should be able to slow down and hide.

Glancing toward the others, he noticed Bertran and Quinn were flagging. Only Rhiannon seemed not to be winded, though her face was drawn tight with anger. Alexander looked away. He dreaded the inevitable showdown to come.

They ran until they thought they were going to collapse, but finally made it to the edge of the woods. Only then did Alexander dare to look back. Relief filled him as he saw there was no pursuit. Hopefully the guards at the side gate would not consider four fleeing kids cause enough to leave their posts. Walking now, he led them deeper into the woods. The temperature felt much cooler in the shade of the overhanging boughs and many of the open spots were spotted with puddles of standing water.

"We have to go back," said Rhiannon, trying to cut in front of Alexander.

"No. At least not yet."

"We *have* to! We have to help Mistress Melinda."

Alexander shook his head and continued walking deeper into the woods. There were countless trails he and Quinn had explored over the years. Several possible hiding places flashed into his mind.

"What if the men we heard were also with Vareen? *They will kill her*!"

"Then they would have killed us too!" Alexander snapped back, losing his temper. "We're not going back yet!"

"But we…I…" Rhiannon's mouth moved, but no words came. Instead, tears began to flow again. She stopped walking and collapsed on a small rise, covering her face with her hands.

Alexander stopped as well and hoped they were deep enough in the woods. Turning to Quinn, he asked, "What in creation happened back there?"

Quinn was still struggling to catch his breath. Between gasps, he said, "I don't know. I was in my room and Vareen came with those two guardsmen to get me. I was scared, so I hid. They chased me to the kitchen and then…well, then they started attacking everybody."

"Why? That doesn't make any sense. Why would they start attacking people in the castle?"

Behind them, Bertran sat on a fallen tree and stared at the sword in his hands. He seemed hesitant to put it back in the sheath, even though there was little use for it at the moment.

Quinn looked at Rhiannon, who sat quietly sobbing. "Rhiannon threw a knife at Vareen."

"And hit him in the leg?" asked Alexander. "Is that why he was limping?"

Quinn nodded in answer. At first he thought Alexander was going to explode, but the older boy only looked down shaking his head. When he looked back up, he had his old grin back on his face.

"I wish I could have seen that. If you ask me, he's had it coming for a long time. Well, that explains why he suddenly felt like killing everybody, but what did he want with you in the first place?"

"He said something about using me to get out of this land. I think maybe he's a spy or something."

Alexander huffed sarcastically. "Boy, wouldn't *that* be a surprise. By the way, someone broke your father's bow."

Quinn blinked. He had forgotten all about it. "I did," he said simply.

Alexander grinned. "Not exactly your day, is it?"

Suddenly, Quinn remembered the note he had taken from inside the bow. He fetched it from his pocket and turned to Rhiannon. Her head was still buried in her drawn up knees, her arms around her shins. Quinn swallowed and called her name.

Raising her head slowly, Quinn thought she looked much like she had the first time he had met her in Bridgetown. Her face was hard and devoid of expression. Only the redness around her eyes betrayed that she had been crying.

Swallowing, Quinn said, "I found a note in my father's bow. I still can't read well enough…"

Rhiannon stared at him for a long moment. It was long enough that Quinn thought he was going to have to ask her directly for help. Just as he was about to, she held out her hand. Taking two steps toward her, he handed her the small rolled parchment. She carefully unrolled the note and scanned it quickly. She was not completely successful at covering her reaction when she reached the bottom.

"*Where* did you find this?" she asked.

"It was in a hollowed out part of my father's bow."

She looked back down at the note again before looking back up.

"It's from my father."

Tears welled again, but Rhiannon stiffened her resolve and proceeded to read without emotion:

Quinn,

If you are reading this, then I am sorry, for I have failed you as I did your parents before you. Know this: despite whatever histories have been written, your parents were murdered as surely as the sun will set tonight and rise tomorrow. As such, my legacy will forever be that of a man who failed his friends. I was responsible for their safety, but my daughter was sick with the fever. I did not make that last voyage with them. Perhaps I might have saved them. If not, I would have died in the attempt.

In my grief, I have mourned them as I would my own family, for in all but lineage, they were family to me. My grief only grew when I discovered your mother's jewelry box in the hands of a thief and your father's sword on the belt of a mercenary. This was <u>no</u> accident. This was murder.

I have spent my life searching for those responsible, to mete out justice, but deceit and danger face me at every turn. If you have found this on the day you had the strength to pull your father's bow, then know I am dead and my quest has ended unfinished. If you are not Quinn Hawk, but a friend, then I beg you to take up my quest. If you are an enemy to Eastcastle, then may the Creator of heaven and earth exact His justice on your soul.

— Marcus

When Rhiannon finished reading, she slowly re-rolled the parchment. Her face was once again unreadable as she handed it back to Quinn.

"Thank you," he said. Not knowing what else to say, he added, "I'm sorry."

She shrugged and then stared down at the carpet of needles and small ferns. As Quinn put it back into his pocket, Alexander looked back up the trail.

"We should probably keep moving until we find somewhere we can hide for a while. We'll need a place where we can see enough to not be surprised."

When neither Bertran nor Rhiannon moved, Quinn looked to his friend and said, "How long do you think we need to stay out here?"

"I don't know. I don't know how many people Vareen has with him, or what he has told everyone. It might not be safe for a while, maybe not even until the duke and your father return."

Quinn shook his head. "We can't stay out here that long. We don't have any food or blankets or anything. Besides, Melinda will tell them what happened. I mean, if…" Quinn left off miserably.

"We have to keep moving. We can try to think of something as we go, but we need to find somewhere better than here."

Reluctantly, the others joined him, and Alexander led them deeper into the woods. The ground rose and fell as they cut across small gullies and washes carved by gurgling creeks. By the time the light began to fade, they had gone further than Quinn had ever been. In fact, he found it harder and harder to convince himself that they were not completely lost. He wondered if nature was going to succeed where Vareen had failed.

Throughout the day, no one seemed interested in talking. Bertran had not said a word since leaving the kitchen, and Rhiannon only answered when spoken to, but never to Alexander. Their earlier animosity was back in full force.

Finally, when the shadows were stretching, Rhiannon blurted out, "You're going to get us killed, aren't you?"

Alexander whirled around, pent up emotion exploding. "No, but it sure sounds like a good idea for some of you!"

To Quinn, it was clear his friend was lost and fear was beginning to take him. Quinn was remembering that awful night in the Castlerooks, but this time, Rowan–no *his father*–was not here to save them.

"Where are we?" asked Rhiannon.

"You know exactly where we are. We're in the woods behind Eastcastle."

"And you know what I mean. Where is Eastcastle from here?"

"That way," said Alexander pointing off in a direction so quickly Quinn almost believed his friend was not lying. Unfortunately, the thought was crushed when Rhiannon pointed out that the shadows thrown by the fading sun were running the same way he was pointing.

"You don't know where we are, do you?" she challenged. "I told you we should have gone back."

"And been killed? You're right, maybe *you* should have."

"I would have had a much better chance of staying alive in the castle than out here in the middle of nowhere."

"Oh, really?"

"Yes, really!"

Quinn felt torn between trying to stop the argument and ignoring it completely. Choosing the latter mostly by default, he was the first one to see the man standing in a small clearing. Any hope of not being seen was lost with the rising voices of Alexander and Rhiannon.

"Alexander," Quinn hissed. "*Alexander!*"

"WHAT?!"

Quinn gulped and pointed toward the man who was now approaching them. Upon seeing him, Alexander pulled out his sword with a metallic ring. Bertran, who still carried his, stepped forward as well, eyes hard.

If they had hoped the show of arms would stop the man, they were disappointed for he continued toward them. He wore a white woolen robe and had a beard that was more white than gray. Even in the waning light, his face seemed illuminated, his eyes bright. He wore a small smile, as though he saw something humorous; however, it was an inclusive smile that put Quinn at peace.

"Put away your swords," Rhiannon said softly.

Both Bertran and Alexander looked at her, but neither lowered his weapon.

Turning, she repeated, "Put them away. You won't need them. He's one of the Travelers."

Chapter 16

Shepherds Pass stood before them, its recesses etched starkly by the fading sun. As they waited on its edge, a single rider approached, cloak flapping wildly behind him. It had been a long journey to the pass, but all things considered, it had gone well enough. Given the wrath of the earlier storm, the roads had at least been passable, with only a handful of low points near the castle offering trouble. However, Rustan found himself hoping they would not need to make a speedy retreat. An army this size would have torn up even a perfectly conditioned road.

As he waited for the rider to reach them, Rustan turned and glanced at his brother's tall and stoic bodyguard. He was surprised at Petric's presence. When they had reached the Lower Crossroads, Renard had taken a small knot of men on to Riverton to meet with any men Anthony might send. Renard had not been pleased with Rustan's suggestion that he, as the standing duke, would be the most logical emissary to meet them. He was even less pleased when Petric asked his leave to accompany Rustan to the pass. In the end, the preciousness of time had made arguing impractical and Renard had gone on alone.

Rustan rubbed his face with his hand and silently wished his brother luck. In Rustan's absence, the Dalatians appeared to have gained no more respect for their adopted land than when he had first proposed their union. Even if Anthony had sent an army, they were not going to be very happy about it. He chose not to think about the other possibility.

The rider came directly to Rustan. His face showed some surprise, but not as much as meeting a dead man might have warranted. The previous messenger had obviously carried more news than just communicating their approach. The rider scanned the other faces, presumably in search of Renard before addressing Rustan.

"Milord, thank the Creator you have made it. The Pass remains ours, but the men are tired. They have repelled several attacks, the first of which began early this morning. The news of your approach bolstered them to hold at all costs."

"The men are to be commended for their service to Eastcastle," Rustan said with a tight smile. "Tell me what news you have from your southern watches."

The man's face wrinkled in sudden distress. "The southern watches? Nothing of note, milord. The attacks have all come directly from the pass."

"Nothing of note meaning you *have* received southern reports?" Rustan pressed.

The man's demeanor changed from awe to awkwardness in the blink of an eye. "I...believe we have received reports, but, given the conflict milord, I cannot state that with full assurance."

Rustan's jaw clenched for a moment. "It is well enough. Return to your men and offer the thanks of Eastcastle for their vigilance. However, send riders immediately to the southern watches. Bring their responses directly to me."

"Yes, milord."

The man saluted and quickly turned his mount. His rapid departure was likely more indicative of his desire to leave than a sense of duty.

"You fear a trap," the tall bodyguard said from beside him. "As well you should."

Rustan hid his surprise as he turned to meet Petric's piercing gaze. The man had not spoken since Renard left for Riverton.

"These same stone walls, which so conveniently thwart Maldria's aggressions, will easily become a pestle's stone to grind our armies. Unfortunately, I fear the pestle will only appear when the grain has been poured."

Whistling, he signaled a captain forward.

"Take your men south, carefully. Proceed as though you were walking through Elksheart manor itself. Do not engage the enemy if you find them, but return with all haste. The survival of the army and all of Eastcastle may well depend upon your actions."

A small detachment of men rode forward and disappeared into the growing shadows.

Turning back to Petric, Rustan said under his breath, "On to the threshing floor, then."

He signaled the men forward and the long, undulating snake began to move into the valley.

*   *   *

The old man gave them a big smile. "Imagine running into a group of children in the middle of the woods." The twinkle in his eye hinted he was not surprised at all. "Would you humor an old man by sharing the evening meal with me? I am afraid I have grossly overestimated my appetite."

Alexander looked from face to face in indecision, but Rhiannon stepped forward immediately.

"We would be most grateful," she said, casting a scowl back at the older boy.

"Delightful! I have set up camp not far from here. I was just gathering some wood for the morning. If you would be so kind as to grab a stick or two along the way, I would be most appreciative."

The youth followed him back the way he had come, each trying to collect deadwood in the fading light. Before long, they came to clearing near a small brook where a fire was already burning. A pot sat atop it. The aroma of spices filled the air, causing more than one stomach to grumble loudly.

"And here we are! Probably not very wise to leave an open fire, I know, but old Augustine was keeping watch." The old man nodded toward an old gray horse munching on the grass. Quinn smiled in spite of himself. The horse was ignoring both the fire and the newcomers.

"I hope you do not mind vegetable soup. I am afraid it is all I have."

This time Alexander piped up, hoping to appear somewhat in charge. "Vegetable soup will be fine, good sir."

"Sir?" the old man laughed a comforting laugh, the kind that encourages you to join in. "Sir will not do, I'm afraid. You may call me Timothy, for that is my given name."

As they gathered around the fire, Quinn realized first he was cold, and second, he was very hungry. His stomach growled loudly, causing Timothy to laugh once again. This time they all joined in.

"Give me a moment to dig through my things. I am certain I have some utensils and bowls around somewhere. One never knows who he might run across on his travels." He winked at them, before digging through some packs on the ground. "Oh yes, these will do," he said pulling out several bowls neatly stacked together.

He distributed the eating utensils and then filled their bowls using a large ladle. The warmth of the soup permeated through the bowls and warmed their hands. As he handed them out, he asked for each of their names. Only Bertran was silent when asked. Quinn finally answered for him when it was clear Bertran was not going to speak.

The old man's eyes tightened ever so slightly, and his smile faded a bit. "Well, Bertran, you must be the shy one in the group. Welcome to my camp."

Quinn stabbed a large piece of carrot, blew on it, and was about to pop it in his mouth, when he heard Timothy say, "May I ask a blessing on the meal?"

Embarrassed, Quinn replaced the fork in his bowl as inconspicuously as possible and looked up at the Traveler. The old man simply smiled at him warmly before bowing his head. The others followed suit as the man talked with his Creator.

Quinn was amazed how normal it sounded, as though he were talking to an old friend. It reminded him of Elias. Timothy thanked the Creator for the blessings of health, food, and friends as though he were talking to someone standing beside him. It made Quinn feel warm and strangely at peace. After closing in the Lord's name, he motioned them to begin eating.

The soup tasted wonderful, and the warmth was an added blessing. Each of them asked for seconds, which Timothy freely gave. As they ate, he also brought out some hard bread, which they used to sop up the broth. They ate until they were full.

When they were done, Timothy collected the bowls and forks and took them to the creek. He carefully filled each bowl with water and scoured and rinsed them several times. He then turned them over in the grass and left them to dry. Standing, he made his way back to the fire.

"My friends, I am thankful for your unexpected company. It is always better to share a meal with friends than with a horse. Not that I do not enjoy your company as well, dear Augustine," he said turning to where the horse stood lazily batting his tail in complete ignorance. The old man laughed in merriment before turning back to face them. Suddenly, his brows crumpled.

"I am sorry; I have been rude in my selfishness. Are you expected somewhere? I fear now that darkness has fallen, it will be difficult to return."

Turning away from the fire, Quinn was surprised at how quickly and completely the darkness had settled in. He had been so intent on eating that he missed the onset of night.

"No, si…Timothy," Alexander said. "Um, we're not expected anywhere."

The old man pursed his lips together. "Are you spending the night in the woods, then? How far is your camp? Perhaps, I can help you find it."

"Um," Alexander started, but Rhiannon cut him off.

"We don't have a camp. We are pretty much lost."

"Oh," said Timothy, his face flashing surprise only for a moment. "Well then, you are welcome to share my camp as well as my meal. I believe I have enough blankets to go around. Young lady, if you would be so kind as to help an old man?"

Rhiannon followed him to a small pile of packs from which he pulled several woolen blankets.

"They are not much to look at, I am afraid, but they will keep the autumn chill out."

Alexander and Quinn each thanked him as they were handed a blanket, but Bertran only nodded. In the firelight, a sad look momentarily crossed the old man's face. After stacking more wood on the fire, Timothy wrapped himself in another of the blankets. He then knelt, closed his eyes, and was silent.

As the time passed, the youths all looked at one another, unsure what to do. No one dared say anything.

Finally, Timothy opened his eyes and with a soft, reassuring voice said, "Sleep in peace this night. You shall be safe."

He then laid his head down and closed his eyes again. He was breathing deeply within moments. After another round of looks to each other, Alexander, Bertran, Quinn, and Rhiannon followed his lead.

Quinn awoke to the sounds of birds and the dampness of fresh dew. Firewood snapped and popped nearby as he tumbled out of the wool blanket. He immediately regretted it and pulled it tight around him as he sat up. The air had a definite chill.

"Good morning," Rhiannon said. She was sitting near the fire poking at the coals with a long stick.

"Good morning," Quinn answered. Looking around he was not surprised to see a large lump under the blanket where Alexander had fallen asleep. "Are you the only one up?"

"No, Bertran and Timothy are over by the creek making breakfast. I asked if they needed help, but Timothy said no." She sounded sort of put out.

"Oh." Quinn looked toward the creek and saw the two mixing something in a large wooden bowl. Their backs were to him.

"How long have you been awake?"

"Not very long. I must have been tired, because I slept pretty well."

Quinn stretched his shoulders and arms under his blanket and yawned. "Me too. Is there more wood? It's pretty cold."

"There is, but I am supposed to make a coal bed for breakfast. I didn't want to add any more wood and have to wait for it to burn down again."

Quinn nodded and yawned again. Looking around at the trees, he asked, "Any idea where we are?"

"Yes. We're lost."

"We're not lost," came a mumbled reply from under Alexander's blanket. "We can just walk west until we meet the road to Eagles Nest. It can't be that far."

"Unless, of course, you don't know which way west *is.*"

Alexander sat up, his head poking out above the blankets. His hair was sticking up everywhere. Quinn could not help but laugh. Alexander turned toward him rubbing his hand through his locks, his customary grin firmly back in place.

"However bad I look, rest assured you don't look much better."

"Sorry," Quinn managed, but chuckled again.

"And as for going west, you simply walk away from the mountains."

Rhiannon made an exaggerated scan of the trees around them. "Only one problem—I don't see any mountains."

"Well they're there. You might have to climb a tree or something."

"Of course, why didn't I think of that?" Rhiannon said sarcastically.

"Good morning, good morning," Timothy said as he came back from the creek carrying a small platter. Bertran was carrying a bowl. His face showed signs of tears hastily rubbed away.

"I sincerely hope you like ash cake turnovers." Viewing Rhiannon's work at the fire, he added, "Marvelous work, young lady. I could not have done better myself."

Sitting down with an exaggerated grimace, the Traveler said, "I am afraid these old bones are not what they used to be." He then motioned for Bertran to sit near him.

"Have any of you made ash cakes before?" When they all shook their heads, he said, "Well, they are really quite simple. You take a spot of dough, which Betran has so masterfully mixed up, and spread it out like so. Once it is flattened, I have some berries or a slice of apple that you may put inside. Then, you simply fold it over, mash the ends together, and pop it onto the coals."

He dropped the dough cake on top of the coal bed causing a small plume of ash to spurt up. "Well, come on then. Making them is half the fun."

They each took turns flattening out small globs of dough as he had shown them and making turnovers. Alexander of course added both berries and an apple slice to his, which the others copied on the next round. Before long, they were all munching—after Timothy's blessing, of course.

When they each had their fill, the Traveler said, "I know I mentioned this last night, but I cannot tell you how nice it is to have shared your company these past few hours; truly, a most pleasant time. Alexander, I understand you are the leader of sorts for the group. What are your plans?"

Alexander had just popped the last of his turnover into his mouth. "Uhm," was all he could get out.

"We need to return to Eastcastle," Rhiannon answered for him.

"Ah yes," the old man said with a nod, "Bertran has told me a little of what has transpired there. Are you sure that is the best course of action?" he asked Rhiannon directly.

Rhiannon met his look for a moment, before looking down. "We need to get back," she said quietly.

"Of course you do, in time," the Traveler said kindly. "But sometimes, when we think we have made a mistake, we need to be careful we do not follow it immediately with another—especially when we feel we might deserve terrible things to happen to us. I like to think of such progressions of mistakes as a big snowball rolling down the mountainside, where each new one is bigger than the last. At these times, it never hurts to stop and let the snowball set awhile."

Rhiannon looked up again and was relieved to find the man's face devoid of judgment. His smile was as kind as it had been the first time they met him the night before.

Turning back to Alexander, Timothy said, "I do not mean to thwart your plans, but I wish to make you an offer. You are all more than welcome to travel with me for a while if you wish. It has been so nice to spend time with you. You each remind me of my grandchildren."

"You have children?" Rhiannon blurted out before thinking how rude it might sound.

Timothy laughed good-naturedly. "Of course! Children, and grandchildren, are the true miracles of life. They provide a fresh view of the future and a hope that maybe, just maybe, they will live their lives better than we have lived our own. I love them each and miss them dearly."

"Then why are you out here?" asked Quinn.

The Traveler's eyes twinkled as he answered. "In my life, I have learned what it means to love my children unconditionally. They make mistakes—we all make mistakes—but that does not change the bond of love that connects me to each of them. In fact, it strengthens it.

"What took me longer to realize was that same love connects each of us to our Creator, only magnified hundreds and hundreds of times. When I realized the immensity of the love He has for me is the same that He has for each of His children, I came to understand that the only real way I have of returning that love is to love all His children the way He loves me. Unfortunately, that love is not best shown locked away in a room with a good book and a fresh loaf of bread." Leaning forward, he added mischievously, "Though I must admit, I do enjoy both immensely."

Standing, Timothy asked, "Shall we be off then?"

Alexander looked to each of his friends before grinning. "Sure."

"In that case, I have one more favor to ask. If you would be so kind as to keep the blankets with you; perhaps you can wrap them around yourselves as you walk. I am afraid poor Augustine simply refuses to carry them one step further. His bones are nearly as old as mine," he said with a wink.

Quinn could not help but look over to where the gray horse was once again munching on the grass along the creek bed, completely oblivious. He stood with a smile, glad to have the warmth of the blanket still wrapped around him.

They helped Timothy put together his packs and load them onto Augustine, who was as passive a horse as Quinn had ever seen. As they were strapping down the load, Quinn noticed there was no saddle.

"Do you ride him bareback?" he asked.

Timothy chuckled. "Oh, no, I am afraid we are both too old for that. I am sure we would both end up with broken bones. No, I am content to walk beside my old friend."

He patted the horse's neck and got a nicker in return. Picking up a gnarled walking stick, he said, "Well, I think I am ready. I thank you each for your help. Alexander, please lead us out of camp!"

Alexander's brow knitted and he looked embarrassedly at the others. Taking a deep breath, he scanned the woods trying to decide which way to go. He was about to simply pick a direction when Timothy spoke.

"Actually, Alexander, I am sorry to be a burden, but could I ask just one more favor. Augustine really does hate to climb hills, and he is always thirsty. Would you mind if we followed this creek downstream to the main road? I only ask for Augustine's sake. He really can be quite moody," he ended, giving Alexander another wink.

The grin returned to the older boy's face and he turned and led them down the side of the creek.

'There you see, Augustine, it never hurts to ask."

They followed the creek throughout the morning, often leaving its side to skirt around thick clumps of bushes. Birds, squirrels, and other small animals chirped and whistled as they walked among the trees. It was one of those wonderful days where the direct sun took the edge off of the cold. In fact, the morning chill soon eased to where they each bundled up their blankets and carried them.

As they walked, Timothy told stories about his family and his travels. They ranged from funny to fascinating, but each was entertaining. Before long, the fears and memories of the day before disappeared with the dew.

Around what must have been midday, Timothy asked if Augustine might rest his legs for a while and they stopped. Fiddling in the packs on the horse, he brought out several apples and passed them around. They sat on the ground and enjoyed listening to the gurgling sounds of the creek. Timothy sat next to Quinn. "I understand you have had quite a momentous event occur in your life."

Quinn felt a lump form in his stomach. He quickly took another bite of apple to avoid having to answer. For some reason, he really did not want to talk about his father's return. In fact, part of the reason it had been such a pleasant morning was because listening to Timothy's stories made it easy to forget.

"I also understand you met your father several months ago, but he did not reveal himself to you. How do you feel about that?" His question was asked bluntly, but not unkindly.

Quinn shrugged. "It's alright."

Timothy chuckled his infectious laugh and patted Quinn on the knee. "Well, you are a better person than I was at your age. I am afraid I would have been quite upset."

Quinn looked at the old man and realized he was watching him intently. "Well, maybe I am, a little."

Timothy chuckled again. "Did he tell you why?"

"No, not really. He said we could talk more when he got back from…well, from going to war."

"I see."

The old man sighed heavily and his smile faded. He looked out at the stream where the sunlight danced along the ripples, creating hundreds of miniature starbursts. "War is a terrible, horrible thing. I must say, I will not miss it when I have passed on."

Turning back to Quinn, he said, "Well, when he returns, you must be patient with your father. Coming back home may be one of the most difficult things he ever has to do."

Quinn looked away and gave a quick, but non-committal nod.

"Will you promise me that you will be patient with him?"

Quinn scrunched up his face, surprised at the question. "I guess," he finally said with a shrug.

The Traveler patted him on the knee again. Quinn thought he was done talking, but after a moment he asked, "Do you know what a killdeer is?"

"A kill deer? You mean like hunting?"

Timothy laughed, but in his unique way that made you want to join him. "Yes, I suppose it does sound like that, but no. A killdeer is a small bird, which I am sure you have probably seen without knowing its name. They are not like most birds, however, in that they make their nests on the ground, many times right out in the open."

"Really?"

"Yes. Because of that, they have developed a very unique way of handling predators. If the bird senses trouble, he will begin to hop around as though he has broken his wing or something."

"Why?"

"Well, as they are fluttering about making a terrible noise, they hop further and further from their nest so that whatever is coming for them will not see it. Instead, the predator thinks to himself, 'Ah ha, here is a hurt bird just waiting for me to eat him.' The predator concentrates so much on the bird, that he never sees the nest. Then, just when the predator thinks he has a fresh meal, the killdeer flies away. When the danger has past, he comes back to the nest. They are quite remarkable, really."

Quinn smiled as he thought about a bird being smart enough to fake an injury to save its nest. Turning to the old man, he noticed he was still watching him thoughtfully.

"You see, Quinn, sometimes parents pretend to be something they are not because they think it is the only way they can save those they care about the most. But, when the danger is past, they will always come back if they can."

The Traveler smiled and winked at him before standing. Stretching his back, he said, "Well, Alexander, shall we continue on our way?"

Alexander stood quickly and said, "Yes, sir. I mean, yes, Timothy."

"Well put, young man, well put. Come along, Augustine. Alexander has chosen a good course. I believe the road is just ahead, though I am sure you will miss the softness of the needles and the grass once we find it."

As Timothy had predicted, within a mile they came to the edge of the woods. Across a small field, they could see the road that led from Riverton to the passes above Eagles Nest. Neither Alexander nor Quinn recognized exactly where they were along the road, but they knew Eastcastle was somewhere to the left.

"Well Alexander, I must thank you for your excellent navigation. Who knows how long Augustine and I might have wandered in those woods."

Alexander rolled his eyes, but smiled at the old man. Timothy winked and smiled back, but then his face grew more serious.

"I am sorry to see our time together has come to an end, but I want you to know, in all honesty, it has been a great pleasure to be with each of you. You are beautiful children, and I believe you have great and wonderful things ahead of you. I hope you remember and treasure the past day as I do. Please keep the blankets. Augustine will only fret if I try to return them now."

He gave them each a hug, and Quinn was amazed at how emotional their parting was when they had only met the man the night before. He fought down his own tears, but was surprised to see them running freely down the cheeks of both Bertran and Rhiannon. Even Timothy's own bright eyes seemed to water. Only Alexander seemed emotionally stable, though he appeared happier than Quinn had seen him for some time.

When the hugs and goodbyes were done, Timothy said, "I have just one last request. Will you stay here, in the woods, until the time is right?"

Quinn looked around and saw everyone looked as perplexed as he felt.

"When will that be?" asked Alexander.

"You will know it when it comes. But, trust me on this one last thing and wait until it does."

Shrugging, Alexander said, "Of course."

"You really *are* a good boy, Alexander," Timothy said putting his hand on his shoulder, "And some day you will be a great leader, as well."

Alexander's face tightened in his first real show of emotion.

Waving to the others, the Traveler said, "Farewell, my young friends, and take care of each other. May the Creator watch over us all."

He then turned and led the old, gray horse across the field toward the road. They each watched silently as he reached it, turned right, and finally disappeared around the bend.

"When the time is right? What do you suppose that means?" asked Alexander, breaking the silence.

Quinn plopped down on a log. "I have no idea."

"I think…" began Rhiannon.

"We should go back to the castle?" finished Alexander, only slightly sarcastic.

Rhiannon stuck her tongue out at him, but through a smile. "No," she answered, sitting down next to Quinn. "I think we should just wait and find out."

"Well, I guess we said we would, so we might as well get comfortable." Instead of sitting, Alexander spread out his blanket on a grassy area near the edge of the field and flopped down. "Do you think all of the Travelers are like Timothy?"

"Probably," Quinn and Rhiannon both answered together and laughed.

Bertran decided to follow Alexander's lead and spread out his own blanket before lying down.

"Are you going to sleep?" Rhiannon asked.

"I might," answered Alexander twisting to get more comfortable, "Unless whatever it is we are waiting for turns up. I can't think of a better way to wait."

"Figures."

"Hey, Timothy said we would know it when it comes. I don't think a small nap will change that. Besides, it may be a long time coming."

"Whatever."

"Suit yourself." Alexander turned away from them and lay still. Bertran was already sleeping.

While they waited, Rhiannon and Quinn talked about the Travelers, the war, Maldria, and the note Quinn had found in his father's bow. Quinn told her how strange it was to read something written from someone who had been dead for several years, before remembering he was Rhiannon's father. He wondered how she felt about it, but was too embarrassed to ask.

After a while, they ran out of things to talk about, and the log grew very uncomfortable. Not knowing what else to do, they spread the blankets Timothy had given them and stretched out. Before long, they too were sleeping.

Chapter 17

"Quinn. Quinn."

Somebody gently shook him. He had been dreaming about Timothy, and as he sat up, he half expected to see the old man's face. His heart jumped when he saw a large man instead, until his eyes focused.

"Asher?"

The man nodded. The hood of his ranger's cloak was back so his round, babyish face and curly locks were visible. "What are you doing out here?" he asked.

"I guess we're waiting for you."

The ranger sat back, scrunching up his face. "Waiting for me? Is Rowan with you?"

Quinn's face immediately hardened. He was not quite sure why he suddenly felt so angry, but he was.

"No, my *father* is not here. He has gone to Shepherds Pass."

Asher winced slightly and looked down for a moment. Casting his eyes back to Quinn, he said, "I am sorry, Quinn. I would have told you earlier, but Rowan…your father…wished to keep it secret."

"So he told me," Quinn said curtly.

Their conversation awoke the others, who each sat up, surprised by the ranger's appearance. Asher gave a nod to each of them, before asking again why they were in the woods.

Rhiannon, Alexander, and Quinn told him about the events of the previous day, which had led to their meeting Timothy and eventually ending up here. The ranger listened carefully without talking, though his face showed surprise when they first mentioned Vareen's treachery.

When they were done talking, he asked, "Was one of the men who attacked you in the kitchen named Petric?"

"Petric?" laughed Alexander, "The duke's bodyguard?"

"Yes, though I take it from your reaction, he was not. However, do you know if he is still at the castle?"

"Of course not!" said Bertran, finally speaking. "He is my father's bodyguard and is always with him. He has gone to the Pass with the army."

Asher raised an eyebrow as he looked at the boy, perhaps just now realizing who he was. After a moment, he gave Bertran a small smile and said, "Yes, of course. I guess he would."

Struck by the odd way the ranger was acting, Quinn asked, "Why?"

Asher turned back to face Quinn, his expression unreadable. He shrugged and said, "No reason, really. Just curious is all."

Quinn felt a sudden annoyance with the man in front of him. The anger that had flared when he had first mentioned his father continued to grow. Why had his father lied to him? Why was Asher lying to them now?

"You're lying," he blurted out. The large man blinked in surprise. "Why are you lying to us?"

Quinn's friends were shocked at his sudden emotion, but he did not care. He was tired of all the secrets, tired of being treated as though he were not old enough or smart enough or *whatever* enough to be told the truth. Inside, he knew he was really angrier with his father for the way he had hidden his true identity from him, but he did not care. Asher had known. He could have told him.

The large ranger stared at Quinn long enough that Quinn's heart began to beat loudly. He wondered if he had gone too far. Just when he thought he was going to completely lose his nerve, Asher burst out laughing, his cherubic face reddening.

"Quinn, you are indeed your father's son. I am sorry. Here I have just told you I would not have hidden your father's identity and yet, I am doing the same thing." After a pause, he said, "Since you asked, Petric is Paddock's brother."

Quinn felt as though he had been punched in the stomach. A "What?" came from Alexander at the same moment Bertran said "No!" Of the four of them, only Rhiannon did not react.

"Well, half-brother really. They have different mothers, but share the same father."

Quinn was vaguely aware of Bertran saying it was not possible, but he was thinking back to the night before leaving for Maldria. Somehow, what the ranger said made perfect sense.

"Well," said Asher, "I *was* going to ask whether either of you thought your fathers knew of Petric's family ties, but I will take your reaction as answer enough. Unfortunately, that makes time even more critical." Pulling his hood over his curly hair, he said, "I am afraid I must take my leave. Be careful."

"Wait!" cried Quinn, "We'll come with you."

The ranger paused and gave a short laugh. "I don't think that would be a good idea. Try and get back to Eastcastle and among the guardsmen left there. They cannot all be working for Vareen."

Asher started to leave again, but Alexander joined the fray.

"Let us come with you. With Vareen still loose at the castle, who knows what he has said or done? The only time it will be absolutely safe for us to return is when the duke does so himself. We might as well go and meet him."

"Your fathers saw fit to leave you behind. I am not so arrogant to think I know better. Go back to the castle. Hide if you must, but you will certainly be safer there than in the middle of a war."

"We'll follow you then. I was already thinking of going to the Pass, anyway. This will just be easier."

The ranger yanked down his hood, his red face stern. "Listen. Anthony's men think the duke and your father may be betrayed by Petric…"

"They won't be," interrupted Bertran.

"Be that as it may, the king's men are not so sure and I am inclined to give their arguments credence. Regardless of who is right or wrong, I have an obligation to fulfill, and circumstances being what they are, I must do it quickly."

"Then lead on," Alexander said in quiet challenge.

Asher glanced from one face to the next; obviously hoping one of them would provide him backup. Unfortunately for him, no one was willing to offer it.

"Do you have any idea what war is like? Any of you? You cannot simply go charging into a battlefield as though it were a dining hall. It is madness and chaos, the lowest depravity that can ever be associated with humanity. Men die in war! And for those of us who do not die, it is hardly better. Grotesque images are seared into your mind, only to erupt unbidden as nightmares or even fully conscious memories. Far more devastating than the loss of life is the shattering of spirits and hopes. Some are never regained. You have no idea what you are asking."

Quinn swallowed, but tried to stand firm. To his left, Alexander stood defiantly, facing down the ranger. Bertran and Rhiannon both looked as if they wished they were somewhere else.

Finally, the ranger shook his head and pulled his hood down. "Very well, but you will follow my lead. You will do what I say, and when I say it, without argument. I will try and take you to your fathers, but I will not risk taking you to your deaths. War is a very unforgiving master, with no mercy for mistakes, no matter how small or unintentional. I will have your word on this, each of you, or I will tie you all to these trees."

Unable to see the ranger's face, Quinn was unsure whether his threat was real. Given the finality in his voice, he guessed it probably was. Each of them promised Asher they would obey him. Alexander was last and only did so after some hesitation.

Apparently satisfied, the ranger said, "You will have to try and keep up. I have lost too much time already."

With that, he turned and started south at a quick pace. The youth each quickly gathered together their blankets and ran to catch up.

For the first couple of hours, no one talked. The ranger was clearly not happy about the arrangement and kept his face buried in his hood. Quinn and the others could barely keep up with his lengthy stride and were averse to wasting breath on words. It was not until the sun started to sink behind the trees that Asher slowed.

"We will need to move out of the woods in order to see. Obviously, this increases our risk of being spotted by unfriendly eyes, so stay close to me and whisper when talking. In fact, try not to talk at all."

"Do you think we're in any danger here?" Quinn whispered. "We're not that far from the castle."

"One of the biggest problems with war is there are no rules. Generally, the more unexpected a move, the better chance it has of success. If you want to increase your odds of living, you learn to expect the unexpected. I doubt there is much risk here, but then I also doubted Paddock would be so rash as to follow in his father's reckless footsteps."

As they broke free of the trees, they could see the road as a dark band in the moonlight.

Asher's last comment sparked something Quinn had not thought about before. Whispering, he said, "If what you said about Petric is true, then he betrayed his own father."

The ranger's surprise was evidenced in a single faltered step. "Yes."

The others looked at them both in confusion.

"Why would he do it?"

For a moment, Asher was silent and Quinn thought he was not going to answer his question.

"I don't know." The ranger stopped and turned, the cowl of his cloak facing Quinn. "Perhaps his father made him angry."

Quinn swallowed and looked down, wondering whether Asher had deliberately directed the comment at him or whether it was merely a coincidence. He hoped it was the latter. *I would never betray my father,* Quinn thought to himself. *Even if I were really mad, I wouldn't do it.*

They made their way down the side of the road, the thin light weakened further by the overhanging boughs. The only sounds were those of the night animals foraging in the woods. The temperature dropped quickly as the night deepened, causing each of the youth to pull their blankets around them tightly. Quinn offered a silent prayer of thanks for the chance meeting of the Traveler. Actually, he wondered just how chance their meeting really had been, and what that meant.

"Is anyone tired?"

The question from the ranger interrupted his thoughts. Quinn wondered whether he meant sleepy tired or simply tired of walking. The late nap and the cold temperature were enough to keep him awake, but his legs were not used to walking all day. It brought back memories again of the trek across the Castlerooks. He was glad when Alexander spoke.

"Are you asking if we need to stop and rest for a while or go to sleep?"

The ranger chuckled. "I am afraid I can only stop for a moment. If you are still determined to follow, you will have to continue on through the night."

"That's fine with me," Alexander answered challengingly.

"Very well. We will rest for a minute. Did any of you bring water with you?"

"We were not planning on staying outside," Alexander said.

"We were not *planning* anything," Rhiannon rejoined.

"Here then, take a little and pass it around," the ranger said taking a water skin from around his neck. "Do not worry about drinking it all. There are plenty of streams along the way where we can refill it."

The youth all sat and took sips from the water skin. The ground was already damp with dew, but it felt good to be off their feet. As they rested, Bertran asked Quinn quietly, "What did you mean when you said Petric betrayed his own father?"

Quinn looked at the barely illuminated face of his cousin and shrugged. "It was something Paddock told me when I was in Maldria. He said Petric was the one who told our grandfather about the plan to attack Eastcastle. That's when my father asked King Anthony for help."

Quinn could not read Betran's face in the near darkness, but his voice was hard. "I don't believe it."

"You should," Asher said quietly, "Because it is almost certainly true."

"How do you know?"

The ranger leaned against a tall tree. "As I said, the king's spies have been finding out all they can about him. Apparently, he made quite an impression on Anthony during the sword tournament at the Spring Festival."

Bertran felt his face redden and was suddenly glad for the darkness. He hoped no one noticed.

"Petric *is* Philip's son and he *did* betray him."

"Why? Why would he?"

The ranger took a deep breath and let it out. He seemed to be debating something. Finally, he shrugged as if deciding it was of no consequence.

"I will tell you what I was told in Roseland. I cannot vouch for any of it personally, but I *will* tell you I am convinced it is either the truth or not far from it.

"It seems Philip's arrogance stretched all the way back to his youth. He was not much beyond manhood when he got married— secretly. He had fallen in love with a villager, the daughter of one of the manor's smiths. From all reports, she was beautiful, the light of any room she was in. Knowing his father would not give his approval, Philip never asked. He married her at night without his consent or knowledge. Unfortunately, all secrets eventually come to light.

"Philip's father was enraged and the marriage was immediately annulled by his command. The girl, her parents, and the entire family were moved to Southreach, the furthest barony from Elksheart. Apparently, this angered the baron even more as the young lady's father was one of the best smiths in all of Maldria. But he knew Philip was resourceful and did not trust them to be near. I suppose it was a mercy he did not have them killed on the spot."

"What does this have to do with Petric?" Bertran interrupted.

The ranger smiled, his white teeth dimly reflecting the moonlight. "*Everything.* What the baron did not know was that the young girl was already pregnant. It was kept hidden for fear of what the baron would do if he suspected anything. Several months later, Petric was born.

"Sadly, his young mother, heartbroken and exhausted, died several days later. Her parents, still fearing for the child's life, placed him with another family in the village who had several children. They raised him until he was old enough to be apprenticed—as a smith to his own grandfather."

The ranger took a small sip from the water skin when it was returned to him. He chuckled as he realized that was all that was left. The youth waited impatiently for him to continue.

Finally, Quinn whispered loudly, "How did he end up betraying his father?"

Asher replaced the water skin around his neck before beginning again. "The smith trained his grandson how to work with metal, but more importantly, he trained him how to *use* it. He was an expert swordsman, and Petric proved to be a model student. Within just a few years, the boy could best his master. He excelled at all weapons, but he was deadly with a sword. His grandfather taught him all he knew about fighting, but it was his grandmother who taught him everything else.

"She had a keen mind and taught him what she knew of the baronies, the land, the politics—basically, Maldrian life in general. When she thought he was old enough, she told him who he really was."

The ranger pushed himself away from the tree and motioned for them to stand. "We need to keep moving."

Quinn stood and stretched his muscles. The cold night air had made them tight, but his mind was absorbed with Petric's story. He wondered how much of it was known by his father. Obviously, whatever he did know, he had not shared with Asher. Like Bertan, Quinn doubted Petric would betray them, but still, he wondered whether his father knew all of Petric's history.

The youth gathered closer to the ranger as he once again started them moving south. They each silently hoped he would continue with the story not only because it was interesting, but because it helped keep their minds off their tired limbs. Asher granted their unvoiced wish.

"At various times of the year, Maldrian villagers are allowed to travel to other baronies to visit family and friends or to conduct trade. The smith and his family were obviously blacklisted. They were prohibited from ever leaving Southreach. However, as an anonymous apprentice, Petric *was* allowed to travel and his grandfather sent him to Elksheart.

"Before he left, the smith gave Petric a small silver locket, the only token he had from his mother. She had received it from Philip, who was now the baron of Elksheart, his father having died of the ague. The smith offered Petric the choice of showing the locket to Philip and trying to claim his heritage, or returning to serve as a full smith. Petric must have decided upon the first.

"Unfortunately, in Maldria, it is not an easy thing for a villager to approach a baron, especially one of a different barony. As fate would have it, a sword tournament was being held in Elksheart several days after his arrival. Taking leave from the travel group, Petric stayed and fought. He bested every man easily and was brought before the baron as part of the celebration.

"The baron presented him with a small bag of gold and a champion's sword. During the exchange, Petric secretly slipped the locket into the baron's hand. Surprised, the baron looked at the small charm. He recognized it immediately. Some who were present knew something had happened, but the baron recovered quickly and led them in another cheer for the young man from the south.

"Later, the baron secretly arranged a meeting with Petric. Philip was united with the son he never knew he had. The locket would have been enough, but Petric is also said to look very much like his mother. There was no doubt in Philip's mind who stood before him. Having won the sword tournament, it was a natural thing for Philip to secure Petric a place on his personal guard. Unfortunately, Philip was overly attentive to his new master swordsman, and people began to notice—particularly his other son."

"Paddock," Quinn whispered.

"Yes, Paddock. Paddock was a power-thirsty creature from his first breath. Everything he did was aimed at gaining power over something or someone. Nobody was safe from his schemes—nobody except his father.

"Paddock idolized his father. To him, he represented everything a leader should be—quick with decisions, magnanimous to one's friends and allies, but utterly ruthless to one's enemies. Only one person in the world could make Paddock back down, and that was his father. At least, up until the day Paddock felt Philip's attentions had turned elsewhere."

A snapping sound in the woods stopped them all. Asher peered toward the source of the sound, but could see nothing. Soon, another crackling sound came from further away as some nocturnal creature scurried away from them. After determining it was safe, the ranger motioned for them to continue.

"Petric's presence would have probably been nothing more than an annoyance had Eastcastle not revolted and left the baronies. Paddock was incensed and immediately joined the cause to depose the Hawks and restore the lands to Maldria. He expected his father, as one of the more powerful barons, would figure prominently in a leadership role.

"Petric had a different view, however. Having been raised on the other side of the fence, he saw the revolt as progressive. Here were two large baronies combining into a kingdom and granting freedoms and liberties he could only dream of. Eastcastle was granting common people the right to own land, freedom to choose a profession, and the liberty to travel when and where they wanted. To one who was not even able to visit his family without permission, this must have been incredibly intriguing.

"As Philip joined in the war councils, Petric began his own campaign to steer his father toward acceptance of the new kingdom. He never did so outright; he was too shrewd for that. Instead, he limited it to a thought here and a comment there. Philip would likely never have agreed to what Petric was ultimately striving for—recognition of Eastcastle followed by similar changes to the other baronies—but he was never really given the chance.

"It was not long before Paddock was told of the tall guardsman's veiled comments. He challenged his father as to why one in Petric's standing was allowed to speak at all. His father dodged the question, causing Paddock to wonder even more. Days later, Paddock managed to get his father drunk. Before the night was over, Philip had revealed Petric's true identity. That was when things changed for Paddock.

"Instead of merely being an annoyance, Petric became a very real threat to his inheritance. Paddock challenged Petric to a duel, which Petric wisely refused. By all accounts, Petric would have easily beaten his younger brother in a fair fight, which of course meant Paddock had never intended it to *be* fair. Most likely, he would have staged an interruption and forced his father's hand. Fighting a noble is punishable by death for a commoner, and Paddock would have bought the appropriate witnesses to blame the aggression on his brother. He may have even hoped to carry out the sentence before his father was involved.

"It was sometime later that Petric's luck ran out. Plans of the war preparations were found beneath his cot with several 'communications' from the Hawks. Obviously, Petric denied knowing anything about them. Unfortunately, too many people had heard his comments to the baron. The appearance of the documents suddenly made perfect sense—Petric was a spy. His last hope was that his father would stand up for him." After a pause, the ranger said, "Phillip chose not to."

"So he came to Eastcastle," Quinn said quietly. "The very place he had been accused of helping."

Asher nodded in the dark. "He somehow managed to escape that very night and fled over the Castlerooks. In fact, he probably walked many of the same trails you and your father took not long ago."

As they continued to walk, it became apparent that Asher was done with his tale. The night sounds once again took front stage as each of the party walked alone with their own thoughts. Quinn tried to make sense of all the ranger had said. All his life, he had seen Petric as a quiet, hard statue of a man—someone he had feared more than he let on. It was odd to try and think of him differently.

They continued on until they were stumbling more than walking. Finally, Asher directed them deeper into the woods.

"We will sleep here until daybreak, which will not be very long. Try to get to sleep as quickly as you can."

His request was not difficult. Each was asleep within moments of lying down.

Quinn awoke, startled by Asher's light shaking. He opened his eyes and was shocked to see it was already well past daybreak. He felt as though he had just barely closed his eyes, but the autumn sun shone brightly through the colorful leaves of the trees above.

They shared a small meal of overripe tomatoes and raw zucchini, which Asher had scavenged from a local farm. It was not much, but it tasted delicious, given the lack of food.

When they were finished, Asher gathered them into a small cluster and said quietly, "From here on, we will consider ourselves in the midst of battle. No talking, not even whispering. Our only defense is our ability to stay hidden. If we are discovered, we have no real way to protect ourselves. Do you understand?" He took the time to look for and get a nod from each of them.

"Asher?" Bertran asked just as the ranger was turning.

"Yes?"

"Why does the king think Petric will betray us now? I mean, if the story you told is true, why would he help Paddock now?"

The ranger's eyes narrowed slightly as he searched the young boy's face. "At the tournament, Petric was perceived to be an angry man. They worry his anger may explode at the wrong time."

"So, they do not think he will betray us to Paddock, just that he may cause a problem?"

The ranger shrugged. "They think he is dangerous. Angry men do unpredictable things, and the battlefield is the worst place for that to happen."

Sensing he may not get another chance, Alexander slipped in a question of his own.

"Is the king sending his army?"

The ranger made a face, which was half smile and half wince. "I am afraid I really don't know. I was…*excused*…from the deliberations to return to Eastcastle with the warning about Petric."

"But…," Alexander started.

Asher cut him off. "Save your words. I have thought of nothing else for the past several days. There is nothing we can do now but hope Anthony honors his word."

"Did you meet with him?" asked Quinn.

"For a short time, but he would commit to nothing. I *will* tell you I fear Eastcastle has few friends on the royal council. Most of the dukes were against committing the armies of Dalatia."

"Why?" exclaimed Alexander. "We're *part* of Dalatia!"

The ranger shook his head. "Not in the minds of many. They blame Eastcastle for its own problems and are not interested in becoming embroiled in what they view as somebody else's fight. They were not happy years ago when Eastcastle became a dukedom. The threat of war with Maldria does nothing to improve their feelings. Come, these are the very things Rustan and Renard will need to hear."

He took a few steps before stopping. "Oh, that reminds me," he said. Reaching into a pocket somewhere inside his tunic he pulled out a chain and a large ring. Handing it to Quinn, he said with a small smile, "I believe this is yours."

Quinn thanked him, took the chain, and placed it over his head. Dropping the ring inside his tunic, he fingered it through the material. It felt good to have it back.

His mind thought back on his conversations with Paddock. No wonder he had raised an army and now threatened Eastcastle. He *counted* on a lack of movement from Roseland! As time had passed, he must have seen that Eastcastle was still treated as the adopted child— tolerated, but never quite embraced. A surprise attack would absolutely cripple Eastcastle's defenses and, given a quick victory, King Anthony would likely do nothing about it.

As they walked south through the woods, depression began to set in along with something else. It was several more steps before he realized it was fear. It was the same fear he had felt in front of the wolves and later, battling Petric. The only difference was those had come instantly; he had not been allowed to think, only to react. Now, with nothing but the calm of an unusually warm autumn day around him, the fear was free to grow and fester. In the forced silence, Quinn struggled to fight it.

Asher left the road and took them into the woods. By midday, the ground sloped upwards, gradually at first, but growing steeper as they continued. Periodically, Asher would stop and listen. Twice, he had them sit in a thicket of bushes while he scouted ahead. Each time, he returned and motioned them on without explanation.

About the middle of the afternoon, he left them for the third time. He was gone longer this time. When he returned he had them gather together.

"Over that ridge is the valley in front of Shepherds Pass. We are quite a bit above it; so, hopefully, we will avoid any fighting." He paused and his face was grim. "I am going to take you on top of the ridge against my better judgment. I need to be able to see the valley floor, but I cannot risk leaving you here on your own."

Again, he paused and wiped his face with his hand. Finally he said quietly, "I need you to prepare yourselves. You are about to witness the closest thing man has ever created to hell on earth. The war has begun."

With that he turned and led them back the way he had just returned from. As they climbed, a horrible din grew louder and louder. It was a sickening cacophony of sound. The clash of metal and splitting of wood discordantly mixed with the roars and screams of men and animals.

By the time they reached the ridge line, Quinn was already pale and light-headed. As he looked over the edge, he collapsed against the rocks, fighting nausea. Even from a high distance above, it was easily the most horrifying and disgusting thing he had ever seen.

The entire valley looked as if a violent storm had swept through the camp. The remains of tents, wagons, and other gear lay strewn everywhere. Directly below them, men fought to destroy one another. From above, it seemed to be complete madness—idiocy. Perhaps, this was how the Creator viewed them all.

Closing his eyes, he tried to block out the image while the blood-curdling noises filled the air around him. He felt small and sickened. He wished with all his heart to be somewhere else, *anywhere* else. Glancing up, he saw that Rhiannon and Bertran were sitting down under the trees, their backs against the rock wall. He decided to join them. Quinn had just sat next to his cousin when Alexander turned from the precipice, his face a mixture of anger and fear.

"They're not here," he hissed. "The king's army didn't come."

Chapter 18

Within moments of entering the valley in front of Shepherds Pass, Rustan Hawk sent messengers to gather the officers to the main tent as soon as it was erected. The men of Eastcastle quickly stretched out across the field, setting up tents and lighting campfires in an attempt to beat the full onset of night. Many of them scavenged the surrounding woods for deadfall, which could be used to warm dinners as well as hands and feet. As the last of the sunlight disappeared, dozens of small blazes dotted the valley floor.

Inside the large pavilion, Rustan Hawk waited. He had opted for the portable quarters instead of the more permanent barracks near the mouth of the pass for two reasons. First, he did not feel good about bumping men who had already been fighting from their rooms. Second, he was wary about stationing his command too deep in the valley. Truth be told, it was the latter that bore more weight.

He had just finished a light meal of bread, cheese, and fruit, when a guardsman parted the flap and announced the arrival of Saladar, the commander of the men stationed at the pass. Rustan waved him in. The large grizzly man barely reacted when he saw the man he had accepted as dead for many years.

Saladar gave a slight head bob, but that was the extent of any ceremony. His countenance showed the physical and emotional exhaustion from a day of constant battle.

"Milord, your presence is indeed welcome. The command is yours."

Rustan stood and laughed, extending his hand. "Sal, you old bear, I see Eastcastle is still lucky enough to have you."

Saladar shook his hand, and Rustan gestured him to a small chair. "Have a seat while we wait for the others. How are things going?" he asked, seating himself again.

The man took the offered chair while offhandedly waving those with him to find their own. He sighed heavily as he looked around the room, his eyes tightening ever so slightly as he realized Rustan was not alone. Petric stood quietly, leaning against a small camp table, arms folded. Saladar scrutinized him briefly, before looking back to Rustan.

"So far, we have held off all their attacks, but..." He left off as several soldiers from Eastcastle entered the tent.

"Gentlemen," Rustan said, "Please find a seat or a place to stand. I am afraid accommodations are going to be a bit austere."

The men settled quickly, most standing near the tent walls as only a few chairs were available. When they were situated, Rustan motioned to Saladar to continue.

"As I was saying, we have met each offensive and turned them back, but I doubt we have met their full force."

"I am absolutely confident you have not," Rustan said, eyebrows quirked. "If you had, we would not be having this conversation."

A buzz of murmuring filled the tent, and Saladar's eyes narrowed.

"You obviously have the benefit of better information. What are we facing?"

Rustan's face hardened as he stood. Glancing around the room, he said, "Leaders of Eastcastle, we are about to face the entire force of men and weapons that Maldria has available to throw at us."

The room erupted into exclamations of surprise and disbelief. Rustan raised his hand for silence. "The army Philip threatened us with years ago stands once again at our borders under the leadership of his son. Only, it has *grown*. Besides a vast amount of men, Paddock has assembled a fleet of ships in which he could easily carry every man in this valley, their families, and a good portion of their flocks."

"Then the attacks against our defenses here..." began Saladar.

"Are no more than a ploy to keep you in the bowl. What have you heard from your southern watches?"

Saladar glanced around the room as though looking for someone, but finally turned back to Rustan.

"Milord, the last report I received was before noon. We have held back six different assaults from the pass since then. There was little time for much else." He gave it as a statement of fact, rather than an excuse. Rustan accepted it with a nod.

"I sent out a party of scouts when we arrived and, with the mercy of the Creator, we will know before any trap is sprung. Until that time, we have work to do, for we will not rely solely on good fortune.

"Barret, you will take your men and relieve Sal's front. They have held the line all day and will need rest. Rotate your men on watches and tell them to sleep as much as possible when not on guard. A day's march is not a light task, and they will need to be rested as much as possible by daybreak.

"Sal, rest your men and prepare them to resume their watch in the morning. They are the border guard of Eastcastle, and no one will take that responsibility from them.

"The rest of you, as soon as your men are done with their meals, move them, but leave the fires burning. Paddock will have spies in the hills. Let him think the bait has been taken and the rabbit waits to be snared."

Retrieving a parchment from the table where Petric stood, Rustan held it aloft.

"Each of you will set your companies along the line of the northern hills as outlined here. We will leave the cavalry throughout the deserted camp, each with his horse. Just prior to dawn, these men will throw green boughs on their campfires to help disguise the lack of activity in the camp. With any luck, Paddock will think the metal is still on the anvil when the hammer falls.

"Once his force enters the mouth of the bowl, each man is to take his horse and ride toward the pass and regroup. Sal, you will need to hold the pass until that happens. My guess is at some signal from Paddock, you will face the full strength of the force you have been fighting. You must hold until the cavalry regroups."

"It will be done."

"All others on the northern ridge will be supplied with bows. The cavalry will then lead a break out from the bowl. The men on the ridge will protect their flank with arrows. As soon as the cavalry moves, Sal, you will follow in an organized retreat. Jarrod and Compton, your squads of longbows will be nearest to the pass. Shred anything that comes out of the pass until Sal's men are free. We will then move out of the bowl as a parchment is rolled, each subsequent group defending the retreat of the previous."

"If what you say of the Maldrian army is true," a man burst out, "Then this is a death trap! We have little chance of escaping before their army turns, and even if we do, what hope will we have standing against them outside the bowl? We will all die here!"

"Our objective is not to win…"

The room erupted into angry shouts and cries of disbelief. Rustan drew his sword and slammed the flat edge against the table to quiet them.

"Our objective is not to win," he shouted over the remaining murmurs, "But to hold until my brother returns from Riverton with Anthony's forces."

"The king!" another man scoffed above the din of the others. "With all due respect, milord, if that is your plan then you have doomed us all! You will not see so much as one Dalatian standard-bearer within this valley."

"Milord, Eastcastle is not how you left it," another said. "No offense toward your brother, but we have garnered no favor among the other dukes. I would expect to see a legion of the Creator's angels before the Dalatian army."

Rustan scanned the room, his jaw clenched. Each man's face looked the same—anger masking fear. Finally, a small, cold smirk emerged across his face. Facing the last man directly, he said in a deathly quiet voice, "Then I suppose you should start your prayers. You have your orders. See that you follow them."

He spun backwards and exited the smaller door at the back of the tent, ignoring the calls for more discussion. Petric moved in front of the door Rustan had exited, the set of his stone face changing anyone's mind who thought to follow. His cold eyes made one scan around the room before he too walked out into the night.

The commanders talked quietly amongst themselves as each came forward to view their assignments on the parchment. The mood in the tent had become black, a far cry from the cheers and excitement back at Eastcastle's gates. No one challenged their assignment for they were seasoned men who understood the necessity of order in the chaos of war. Challenging the plan before the final decision was part of their job, but so was acceptance of their responsibilities when the talking was finished. They may not agree with the course of action, in fact they might even think it was doomed to fail, but each was determined not to let it happen because they shirked their duty. War was an unpredictable leviathan that twisted and turned with a life of its own. The best one could hope for was to start with the most favorable plan. After the first clash of swords, you simply hoped it was enough. With the discussion over, each man took his assignment and returned to his command. Before long, the pavilion stood empty.

Outside the tent, Rustan scanned the darkness, letting the cool night air calm the anger inside him. He shut his eyes for a moment, willing a return of balance. Rage, revenge, hatred, and exhaustion—that was all his life seemed to be now. Everything else had ended the night Cat died. He was nothing more than a shell of blackness seeking to fulfill the vow he had made that night at sea.

Opening his eyes, he noticed the stars shown brightly from above. Any other night and the sight would have been tranquil, but tonight the light was his enemy. Their only chance was for Paddock to overplay his hand—a slim hope at best.

"Will they come?"

Rustan turned only his head. His brother's tall bodyguard stood resolutely in the shadows of the tent.

"I honestly do not know," he sighed. "It should have been possible for the king's army to arrive before us."

Silence again permeated the air until Petric broke it. "I know you are aware that your men are correct. Without the king's army, we have no hope of surviving this battle."

"Yes." Rustan turned to face him, his countenance showing nothing but his tiredness. "I am aware of that. So, tell me your thoughts, Petric. Have I done the right thing? The price of freedom is always high, but have I made a fool's gambit? In this case, is the cost *too* high?"

The bodyguard's face did not change, leaving Rustan to only guess at his thoughts and emotions. Inside, the ranger smiled to himself. *At least some things do not change with time.* Finally, Petric shrugged.

"I think it is easier to motivate men to fight to *save* their freedom than it is to try and raise a broken people to reclaim it. When they have tasted freedom and it is fresh in their minds, they will not set it aside so easily. Your men are here because they understand the realities that will most definitely follow should they fail. This is not the first conflict fought for freedom, nor will it be the last. Ultimately, it is a simple matter for each man to decide whether the risk of dying a free man is more favorable than the certainty of life as a slave."

A small smile played on Rustan's lips. It was the most he had heard Petric say at once since his return to Eastcastle. Taking a deep breath through his nose, he looked to the ground before yawning.

"Well, Petric, take what rest you can. Tomorrow, I fear the world will collapse into madness."

The tall man bowed formally. Standing erect again, he said, "Fare well, Rustan Hawk," before disappearing into the darkness with his swift, graceful stride.

Rustan was so surprised by the abruptness and finality of his parting that by the time it registered, the bodyguard was gone. His brow wrinkled in confusion for a moment before he shook his head once and re-entered the tent. He had little time to spend sorting out the demons of others; heaven knew he had enough of his own.

Once inside, he retrieved his ranger cloak and collapsed on his small cot. Using the skills he had learned and mastered over time, he found sleep almost immediately.

Rustan's eyes flashed open as soon as the man entered the tent, his right hand a silent blur as it grasped the hilt of the sword laying nearby.

"Milord?" came a whispered entreaty.

Rustan sat upright, all vestiges of sleep completely gone. "What is it?"

"Sorry to disturb you, milord, but a man has returned from the south. He brings news."

Moving quickly, Rustan fiddled with a lamp on the table. Within moments, a small flame sputtered to life.

"Bring him in."

The guardsman had barely left the tent before another man strode in. He gave a quick, formal bow, which Rustan abruptly waved off.

"What news, captain?"

"Milord, it is as you feared. A vast force lies just south of this valley. We were unable to get an exact count from our position, but we dared not go closer. The entire land was bathed in a half-light as bright as dawn from the bonfires. Milord, we are easily outnumbered ten to one, if not more."

Rustan's jaw clenched. Suddenly, his eyes flashed to the captain's. "Has this been spread to the men?"

"No, milord, at least not before I came here. We have only just returned."

"Good. Tell your men to keep silent. Night is by nature devoid of hope; let the dawn's light show our true standing."

"Yes, milord."

"Get some food and rest wherever you can find it. Both will be scarce after the sun's rays breach the Castlerooks."

The man bowed and dismissed himself. Rubbing his face, Rustan tried to focus his thoughts. Standing, he once again reviewed the scrawled lines on the parchment outlining his army's defenses. He scoured them for weaknesses he knew did not exist. Shepherds Pass had always been the obvious point of attack from Maldria and, as such, every yard of ground had been mapped and studied over the years. The battle ahead had been fought for centuries in the minds of the best strategists of both lands.

Only now, the scenario had changed. His greatest fear had been confirmed. Paddock had landed a ground force somewhere on the rocky southern shores. He wondered how and where he had done it, realizing at the same time that it no longer mattered. It had been done. The natural defenses offered by the bowl they camped in would quickly become a quagmire.

Staring at the dance of the lamplight on the fabric of the tent, he whispered, "Where are you, Anthony?"

The smoke from the fires wafted across the fields, seemingly trying to prolong the night. Already the pale glow over the mountains had brightened enough that Rustan could see the dark slash of the pass from his position near the mouth of the bowl. The army of Eastcastle lined the northern edge of the bowl three and four men deep just inside the trees. Standing or sitting, they waited for the approach of the army they now knew was coming from the south.

Rustan had hoped to keep its presence quiet, but the news had spread like a flame in a dry field. Rumor had piled on rumor and before long, the entire camp knew of the threat coming to meet them. Rustan would not have been surprised to find some who believed every man, woman, and child of Maldria was marching toward them.

Out on the flats, members of the cavalry chatted in small groups or tended to the fires. Rustan hoped they did not appear as sparse to the casual viewer as they did to his knowing eye. It was vital for Paddock to deploy his army as quickly and recklessly as possible. If he chose to hang back and block the west side of the bowl, it would only be a matter of time before he found them. If that happened, Eastcastle's army would be decimated.

He wondered where Petric had ended up. The tall bodyguard had not come to his tent when he awoke. In fact, he had not seen him all morning. He had hoped to review some last minute contingency plans with him, but the man seemed to have disappeared. He had presented the plans to the unit commanders a couple of hours before dawn, in hopes of shoring up the confidence that had fled with the report of the scouting party. From the looks on their faces, he knew he had failed. Unfortunately, there was little time left to do anything about it.

With each of the units in place, it now became a waiting game. However, Rustan knew the longer they waited, the worse the psychological damage would be to his troops. Facing a larger force is always frightening, but letting your mind run free, conjuring up images of impossibilities, was another thing altogether. Even his nerves were beginning to feel fully taxed. The almost indecipherable chatter of the men under their breaths sounded as though they were yelling in his ear. He was annoyed at their lack of silence even though he knew there was little chance of anyone hearing them.

Finally, as the first rays of the sun broke over the Castlerooks, a dark line appeared on the southern horizon. As it slowly grew, the new day's light began to shimmer upon the sea of metal coming toward them. With quick hand movements, Rustan quieted the men around him near the top edge of the bowl. Like a ripple from a stone thrown into a pond, silence traveled down the line. Before long, the only sounds were the light wind in the trees and the occasional distant, almost imperceptible, noise from the counterfeit camp before them.

Glancing once again out onto the flats, Rustan was suddenly struck by the realization that every item of his army's camp gear was about to be destroyed. The concern was only momentary. One way or another, the conflict would end today. There would be little need for an extended camp.

The dark line grew as it came toward them, slowly taking on individual shapes and movements. Even from a distance, he knew the scouting report had not been exaggerated. The body of men was easily ten times that of the Eastcastle force, if not more. Paddock had sold his cause well. The entire might of Maldria approached them.

Time seemed to slow as they watched the horde develop. Irrationally, Rustan was anxious for it to begin. The inevitability of the conflict was already set, so it might as well begin now. As he scanned the men near him, he saw his thoughts reflected on their resigned faces. Some of the younger ones showed fear, but all were prepared to see it through. Rustan's heart fell as he accepted the reality of what this day would likely hold. Forcing his eyes straight ahead, he watched as the Maldrian army filled the western mouth of the bowl and stopped.

Panic began to tickle the back of his mind. Already, the cavalry men were playing their part in the fields below, running wildly and screaming into empty tents, trying in vain to raise an army that was no longer there. Rustan had stressed the importance of making it look real, selling the fear and surprise. He realized with bitter humor that they were likely no longer acting. Any sane man would be running.

Attack, curse you, attack!

Rustan's heart began to beat loudly. In the mild insanity that accompanies all fears, he hoped it could not be heard by the Maldrian army, which now stood a stone's throw from his position.

What are they waiting for?

Through small gaps in the swirling smoke, Rustan could see many of his men were already beginning to mount up. If they moved too early, the deception would be lost, and they would find themselves with no way out.

Why are they not attacking?

Suddenly, Rustan's stomach lurched, and he had to consciously fight to hold down its sparse contents. His eyes scanned the Maldrian line frantically, hoping he would not find the source of the thought that cankered his insides.

Please, do not let me find him there!

As he looked, horn blasts sounded from the Maldrian army and reverberated across the valley. Immediately, the entire mass of soldiers joined in, their primitive yell becoming deafening. Men visibly shrank around Rustan as the cry built in volume. Then, as if one massive beast, the hordes of men moved forward. The ground rumbled with the thunder of feet and horse hooves as the front line seemed to stretch out in a continuous flow of destruction, speeding toward the empty camp.

Rustan let out a quick breath and nearly fell against the rock upon which he was leaning. Swallowing quickly, he watched as the army of Maldria swept forward. The sounds of cracking wood and ringing metal filled the air. The absence of screams of pain was a welcome relief, though he knew that would not remain true for long. Those discordant shrills would soon be added to the deafening noise.

Watching the Maldrian army, Rustan suddenly went cold. The mass of soldiers smoothly divided into two parties as though a huge sword had divided them.

Too many, thought Rustan. *They have left too many.*

Eastcastle's only hope had been that Paddock would deploy nearly his complete force into the valley, leaving the possibility of an escape down the flank. What had been a risky prospect from the beginning now looked to be an impossibility. Rustan bowed his head as second thoughts plagued his mind. He should have guessed better. He should have been ready with an alternative plan, maybe even retreated altogether.

Turning and climbing down from the rock, he battled down his fears. He had done the best with what was available. A retreat would have led to a razing of the entire countryside, something Eastcastle could ill afford with most of the harvest still standing in the fields. Even now, the women and children worked in the absence of husbands and fathers to prepare for the long winter ahead.

Rustan glanced at the men around him and realized they were watching him intently. His face must have shown his trepidation as the countenances of the men had fallen. Drawing heavily on his own reserves, he set a tight smile in place as he drew near them.

"For Eastcastle," he whispered.

Instantly, the men around him straightened. Heads were suddenly held higher, swords and bows gripped more confidently. The men's eyes brightened with determination.

"For Eastcastle, milord!" came the hushed reply.

Rustan walked quickly toward the pass.

"For Eastcastle. For Eastcastle, milord."

With each nod and reply, Rustan could feel the intensity begin to build. The small hairs on his neck began to rise.

"For Eastcastle, milord. For Eastcastle."

No matter the outcome, they would fight valiantly for Eastcastle this day. They would fight to remain free.

When he finally reached the other edge of the line, the horsemen of Eastcastle had already begun their flanking pass. Rustan signaled the men to fix their arrows as hundreds of cavalrymen pounded by, swords and spears raised. Behind them came the border guards, running swiftly in an organized column, arms held ready. Rustan scanned them quickly looking for Saladar, but was unable to find the grizzled warrior. He was sure the soldier did not enjoy leaving the station he had watched faithfully for so many years.

Soon the dull calls of battle horns pealed through the valley. The game was up. Within moments, the great wave of the enemy turned toward the northern part of the bowl. Rustan smiled to himself. The bulk was returning from the pass. They had skirted them after all.

"Notch your arrows, men. Make each of them count. On my command…"

The Maldrians stormed after the rear of the border guards, maddened by the ruse. Concentrating on what appeared to be the back of a full retreat, the Maldrian army began to separate from ranks as they scrambled fiercely to engage the fleeing army.

"NOW!!"

Arrows flew from the depths of the trees piercing men and horses alike. Screams of pain and surprise filled the air as man and beast tumbled to the ground. The wave of soldiers crashed into the unexpected pile of roiling flesh like a sea wave breaking on a spit of land.

"ROLL BACK. FIRE AND ROLL BACK!" cried Rustan and the unit leaders.

The men quickly responded, and by the time the Maldrian soldiers rushed the woods, only the trees remained. Roaring with rage, the enemy surged forward again after the retreating border guards. This time, however, they spread to the edge of the tree line. They had only gone several more paces when another volley of arrows hissed through the air. The Maldrians were not surprised the second time, and instead of faltering as before, the river of men rushed onward.

"FALL BACK! FALL BACK!"

Madness ensued as those retreating were forced into the lines of those waiting to cover their retreat. The response of the Maldrians had been too quick, and the force of Eastcastle was in complete disarray despite the screamed orders from its commanders. Soon the sound of metal on metal replaced the *thwips* of arrows.

Rustan drew his own sword and fought beside his men, using the trees and rocks as natural defenses. The fever pitch of the battle became desperate as the Maldrian army began to fill in around the front line. Before long, the body of the enemy forces would swing around like a hinged gate, and split off a large part of the Eastcastle army from the others. Rustan urged his men to move west as swiftly as possible, but hope was beginning to fade. In fact, it might have been lost altogether if the cavalry had not returned, crashing through the flank of the Maldrians.

"MOVE NOW, MEN. MOVE!"

Men scrambled over the rocks and through the brush as they fought their way west, while the cavalry clumsily circled and tried to fight their way back to the mouth of the bowl. With little speed to protect them, many of the riders were dragged from their mounts and swallowed in the seemingly endless swath of enemy soldiers.

Retrieving his bow from his back, Rustan joined the others as they once again filled the air with the hissing sounds of arrows in flight. They concentrated their aim on the western most side of the enemy in hopes of weakening the force in front of the now embattled cavalry. Finally, a breach opened and the riders surged forward, horse hooves mangling both turf and flesh.

As soon as the corridor opened, Rustan once again signaled the men to retreat through the trees, hoping another wave of arrows would provide them the necessary cover. As he rushed over the uneven ground, he realized another miscalculation. They were tiring.

Even given an escape route, he was not sure that they would be able to physically make it. He had counted on the Maldrians' recovery being slower, and that they would not have to engage them in hand-to-hand combat so soon. The swordplay had drained them much more than he had intended. He was not surprised when the army was once again pinned against the mountains; only this time, he knew there would be no cavalry to the rescue. The Maldrians would be ready for a repeat maneuver.

As he fought with his men, hope began to falter and a maddening rage filled the void. It began to consume him. For years he had plotted his revenge. He would bring his wife's murderers to justice, hunt them down one at a time if necessary, but each would pay. For years, the madness had grown inside him, fueled by hate and fed by anger.

But now, with the imminent capture and destruction of this army, Rustan felt it slipping away. He had failed. Cat had died in front of his eyes, and now he had failed her once again. The weight of his inability to keep his last promise to her stung his memories. A mace glanced awkwardly off his helmet, sending him careening down into the bushes.

I am sorry, Cat, I have failed you.

He fell headlong into the darkness. He did not know at that very moment, his son sat huddled in the rocks above him, trying to block out the sounds of the insanity below. He did not see the knot of men, which swarmed to protect him when they saw him fall. Nor did he hear the piercing sound of hundreds of battle horns reverberating across the valley, carefully fanning the last remaining spark of hope and willing it back to life. Suddenly, at the mouth of the bowl stood the Dalatian army and at its head rode their king.

The march from Riverton seemed slow to Renard; though, years later the army's landing and movement would be considered a model for military operations. The boats ported with near perfect efficiency. The troops came ashore and assembled in a matter of hours—an impressive feat, considering it began in the twilight of the night before. By the half-light of dawn, the column was already moving toward the pass.

The king disembarked from the second ship, much to the surprise of the people of Riverton. There had been rumors, of course, but none of them had said anything about Anthony coming himself. By the time Renard arrived, the town was already in a commotion. The relief the duke felt upon seeing the countless ships in the bay evaporated quickly when he was summoned almost immediately to a late night meeting with the king.

He was glad to at least have Bastian with him, filling in as his bodyguard. It bothered him that Petric had requested to continue on with the army, but he hoped he had kept it from showing on his face. He realized he was having to do that more and more, lately.

The king and his advisors grilled Renard on everything from the return of his brother to where his true loyalty lay—another thing he would thank Rustan for when he saw him again. He was grateful the rider from the border patrol had found them before the crossroads. It provided more proof than the seemingly paranoid theories of a man who had, for all intents and purposes, just returned from the dead.

Had he known the king himself was coming, he would have protested a bit more fervently as to exactly whose responsibility it was to meet the Army of Dalatia. The other dukes and advisors were bad enough, but he would have stood as their equals—at least on paper. The king's presence changed his position to one of subservience; though the other dukes shared a similar fate. Many were clearly not happy to be here, yet here they were.

As he answered their questions, a bevy of silent looks and small gestures carried on an entirely different discussion, which he was clearly not meant to be privy to. The hour-long conference was absolutely exhausting. Renard was not sure whether he was more tired from the all-day ride or the stress of the meeting.

After the audience with the king, Bastian and Renard found a place in the town where they could grab a few hours of sleep. Unfortunately, Renard had barely settled down before a knock came at the door. Apparently, the army was moving out, and their presence was again requested. Replacing their boots and cloaks, they retrieved their horses and joined up with the king and his party.

As they rode, the dukes asked more questions. How big was the Maldrian army? What was the area like? What were the weaknesses? What were the strengths? What would Paddock do? How long could Eastcastle hold?

They came like a hail of arrows, one after the other. Renard did his best to answer each, or at least provide what information he knew. His anger toward Rustan grew with each one. By the time they reached the fields in front of the bowl, he was seething.

At first, Renard thought the large standing army coming into view was his own, but his stomach seized as the banners became distinct. They were the colors of the various baronies of Maldria, and they were on the wrong side of the pass.

He spurred his horse forward to where the king rode, only to be stopped short by his royal guard. Finally, he was able to get a message to the king that the army coming into view was not friendly.

"You are sure they are Maldrians?"

"Yes, your highness. Somehow they have circled the bowl. Probably by boat as my brother suggested."

"They are facing east. One might surmise that Eastcastle's army is trapped between two pincers."

Renard swallowed as his own fears were vocalized. "Yes, your highness."

The king turned and signaled to two men riding nearby. "Edmond, Stefan, take your riders and engage them. Given the banners, the main commanders of Maldria are likely with them. I doubt we still have the advantage of surprise, but let us see how the beast does without its head. Do not let them join with those in the bowl."

The two men immediately relayed the necessary messages and over a thousand riders broke free from the column. They streamed toward the mass of men in front of them. A sudden agitation in the enemy's army confirmed they had indeed been seen.

Turning to face his leaders, the king cried, "Command every man who has a horn to sound it now! Let the world know we are here. Let them know we do not tolerate invasions into *our* land! Dalatia *will* stand by her people! *TO BATTLE!!*"

Several horns rapidly multiplied into hundreds. The massive sound blared across the fields and reverberated off the distant mountains. The column became a swiftly flowing river headed straight into the bowl. There may have been doubts expressed in the late night meetings, with arguments strewn around like leftover food, but here on the plains, all doubts were set aside. The Dalatian army had been called upon to help its own, and they would do so.

Renard rode forward and stared in disbelief across the bowl in front of Shepherds Pass. The remains of what was once the camp of Eastcastle lay strewn across the valley. Tents and carts were decimated and in ruins. His heart sank at the sight until he realized something was missing. Not one single body lay among the destruction, friend or foe. He dared not expect too much, but the realization was enough to foster a small glimmer of hope, which was more than he'd had when they first approached.

Glancing toward the king, he saw Anthony's face reflected more curiosity than concern. Around them, the soldiers of Dalatia poured into the bowl. Perhaps they would find more than just a slaughtered army.

Chapter 19

Quinn's head jerked up when he heard the battle horns echoing off the surrounding hills. After glancing at Rhiannon, he scrambled to the edge of the cliff where Alexander still lay sprawled beside the ranger. Within moments, Rhiannon joined them, leaving Bertran sitting alone against the ridge of rocks with his head resting on his knees.

At first, nothing looked different. The throng of men beneath them was still locked together in battle, their cries and yells mingling with the clanging of metal on metal.

Suddenly, Asher said in a hushed, but ardent voice, "There!"

He pointed to the mouth of the bowl to the west. Following his finger, Quinn could just make out a large standing body of men and banners; however, he quickly realized the colors were all wrong.

"It's just more of the Maldrian army," he exclaimed, nearly collapsing in despair.

"No, not them; the riders, coming from the north."

Quinn looked again and this time saw what the ranger had seen. Two columns of riders thundered toward the army standing at the mouth of the bowl, clouds of billowing dust rising behind them.

Asher looked at them with a grim smile. "They're here. Let's pray it's in time to matter."

As they watched the scene play out, Quinn had the odd feeling he was watching a game of Knights, only with real men and higher stakes. The band of the Maldrian army to the west slowly contorted to face the threat of the Dalatian riders. Horns and signals filled the air with a chaotic cacophony of sound.

Beneath them, the rearmost units of the Maldrian army began to react and move in answer to the calls for assistance. Unfortunately, the distance between the two groups was too great for them to join together in time to meet the first onslaught of the Dalatian riders. Turning an army on a parade field is difficult enough; in the heat of battle, it was nearly impossible.

Quinn watched with a mixture of fascination and horror. What had once been a clear confrontation between the Eastcastle force in the trees and the Maldrian fighters in the bowl transformed into an absurd melee of men and beasts. The Dalatian foot soldiers poured into the bowl like water diverted into the irrigation lines of a farmer's field. The stream of men crashed into the disorganized enemy as it hesitated between responding to the calls from the barons and pursuing the beaten army of Eastcastle up the slopes of the bowl. Before long, utter madness reigned in the valley. Quinn could only imagine what it must be like to be in the middle of it all. He suddenly felt ill when he remembered Bastian and his father were.

"Come with me," Asher said finally. "If the Dalatian army is coming from the north, we can backtrack to join them. There is nothing more to be gained watching this."

Slowly, the three youth pulled themselves away from the carnage below, still struggling with the reality of it all. Joining Bertran, they hurried to catch up with the ranger as he led them back down the slope.

Renard sat helpless on his horse. In front of him, two massive armies were locked in battle and yet here he sat uselessly watching it all. To his left, Bastian sat astride his own horse, probably with similar thoughts. In front of them, Anthony sat easily in his saddle, his arms resting lightly on the horn, his eyes riveted to the events before them. Messengers came regularly, delivering reports and carrying instructions. For the most part, Anthony allowed his field generals to run the battle, overriding their commands only a couple of times when he felt something was amiss.

Renard had requested permission to join the battle soon after the front lines had met the Maldrian army, but his petition had fallen on deaf ears. Anthony had no intention of allowing him or any of the other dukes to join the fray. Instead, he kept them back as "councilors."

The word burned in his gut. Anthony was unlikely to ask his opinion on anything. Renard had effectively lost all leadership responsibilities as soon as the king had set foot in Riverton. Renard could no longer even make decisions regarding his own person, let alone the movement of his army. With no other options available, the Duke of Eastcastle sat in silence, fighting the bile flooding his stomach.

"Riders, your Majesty."

Renard's head turned. Several men on horseback had left the melee at the mouth of the bowl and were riding toward them at a gallop. In clear, but easy movements, the king's guard fronted their liege as the men approached.

"It's Edmond, your grace."

The king nodded his agreement. "Let them in," he said.

The line of men opened briefly for the six mounted men to enter. Renard recognized the lead rider as one of the two men Anthony had sent into battle. His face was red and bathed in sweat, while his armor and cloak were splattered with mud and blood. As the man swung down and bowed before his king, Renard realized only four of the men wore the uniforms of Dalatia. Glancing at the other two, one was clearly a Maldrian while the other was difficult to ascertain as he wore a nondescript, hooded cloak.

"Your majesty, this is Cyrus, Baron of Southreach. He has asked for an audience with you."

The king's jaw clenched at the introduction, but he gave a slight nod. The tall, slim man Edmond had introduced as Cyrus dismounted smoothly from his horse and stood before Anthony. His countenance and the set of his head clearly reflected a lack of obeisance.

"King Anthony, I fear the people of Maldria have been misled."

The corner of the king's mouth edged up in a humorless smile. "I agree. As I remember it, your border lies several miles east of here."

The tall man noticeably winced, and his head bobbed ever so slightly.

"Yes, but what I mean is most of Maldria is under the impression we are freeing Eastcastle from a despot who has usurped power from his nephew—a man who is seeking to reestablish the

Kingdom of Eastcastle. Such an action would surely disrupt the balance in the area and..."

"Lead to war?" the king interrupted, sarcastically.

The man's face reddened and he took a moment to compose himself. "We were told we were answering a call for aid."

"From whom?"

"From Quinn Hawk, the heir of Eastcastle."

"Quinn?" The name slipped from Renard's mouth and all eyes turned to him. Feeling their stares, he added, "That is insane."

"Baron Cyrus," Anthony said, "I suppose you know Renard Hawk—your so-called usurper."

The tall man looked at Renard as the duke edged his horse closer. Turning back to Anthony, he said, "The boy and the daughter of Baron Paddock were abducted by two rangers. We were led to believe it was his doing. We are here to avenge the kidnapping of his daughter, to ensure the rightful heir is returned to power in Eastcastle, and to see our two lands are not once more plunged into years of war."

"One of those *rangers* was the boy's own father!" Renard retorted, anger building at the deception that had cost so many lives.

The baron glanced ever so slightly at the hooded man to his side before responding. "So we have been told."

Anthony coughed, pulling the man's attention back to him. "So, Baron Cyrus, what would you have us do?"

"Pull back your men. End the fighting."

The king gave a dry laugh. "You would have me call a retreat? One might question the wisdom of that, considering your army is currently divided and at a disadvantage. What would I possibly gain in ordering such an action?"

"If you pull back your men, most of the barons will do the same."

"*Most?* But not all."

"We will deal with the others when your armies have moved back."

Anthony stared at the man and tried to gage his honesty. Finally, he said, "Why call for a truce now? Clearly, you had the option of correcting your wrongs earlier when the field was in your control. Why should I accept your sudden acknowledgment of error when the risk is all against me? How do I know you will not simply use it as a stratagem to pull your army back together?"

"You have my word and the word of the other barons whom I represent."

"And is that enough?" the king challenged dryly.

The baron and king stared at one another, but neither spoke. The sounds of the distant battle floated into the silence like a macabre background song of a bard. The cloaked man who had ridden with the baron suddenly spoke.

"It is enough," said a quiet, cold voice. The man pulled back his hood.

The king's jaw clenched again when he recognized Renard's bodyguard. He stared for a moment before the small, humorless smile crept again to his lips.

"Ah, Petric. And whose side are you on today?" he asked in an icy tone.

"I am on whichever side has the best chance of ending this senseless killing."

The eyes of the two men locked. Time passed slowly as the air became electrically charged around them. Within the silence, fates were aligning and each man challenged the other to wither from them. Finally, without looking away, Anthony spoke softly.

"Captain, sound the retreat."

"Your majesty?"

"*Sound the withdrawal!*"

The Maldrian baron nodded his head and climbed back upon his horse. He was barely seated before turning his horse to return the fight. Petric pulled his reins to do the same, but the king called out.

"Petric! You will stay here. Should your *friends* play false, know that your life is forfeit."

Petric faced the king, his stone face devoid of all expression.

"Anthony, should they *play false*, I will take my own life and save you the trouble."

Petric glanced back to Cyrus, who gave him a quick nod. After a final look to Anthony, Cyrus spurred his horse forward.

"Edmond!" Anthony called. "Take your men and see that the baron returns safely. However, if he so much as draws his sword against one of our men, cut him down."

"Yes, your majesty."

The riders turned and followed the fluttering cloak of the baron. As they rode, a staccato of horn blasts echoed across valley.

At first nothing happened, the battle continued to rage in front of them.

"Sound it again," Anthony commanded and the horn blasts again reverberated around them.

Slowly, the Dalatian army changed. The front lines switched from an attacking position to forming ranks in preparation for an organized retreat. Already, the rearguard had fallen back, maintaining a formation that could easily return to the conflict if necessary. Soon the entire army extracted itself as a tide retreating back into the ocean. Instead of rocks and shells however, dead and dying men were exposed in the gap.

Despite the retreat, the Maldrians continued to fight in desperation. They understood the danger of their predicament as soon as Anthony had arrived, and they were now fighting for survival. It was not long before they recognized the battle horn signals for retreat, and a cheer erupted from their ranks. A visible bolstering was seen across their lines.

As he watched the scene before him, Anthony's nostrils flared and his cheek muscles flexed over clenched teeth. The Dalatian army was now disengaged from the combat with the cavalry running flanking movements to cover the retreat. The Maldrians, on the other hand, appeared to be gathering for a run at the withdrawing army. Men scrambled together, forming ranks and reorganizing their units. Just as they appeared ready to launch the attack, more horn blasts filled the valley.

Renard breathed an audible sigh of relief. He looked toward his old bodyguard and was surprised at the lack of emotion on his friend's face. Even now that Cyrus had proven true to his promise, the tall man was completely calm. He showed no sign of surprise or relief—in fact, his face showed nothing at all. Petric might have been watching grass grow for all the outward signs of expression he showed.

Renard turned back to watch the two armies pull back from each other. He had grown to trust Petric explicitly and knew he had a multitude of skills; however, for the first time, Renard realized he did not really *know* his bodyguard. The man who sat resolutely on the horse near him was obviously his old bodyguard, but he was now also more— bigger, more complex. Whereas before, the duke had seen Petric's skill as a fighter, he now saw his bodyguard in his complete potential. The man before him was a leader and a formidable one. For years, Petric had taken commands from him, but Renard now knew instinctively he would never do so again. He had faced Anthony, not as a defiant, rebellious servant; he had challenged him as an equal.

The front lines of the Maldrian army fell into disarray. The commanders looked baffled by the horns, which continued to blare behind them. Suddenly, without warning, the middle of the army imploded as arms were raised against earlier allies.

With one final look toward Petric, Anthony called several riders to him.

"Tell every captain to keep their men out of that conflict. Let the Maldrian's destroy themselves if they wish—it is no longer our fight. However, tell them to keep their watch should they turn once again."

The riders sped across the field toward the now idle Dalatian army. Up and down the lines they rode, spreading the word that for now the fighting was over. Anthony watched for a moment before signaling another servant.

"Have a pavilion set up there. With any luck, we will be discussing terms by nightfall."

The servant bowed and excused himself.

"The rest of you may see to your men. Renard and Petric, you will stay with me until we determine what has become of the Army of Eastcastle."

The silence of the night struck Quinn more than the hundreds of fires and torches that lit up the darkness. When he had seen the bowl of Shepherds Pass from above, the gruesome sounds of battle had assaulted his ears. Now, with the blackness of night blanketing the valley, he could almost pretend none of it had been real. *Almost.* Deep down he feared the awful scenes would be forever etched into his mind.

Asher led them to the picket lines, walking slowly and whistling a horrid performance of a lively air. As expected, they were hailed immediately and questioned. As soon as they stepped into the ring of light from a nearby fire, they were ushered through the lines without much thought. Apparently, four youth traveling with a ranger were not deemed much of a concern.

Asher asked the nearest of the guardsmen where the Eastcastle army was camped.

The man snorted before pointing, "You can find what's left of it over there."

Asher thanked the man, while Quinn tried to keep his stomach. From the look of his friends' faces, he knew they felt the same way.

They were silent as they walked through the haphazard mix of tents and fires. The men sitting around them talked in hushed tones. The evening had a somberness that made Quinn wish once again they had never left the woods above Eastcastle.

The camp was unbelievably large. They seemed to walk forever, partly because the darkness hid the extent of the camp and partly because they were exhausted. Finally, after passing several posted colors, they found the scarlet and gold of Eastcastle. Quinn avoided looking at the huddled men sitting around the fires. There were clearly fewer than had left the gates of Eastcastle. Many were bandaged, their clothes stained with blood.

Asher paused a moment scanning the surrounding area before leading them toward a large tent with sentries posted. Whoever was now in charge of the Army of Eastcastle was likely there. He walked with a deliberate step toward the two men posted at the front flap.

"What do you want?" the first asked, his voice tinged with irritation and exhaustion.

"We need to see the duke. Is he here?"

The man looked at the ranger as if trying to recognize him. Failing to do so, he glanced past him into the faces of the youth behind. The limited firelight momentarily obscured their faces from his view, but he soon recognized Bertran.

"Lord Roland's ghost! Just a moment."

Taking a step back, he parted the flap of the tent with his left hand.

"My apologies, milord, but your…well, you have visitors, milord."

The sentry listened for a moment before saying, "With all due respect, milord, I think you should see them tonight."

After a short pause, the tent flap flew open and Renard stepped out into the evening air.

"For land's sakes, who is it, Caleb?" The duke's eyes took a moment to adjust before recognizing his son. "Bertran?"

The suddenly very young looking boy flew to his father and clasped him about the waist, completely breaking down. His small body began to shake with his sobs. The surprised duke hugged his son close before kneeling down and catching Bertran's head between his hands.

"Bertran, what are you doing here?"

"I…we…father, I'm sorry." Once again the sobs took over.

Renard hugged his son close again and looked from one face to the next. "Alexander, Quinn, what are you doing here?" After spotting the large ranger, he asked him, "Why have you brought them here?"

At first no one spoke and then, as if on cue, they all spoke at once.

"Just a moment, just a moment!" the duke said, trying to listen and console his son at the same time. "Please, just one at a time. In fact, come inside first."

He opened the flap and stepped inside before stopping so abruptly that they almost ran into him. When he turned back, the flickering torchlight deepened the seriousness etched on his lined face.

"Quinn," he said somberly, "Your father is inside. He is alive, but badly hurt. We found him unconscious in the woods, and he has not awakened since. I am sorry."

Quinn felt the tears begin to form, but fought them down. Stiffening his resolve, he nodded at his uncle, unwilling to risk talking. His uncle nodded back and led them into the tent. Candles burned throughout, filling the tent with the smell of burning wax. A small camp table and chair stood on one side while two cots were on the other. A still figure lay on one of them.

"They have done everything they can for him," said Renard, following their gazes. "If he recovers, it will be his own doing."

Asher and Quinn walked slowly toward the cots, followed by Rhiannon. The others wandered toward the table and lone chair.

"I am afraid camp furniture is scarce at the moment. Much of what was available is scattered from one end of the Bowl to the other."

Asher nodded and knelt down near Rustan's cot, his fluidity inconsistent with his size. As the large man checked on his friend, Quinn and Rhiannon stood together looking into the face of the man each knew better as the ranger Rowan.

The ugly scar down the side of his face looked even worse in the flickering candlelight, but it was slight in comparison to the angry, purple swelling on the other side. Quinn stared down and felt something begin to stir within him. He was surprised when he realized it was anger. In fact, his fury continued to build until his hands clenched tightly into fists, his fingernails digging into his palms.

"I'm sorry, Quinn," Rhiannon whispered beside him. Quinn nearly jumped. His rage was so complete he had forgotten she was standing so near.

"Don't be," he hissed.

He immediately regretted the words when he saw her reaction, but he no longer cared. This man professed to be his father, but for the better part of a summer, he had wasted every opportunity to tell him. Even when they had been alone crossing the Castlerooks, he chose to keep his secrets. And now, lying on an old battle-scarred cot that may well be his deathbed, he *could not* talk. All the things he could have told him about his mother, how they had met, what they liked to do—all of it was lost. Quinn now had to deal with his death all over again without the benefit of having spent time with him.

Quinn felt the sting of tears in his eyes. He hoped the others took them as a sign of sorrow instead of the anger that burned inside him.

Finally, Asher stood.

"He is sleeping well enough. I believe his mind has simply locked itself for a time while his body heals. It happens sometimes, after severe injuries. He may wake up after more rest."

"Or he may not," Quinn challenged roughly.

Asher nodded. "Or he may not," he conceded.

The ranger moved away from the cot toward where the duke was now sitting at the table, his son standing and leaning on him.

"So, tell me, ranger, what in creation would possess you to bring four children into the madness of war?"

Asher's blue eyes locked with Renard's, but his face remained calm.

"It wasn't his fault," Alexander piped in quickly. "We sort of, well, helped him decide to bring us," he ended lamely.

The duke looked over at Alexander, his face clearly not surprised by the confession. "And why would you do that?"

Alexander recited the treachery of Vareen and the events that followed. Throughout, Bertran interjected comments, but the ranger stood silent. When the narrative was over, the duke sighed heavily and dry washed his face with his hands. He was clearly tired.

"Of course—Vareen. It makes perfect sense in hindsight. So many years he was with me. I should have seen it before, but I had always hoped..." He sighed. Looking at Asher, he said, "Sir, please accept my apologies. I was rash."

Without changing his expression, Asher bowed slightly.

"No need, milord. I do have one other message I was to bring; however, since the Dalatian army is currently surrounding us, I doubt it is of much relevance. Your bodyguard, Petric..."

"Is of Maldrian descent," the duke finished. "I am aware of his heritage and his loyalties. Not many know his true story, and I believe he would like to keep it that way," Renard added, looking meaningfully at the ranger.

Asher nodded.

Accepting the matter as closed, the duke said, "You may leave the children with me with my thanks for their safety. Feel free to search for food or whatever you need. You may use my name if you are given any trouble."

"Thank you, milord."

With another slight bow of his head, he excused himself and left the tent. Quinn felt a slight sadness at his parting. He had come to view the large man as the protector of their small party.

"Well, there is not much room, but it should be sufficient," Renard said. "Luckily, you appear to have your own blankets, as I imagine it would be quite difficult to round some up. Go ahead and spread out wherever you can find space. We should probably all try and get some sleep. I expect tomorrow is going to be an interesting day for all of us."

They each spread the blankets they had received from Timothy. Side-by-side, the blankets took up more than half of the tent's floor space. The duke prepared his own cot as well, and soon only the sounds of sleep were heard.

Chapter 20

"Zander. Zander."

Quinn opened his eyes and saw a large, stocky shadow of a man on one knee gently shaking his friend.

"Wake up, son!"

"Father? *Father!*"

Father and son embraced in the dim light filtering through the flaps of the canvass tent.

"Zander, thank the Creator you are safe. And Quinn too," Bastian added as he sat up. "How are you?" he asked coming over to him.

Quinn stretched. "A little stiff and very hungry."

The weapons master laughed heartily. "Good—you sound well enough. I hear Bertran and Rhiannon are also here."

"Yes, father," Alexander answered, standing and stretching as well. "We were attacked. Well, Quinn was attacked. We fought them off, but didn't know where else to go."

Even in the bad light, Quinn could see that Bastian's face was beaming.

"I know, son. The duke told me as much as he could remember. You will have to tell me the rest later. I'm proud of you, son," he finished, his hands resting lightly on Alexander's shoulders. "Now we need to hurry and find you some breakfast and get you to the council."

"To the council?" asked Alexander.

"Yes, well, actually, more specifically, we need to get Quinn to the council."

Quinn's stomach flip-flopped as he spun to look at the weapons master.

"*Me*? Why me?"

"Apparently, the king has some questions about your time in Maldria. Come on, all of you, or you won't get anything to eat."

Rhiannon and Bertran rolled out of their blankets and they all followed Bastian to the flap of the tent. Quinn was so flustered that he barely noticed the empty cot on the other side. In fact, he had to look a second time.

"Where's my father?" he asked abruptly, stopping so quickly that Bertran almost ran into him. When they all looked at him, he asked again, "Where is my father?"

Almost as one, they turned to the weapons master.

"I honestly don't know, Quinn. The duke doesn't either. He disappeared sometime in the early hours of the morning without leaving word with anyone. The duke sent out scouts, but no one seems to know where he went after he left the camp."

Inside, Quinn felt a jumble of conflicting emotions. On the one hand, he was relieved his father had awoken and was well enough to walk, but the residue of his anger still burned like banked coals. His father would have had to know they were there—you could barely move inside the tent without walking on one of them—and yet he did not even wake them when he had left. Once again, his father had completely ignored him.

They walked to a nearby fire where the aroma of cooking meat and onions wafted from several pans. Bastian gathered up several plates and forks and managed to get small helpings of potatoes, onions, and salted pork for each of them. They ate hungrily, leaving the plates nearly as clean as they started.

Rhiannon and Alexander tried to talk with Quinn while they ate, but he only answered their questions with one or two words. His thoughts were too focused on where his father had gone, and why the king wanted to see him. When they gave up, everyone finished in relative silence.

After returning the plates and utensils, Bastian motioned for them to follow him. Quinn felt his body begin to shake and it was all he could do to put one foot in front of the other. He hoped no one would notice, but Rhiannon took his hand for a moment while they walked.

She whispered, "Don't be nervous. He's just going to ask some questions."

Quinn nodded and tried to smile, but the muscles in his face did not work very well.

She smiled back. "You'll do fine."

Bastian led them through several different camps, each marked by the colors of the some dukedom or another. They walked toward the center of the encampment. During their approach, Bastian tried to reassure Quinn while Alexander made jokes. Neither was any more successful at calming his nerves than Rhiannon had been. Only Bertran remained as quiet as Quinn. In fact, other than talking to his father, Bertran had barely said a word to anyone since fleeing the kitchen at Eastcastle.

They reached the large pavilion at the center of the camp. Guardsmen in the king's personal regalia stood all around the large tent. Bastian slowed as though to speak with them, but they simply waved them through. Bastian gave Quinn one last reassuring smile before ushering them all in.

The heavy material of the pavilion blocked out much of the bright, late autumn sun, causing them to blink for a moment until their eyes adjusted. The smoke from a number of lanterns made everything look hazy compared to the crisp air they had just left.

Stopping just inside the doorway, Quinn swallowed heavily. At the other side of the tent sat King Anthony. His face was unreadable, but his eyes instantly fastened on Quinn. To each side sat several men, the furthest on the left being his Uncle Renard. The duke smiled and motioned him forward with a small hand gesture. Quinn decided the other men must be dukes from the other parts of the kingdom.

He looked back at Bastian and his friends, but they had already filtered down along the side of the tent. Swallowing again, he started forward, but froze almost immediately. As he turned back toward the king, his eyes locked with another set so filled with hate and anger that he almost cowered on the spot. In a blink, Baron Paddock's eyes were normal again, his face expressionless. The change was so abrupt that Quinn wondered whether he had only imagined the anger.

"Young Hawk, please come a little closer so we do not feel as though we need to yell to one another."

Quinn jumped slightly at the king's address. Bowing quickly, he hurried forward to stand in front of Anthony and the surrounding dukes.

"Now, Quinn, your presence here is somewhat fortuitous, though unexpected. From your reaction a moment ago, I believe we are safe in stating you have met the Baron Paddock before. In fact, your visit to Maldria is precisely what we wish to discuss. Primarily of interest is how you came to meet the baron and how you spent your time in Maldria."

Anthony paused, his fingers templed in front of him, his elbows resting on a small camp table. He then added less formally, "You do not need to be nervous; you will not come to any harm here. Just answer the questions as best as you can, understood?"

"Yes, your majesty."

"Good. First, do you know these men?" he asked, gesturing to the men on each side of him.

"I suppose they are probably all the dukes of Dalatia."

King Anthony smiled. "Yes, nearly. Actually, due to the necessary haste, some of the dukes are not here, but these men represent them."

The king then pointed behind Quinn. "And do you know these men?"

Quinn turned and looked back to where Paddock was standing. Several men stood together, surrounded by many others. He recognized some of them from his time in Maldria.

"The barons of Maldria?" he guessed.

The king nodded. "Yes, very good. All of the others are soldiers, mostly Dalatian, but a few from Maldria. As things stand at the moment, we are currently in the midst of a truce. Do you know what that means?"

Quinn shrugged, "I think so."

The king raised a hand to his mouth to hide his smile. He wondered whether the boy realized how politically adept his response was. He had certainly given a valid reply, but in so doing had not really answered the question at all. Perhaps there was more of his father in him than he had thought. Anthony decided to let it slide.

"Very well, let us start."

"Whose idea was it for you to live in Maldria?"

Quinn almost jumped. The question had come from one of the dukes sitting to the right of the king. He had expected Anthony to ask all of the questions. Turning toward the duke, he said, "I think it was Baron Paddock's idea, sir."

"You *think*?"

"I mean, the baron told me he had arranged for me to come to Elksheart."

"Why would he do that?"

"He said…, well, he said I was not being taught well and that…" Quinn left off. He licked his lips and tried to avoid looking at his uncle.

"That what?"

Swallowing, Quinn said, "He thought I was not being trained so I would never have the chance to be the next duke."

"Can you read?"

This time the question came from the other side of the room, the side he was consciously trying to avoid. In fact, the question came from a man sitting just two seats down from Renard. Quinn turned and tried to keep his eyes from straying toward his uncle.

"Yes, sir. A little."

"Who taught you?"

"Alysse."

"And who is Alysse?"

"Baron Paddock's…daughter." Quinn hoped the pause was brief enough that no one noticed it.

"In other words, you did not know how to read *before* you went to Maldria?"

Quinn looked down at his feet. "No, sir," he said quietly.

"How old are you?" the second duke continued.

"Almost fourteen."

"Almost fourteen and you were *never* taught to read before going to Maldria earlier this year?"

"Yes, I mean no." Quinn looked at the duke. "No, I *was* taught to read at Eastcastle, I just couldn't seem to learn how."

"And who was teaching you?"

"Vareen."

"Vareen?"

Quinn finally ventured a look toward his uncle. He was watching Quinn with a sad expression on his face. When Quinn made eye contact, Renard looked down briefly before deliberately turning to the questioning duke.

"Vareen is…*was*…one of my councilors. He is the same man whose attack on Quinn led to his being here now."

The eyes of the man questioning Quinn tightened slightly as he looked at Renard. Soft murmurs could be heard around the room. Raising his voice, the man asked, "And you were aware of the boy's inability to learn his letters?"

Renard hesitated for a moment before answering, as if organizing his thoughts. Sighing, he said, "Yes, I was aware of his struggles. Quinn and I came to a mutual agreement to…" He paused and turned to look directly at Quinn. "Discontinue his lessons. Quinn, I am truly sorry."

Another question shot from the other side of the tent. "Two rangers took you from Elksheart. Who were they?"

Quinn's mind was still trying to come to terms with the sadness on his uncle's face as he looked to the new questioner.

"Only one was a ranger. His name is Asher. He is the same man who brought us here. The other man was my father."

The room erupted into skeptical chatter and outright disbelief.

"Silence!" Anthony's voice boomed as he stood. "Silence." When the pavilion quieted down, he looked directly at Quinn and asked, "Quinn, where is your father now?"

Again, Quinn looked to his uncle before answering, "I don't know."

Anthony knitted his brow, his eyes narrowing as he stared at the boy in front of him. Without changing his expression, he turned his head to look at the Duke of Eastcastle.

"Renard, where is your brother?"

Quinn's uncle again considered his words before speaking. After several moments, he said, "My men found Rustan just before dusk. He was alive, but unconscious. Most of those who were with him were dead or too injured to seek help. They probably expected to face death in the morning. The men who found them brought Rustan to my tent in the darkness. We did what we could for him, but all we could really do was wait."

"However, as Quinn professes not to know where he is, I gather he is no longer in your tent."

"No, milord, he is not."

The pavilion grew eerily quiet compared to the murmuring before. Everyone's eyes were fastened on the two men.

"I ask again, where is your brother?"

Renard met and held the gaze of his king, his face void of all expression except perhaps fatigue.

"I am afraid I do not know either."

Instantly, the silence was broken with more hushed whispers. Renard raised his voice slightly as he continued.

"He must have left sometime in the early morning hours. I did not hear him leave, nor did he leave any indication of where he was going."

The king stared at Renard. The muscles flexing in his cheek were the only indication of emotion.

"Enough of this," Paddock's strong, but irritated voice came from behind Quinn. "How much longer must I be subjected to these lies and rumors? The boy has verified everything I have told you, though the actions of Eastcastle's duke should have been clear enough. He has subjugated the rightful heir while throwing up flimsy walls of deceit on every side, the latest being the specter of his dead brother."

"Had this been his only crime, obviously I would have waited for a direct call from Quinn to restore him to his rightful place. But I will not sit idly by while Renard's fiends kidnap my daughter! You blame me for this war, but I did not start it—I only responded to Eastcastle's challenge. Maldria will avenge itself against those who threaten it with harm! If you want a cause for this bloodshed, look no further than Renard Hawk!"

"Enough, Paddock!" Anthony said sternly. "Our agreement called for your silence. Do not mislead yourself into thinking I will not withdraw the truce and settle this with the sword."

The two men stared at each other, neither willing to back down. Finally, with a mocking bow and a sneer, Paddock retreated. Anthony looked back at Quinn.

"Why did the rangers take Paddock's daughter when they took you from Elksheart?"

Quinn fidgeted and wished he were somewhere else. His mind began to race as he tried to think of how to answer the question, knowing Paddock was only several steps behind him.

"They did not take her, she chose to come along."

For the third time, the hum of chatter and whispers filled the tent. Quinn spoke louder. "Alysse forced my father to take her. She *wanted* to go with us."

"Anthony, I say enough! I will not stand and listen to any more lies!" Paddock hissed loudly. "The boy has obviously been coached. Everything that comes from a Hawk's mouth is as substantial as smoke from a funeral pyre. First stories of dead men returning and now we are supposed to believe my daughter asked...*asked*...to be kidnapped from her home. Anthony, break your truce if you will, but I will not stand and listen to this anymore. The boy has validated my words; no one has done the same for Renard."

Anthony glared across the pavilion at the large man in the fur-lined coat. His face showed the signs of the inner battle he fought to keep from releasing the rage building inside him. Instead of responding to the baron, however, he looked at Renard.

"Renard, you have heard your accuser. What say you?"

A sad smile crept across the Duke of Eastcastle's face. "Your majesty, I have only my word and my honor to present in my defense."

"Then he has *nothing!*" spat Paddock. "*We are done*," he added, emphasizing each word.

The tent erupted into angry shouts and raised voices. The small group of barons standing with Paddock glared at their countrymen behind them as they turned to make their way to the exit.

"Paddock!" Anthony roared above the din. "We are *not* done! *Paddock!!*"

But the tall man ignored him and pushed toward the tent flap. He had almost made it when a small, disheveled figure came flailing into the tent as though he were pushed. He collapsed in a heap, his stringy, sweat-filled hair hiding his face. A sound somewhere between a hiss and a whine came from his mouth. His entrance caught everyone off-guard and silence spread throughout the room.

As the people jostled to get a better look, the tent flap opened again. Rustan Hawk entered first, followed by the ranger Asher. They both stood for a moment as their eyes adjusted from the bright sun to the dim light in the tent.

Quinn watched the reaction of the men in the tent to the appearance of his father. Their faces reflected shock, surprise, or disbelief, until his eyes came to Paddock. The face of the baron of Elksheart had turned purple with rage. The hate Quinn had seen when he first entered the pavilion was redoubled.

"Where is my daughter, Hawk?!"

Rustan blinked a couple times as he turned his head toward the source of the roar. As his eyes fixed on Paddock, his customary smirk crept across his face.

"You *have* no daughter, Paddock," he said in a soft voice as cold as death.

"You filthy…"

"Save the dramatics. You have no child by birth, just one by death—the mysterious deaths of her parents, which conveniently granted you rights to another barony."

Paddock's rage grew even greater. In fact, if his eyes had turned red and fire had shot from his mouth, it would not have surprised Quinn. He had never seen anyone so filled with rage, not even his uncle after one of Alexander's worst stunts. It made his stomach hurt.

"I *will* kill you," Paddock hissed, his eyes trying to put his words into immediate action.

Rustan's smirk grew wider. "I believe you tried that once already."

"Rustan."

Anthony's voice carried across the room, momentarily slicing through the war of words in front of him.

Quinn's father turned his head toward the king and for once, the smirk disappeared off his face. With a slight bow, Rustan Hawk said, "Well met, my lord king."

"I see the rumors of your return were not unfounded."

"No, milord."

"Anthony, I demand this man be detained until he returns my daughter or tells me of her whereabouts. It is his crime that has led to the bloodshed of so many men on both sides."

Quinn was amazed at how quickly Paddock transformed back from the dragon he had appeared to be a moment before. Once again, he stood as the powerful, self-assured noble Quinn knew at Elksheart.

Without looking toward Paddock, the king asked his former duke, "Where is Paddock's daughter? Where is Alysse?"

"She is where she wants to be."

Anthony winced slightly. He was not in the mood for Rustan's games. His absence had clearly not changed that aspect of him; however, there was now a tint of callousness in the former duke.

"And where would that be?" he asked evenly.

Rustan stared momentarily at the king before answering softly, "Paddock's *daughter* is with friends. She is safe enough and will remain so, given her exact location is allowed to remain secret."

"By his own mouth then, he has confessed his guilt," boomed Paddock. "Look no further for the cause of this war."

Rustan whirled on the baron. "A war you were astoundingly well prepared for, Paddock. One might just think you simply needed a cause."

"You steal *my* daughter and accuse *me* of looking for war? You are deranged."

"It was Alysse's choice to leave, not mine, so you can drop the protective father routine—it does not suit you."

Paddock's face once again grew red.

"Oh, cheer up, Paddock," Rustan mocked. "After all, I have brought back your man."

Paddock turned to the man still crouched on the dirt floor. His eyes were just visible through his stringy hair. They had an intense, feral look to them. From the baron's confused expression, he obviously did not recognize him.

"Well met, my lord Paddock," the man hissed in a whiny voice.

Paddock eyes blinked in recognition and then a laugh escaped his lips. Looking to Rustan, his laughter grew louder until it turned into a boisterous guffaw.

"You really *are* deranged, Hawk. I am afraid you will need to look a little closer to home for this creature's owner. Vareen is not *my* man; he serves your brother."

Quinn and most of the others in the tent looked again at the man who seemed more animal than human. Even knowing who he was, it still took Quinn several moments to see Vareen in the man squatting in the dirt. His face was severely drawn and his hair was matted with sweat.

"Or so you would have us believe," Rustan challenged. "Unfortunately, my brother's poor councilor is not doing too well. It seems he was on the receiving end of a rather unclean kitchen knife. We *convinced* him his best chance for aid was here—after a short audience with the king, of course."

Paddock scoffed and motioned to the men around him. "Then we will be on our way so the poor man can meet your sadistic conditions for help."

They began to walk toward the tent opening, a good portion of which was now blocked by Asher. Rustan stepped into their line of progression.

"Perhaps before leaving, you can explain why he carried this hidden in a secret pocket in his cloak?"

Rustan pulled a folded parchment from his own pocket and held it out to Paddock. The baron looked down at the proffered document, but did not take it.

"They are papers guaranteeing entry into *your* barony. Signed and sealed by none other than one Baron Paddock."

Paddock shook his head. "Oh please, Hawk, you will have to do better than that. The man brokered the arrangements for your son's stay at Elksheart. He had ample time to steal or forge those on any one of several visits. Now, if you will excuse us, I am growing tired of your conspiracy theories."

Neither Rustan nor Asher moved as the baron and his men tried to push forward to the flap of the tent.

"Anthony," Paddock called without turning, "I believe our discussion is over. Please tether your bird of prey."

The tension in the tent grew, but no one moved. Quinn swallowed and looked to the king, but Anthony simply stared at the scene before him over his templed fingers, tapping them together lightly. If he was feeling any of the stress Quinn was, he did not show it.

Suddenly, a sickening laughter filled the air. Vareen's face was an odd mixture of pain, hate, and amusement.

"You fool, Paddock! Do you really think I will take the fall for you? Twelve years I have played your lackey and for what? To be discarded like a captured knight in your game of domination?"

"You are clearly unwell, my friend," Paddock said in a voice that conveyed anything but concern for the suffering man.

"*Friend?*" Vareen scoffed, his face a mask of madness. "You are incapable of even *understanding* the word! You left me to rot in Eastcastle, always promising rewards and wealth when your plan came to fruition. I have done everything you asked, but now I am to be cast off?"

Paddock took a step toward Vareen, his voice low and ice cold. "Stop your libelous tongue, lest I do it for you."

Vareen cowered back, scampering in the dirt like an injured spider, but he continued to challenge the baron. With a screeching laugh, he said, "What's wrong, Paddock? Not used to one of your pawns turning on you? Are we just supposed to be sacrificed for your game? Am I supposed to be like one of your pet barons who have tied their lives to your schemes? Buchart, Martin, Stephan, Malathor—I know them all!"

To their credit, only one of the named men flinched.

"Enough!" Paddock roared. "I repeat, I will not be subjected to lies spouted by an obvious servant of the Hawks! This conference is at an end!"

"Hold, Paddock! You have no authority to declare such a thing." Cyrus moved forward from his place at the back of the tent. "May I remind you that you also stand challenged by the majority of the Council of Barons as to your right to rule Elksheart. Starting a groundless war for your own ambitions is not in the best interests of your people."

Paddock whirled on the older baron. "I will not stand and answer to that charge in the tent of an enemy," he hissed in a voice barely above a whisper. "If you must persist in your accusations, then we will finish this in Maldria in a formal meeting of the barons. I am done listening here."

"No, Paddock," Cyrus responded calmly. "We will finish this here, and we will finish this now."

The two men stared at each other until Paddock finally forced a smile onto his face. "As you wish, Cyrus, but know that I will remember this day—*forever.*"

Cyrus responded with his own easy smile. "I expect you will, Paddock. It is an infrequent thing for a baron to lose his manor."

Paddock's smile soured, but he retained his silence.

"Now, Vareen," Cyrus continued, "Or shall I call you Fenton?"

The sneer grew on the snarling man's face. "I once went by that name. Before I sold my soul to Paddock—the price I paid for *freedom*." The sarcastic emphasis on the last word was clear.

"For your benefit, Anthony, this man is a common criminal and murderer. He mysteriously disappeared years ago just before his sentence was to be commuted. Apparently, he found some friends in high places."

"*Common?*" Vareen cackled inanely, "There is nothing *common* about me! My brilliance was unparalleled before I was betrayed."

The ridiculousness of the statement was heightened by the fact that it came from the mouth of one with only a tenuous hold on sanity.

Paddock ignored the babbling, his hands clenched into fists. "Cyrus," he hissed, "If you wish to make an accusation, make it. The condemnation and retribution you face will not change with one more foolish action."

"Fool, Paddock! You are the fool!" Vareen screeched, apparently bolstered by Cyrus' intervention. "Do you think I *trusted* you? Ever?" His shrieking laughter filled the pavilion. "I wrote it all down! Everything! The plot to kill the Hawks, the murder of Marcus, the 'schooling' of Quinn…aagghh!"

Paddock whirled so quickly that few in the tent had time to react. From somewhere in the recesses of his fur-lined cloak, the baron pulled a knife and turned on the cackling man in the dirt. Vareen scrambled back, his face draining of color. Paddock closed the gap in two strides and would likely have killed the cowering madman had Petric not intervened.

Renard's old bodyguard leapt forward, quarterstaff in hand. With a blur of motion, he landed a blow solidly on Paddock's extended forearm with an audible crack. Petric then smoothly reversed the staff's motion and caught the baron behind his knees, collapsing him to the ground.

As the knife skittered into the dirt, Paddock rolled quickly to his left, sheltering his right arm. His face was drawn in pain, but his eyes burned with rage. From a fighter's crouch, he scanned quickly for his attacker. An evil smile crawled across his face as he recognized Petric.

Before either man could do more, the tent filled with Anthony's personal guards. They quickly relieved Petric of his quarterstaff, which he offered up without resistance. Two guards flanked Anthony as he made his way over to them. With a disgusted glance at the cowering Vareen, Anthony reached down and picked up the knife Paddock had dropped. Hefting it lightly in his grip, he turned to Paddock.

"You have broken the rules of the truce by exposing a blade. Even without the revealing words of your accomplice, I find you reprehensible. With them, I judge you guilty in the unwarranted and unprovoked attack on our kingdom. You will rot in a dungeon for the remainder of your years."

Paddock reared up between the guardsmen. "You have no authority over me! This is no trial and you are no judge! I demand safe conduct back to my men as outlined in our agreement."

"An agreement that included no blades! Why should I honor the rules you have just trampled under your feet?"

"I demand safe passage!"

The two men faced each other once again, neither giving quarter to the other.

"Anthony, may I speak?"

Anthony turned his head in surprise at the request from Petric. Although he fought to keep it off his face, he clearly struggled with his preconceptions of Renard's bodyguard. Finally, he gave his consent with a nod.

Petric walked forward, but instead of speaking to the king, he turned to the other Maldrian barons.

"My countrymen, you have been deceived and betrayed. You have been tricked into a war with talk of noble causes and appeals to good conscience. They are all lies.

"The man before you has forfeited his right to rule. By our own codes and precepts, he was sworn an oath to protect the people of Elksheart and Northridge. Instead, because of his greed and insatiable thirst for power, he has brought you into this needless war. He has caused the pointless deaths of hundreds of men, both Maldrian and Dalatian. Dead men who will not return to their families, bring in their harvests, or provide for their children. He has made a mockery of his charge, as have those who stand with him. In Paddock's eyes, all people are irrelevant pawns to be used and spent in his service.

"Barons, I call upon you to revoke his stewardship here and now. There is no need for a Council. The facts are laid bare and his guilt is clear. Act now and repair that which has been so foolishly broken."

"This is not proper," one of the barons voiced from the back of the tent. "Maldrian concerns should be resolved in Maldria, and not in the tent of an enemy."

"And why *are* they enemies?" Petric shot back. "And why are you in this tent? Because of the lies of this man!" he said, pointing to Paddock. "Cast him out as he would surely do to you if it served his purpose. Paddock is loyal to one person and one person alone."

Paddock scoffed. "And who are you to talk of loyalties? Your words are as flimsy as sea grass in the wind, unsupported by honor."

Petric whirled on the baron.

"Yes, who *am* I, Paddock? Why not tell them who I am?"

Again, Paddock laughed. "I hardly think I need to introduce the Betrayer of Maldria! Any child old enough to talk knows you by name."

Petric shook off the restraining guardsmen and strode to the baron's side. The soldiers looked to Anthony for guidance, swords held ready. With a quick, dismissive wave of the king's hand, they stood down.

Petric edged closer so his face was no more than a breath away from Paddock's. He grabbed the baron's right arm causing him to wince and breathe in sharply.

"No, Paddock," Petric said in almost a whisper, "Tell them who I *really* am."

Paddock's face filled with rage and pain, but he held his tongue.

"*Tell them!*"

"You are the Betrayer of Maldria! You betrayed your own father!" Paddock spat, causing an eruption of surprise.

Petric roughly released his half-brother's arm and turned back to the barons, who were looking at one other in confusion.

~ 301 ~

"I am Philip's eldest son and heir. By right of birth, Elksheart belongs to me."

"You forfeited your rights when you sold out your family and your country to the Hawks!" roared Paddock. "You are no more Philip's heir than you are Maldrian. You deserve nothing except a traitor's death!"

"I served my people more than they will ever know. I gave my *very life* to protect them from a pointless war that would have proved a hundred times more costly than this fiasco. My only regret is I could not stop your idiocy sooner. Barons of Maldria, I submit my claim to the manor and barony of Elksheart."

"This is not protocol!" began the same baron who had spoken before. "I will not…"

"I say yes," Cyrus intoned, cutting him off. "Paddock's treachery is clear, and I believe there is honor in Petric's words. I say yes," he repeated.

"Have you lost all sense of reason?" another baron asked.

Within moments, a full debate broke out among the barons. Anthony returned to his seat and laid the knife on the small camp table in front of him. He watched the proceedings with feigned interest while the dukes talked quietly among themselves.

Quinn drifted over to stand near his uncle. Facing the barons, he watched Petric, who had returned to his familiar demeanor—still as a statue, his face unreadable, his eyes constantly scanning. Even as Paddock and his coconspirators railed against him, he stood resolute, content that his brief defense had relayed everything that needed to be said.

While watching his uncle's bodyguard, his eyes stopped on his father. The smirk was fastened on his face, but it appeared to be nothing more than a cheap mask. Everything else from his stance to his eyes, radiated something else—an overpowering aura of hatred and rage. The anger he exuded was so great Quinn had to look away for fear their eyes would meet.

In doing so, he found he was not the only one who had noticed his father's demeanor. Chin resting lightly on his clasped hands, Anthony's intense gaze was also fastened on his former duke. His regal face did not show the fear Quinn imagined was on his own. Instead, there was a mixture of concern and sadness, which Quinn found nearly as unsettling as his father's visage of hatred.

Alexander, Rhiannon, and Bertran stood across the tent from him. When he caught their eyes, Rhiannon gave a half wave and Alexander raised his eyebrows, making a mock grimace. Quinn smiled in spite of himself. Bastian turned and flicked Alexander's ear, which caused Quinn to smile even more. He covered his face in a fake yawn in hopes of disguising it.

The debate dragged on until finally Cyrus raised his voice above the others.

"Enough!"

When the noise settled to nothing more than whispered conversations, Cyrus strode out to face the barons.

"We have discussed enough. No further benefit can come from finding new words to express old thoughts. We must move beyond these arguments of protocol and precedence and act on what we know.

"These men have broken their oaths. That much is clear. They have knowingly led all of us into a war of their own manufacturing for their own greed. They have trampled on their most basic stewardship of providing for their people. What more is there to discuss? They are guilty of neglect, if not treason, and I say be done with them. Remove them from the Council of Barons."

Murmurs and shouts of agreement filled the pavilion. Cyrus pulled a small leather bag from his pocket. Loosing the cord, he opened the bag and turned it upside down to show that it was empty.

"As is customary, a gold coin is a yes vote while silver is a no. Accused barons do not vote."

He then pulled some coins from another pocket, sorted them in his hand, and placed one inside the bag before handing it to the nearest baron. This process was repeated until each of the remaining barons had placed a coin in the bag. After the final coin was given, the leather bag was returned to Cyrus, who unceremoniously dumped its contents into the dirt. Squatting, he spread out the coins.

"All gold, no silver—the accused are deemed guilty and are relieved of their baronies."

"Fools!" roared Paddock, straining against the men who held him. "There is no legal precedence for such actions outside a chamber of council. None of this is binding! I refuse to accept any ruling made outside of Maldria as is dictated by our codes and reinforced by centuries of tradition."

Cyrus ignored his ranting and once again addressed the barons. "On the matter of the baronies of Elksheart and Northridge, I submit the name of Petric, Philip's oldest son, to procure and maintain the role of baron."

Again, he placed a coin in the leather sack and passed it around the room.

"You have no right!" screamed Paddock. "Cyrus, you are out of order! *Cyrus!*"

The bag passed quickly through the barons and Cyrus once again spilled the contents into the dirt. After a momentary glance, he stood and said almost tiredly, "Two silvers, all others are gold. Petric will take his brother's stead as baron and lord of Elksheart."

"Fools! Everyone of you! You will all regret this," fumed Paddock. "You will all pay for your stupidity!"

Cyrus ignored him completely and replaced the bag into his pocket.

"We will replace the other barons in Maldria after a suitable heir has been found for each. Now, if you will excuse me, winter is at our doorstep and I do not wish to lose my ships on the southern shoals. Farewell."

Without further ceremony, Cyrus walked to the tent flap and left. Several other barons did the same before Anthony could even stand and object.

"*King* Anthony," Petric called out with an emphasis on the title. Anthony looked at him with a hint of surprise. "The Barony of Elksheart has initiated and enacted an unjustified war upon your kingdom under the direction of its former leader. He has subsequently been tried, found guilty, and removed from his stewardship. I offer the traitor Paddock to you to exact your king's justice upon him. Treat him as you will."

Not knowing what else to do, Anthony bowed his head slightly in acknowledgement.

"Further, in an attempt to rectify that which obviously cannot be rectified, I offer the forces of Elksheart to your Duke of Eastcastle. We will help restore order and properly care for the fallen, as well as bring in any remaining harvest in preparation for winter."

Anthony eyed Maldria's newest baron carefully. After an extended pause, he said, "Your offer is admirable, though likely unrealistic. Do you really think men who have spent these past hours locked in battle, who have seen friends and family fall, will now stand side by side with their enemies?"

"Your majesty, the men of Elksheart will learn the price of restitution. By so doing, perhaps their children will be spared a similar lesson."

Again, Anthony considered the man in front of him. Finally, he turned to Renard.

"I will leave the decision to the Duke of Eastcastle."

A slow smile crept across the face of Quinn's uncle as he looked at his old bodyguard.

"Eastcastle accepts any and all offers of help."

Expressionless as ever, Petric nodded to his former employer. "Then it is decided. I will go and make my men aware of their obligation. As for this despicable creature," he said pointing to the man who was both Fenton and Vareen, "I leave his fate to you and the remaining barons. I have neither jurisdiction nor interest in his demise. By your leave."

With a bow to both Renard and Anthony, Petric turned toward the exit. As he walked past his brother, Paddock hissed, "This is not over."

Petric stopped.

"Actually, brother, I believe it is. You see, that is how the game is played."

"I will kill you. I will return and find you and I *will* kill you!"

Petric calmly faced him. "There was a time when your threats meant something, when they might have influenced my actions. But those days are gone. Farewell, brother."

"This is not over, Petric! *This is not over!*" roared Paddock, still bound between two of Anthony's guardsmen. Petric ignored him completely and walked toward the sliver of sunlight slicing across the dirt floor. Just before he reached the exit, a large, square man caught him.

"Welcome back, my friend, welcome back. My name is Trimble. I am the baron of Silver Flats just south of Elksheart. When you return, please stop by. I would like to talk with you regarding a matter of some beavers…"

Chapter 21

The snowflakes fluttered through the wind, writhing and changing in the breeze like some insubstantial creature of magnificent size. The whiteness was a welcome change from the dreariness of the rain that had engulfed Eastcastle soon after the army had returned. Even with the help of the Maldrians, some of the fall harvest had been lost. A few minor incidents had occurred with fault being found on both sides, but Petric was quick and exact in his retributions. Those who had supposed him softer than his treacherous brother soon learned their error.

Within the walls of Eastcastle, the residual gloominess from the war started to break as the snow spread its comforting white blanket across the countryside. The grieving, which had harrowed the land for so many days, was buried below the pristine white snowfields. Already, the bards were immortalizing the deeds of many in such ballads as *The Last Stand of Saladar* and *Renard's Ride*. The people of Eastcastle began to soothe their heart-wrenching sorrow with soul-building pride. They had been tested, but they had endured and they had triumphed.

Quinn watched the snow as it weaved its intricate patterns, spinning right and left without order. As the drifts continued to build, he remembered back to earlier winters when such storms would have brought promises of sledding and snowball fights. Now, it just seemed to be one more reminder of how much things had changed.

He sat outside in his fur-lined clothes, as he did most days. When they had first returned, Rhiannon and Alexander had tried to break him out of the cloud of gloom that surrounded him, but even they had finally given up—at his suggestion, he reminded himself. Most days, he simply tried to sleep, but he could only do that for so long before his eyes would not stay shut. He was then forced to get up and wander the castle, looking for a place where people would leave him alone.

Ironically, he grew even angrier when they did just that, especially one person in particular.

Justly or not, Quinn had focused all his pent up anger on his father. He had tried to talk with his father many different times, but each had the same result: something had to be done; someone had to be talked to; someplace had to be visited. After the meeting in Anthony's pavilion, Quinn had been handed back over to Bastian's care with instructions to take him back to Eastcastle. Quinn had wanted to stay; to help where he could, but his father had refused with the words he had grown to hate—"We will talk later."

Later. The word set off a chain of grievances. 'Later' was what had led to his not being taken to Shepherds Pass. That of course had led to the attack on Melinda, who still lay in a coma from which she may never recover. In fact, 'later' was what caused him to be sent to Maldria in the first place. Had his father simply told them who he was on the way to the Festival, the whole stupid war might have been avoided, and Melinda would still be cooking in the kitchen.

Quinn made a snowball, the wet snow stinging his bare hands. When he was done, he threw it as hard as he could against the castle wall where it exploded with a mushy splat. Some part of him had hoped it would make him feel better, while the rest of him laughed at his stupidity for thinking so. Even his lengthy shadow from the winter sun seemed to mock him. Drying his freezing hands, he stormed back into the castle, wearing his anger like a mask in case someone felt the need to try and talk with him.

In the weeks since the end of the war, Rustan Hawk had "needed" to talk with seemingly everyone—everyone that is, except Quinn. He disappeared for a time with Asher, spent a few days with Anthony before the king returned to Roseland, and met with Petric, Renard, and countless soldiers and advisors. He had even spent time with the farmers and villagers. But whenever Quinn found him, the answer was always the same—"Later; we'll talk later."

Quinn rubbed his hands as he walked through the cold hallways. Each of the large fireplaces throughout the castle burned non-stop, but the heat seldom reached further than the room in which they were situated. As such, the hallways were usually the coldest parts of the castle.

He walked past the kitchen and debated about scavenging some food before dinner, but changed his mind when he realized it would be full of kitchen staff preparing the evening meal. Walking quickly in case Rhiannon was one of them, he headed toward the library instead.

The library was always kept warm to protect the books and manuscripts from the dampness that seeped throughout the rest of the castle. This close to the dinner meal, his chances were good in finding it empty.

He eased open the solid wooden door and felt a blast of warm air hit his face. The room appeared to be empty. He slipped in and shut the door. An inviting fire burned in the large fireplace, casting shadows around the dimly-lit room. Quinn was just taking a chair near it when a cough spooked him and he jumped.

"Hello?"

A figure straightened up from one of the chairs facing the wall and turned to look in his direction.

"Quinn?"

"Yes, sir," Quinn answered, recognizing his father's voice.

"Sorry, I did not hear you come in. Did you need something?"

"No, sir, I was just trying to find someplace to get warm."

"Well then," he said, "I will not stop you." He turned back around in his chair.

Quinn stayed where he was, staring at the back of his father's head. Part of him wanted to go back to his bedroom and sit by the smaller fireplace there, but the rest of him could feel the anger building once again. In the end, the anger won out.

"Father, may I ask you a question?"

Without turning, his father answered, "Quinn, today has been a challenge. Would it be all right if we talked another time?"

He had known what the answer would be before his father had given it, but it still pushed him over the edge. The silent rage that had been building for weeks finally peaked like an overheated soup pot.

"No! No, it would not be all right!"

With a sigh, Rustan Hawk slowly raised himself from the chair and circled it. Leaning against the back, he asked, "Very well, what is your question?"

Somewhat shocked by his father's concession, Quinn was a bit flustered as he tried to decide which of all his questions he wanted to ask. Finally, anger barely in check, he sputtered, "Why didn't you tell me who you were? I mean, when we first met or even later on. Why did you tell me you were a ranger?"

His father gave a small laugh. "Why did you not recognize me? My picture is on the wall behind me. Surely you must have seen it before."

"That's not an answer. Besides, you don't exactly look like that anymore."

Rustan turned with a mock look of surprise. "Really? I cannot be *that* different. Except perhaps for this," he said, gesturing to the ugly scar along the side of his face. "Do you know where I got this?"

"No."

Rustan's face instantly turned hard and his eyes burned with an anger that surprised Quinn.

"This was a gift from the man who murdered your mother, a man whose name I still do not know to this day. Until recently, I did not know who he worked for, or why he sought to kill me at all. Do you know what it feels like to be hunted?"

Quinn swallowed and shook his head. The man before him had transformed from someone who looked somewhat like his father's painting to a devil in men's clothing.

"Good, be thankful, for it is an awful feeling. As to your question, the answer is actually fairly simple. I did not wish to be hunted again, nor did I wish for you to become a target. Is that too hard to understand?"

The tone of his father's voice was barbed and condescending. So much so, that Quinn could feel his own anger rising to meet it.

"But you *did* put me in danger!" he spouted. "You let me be sent to Paddock and later, left me here with Vareen!"

"*Let* you be sent to Maldria? Search your memories, boy. I did not send you to Elksheart—that was your uncle. In fact, in case you have forgotten, I was the one who brought you *out* of Maldria."

"But you did not take me with you to Shepherds Pass. You left me here in danger instead of taking me with you."

Rustan stared down at his son, his face contorted in a rage of madness. Suddenly, in the time it takes for light to leave an extinguished candle, his face softened again.

"Fine," he said, his voice lower once again. "I made a mistake. Is that what you wanted to hear? Then fine, yes, I made a mistake leaving you alone at Eastcastle."

"Why did you?"

Again, Rustan paused, not answering immediately. Twice, he began, only to clamp his mouth shut tightly. Finally, he said, "Because long ago I made a promise."

"But I could have fought," Quinn said, knowing inside that he would have done no such thing. Memories of the view from the cliff above the battle still haunted his dreams. But he continued anyway. "I've had training."

His father's odd smile grew and he called Quinn's bluff.

"Do you think smashing other boys with cloth-covered sticks qualifies you as a soldier? Do you think you could have stood in battle and not run like a spooked rabbit? Do you really think you could *kill* a man who is trying to kill you? You are not a soldier, Quinn, just a dream-filled boy, and that is why I didn't take you to war."

Embarrassment flooded Quinn, further reddening his face. Trapped by the knowledge that his father had seen through his charade, Quinn could feel the tears forming in his eyes. Steeling himself so his father would not see him cry, he hissed, "I wish you had never come back!"

He quickly ran to the door and slipped out, slamming it with a dull thud. Only then did he allow the tears to flow. He started for his room, but had only gone a few steps before he heard his name called.

"Quinn. Quinn."

Great, thought Quinn, recognizing Rhiannon's voice. He kept walking away from her.

"Quinn!" she called again, and he could hear her footsteps speed up as she ran down the hallway. As soon as he heard her grow close, he whirled around.

"What!?" he barked.

Surprised, Rhiannon took a step back and asked, "What's the matter with you?"

"Nothing, okay?"

For a moment, Rhiannon looked as if she was going to walk away, but then she shot back.

"No, it's not okay. Ever since we came back from Shepherds Pass you have been sulking around, avoiding everyone. What's bothering you?"

"Right now, you are."

Quinn regretted it as soon as he said it, but he was too angry to care. He just wanted to be left alone. Even so, he could not look at her. She had tear tracks streaking her face, and he would not let guilt curtail his rage.

Rhiannon fought down her own anger. She thought about just leaving him to his own misery, but decided she would not give him the pleasure.

"Good, I'm glad to hear it. So, what are you crying about this time?" *If he can be a twit, then so can I*, she thought to herself.

Quinn turned red, but could not think of anything to say. Instead, his eyes trailed over to the library door, before snapping back to Rhiannon.

"Who's in there?" Rhiannon asked, following his eyes.

"Nobody," he answered and began to turn away from her.

"It's your father, isn't it?"

Quinn halted, still facing away from her. Finally, he said, "He's changed everything. I wish he'd never come back."

Rhiannon scrunched her face in confusion. "What?"

Whirling around, Quinn repeated with more force, "I wish he had never come back. He doesn't ever want to talk to me and when he does he treats me like I am still three years old. I hate him."

At first, Quinn thought Rhiannon was too shocked to say anything. It was only a few moments later he realized it was not shock, but anger.

"Hate? *Hate?!*" She gave a short, humorless laugh. "You don't know anything *about* hate!"

Her voice was raised and her expression was furious. Quinn tried to leave, but she grabbed hold of his tunic and turned him around.

"Do you think that's what he needs, someone to *hate* him? Quinn, he's so completely full of hate already—it radiates off him! If you really want to learn how to hate, you should stick close by him. He'll teach you all you need to know."

"What do you know? What makes you the expert?"

"I don't need to be an expert. It's obvious. Your father is so filled with rage and hate he's forgotten how to care for people. It's not you he's mad at, it's the whole world! Right now, I don't think he's capable of being nice, let alone loving anyone. Maybe that's why he avoids you. He doesn't need you to hate him; he does enough of that himself. He needs you to show him how to care again, how to love again."

Quinn tried to pull away again. "You don't understand."

"Understand what?"

Glaring into her face, he said, "I can't do it! I can't!"

"Can't or won't?"

Again the tears started to flow down Quinn's cheeks. This time, he was unable to stop them.

"I can't! He left me here where Vareen could get me. He…he…"

"What? Made a *mistake*? So what! People make mistakes everyday, and sometimes those mistakes get people hurt. Because of me, Melinda…"

Rhiannon suddenly choked up and tears burned down her cheeks. After several moments of fighting for control, she said softly through her tears, "I was coming to tell you. Melinda died. Because of me, Melinda is dead."

Quinn felt like he had been punched in the stomach. Her tears had not been because of him. He felt as though he was shattering in a hundred different pieces. One part of him wanted to scream, and another wanted to collapse in tears. One wanted to console his friend, while another wanted to blame her. Instead, he simply stared at her, unable to bring himself to accept what he had just heard.

Rhiannon, crying freely now, whispered, "I'm sorry, Quinn. I'm so sorry."

Finally, the unbridled anger that had taken control over the past several weeks reared up again.

"It's his fault," he whispered. "It's not your fault, it's *his*. If my father had not left me here, none of this would have happened."

Stepping around Rhiannon, he headed back to the library. Melinda was dead and it was his father's fault. He should know that.

"Quinn, wait! What are you going to say?"

Turning his head, he said, "It's his fault, Rhiannon. He needs to know that, and I am going to tell him."

"Quinn, wait until later. Don't tell him now."

"No, I *am* going to tell him now. He needs to know what his little games and secrets have done. He needs to be told."

"Quinn, he's your father. Your *father*!"

"He's *not* my father. My father is dead. He died with my mother. I don't know who that man is, but he is *not* my father."

Tears still streamed down Rhiannon's face as she grabbed Quinn's arm. "All your life you've wanted to belong to a family. All your life you have missed your parents, and now you have a second chance. Don't throw it away, Quinn."

"How would you know what I want?"

Rhiannon's face softened as she looked at him.

"Because," she whispered, "It's the same thing I want. It's what I have wanted everyday for years. I want to see my mother's face again. I want to hear my father's laugh. Every day, I wish I could have my family back again, Quinn. *Every single day.*"

Quinn looked at her one last time before steeling himself. He walked purposefully toward the door, pulling his arm free from her grasp.

"Quinn, don't," she called after him. "Do you think families are perfect? That they never have problems? Do you think you don't have to work through them? You don't *get* a great family, Quinn, you *earn* one! *Quinn!*"

He pulled open the heavy door and walked in. He only managed one step before the clear sound of a wooden flute stopped him as though he had run into a wall. He had heard the tune before, years ago, when his mother sang it to him every night, but it was different now. The melody had been set in a minor key and its notes now carried pain, anguish, and heartache. Within moments, he felt his anger seep away from him, even though a part of him fought to hold it. The rage escaped from him like water running through fingers. Transfixed, he listened to the haunting tune.

Closing his eyes, he could once again hear his mother's voice, could smell the flowers she wore in her hair, could see the deep blue of her eyes. Tears welled up and fell, ignored, on his tunic. He knew the hand that came to rest on his arm was Rhiannon's, but in his mind he pictured his mother's hand and the tears fell freer. A mother's love, so carefully wrapped and preserved in a simple tune, reached out from beyond the veil of death and whispered to her son, soothing his fears and bringing him comfort. He was sobbing quietly when the song ended, his eyes still closed, and his mind trying to grasp the fading embers of his memories.

He was unprepared for the roar that followed. It nearly knocked him to his knees. It was a cry of anguish, sorrow, hate, rage, and despair all mixed in one power surge of volume. It reverberated off the stone walls and pierced him to his very core. He knew its source before opening his eyes, but was still surprised to see the battered soul weeping as he knelt before the portrait of his mother. Violent sobs racked his body as pure emotion tried to tear him limb from limb. It was the most pitiful image of loss Quinn had ever witnessed, and it would haunt him for years.

"*I cannot do this, Cat. I need you!*"

"Father?" he whispered with a crack in his voice.

Rustan Hawk turned his face toward his son. Deep lines etched his face as though he had aged twenty years in just a moment's time. His dark eyes no longer held their sharpness, but instead appeared to be deep pools of eternal sadness. Gone from his face was the characteristic smirk that had dominated it from the time Quinn had met him. It was as though a mask had been torn forcefully from his face, leaving a raw, vulnerable visage of shame.

"Quinn," he said hoarsely. "I am sorry."

He opened his arms and Quinn ran to his father.

"I am truly, truly sorry."

Epilogue

The light of the spring sun danced playfully on the surface of the sea below him. Closing his eyes, Quinn breathed in the crisp sea air, letting the sun warm his face. The winter had seemed to last longer than normal. Even now, two days before the Spring Festival, small drifts of snow remained in the shadowed parts of Eastcastle. Below him, Quinn could hear the distant sounds of Gulls Bay mixing with the calls of the birds which gave the town its name.

"I thought I might find you here."

Turning, he smiled at Rhiannon. "You remembered too, then."

She shrugged and smiled back, though her face was still a bit splotchy from crying. "Of course."

Becoming more serious, Quinn asked, "How are you doing?"

"Fine. No, better than fine. Really, I mean it," she added, seeing his concern.

They had spent the morning placing headstones on the gravesites of her parents and conducting a small service. The townspeople of Gulls Bay had been hesitant to tell them where they had buried Marcus, his wife, and his small daughter; at least until Rustan presented Rhiannon to them. Quinn could still see the shock on their faces when a well known dead man introduced them to Marcus' equally dead daughter. They had been wary at first, but by the end of the service several offered Rhiannon hugs and condolences.

"Have you changed your mind?"

Looking out to the sea, Rhiannon shook her head. "No."

"I know my father would let you come."

Rhiannon laughed. "I know that, too. He just asked me again."

Quinn laughed as well. "Oh."

"No, I think you need some time alone with your father, and he needs time to be alone with you. Someday I'll come to Roseland when you least expect it."

"Promise?"

Rhiannon looked at him, with a curiously mischievous smile. After a moment, she said, "Promise."

Suddenly uncomfortable, they both looked out to the sea. Below them, the ship taking Rustan, Quinn, Alexander, Bastian, and Petric to Bridgetown for the festival sat docked at the wharf. Alexander was competing in the sword tournament, while Quinn was going to shoot in the archery meet. He had spent most of the winter working with his father on perfecting his technique and was good enough now that Alexander no longer offered to challenge him.

Petric was also competing in the tournament in an attempt to become the first Maldrian ever to become a king's champion. Rustan had made the suggestion to King Anthony during one of his many winter trips to Roseland, and the king had agreed. It was one of Rustan's first acts as the king's new foreign relations advisor.

After the Festival, Quinn and his father would travel back with the king's court. His father had accepted the invitation from Anthony to leave Eastcastle in order to relieve the stress his presence put on his Uncle Renard. It also offered Rustan an escape from the demons of his past. Occasionally, the old smirk crept back, but he usually fought it down. Only time would fully heal the damage to his soul.

With Rustan's appointment in Roseland, Renard remained the Duke of Eastcastle. He had opted out of attending the Festival due to his wife's pregnancy. Besides, his absence would give Rustan one last opportunity to serve as the representative of Eastcastle. He also wished to stay with Bertran, who had ended his weapons training after returning from Shepherds Pass.

Petric had arrived several days earlier in order to visit Eagles Nest. He had met with Alysse, the heir of Northridge, and tried to convince her to return with him after the Festival, but she had declined. Apparently, she had found a fondness for innkeeping, or at least for Tomkin, the innkeeper's hand. She had gradually recovered over the winter and was now able to help out around the Golden Boot. In fact, she had become the object of Gwendolyn's pride and attention, which of course, suited Grobeck just fine. With someone else receiving his sister's full attention, he was the happiest he had been in years.

A quiet cough caught both of them by surprise. "Am I interrupting anything?" Petric asked.

Both Quinn and Rhiannon shook their heads as their faces reddened.

"Well, I'd better go. Even riding, it will still be dark before I get back to Eastcastle," Rhiannon said. "Good luck at the tournament, Quinn. Come back and visit when you can."

She gave him a hug and he noticed that her eyes were moist once again. Hugging her back, he whispered, "Thanks—for everything." She pulled him tighter before letting go and disappearing into the brush. Quinn tried to casually wipe the tears from his own eyes, knowing Petric was watching him.

"Sorry," he said. "I did not intend to end your visit."

"No, it's okay."

Taking a step closer, Petric said, "I misjudged you; though, in hindsight, I suppose that was precisely Paddock's intention. It was unbelievably infuriating to watch you throw away every opportunity that had been stolen from me. Perhaps, I recognized the worst parts of myself displayed in your weaknesses."

Quinn looked out at the sea, unsure of what to say. If this was supposed to be an apology, it had certainly missed the mark. On the other hand, he guessed it was as close as the tall man would ever get to contrition.

"I have something for you."

Quinn looked at him with a confused expression on his face. "For me?"

From underneath his cloak, he pulled out a small, sheathed sword. Holding it in both hands, he said, "I was told this belongs to you."

Quinn looked at the sword carefully. It was the one he had left at the manor when his father had taken him from Elksheart. Quinn swallowed, but made no attempt to take the weapon.

"Thanks, Petric, but you can keep it. Perhaps you know somebody who can use it back at Elksheart."

Petric stared down at him, his stone face resembling a statue. Only the tightening around his eyes betrayed any emotion.

"Take it, Quinn. It is your sword."

Quinn looked again at the sword, but still made no effort to retrieve it.

"The Creator forbid, but someday you may need to use it…For Eastcastle,…For Honor…"

Quinn's eyes flashed up in surprise at Petric's recitation of Eastcastle's battle cry, and Petric smiled.

Character List

Alexander	*Son of Bastian; Quinn's best friend*
Alysse	*Daughter of Baron Paddock*
Anthony	*King of Dalatia*
Asher	*A ranger, friend of Rowan*
Bastian	*Weapons master of Eastcastle; father of Alexander*
Bertran Hawk	*Son of Renard; Quinn's cousin*
Carmen	*Wife of Paddock*
Catherine Hawk	*Wife of Rustan, Quinn's mother*
Cyrus	*A Maldrian baron*
Dominic	*Weapons master of Elksheart*
Grobeck	*Co-keeper of the Golden Boot in Eagles Nest*
Gwendolyn	*Co-keeper of the Golden Boot in Eagles Nest*
Jens Hawk	*Son of Renard; Quinn's cousin*
Landon	*A ranger; former bodyguard of Rustan*
Marcus	*Weapons master of Eastcastle under Rustan*
Melinda	*Kitchen master in Eastcastle*
Paddock	*Maldrian Baron of Elksheart*
Petric	*Renard's bodyguard*
Philip	*Former Maldrian baron*
Quinn Hawk	*Orphan son of Rustan and Catherine*
Renard Hawk	*Duke of Eastcastle; Quinn's uncle*
Rhiannon	*Orphan girl Quinn meets in Bridgetown*
Rowan	*A ranger, friend of Quinn and Asher*
Rustan Hawk	*Previous Duke of Eastcastle; Quinn's father*
Saladar	*Commander of the Eastcastle forces at Shepherds Pass*
Timothy	*A Traveler*
Tomkin	*A servant at the Golden Boot*

Trimble	*A Maldrian Baron (of Silver Flats)*
Tucker	*Coach driver of Elksheart*
Vareen	*Councilor to Renard; Quinn's former tutor*
Vespian	*Father of Rustan and Renard; Quinn's grandfather*

About the Author

Jim Pugmire was born and raised in the Pacific Northwest, where his imagination grew up among the evergreen trees and clear mountain lakes. Though his employment planted him firmly in the world of statistics and semiconductors, he never really lost his interest in exploring new places in his mind. Over the course of two decades, imagination progressed into a hobby, which in turn became his Quinn Hawk series of books. He now lives in Utah with his wife and five children.

Made in the USA
Lexington, KY
11 December 2018